"Simply riveting. Kent Nerburn has the ~~very rare ability to gently~~ and compassionately teach in a respectful way. I love this book. And so does the rest of our staff."

— Susan White, manager of Birchbark Books

"How do you live when you don't know what spirits to believe in? *The Girl Who Sang to the Buffalo* poses this question for Natives and non-Natives alike. In it, a mysterious Native American girl named Yellow Bird from an Indian boarding school shows us what we already know within ourselves about which spirits to follow. With this book, Kent Nerburn leads us on a search through old and new Native America in a touching and enlightening pursuit of spirit."

— Chris Eyre, director of *Smoke Signals*

Praise for *The Wolf at Twilight*

"Emotionally arresting...Nerburn shines when describing the humor and heartbreak he finds on South Dakota's Pine Ridge Indian Reservation....Heartfelt wisdom is found throughout Dan's quest for closure and the tale is beautifully told."

— *Publishers Weekly*

"After my prison cell began to cool from the day's heat, I opened Kent Nerburn's creative and compassionate book, which I found humorous, hilarious, and at times very sad. Thank you, Kent, for a good book to read. *Doksha.*"

— Leonard Peltier, author, artist, and activist

"Elegant, yet powerful...Nerburn crosses borders with a single-minded dedication to preserving an oral tradition. The emotional truth that resides in the rich storytelling is a testament

to the strength and endurance of Lakota culture and…removes barriers to understanding our common humanity."
— Winona LaDuke, founder and executive director of the White Earth Land Recovery Project

"The story of this unique and captivating journey should be accepted with an open heart. It is a remarkable gift that we are honored to receive and obligated to pass on."
— Steven R. Heape, Cherokee Nation citizen and producer of the award-winning documentary *The Trail of Tears: Cherokee Legacy*

PRAISE FOR *Neither Wolf nor Dog*

"A chronicle extraordinary for its difficult truths and its stunning depths…This is a sobering, humbling, cleansing, loving book, one that every American should read."
— *Yoga Journal*

"I expected to find Black Elk between these covers. What I found instead was more modern, more alive, and every bit as poignant and moving."
— *NAPRA Review*

"This is one of those rare works that once you've read it, you can never look at the world, or at people, the same way again. It is quiet and forceful and powerful."
— American Indian College Fund

The Girl Who Sang to the Buffalo

ALSO BY KENT NERBURN

Calm Surrender
Chief Joseph and the Flight of the Nez Perce
A Haunting Reverence
Letters to My Son
Make Me an Instrument of Your Peace
Neither Wolf nor Dog
Ordinary Sacred
Road Angels
Simple Truths
Small Graces
The Wolf at Twilight

EDITED BY KENT NERBURN

The Wisdom of the Native Americans
The Soul of an Indian
Native American Wisdom

THE GIRL
WHO SANG
to the BUFFALO

A Child, an Elder, and the
Light from an Ancient Sky

KENT NERBURN

New World Library
Novato, California

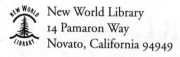 New World Library
14 Pamaron Way
Novato, California 94949

Text design by Tona Pearce Myers

Photograph on page 389 courtesy of the South Dakota State Historical Society.

Library of Congress Cataloging-in-Publication Data
Nerburn, Kent, date.
 The girl who sang to the buffalo : a child, an elder, and the light from an ancient sky / Kent Nerburn.
    pages   cm
 ISBN 978-1-60868-015-3 (pbk.) — ISBN 978-1-60868-017-7 (ebook)
 1. Dan, 1913-2002. 2. Dakota Indians—Biography. 3. Dakota philosophy.
 4. Dakota Indians—Social life and customs. I. Title.
 E99.D1.D345 N 2013
 978.004'975243—dc23   2013030970

First printing, November 2013
ISBN 978-1-60868-015-3
Printed in Canada on 100% postconsumer-waste recycled paper

 New World Library is proud to be a Gold Certified Environmentally Responsible Publisher. Publisher certification awarded by Green Press Initiative. www.greenpressinitiative.org

20 19 18 17 16 15 14 13 12 11

In memory of Richard Twiss and Vine Deloria Jr.,
two exemplary men who understood, in very different ways,
that what we believe is who we are;
and
Harold Iron Shield,
who would not let the dead go unremembered

There are more things in Heaven and Earth,
Horatio, than are dreamt of in your philosophy.
— WILLIAM SHAKESPEARE, HAMLET, ACT I, SCENE 5

Contents

Part 2. Into the West

Part 3. Northern Light

A World beyond Our Understanding

We will stir the waters
Until one remembers
— Ojibwe ceremonial song

For more than two decades I have tried, honestly and respectfully, to walk the difficult line between the world of
Native America and the world of those of us whose people came,
willingly or otherwise, to these American shores.

I have done this because I believe that we, as Americans, are
poorly served by our willful avoidance of the true facts of our
national experience, and also because I believe that the lives and
ways of the Native American peoples have much to teach us all.

It has been a fascinating and deeply rewarding journey. It has
taken me into classrooms and sweat lodges, onto basketball courts
and to kitchen tables. It has found me on dusty reservation back
roads, in deep northern forests, and on lonely mountain passes.
Most of all, it has taken me into the hearts and lives of some of the
kindest, most fun-loving, most thoughtful people I have ever met.

But it has also taken me to places that challenge my way of
understanding. Lying in the shelter pits on Chief Joseph's final

battlefield on the lonely Montana high plains, I was touched by a force, almost palpable, telling me to leave, because I did not belong there. On a wintry day on a great frozen marsh in northern Minnesota, where a battle between the Ojibwe and Sioux left hundreds dead more than a century ago, I heard what sounded like voices, or cries.

Projections? Maybe.

Fantasies? Possibly.

But, perhaps, something else.

The book you hold in your hands — *The Girl Who Sang to the Buffalo* — takes you to the edge of this world so far from our own. It weaves its way through lands of the heart and the spirit, where reality takes different shapes and truth is often better revealed by the power of story than by the simple recounting of fact.

At its center, of course, is Dan, the Lakota elder you have come to know if you have followed my journey through *Neither Wolf nor Dog* and *The Wolf at Twilight*. Dan was a gift — a person who gave me the opportunity, through stories well told, to reveal the world of Native people in a way that would touch minds and change hearts. Through him, I have been able to lead you into the heart of Native America in a way that few non-Native readers ever experience.

You traveled with us across the Dakota high plains and into the dark confines of the Indian boarding-school system. You learned of the beliefs and struggles of the Native people as our American culture moved across the land that was once their own. You saw how they lived, how they laughed, how they honored their Creator, and how they cared for one another. You learned of Dan's life, his friends, and the world through which he passed in his almost ninety years on earth. You came to know his humor, his insight, his anger, his sadness.

What you don't know — and what I am going to share with you in this book — is the deeper dimension of the world in which he lived, a world that remains a mystery and impossibility to those of us who come from the world where the European mind and spiritual tradition hold sway.

All of us who have spent time in Indian country know that beneath the myths, misperceptions, and stereotypes that make up so much of our understanding of Native life lies a world that beats with a different and indomitable heartbeat. It is what has kept Native cultures alive and vibrant in the face of half a millennium of policies and practices dedicated to the extermination of their peoples and their ways of life.

In *The Girl Who Sang to the Buffalo* I want to bring some of this world to you. It is a task I undertake with trepidation. The essence of a respectful approach to Native life, for both Native and non-Native people, is an honoring of boundaries. There are things that are not meant to be shared, known, and even understood. You must earn the right to approach them, and you go only if called. And despite the claims of many non-Native writers, there are places where no non-Native person is ever called, or ever should be. This is simply the way it is.

But this does not negate the truth of these places, nor does it mean we should not honor their presence. They merely must remain, to those of us on the outside, part of the realm of the mysterious, a realm that flies in the face of what Dan once called our "square-cornered understanding of life."

The Girl Who Sang to the Buffalo brushes against these places. They are not places for spiritual dabblers. They are a taproot to a world that runs deeper than our presence on this continent.

But, more than that, they are an incursion into a spiritual realm where there are powers and forces that neither can nor should be taken for granted.

Whether it be as simple as a group of eagles suddenly appearing and circling overhead during a ceremony, or *tatanka*, the buffalo, showing himself on a hillside where moments before there had appeared only trees and bushes, or the whispers of forgotten voices on the Montana high plains, there is a world out there that stretches far beyond our understanding.

The Girl Who Sang to the Buffalo is a journey into the border regions of that world. It is not a journey that admits of easy understanding or easy acceptance. But it is a journey that I believe we should be willing to take. For only by exploring these realms, and acknowledging them with humility and grace, can we truly understand how small and fragile is this piece of earth, both physical and spiritual, that we have come to know and embrace as home.

Kent Nerburn
Bemidji, Minnesota
2013

Part One

Forgotten Secrets

CHAPTER ONE

A Shout in the Night

It was early spring when the dreams began.

They were not ordinary dreams. They had none of that unreality that separates night from day. Their colors were the colors of sunlight, their sounds as real as everyday life. I would wake from them with my heart pounding and my palms sweating, not knowing where the dream left off and the waking world began.

But there was something else about them. They were always the same — Dan's sister, Yellow Bird, with her little bowl haircut, standing in front of a monolithic red-brick building wearing a faded white dress; Mary, the old woman I had visited when I was searching for her, standing by her side.

Mary smiles at me. I see the wrinkles on her face and the yellow stains on her teeth. She begins talking, but no words come out of her mouth. Yellow Bird stares at me with mute, expressionless eyes. She turns and begins walking toward a field filled with large boulders or hay bales. There is steam rising from them into the night. A feeling of dread comes over me. I shout at her but get no response.

Mary continues smiling. She points at Yellow Bird, who is disappearing into the mist-covered field. I keep shouting, but Yellow Bird doesn't hear me.

Mary reaches her bony hand toward me. She keeps gesturing toward Yellow Bird and nodding. I want to run, to catch her, but I can't. Yellow Bird turns and looks directly into my eyes. She beckons me to follow her as she disappears into the field.

Then I wake up.

Mary and Yellow Bird had been part of a sad and poignant episode in my life.

Twenty years earlier, I had done two books of oral history with students on the Red Lake Ojibwe Indian Reservation in the pine forests of northern Minnesota. Those books, *To Walk the Red Road* and *We Choose to Remember*, had traveled around the country on the powwow circuit and landed in the hands of many people. One of those people was a Lakota elder named Dan who lived on a reservation far out on the high plains of the western Dakotas.

Dan had asked me to visit him. I did so, and our meeting had resulted in a book — *Neither Wolf nor Dog* — in which Dan revealed his thoughts about subjects ranging from his understanding of history to how Indians felt about being called by that name. Over the years he and I had developed a friendship that had culminated, most recently, in his asking for my assistance in helping to find out what had happened to his little sister, Yellow Bird, who had disappeared from a government boarding school when they were both children.

Mary, the other presence in my dream, was an elderly part-Ojibwe, part-Cree woman who lived in the heavy pine and lake country near the Canadian border in my home state of Minnesota. My search for Yellow Bird had led me to her home, and, ultimately, to information that had helped solve the mystery of Yellow Bird's disappearance. Though I had only visited her once, her kind manner and haunting face had stayed with me.

Now they were both returning in my dreams, and I could not figure out why.

"But there's something different about them," I say to Louise. "They're like echoes, as if there's something real behind them, and I just can't get to it. It's like they're calling me."

She takes a sip of her morning coffee. "It's probably just guilt," she says.

"Guilt? Guilt at what? I did what I could. I found out about Yellow Bird. I gave Dan such peace as I could at the end of his life."

"I don't know. Maybe at not having done enough? About getting there too late?"

The answer is too facile, too full of modern psychology. This is one of those dreams that touches some taproot of terror, like the fear of the depths below you when you swim in dark waters. It doesn't respond to rational analysis or admit of easy dismissal.

"This isn't some cheap psychological thing," I say.

"I didn't say that it was," she answers. "I just don't know what to say."

I put my head in my hands, rub my eyes with my knuckles. "They're just not normal. They seem too real. And they stay with me all day, like they're haunting me, or following me. Sometimes I think I went someplace that I didn't belong."

She puts her hand on my shoulder. I know she thinks I'm being overly dramatic. "You did what you were called to do. You helped an old man find out about his sister. You told a story that he wanted told, and you opened his world to a lot of people who needed to hear what he had to say."

"I know," I say. "But maybe I went too far. Maybe I opened some doors that were meant to be left closed."

The room fills with silence. We are both at a loss. She walks to the window and looks out at the morning sun.

"Do you remember that woman you worked with at Red Lake?" she says. "The one who baked the rolls for our wedding?"

"Lurene?"

"You remember what she told you when your dad was sick?"

Lurene was a gentle Ojibwe woman who had prepared meals for the elderly and shut-ins on the Red Lake Indian Reservation. She had been raised in the traditional manner and still practiced many of the old ways. She and I had gotten to be friends when I brought my students in to help serve meals to the elderly.

One time when my father was ill I had experienced a disturbing dream about him that had seemed almost real. I made an off-hand comment to Lurene about how much it had bothered me.

"You should call him," she said quietly. "He's probably reaching out to you."

That evening when I got home I picked up the phone and dialed my father's number. Though my father was one who held his emotions close, I could hear the relief in his voice. "I was hoping you'd call," he said. "I've been thinking about you for the past several days."

The next morning I went in to thank Lurene for prodding me to make the call. I found her making sandwiches to deliver to the elderly shut-ins.

"Thanks for telling me to call my father," I said. "It was a good thing that I did."

She kept her eyes down, but I could see a small smile creep across her lips.

"You need to pay more attention to dreams," she said. "They aren't just playthings. They carry messages."

As summer progressed, the dreams grew more intense. I struggled with them, anguished over them, did whatever I could to avoid them. I would not give in to the possibility that they were trying to send me a message.

Then one night in late August everything changed.

I had gone to bed slightly before midnight, hoping this would be one of the rare nights when the dream would leave me alone. I lay in the darkness, trying to claim a few hours of quiet rest. I do not remember if I had fallen asleep or was simply drifting in that liquid state between sleep and consciousness. I only remember the sound, like a shout or a thunderclap, that shook me with a violence that left me gasping for breath.

It was loud, almost human. I could not identify its source. I was not sure if it had taken place outside the house or inside my head. I sat up and tried to calm myself. My heart was racing and my pulse pounding.

I looked over at Louise. She lay quietly next to me; her breathing was deep and regular. Our dog, Lucie, was still asleep at the foot of the bed. Neither of them appeared to have heard anything.

I sat for a minute until my heart slowed, then pulled on some clothes, grabbed a flashlight, and went out into the yard, Lucie at my heels. I thought perhaps a tree had fallen or some part of the house had cracked and broken.

It was a dark night with only a sliver of moon and high, racing clouds. The pines surrounding the house were alive with moving shadows. I walked among them, shining a flashlight in all directions. No trees were down, and the house appeared to be fine.

Lucie snuffled happily in the trees and grasses; nothing in particular piqued her interest or caught her attention.

Eventually I became convinced that the noise had not come from outside. I went back into the house, still unnerved and agitated, and sat in the living room in the darkness, trying to calm myself.

At some point, I fell into an uneasy sleep. The dream of Yellow Bird and Mary came and went, but it was distant and fractured, like disembodied laughter heard around a corner. Every time I drifted into heavy sleep, Mary would appear before me with her yellow teeth and wrinkled smile, pointing toward Yellow Bird. I would snap back awake and try to chase away the image. But soon enough exhaustion would overtake me and I would drift off again, and she would rise up before me, smiling and pointing, like an image in the fog.

Eventually, the eastern horizon filled with a thin, grey light, and the shadowy shapes of the trees began to emerge in the dim illumination of the dawn. By the time the full light of day flooded through the windows, I had made a decision: this dream and its nightly hauntings could not go on. If, indeed, it was carrying a message, I needed to find out what it was. If it was just guilt, I needed to put that guilt to rest.

My plan was simple: I would make the three-hour trip north to Mary's house, make a casual visit under the pretense of thanking her for her help in finding out about Dan's sister, and pass along what Dan and I had discovered. If, in the process, she brought up anything about having wanted to see me, so much the better. If not, it would still be a visit worth making. It would be a closure of sorts and would perhaps put to rest any subliminal guilt I felt at not having contacted her after she had been so helpful in providing me information during my previous visit.

So, on a warm early September morning, with the wind blowing whisper-soft through the trees, I loaded up the car and headed north toward the Canadian border. Though I was feeling a bit self-conscious about my willingness to entertain a vaguely super-natural interpretation of what was probably an ordinary dream, I was feeling good about my decision. At least I was taking some positive action.

As I drove along the thin ribbon of roadway through the sun-lit forests, the weight of the dream seemed to lessen. Perhaps, I told myself, Louise had been right; perhaps I was overreacting and the dreams were just the logical subconscious response to a trau-matic event that had never been completely resolved.

I knew I had never quite come to grips with the deep pain and sadness that had resulted from my lonely search for Yellow Bird. And I had never reconnected with Mary to thank her for talking to a strange white man about something so personal and painful. These issues lay there, unspoken, unaddressed, at the center of my life.

And then there was the specter of Dan, who was now almost ninety years old — if indeed he was still alive. I had always known that my feelings for him were bound up with feelings for my father, who had died at about the same time Dan and I had met. The two of them were nearly the same age, and, though my father had worn his hair short and Dan's long white hair fell down below his shoulders, something in their physical presences linked the two of them in my mind. Maybe it was the slightly protruding lower jaw; maybe the gentle sadness deep in the eyes. Maybe it was just the common ravages of advancing age — two strong men grown fragile and unsteady and accepting their infirmity only grudgingly.

There had been moments when Dan and I were together that I would catch a glimpse of him out of the corner of my eye and think, for an instant, that I was looking at my father.

By the time I had finished the search for Yellow Bird, they were like one person in my heart. I could no longer separate them, nor did I want to. What I did for Dan, I did for my father. What I owed to my father, I owed to Dan. Perhaps the dream was just the extension of the guilt I felt about obligations left unmet and debts that had been left unpaid to two men who stood like comforting shelters over my own winding path to adulthood.

As the drive to Mary's house came to an end, I had almost convinced myself that the dream was, indeed, nothing more than a confused welter of guilt, memory, and projection, and that I was making more of it than it deserved. Still, I was happy for the visit. That kind old woman who had shared the stories of her childhood with me deserved the courtesy of a visit and a personally delivered thank-you.

I turned down the path to her house with a lightness of spirit that I hadn't felt in months.

The early autumn light filtered through the branches and painted dappled patterns on the hood of my car as I navigated the two ruts that cut through the trees toward Mary's home. The path itself was still soggy from a summer of heavy rain, making the driving slippery and slightly problematic, but nothing like the white-knuckle experience it had been several winters before when I had pushed my way down these same ruts in the snow-covered darkness of a frigid January night.

I splashed my way through the puddles and pools of standing water. Through the openings in the trees I could see the great lake rolling in the distance.

As I turned the corner into Mary's yard, the pristine white trailer, set against the backdrop of the great, shimmering northern lake, formed a breathtaking tableau.

In winter, everything had been dominated by the dark, star-filled sky and the huge, impersonal silence. The frozen lake had been an unseen presence, sleeping like a great animal just beyond my consciousness. Now the same lake, unchained from its winter bondage, was a dancing, playful life force, whispering rhythmically as its waves lapped gently against the shore.

I rolled down my window. The air was filled with a pungent, watery scent. Far out toward the horizon, diamonds of light flashed on the lake's surface. Clouds floated across the blue vault of the sky, forming momentary images, then dispersing as the gentle autumn winds moved them along. Small flocks of birds rose from the wood and lake and congealed into formations — practice for the great fall migration that was just weeks away.

Despite the idyllic beauty of the setting, it was clear that something had changed. The home that had been so neat and tidy at my last visit was now surrounded by a jumble of children's bikes and plastic tricycles. The van that had been sitting half-buried in a snowdrift had become a storage bin filled to the top with boxes, antlers, and items I could not identify. A child's playhouse had been built on a platform behind the house, and a tarp-covered sweat lodge with a deep fire pit stood near the shore of the lake.

At first I thought I had simply missed all this on my last visit because of the winter darkness and the deep blowing snows. But the change was more fundamental. The last time I had been here the house had felt solitary and singular, as if it was holding out against the forest and the lake and the great forces of nature. Now it felt complicated and busy and full of human life.

Three children were jumping on an old battered trampoline at the side of the house. They stopped their bouncing and stood motionless as I parked the car. I was about to ask if their grandma was home when a heavy woman in her midthirties stepped out of the front door and stood staring at me with her hands on her hips. I recognized her as Donna, Mary's granddaughter, with whom I had spoken at the reservation convenience store several years before.

She looked at me strangely, as if trying to remember where she had seen me.

"Hi," I said. "You're Donna, right? I'm Kent Nerburn. Maybe you don't remember me. I met you at the trading post a few years ago. I was trying to find out about a little girl who had gone to boarding school with your grandma."

"I remember you," she said, continuing to stare.

"Is your grandma home?" I asked. "I thought I'd come and tell her what I found out about the little girl."

"She's gone," she said. She continued to fix me with a strangely intense look.

"I'm sorry. I should have called," I said. "Will she be back soon?"

She shook her head. "She's gone," she said again. "Dead. Walked on."

I felt the blood rush to my face. "I'm sorry," I said. "I didn't know."

"A week ago Thursday."

"Oh," was all I could say. A week ago Thursday I had been awakened by the noise that had shaken me like a shout in the night.

CHAPTER TWO

"I Have Something to Tell Him"

" *I* 'm sorry I seemed so strange," Donna said, handing me a mug of coffee. "But I couldn't believe it was you."

We were sitting at the kitchen table in the cluttered trailer that had once been Mary's tidy and pristine home. After the initial shock of my arrival, Donna had relaxed and become the warm, welcoming presence I had remembered from our brief encounter several years before.

"Grandma had always hoped you'd come back," she said. "She was always asking about you. Every time I'd come over she'd say, 'Do you know who that white man was who came to visit me? I have something to tell him.' But I didn't know who you were. I didn't know how to find you."

"I should have come sooner," I said. "I owed her a thank-you for how kind and helpful she'd been during my visit."

"That's all right," she said. "Grandma would understand. She was very traditional. She thought everything happened for a reason."

Donna went over to the refrigerator and returned with a long, oblong block of commodity cheese and set it on a plate with an opened package of saltines.

"It isn't much, but it's all we've got until the first of the month," she said, placing the plate before me. There was a hint of apology in her voice.

"This is fine," I said, sawing off a chunk of bright orange cheese with a butter knife and placing it on a saltine. "Reminds me of growing up."

"Do you want some milk for your coffee? Some orange juice?"

Her hospitality in the face of her poverty was touching. When she had opened the refrigerator I had seen that it was almost empty. Yet she was offering me everything she had. I looked out the kitchen window at the happy children who had gone back to bouncing on the trampoline. This was a woman who worked hard at being a good mother.

"Grandma always felt bad about not telling you everything," she said. Again, there was apology in her voice. "But you were a white man. She didn't know you."

She touched her fingertips together and stared at the lake. There was a distant look in her eyes, as if she was trying to make a decision about something that she wasn't sure she wanted to reveal.

"I have to ask you," she said. "Why did you come back now?"

"It's kind of hard to explain," I said. "And kind of embarrassing. I kept having dreams. Your grandma was in them. She kept gesturing to me."

Donna got up and walked around the room. It was clear that she was nervous. She kept picking things up and setting them down, moving objects from one place to another.

"I think we need to go for a drive," she said.

We piled the three children into my car and headed up the path toward the main road.

"We need to visit Grandma," Donna said. "I want her to see you. We'll drop the kids off at Lori's store. They can stay with her."

I was not sure if she was referring to Mary or a different grandma, but I asked no questions.

"But we want to visit Grandma, too," the oldest child said, bouncing up and down in her seat.

Donna turned and held up one finger in a gesture of quiet admonition. The girl sat back glumly, pushed out her bottom lip, and folded her arms across her chest. She said nothing more but began kicking the back of my seat.

Donna turned again and said something in Ojibwe. Her voice was soft but her manner was stern. The kicking immediately stopped. Donna reached across and touched the girl gently on the side of the head. "Be quiet, child," she said in English. The girl made a pouty face but sat back in her seat. The other kids kept their eyes down and their hands in their laps.

We stopped at the small trailer store where two winters before I had received instructions on how to find the path to Mary's home. The children piled out of the car and lined up at Donna's window for a kiss. She leaned out, taking each of their heads in her hands and whispering something in Ojibwe before kissing them on the forehead and giving them a gentle pat on the cheek. It was obviously a practiced ritual.

"Be good now," she said to the oldest girl. "Tell Lori I'm going up to Grandma's grave. I'll be back in a few hours." The kids nodded and ran off toward a passel of puppies that had emerged from somewhere beneath the footings of the trailer and were barking and squealing with an enthusiasm equal to that of the girls running toward them.

"Good kids," I said.

"They got some fire," Donna answered.

"I would have been okay with them coming along," I said.

"No," Donna said. "This is not for them."

We proceeded westward along the lake. An occasional promontory or finger of land thrust out into the sparkling waters,
breaking the otherwise smooth crescent of shoreline that stretched
to the horizon. The waters glistened in the late morning sunlight
and lapped gently against the thin margin of sand and stones that
formed the water's edge.

After about ten minutes Donna pointed to a path that wound
down through a stand of oak and maple toward the lakeshore.

"Go down there," she said.

I turned the car onto the weedy, overgrown trail. We wound
through the brush and deadfall, pausing occasionally so I could
remove a tree limb or cluster of branches that had fallen during
some recent storm. When we reached a clearing by the shore of
the lake, she told me to stop.

She hoisted herself out of the car and walked into the stand of
trees at water's edge. She was a heavy woman and had a roll in her
gait like someone who had suffered a serious knee or hip injury in
the past. Nonetheless, she moved with confidence and an ungainly
grace through the tall weeds and over the uneven ground.

"This was Grandma's favorite place," she said. "I want you to
see it."

Again, I was unclear about her purpose. She seemed intent
on giving me some insight into her grandmother, but I had no
idea why.

"We used to come here every summer," she said. "This was
our fish camp. Grandpa had a bark house he built. He did it in
the old way, by bending willow branches and covering them with
strips of birch bark. He said that was the way his ancestors had
done it. He wanted us kids to learn the old ways. He was afraid we
would cross over to the white man's world and never come back."

She stared out over the sparkling, lapping waters, lost in thought.

"We fished," she said, almost as if she was talking more to herself than to me. "Oh, we loved to fish. Grandma, Grandpa, all of them. That's what our family did, all summer. We'd move here right when the ice went out. We mostly ate fish and berries all summer, and my mother would make outside bread in a pan that she set by the fire. We had all kinds of nuts and vegetables. Oh, we ate good.

"In the fall we'd go ricing and every spring we'd tap the maple trees. We'd make a big fire and boil the sap in a big iron pot. Sometimes Grandma would sneak a little out and let it cool, then give it to me for a treat. Oh, I loved the taste of that maple sugar."

She walked away from me, out toward the water, speaking softly. I moved along behind her, struggling to hear her words.

"I loved the way we grew up. It was so different. I remember how before the men went out in the spring, Grandma would tie a bundle of sticks together with pieces of all our clothing, a pouch of tobacco, and a little black puppy. She said it was an offering to the lake spirits so the men would be safe. It made me sad to see that little puppy get thrown in the lake. But I loved my dad and my brothers and my grandpa. That little puppy was drowning to save them.

"I remember raising my hand in school when the nuns talked about Jesus dying so everybody else could live. I was really excited to tell them that we had a little puppy that died to save my brothers and my father. They locked me in a dark closet and didn't let me out for the rest of the day."

Her thoughts were moving like the clouds overhead, and her voice was almost dreamlike. She seemed almost to have forgotten I was there.

"I really loved my grandma," she said. "She raised me, even more than my mom did. That was the old way, to give the little girls to the grandmas. They taught us how to cook and sew and where to get good wood for the fire, and how birch bark would start a fire even when it was wet. I used to follow my grandma into the woods. 'Here, my girl,' she'd say. 'This plant will help you if there is something bad in your stomach.' She would show me how to pick the leaves, how to boil them. She told me the things to do and the prayers to say so it would give me its medicine."

She turned abruptly and looked toward me.

"Mr. Nerburn, do you know how hard it was for Grandma to tell me those things? The priests in the boarding school had taught her she would go to hell for believing in the old ways. She was so afraid that she was going to go to hell for teaching me those things. Afraid that I would go there, too, if I learned them. But she was afraid of the old powers, too. How do you live when you don't know which spirits to believe in?"

"I don't know," I said. I was tempted to place my hand on her shoulder or do something to comfort her. She seemed so desolate in her memories. But I held back.

"This is why she couldn't tell you things. She didn't know what you would believe. I don't even know if she knew what to believe herself."

She stared through the trees out at the lake.

"What they did to those little kids was just awful. Just awful."

We walked slowly among the birches at the edge of the clearing. Donna kept pausing and listening, as if there was some distant echo she could not quite hear. I was desperate to ask what her grandma had wanted to tell me. But I kept reminding myself of what Dan had often told me — that white people always want to go in a straight line to any destination, while Indian people survey the whole landscape before they proceed. This was Donna's private journey through the landscape of her memories and grief. Where she wanted to go, and how she wanted to get there, would reveal itself in its own good time.

CHAPTER THREE

SPIRIT LODGE

*W*e returned to the car and proceeded westward along the rutted path that hugged the shoreline. The lake was huge — so large that you could not see the other side. Here on the south shore, eons of winds from the northwest had shaped the land into craggy, scrub-covered dunes. Some of these were fifty feet high and hundreds of feet long and jutted out into the lake like great, sandy fingers.

Donna directed me along the road until we reached a weedy path that led to the top of one of these dunes. "There," she said. "Go up there."

The undercarriage of the car dragged against the scrub grass, and the wheels spun in the sand as I nosed toward the top. It was obvious that few vehicles made this journey.

As we reached the crest, a small village of low doghouse-like structures spread out before us in a long, uneven line that stretched out onto one of these fingers. I recognized them as the spirit lodges that the Ojibwe built over the graves of their dead.

Someone had once told me that these lodges were put in place when someone died, and when the walls finally decayed and collapsed, the spirit was set free. I didn't know if this was accurate, but even from this distance I could see that some of the houses looked new and freshly painted, while others had crumbled and collapsed, leaving only a pile of weathered wood and shingles on top of a mound of earth. All of them had personal shrines of stuffed animals, coffee cups, and various mementos in front of them.

"Go that way," Donna said, gesturing toward the point of land that thrust like the prow of a ship out into the lake. "Grandma's grave is over there."

We drove through the loamy ruts past several small clusters of spirit lodges spread along the dune. The lodges were all long and low, mostly six or seven feet in length and one or two feet high, though several were smaller, about the size of a young child. There must have been about fifty in all. They all had low-pitched, shingled roofs and were painted in different colors, ranging from solid blue to white with red or yellow or black trim. Each had a small hole in the front, no bigger than an inch in diameter, with a tiny platform beneath it.

I recalled from the Ojibwe funerals I had attended over the years that the holes were there to allow the spirit of the departed to travel in and out of the spirit house, and the platforms were there to hold food that was to nourish the spirit on its journey to the afterlife.

"Do you have tobacco?" Donna asked.

Luckily, I had placed a pack of Prince Albert in my pocket before I left — an almost unconscious act I performed before any extended trip into Indian country, where I knew that tobacco was always offered as the traditional gift of greeting and respect.

I had brought it along to give to Mary. I never expected that it would end up as an offering to her departing spirit.

"Grandma will like that," Donna said as I pulled it out and placed it on the dashboard in front of me.

We drove to the end of the promontory and parked in the grass just behind the last gathering of spirit lodges that faced the lake. Donna got out and walked toward them. Her uneven gait was painful to watch. I followed at a respectful distance, holding the pouch of tobacco in my hand.

Mary's spirit lodge was the newest. It had been painted a robin's-egg blue with floral and geometric designs on the side. Fresh dirt from the burial still spread out around its edges.

The ground in front of the lodge had already been decorated with plastic flowers and various mementos, including a feather and a ceramic eagle and the red-and-blue china teapot she had used to serve me when I had visited her before.

On the ground on one side of the small spirit portal sat the little one-legged Barbie doll that Amber, the daughter of Lori, the woman who ran the store where we had dropped the girls, had shown me when I had last visited. Amber had loved that little doll and showed her off proudly. It was a poignant reminder of the Native belief that you should always give away that which you love the most, and a quiet lesson in how this belief was being passed along from generation to generation.

Perhaps most poignant and disconcerting was the metal crucifix I remembered hanging on the wall of Mary's trailer. It was leaned up against the front of the lodge on the opposite side of the spirit portal from Amber's Barbie doll. On the ground next to it was a stake with an emblem of a bird, signifying the clan to which Mary had belonged.

Donna was standing in front of the grave with her hands clasped and her eyes cast down. She was speaking softly.

I remained at a distance, not wishing to intrude on, or even witness, this private moment. I walked slowly among the other graves, looking at the private shrines of children's toys, baseball caps, favorite coffee cups, and pieces of candy. It cut to the heart; there was love here in every amulet and small object.

I thought of the austere and bloodless geometry of the military cemetery where my father and mother were buried. There were no personal shrines there, no personal mementos, only a sea of anonymous humped white stones marching in martial precision over a treeless hillside. At the time of their burials, we had been handed a list of regulations about what could and could not be put on the graves, and how long the permitted objects would be allowed to remain. Had we tried to put a personal note, one of my sisters' little dolls, my father's favorite pipe, a copy of one of my mother's favorite poems — even a photograph of our old orange cat — it would have been summarily removed for violating cemetery regulations.

"This is the way I wish I could have buried my parents," I said to no one in particular as I watched Donna speaking softly to the spirit house of her grandmother. I was feeling lonely and forlorn and a long way from home.

In the distance a ragged, emaciated dog loped along the path we had just driven. He moved swiftly, stopping every few steps to stare at me, as if trying to identify me or determine my purpose in being here. I walked toward him, hoping for a moment of friendship, but he darted off into the weeds. Soon he appeared again, stared at me, and disappeared.

Donna was finishing her private moment with her grandma. "You should come over now," she said.

I made my way through the patchy grass to the front of the grave. "Do you have the tobacco?" she asked.

I quickly removed the Prince Albert from my pocket and placed a few pinches on the small platform in front of the spirit hole. The wind whisked in and picked it up, sending it scattering through the air.

Donna smiled at me. "Grandma is with us," she said. "This is good."

She reached into the bag she had carried over her shoulder and removed a deer-hide packet bound up with rawhide laces.

"You open this," she said. "Then give it back to me."

I took the folded-over deer hide and carefully began untying the laces that had been tied into tight bows.

"Grandma tied those," she said. "You are touching Grandma's hands."

The realization gave the task an unexpected significance.

"Grandma said that if you came back she would tell you something. But if she died first, I should give you this. I think it's time you saw it."

I finished untying the laces and opened the stiff, fur-covered hide. Inside was a sheaf of notebook pages held together by pieces of rawhide looped through the binder holes. On the front page, in a small but precise penmanship, gone shaky with age, was written,

What I Remember

Mary Johnson

Ozhaawashko-binesiikwe

CHAPTER FOUR

THE NOTEBOOK

"*G*ive it back to me now," Donna said. "Grandma said that I should read it to you. She said that in our way, if someone is there to witness, you need to speak the truth. She said that I should read this because that would be her voice talking and my reading would be the witness. That way you would know it is the truth."

"I would always believe your grandma," I said. "No matter who read it."

"It doesn't matter. This was her way. The way she wanted me to do it. Sit down now. We need to do this in Grandma's presence."

I handed her the folded deer hide and sat down in the sand and wiry grass, facing the spirit lodge. The wind off the lake whispered from far distances.

"I'm not a good reader," she said apologetically as she lowered herself onto the ground next to me.

"It's your grandma's voice," I said. "I'm sure it will be fine."

"Put some tobacco on the ground between us."

I did as she requested, then asked, "Do you know what's in it?"

"No. She never told me. I watched her tie it with her own hands. She said I should only open it if you came. Otherwise I should burn it."

"I'm glad I came," I said.

"So am I," she said. "So is Grandma."

Donna shifted herself several times in an effort to get comfortable. I could see that her bad leg was causing her pain. Then she opened the deerskin and, like a mother telling her children a bedtime story, began to read:

My name is Mary Johnson. That's my English name. My Indian name is Ozhaawashko-binesiikwe. I knew your friend's little sister. I think she was a very good person. I want to tell you these things. I did not tell them all to you before.

Your friend's sister was called Sarah. That's the name they gave her in school. I am Anishinaabe so I couldn't speak Lakota. But another student told me that her name was Zintkala Zi. She said it means Yellow Bird. That was a beautiful name. It made me like her because my name means the Bluebird Woman in our language. It made me feel like we were sisters. I wish we could have called her that. But they would have beaten us or put us in the closet, so we just called her Sarah.

Sarah couldn't learn English. There was something wrong with her ears. Maybe with her voice, too. She couldn't speak except to make loud sounds. Maybe they meant something in Lakota, but we couldn't understand them at all. I thought she was a very pretty girl. She had her hair cut short. We all did. They did that to us there.

But it looked so good on her. She looked like a little doll with her beautiful skin and big eyes. She had very speaking eyes. Maybe that was because she couldn't use words. Her eyes could say everything.

The nuns, some of them, tried to be nice to her. I think they felt sorry for her. But she would never do what they said. That made them angry. They would tell her to do something, and she would just stare at the ground. I don't think she understood. But in that school, that didn't matter. You were supposed to understand, no matter what. If you didn't it was because you were a bad person or weren't trying. Then you got beat or punished. They didn't care if there was something wrong with you.

In that school they had lots of ways of punishing. Sometimes they would make you go down to the basement and sit on the cold stove with your underpants down until you got blisters. Sometimes they would beat your hands with a belt until you couldn't move your fingers. Sometimes they would just lock you in the closet or not give you supper. They did whatever they wanted to. There was no one to stop them. We were all scared, but there was nothing we could do.

I remember one time Sarah wouldn't do what the nuns said. I don't think she understood them. They called the Indian man who worked there. He took her out behind the school building where there was a big hole. It was for punishing. They put her down in there and covered the top with boards. When it was time to eat they lowered food to her on a rope. They kept her there for three days. She was only six or seven.

Another time they put her in a dark closet. That was because she started crying and wouldn't stop when they

burned up a doll another girl had. That girl was from
Turtle Mountain, I think. An Anishinaabe girl, like me.
Her mother had made her new clothes and a little doll to
bring to the new school. Her mother thought that boarding school would be good for her because it would help
her learn English and the ways of the white people. She
wanted her to have a good life, not like the life on the
reservations, where everyone was starving.

She had made a beautiful dress for her daughter and a
beautiful doll. I remember seeing them when she came in.
Sometimes we would watch when a new girl came, to see
what she was like. That little girl had the most beautiful
dress and the most beautiful doll.

When that girl from Turtle Mountain got to the
school they did the same thing they did to all of us. They
made her take off all her clothes and gave her a bath in
kerosene. Then they cut off all her hair and washed her
head with kerosene, too. They said it was to get rid of
lice. They did it to the boys, too. The girl was crying. Lots
of us cried when they did that to us. The kerosene burnt
really bad. Then they made her take the dress her mother
had made for her and throw it in the fire. Her mother had
beaded flowers all over it. Those were the designs from
our people, flowers and plants. But the priests didn't like
them. They said they were designs from the devil. Then
they made her throw the doll in, too, because the mother
had made the same designs on it.

This hurt little Sarah really bad. She loved dolls. They
were her only friends. She would make sounds to those
dolls and talk to them like they were real. It was her own
language for just her and the dolls.

When Sarah saw the new girl throw her beautiful

doll in the fire, she started crying and wouldn't stop. For her it was like burning up a person. I think maybe she thought that the new doll would be friends with her doll. Or maybe it was like our old ways, where our grandfather made us a doll when we were very young so we could practice the ways of motherhood. Our doll was our child. Maybe when Sarah saw that doll thrown in the fire it was like seeing a child being burned. She cried until a mean priest with crooked teeth and a big white beard all covered with tobacco stains came and grabbed her by the arm. He took her away and locked her in the cellar. There were rats down there. We knew because we could hear them moving around at night.

That was the kind of thing they did to her. I only saw some of it. I think it happened to her all the time. I want you to know that I don't think they did any of the really bad things to her that happened to other kids. Like I know one girl whose fingers froze when they put her outside in the winter. When she came in her fingers got all black and hurt so bad that they had to be cut off. But that was at a different school. I never heard of anything like that at our school. I don't know how I could live if I had seen any of the really bad things, like babies being buried or boys being made to do things with some of the men. I want your friend to know that they didn't happen to your friend's sister. At least not the really bad things.

I'm sorry I didn't tell you these things before. I didn't want your friend to have a heavy spirit. So I just told you that they took her away.

Now I think I have to say the other things, though. The things I didn't say. It was not right that I did not tell you everything. If your friend is still alive he is old like I am. He has seen many things, like I have. Some of those things are bad and make our hearts heavy. Sometimes it is good to know these things because when we know them we can put them on the ground and walk away from them. I know this. I have placed many heavy things on the ground in my life. I still feel their sadness. I should not have tried to decide for your friend what he should carry and what he should put on the ground. I will tell them to you now.

I told you before that his sister could not learn English. That was the hardest part. I told you she could not hear. It was like she was in a dark room with no light. It was good to learn English in the boarding schools. When we learned English we could all talk to each other, even if we were from different tribes. If you could not speak English you were all alone, except for when no one was around and you could talk to your friends who spoke the same language as you.

That little girl Sarah couldn't hear, so she was all alone all the time, even when people who spoke her language tried to talk to her. I think that must have been the worst — being all alone. I wanted to be her friend, but if they saw you becoming friends with someone they separated you. They did not want you having friends. They thought that would keep you being Indian longer. They wanted everyone to be all alone. Sarah was the most alone of anyone.

I used to see her hugging her dolls all the time and saying things to them. I think she was pretending she was their mother. She must have had a very kind mother because she was very kind to her doll children. She would have been a good mother.

It made me sad to see her hugging her dolls. It made me miss my home. When we were at home with our parents we were hugged all the time. The grandmas were always touching us and hugging us and fixing our hair. Our people like to use our hands. When we got to the boarding school no one hugged us. We got no good-night kisses. No one stroked our hair.

This made my spirit turn hard. We learned to be good. But we forgot how to love. We had the love ripped away from us when they took us away from our mothers and fathers and grandmas. If we had any love left in us, they beat it out of us. This happened to me. I didn't know how to love. I only knew how to hurt. We knew how to punish because that was all we had ever known. My own children know this. I couldn't even hug my own daughter until she was fifteen years old. That's how far inside myself I was.

I'm telling you this because your friend's little sister did not forget how to love. She had her dolls. I saw how she loved them. She loved them like my mother loved me. I wish I could have kept that love in my heart. But they scared it out of me. They beat it out of me. They didn't beat it out of your friend's sister. I think she was very strong.

It was bad what they did to us. They made us shut down our spirits until we didn't even care what went on around us. Kids were always sick and kids were crying and new kids would come and there would be sicknesses and no one would even care. When you are little and you get sick you just want someone to come and hold you and tell you you're going to be all right. But we had no one to hold us. We had no one to tell us we were going to be all right. When we saw other kids get sick like us, then get taken away, we got so scared that we were going to die and never get to see our mothers and fathers again. Then they told us that if we weren't good we were going to go to the place where there was a fire and we would burn up forever, so we were afraid of that, too.

When I got the sickness with the spots — that's what little Sarah got, too — I was scared I was going to die and go to that fire place and burn up forever. It made me hide in my bed and cry all night. But I would have gone there if I only could have seen my mother and father one more time. That's all I wanted. To have my mother and father come and hold me. Then I would have gone to that fire place forever. I really would have. I just wanted to be held one more time by my mother, to have my father lift me up like he used to and hold me in his arms and call me his little girl and run his hand through my hair. I was so afraid. I was so scared.

When I remember that I think of little Sarah. How she didn't even have anyone, how she couldn't talk to anyone, how she was so alone all the time. That's why I didn't tell you everything I knew, because I didn't want your friend to know how sad she was. But I thought about it every day after you left. It is not good to have something in your heart and not tell it. So that is why I am writing this. I want to get it out of my heart.

Now I'm going to tell you the hard part. This is the part I didn't want to tell you. It is about the place they sent her. I told you when you were here about the time she fell down and started crying and saying sounds like, "*Shunka, shunka*" that day we were walking along the road by the big field, and how we all thought she was saying she wanted to ride on a horse instead of walking. I told you how we found out later that there had been some horses frozen to death in that field and that she was feeling their spirits. I only told you that one story. But there were lots more. There was the time she made a bird come to her hand and she said things to it and it said things back to her.

The nuns and priests didn't like these spirit things she was doing. They said she was doing devil things. They wanted her out of there. I think they were scared of her. They didn't like her power. They tried to give her to a white family, but no one would take her. People didn't like that she couldn't say real words and couldn't hear.

One day a woman came to the school. She was from a doctor place. She spoke English different from the other people. Someone said she was from Germany. She came to us to see about how many of us were sick. That was when we were all getting the disease with the black spots. We were all getting it. They made us all take baths in the same water and use the same towels. So when one of us got sick we all got sick. Lots of kids were dying. Some of them the parents came and took home so they could bury them in the Indian way. The other ones were buried out in back in the corner of the schoolyard. We all had to go out and fold our hands and pray while the priest said words and they put the child in the ground. We were all so scared. We didn't want to die from the black-spot sickness and be buried where our families would never find us. Lots of kids tried to run away at that time. They mostly got caught and brought back and punished. They would tie a log to our legs and make us walk around the schoolyard until we had walked as far as we had run. Some kids had burns on their legs from the ropes that never went away.

That nurse who came to see us that time made us all line up. She looked in our throats and made us take off our clothes to see if we had spots on us. When she told your friend's sister to open her mouth and she didn't do it, the nurse looked in her ears and then went behind her and clapped her hands behind her head. Your friend's sister didn't move. That nurse said she shouldn't be there.

That night I was in the kitchen doing my work when I heard one of the nuns say they didn't like that nurse. I was peeling potatoes and pretended I wasn't listening. I don't think they cared anyway. They said the little girl Sarah had a bad spirit. They did not like that the nurse was blaming them and telling them that Sarah shouldn't be there.

The next day that little girl Sarah was gone. Someone said they took her to a place in South Dakota that was like a prison for Indians with bad spirits. I did not believe they would take a little girl there, but that's what I heard. She went with a man who came to get her in a black car.

If you get this book there is a person I want you to go see. His name is Benais. I have heard he was in that place for Indians with bad spirits. I have never talked to him about it. I did not want to make it come alive again for him by making him talk about it. I think he knew that little girl Sarah.

I was raised to only tell those things I have seen with my eyes. That is why I am only telling you these things I have seen. I am writing them because you have come back.

When someone asks for something twice you must give it to them. If you have come back, that is the second time. Now I must tell you. I ask *Gichi Manidoo* to help me speak the truth. I hope what I say will not give your friend a heavy spirit.

Donna shut the book and closed her eyes. She stayed that way for several minutes.

Far in the distance the golden afternoon light shimmered and glistened on the lake. I sat, chastened, contemplating what I had just heard. From behind one of the spirit houses the ragged dog reappeared and looked at me, then disappeared into the brush.

Eventually Donna opened her eyes. "It was hard to hear her voice," she said quietly.

"Your grandma was a very good person," I said. "It must have been very hard for her to write that. This must have been difficult for you."

She nodded and looked down again.

"Do you think I could take that book? To read to my friend?"

"I am glad you asked," she said. "That's what Grandma wanted. But she said I should only give it to you if you asked. Now you have asked." She was carefully retying the rawhide laces, caressing them gently as she formed them into bows, as if this was the last touch she would have of her grandmother's hands.

"Do you know who this Benais is?" I asked. I didn't want to push, but I needed to know who it was I was supposed to see.

Donna nodded but said nothing.

She struggled to her feet; I stood up quickly and gave her my hand.

"Take me back," she said. "I need to start supper." She was clasping the notebook tightly to her chest.

We rode in heavy silence around the broad rim of the lake until we arrived at Lori's store. The kids were running around the dusty yard, shrieking and laughing. I recognized little Amber, the girl who had once shown me the broken Barbie that was now propped up against the small platform of Mary's spirit lodge.

Donna opened the door and began to get out. She turned and looked directly at me. Her face was blank, like someone who had retreated out of sight. She carefully placed the folded animal skin containing the notebook on the passenger seat of the car. She kept her hand on it for a moment.

Then slowly, hesitantly, she removed her hand and turned toward the house. She took several steps in her painful, hitched gait before turning back to me. "Benais lives on the other side of the lake," she said. "He's one of the old ones. He's not like us. I wish you luck, Mr. Nerburn."

CHAPTER FIVE

"I Knew You Were Coming"

I drove off feeling forlorn and unclean. For reasons I could not understand I felt vaguely responsible for Donna's sadness. She had been so kind and helpful, but her loneliness and the loss of her grandmother had been like open wounds on her heart. By making her revisit her grandmother's words, then taking away the notebook that had been written in her grandmother's hand, I felt like I had stolen something from her and left her even more alone and bereft than she had been before my arrival. It only made me feel more responsible to Mary and to the task of bringing the information to Dan.

I knew I needed to visit this Benais. But the strange tone in Donna's voice when she had said, "I wish you luck, Mr. Nerburn," had left me wary and on edge.

I had no idea how to find this man who Donna said is "not like us." All she had told me was that he lived on the other side of the lake, and that could mean anywhere along hundreds of miles of shoreline.

I drove for about an hour, dropping around the south end of the lake, then heading north along the eastern shore. Gradually the road moved inland, away from the water. The trees became taller, the forest deeper. The pines loomed large on either side of the roadway, their heavy branches shutting out the warm autumn light. Huge crows and other dark birds flew from branch to branch and walked along the side of the road, as if this was their domain and I was just a momentary intruder.

No cars came up behind me or toward me from the other direction. I was alone on a forest road that was getting smaller and darker. Finally, I saw a rural mail carrier driving slowly along the shoulder in an old Buick. I flagged him down and asked him if he knew where a man named Benais lived.

"Yeah, it's up about six miles," he said, leaning out of his car window. "There's a mailbox with a feather hanging off it. I don't know why he's got it, though. He never gets any mail. I've never even seen him."

I thanked him and continued north. I had the distinct sense that I must be heading toward a dead end; there was no traffic and the road had changed from asphalt to gravel. The cut-offs into the woods were few and far apart and almost completely overgrown with brush, as if no one had traveled them for months or years.

I passed a small pull-off area that contained two dented green Dumpsters. White trash bags, rotted mattresses, and old tires were strewn around the ground. Three black bear cubs were climbing in and out of the Dumpsters.

I had almost decided that I had misunderstood the mail carrier's directions when I saw the dented mailbox with the feather dangling from a piece of rawhide. There was no name on it. Next to it was a weedy trail heading off into the forest.

I turned down the trail and headed back through the trees.

I was feeling increasingly uncomfortable. There was something dark and brooding about the forest. I had been fine so long as I was on the main road, even though I saw no other cars. I trusted my little Toyota; it had seen worse.

I had not even been bothered when the asphalt turned to gravel. But now I was on a weedy, poorly traveled path with jagged rocks jutting up through the dirt like sharp, grey animal fangs. I wasn't sure my spare was any good, or that it would even be possible to change a tire on this uneven ground. And the prospect of a man who received no mail, lived alone at the end of a road, and had been described as "not being like us" made me think that I had made a serious mistake. But I kept telling myself that if Mary had wanted me to see him, it was only right that I accede to her wishes, and that perhaps by visiting this Benais I would learn something I could share with the old man out in the Dakotas who meant so much to me.

The trees and bushes crowded the path. Here and there the woods opened to the left, revealing a marshy field with a small oxbow creek meandering off into the distance. Red-tailed hawks floated overhead, and songbirds darted in the reeds and rushes at the edge of the creek. Once a beaver or an otter slipped off a bank and hit the water with a splash, surprising me and further setting my nerves on edge. I began to look for a place to turn around in case I decided that this was not a course worth pursuing. But at no point did the road widen enough to allow me to reverse my direction.

I kept thinking I should somehow have tried to communicate with Benais before attempting to visit him. I was nervous about intruding uninvited on a man who so clearly valued his privacy. But given the narrowness of the path and the distance I had traveled, I had no option but to proceed. I had to hope that Mary's instruction to go visit Benais had been based on sufficient knowledge that he would not take offense at my intrusion.

At the convenience store at the base of the lake, I had armed myself with another pouch of Prince Albert tobacco and a large can of Folgers coffee as gifts. But suddenly they seemed too "white," like some kind of peddler's trade goods. I wished I had been able to find *kinnikinnic*, the Indian tobacco made from the inside of willow bark, but it was too late to worry about such things.

The undercarriage of the car scraped excruciatingly against the center hump on the path. I tried to avoid the deepest depressions. But the thick growth of dwarf aspen and berry bushes pushed to the very edge of the road, so there was no real way to avoid bottoming out other than by driving very slowly and hoping that the scraping of the underside was causing no serious damage.

My discomfort was rapidly increasing. I was like a man who had crawled into a cave and was now unsure if he'd be able to back out. But just as my discomfort was turning toward panic, the path opened into in a wide clearing with a tiny metal trailer at its center. The trailer was old and dented and missing pieces of skirting around its base. It was more like a construction shack than a trailer intended for human habitation. Chickens were walking in the clearing, pecking at the dirt. The whole setting had an unnerving primitiveness about it, with skulls nailed to trees and raw animal skins hanging over branches.

Despite the primitive nature of the compound, there was a definite sense of order to the setting. A number of small garden areas were fenced in with chicken wire. Behind the trailer were frames with hides stretched taut inside them. Throughout the clearing and off into the woods stood a series of structures covered with old army tarps. Their rounded shapes indicated that their frames had probably been made by lashing branches together.

The whole area had been raked and cleared right up to the edge of the forest. It was an environment that had been ordered, shaped, and carefully tended.

A man who must have been well into his eighties was standing in the middle of the yard methodically sweeping a patch of dirt with a broom. He was small and thin, with dark, almost mahogany, skin and a shock of thick, white hair. He had on baggy black cotton pants tucked into heavily worn calf-high moccasins, and a long-sleeve flannel shirt buttoned at the sleeves and at the collar.

He did not bother to look up when I drove in.

I was about to step from the car and make some uneasy introduction when I saw a black bear sitting on its haunches at the rear of the clearing. The man seemed indifferent to its presence.

I sat for a moment, uncertain of what to do, then slowly opened the car door, hoping to scare the bear away. The bear lifted its head and stuck its nose into the wind, then crashed off into the brush. Neither my arrival nor the bear's departure seemed to make even the slightest impression on the man.

"Benais?" I said.

The man moved his head slightly in my direction. His movements were slow and deliberate, neither welcoming nor discouraging.

Even at a distance, it was impossible not to notice his eyes. They were small and vigilant, with a piercing, avian quality, as if he were watching something closely from a great distance.

I walked over slowly and held the tobacco out to him.

He nodded, took it without looking at me, slipped it in the breast pocket of his shirt, and returned to his sweeping. I noticed he was missing the first two fingers on his left hand.

"Mary Johnson — Ozhaawashko-binesiikwe — said I should come and see you," I said.

He remained silent and focused on his inscrutable task.

I thought of what Dan had often told me — that Indians knew that the best way to deal with white people was to stay silent until we become so uncomfortable that we start talking and reveal the true intention behind our presence.

I thought perhaps that he was testing me in this fashion, but his silence did not seem to have any ulterior motive. He was simply invested in his private actions and was pursuing them exactly as he would have had I not been there.

I stood for a while feeling clumsy and out of place. I actually thought of getting back into my car and leaving. But the message from Mary had been clear — "Go see Benais. He knows about the place your friend's sister was taken." For her, if not for myself, I needed to bring this situation to some kind of resolution.

Benais continued his sweeping. There was an almost monastic mindfulness in his actions. Each stroke of the broom was slow and methodical, precise in its focus and intention.

After a few more minutes of sweeping, Benais picked up his broom and carefully pulled the dirt off each bristle. Then he turned slowly toward the house and began walking up the steps, leaving me alone in the yard. I was ready to give up and get back in the car when he gestured for me to follow.

As we neared the steps a small black-and-white bird flew down and landed on a post near the doorway. Benais took some of the tobacco I had given him and sprinkled it on the ground in front of the steps as if he was distributing seed, then said something in Ojibwe. The bird cocked its head and flew away. I was reminded of Mary's words about how little Yellow Bird had upset the nuns by talking to birds.

I followed Benais up the stairs, making sure not to step in the tobacco.

The trailer had a cheap utility metal door with no window. It was dented as if it had been kicked or bent or perhaps salvaged from a pile of construction materials that had been discarded as too badly damaged to be worth saving. There was no lock, only a rope strung through the hole where the doorknob should have been.

Benais took off his shoes before entering, so I did the same.

The interior of the trailer was dark and suffocating, full of the dark musk of man smell and animal skins. All the windows were curtained with sheets and blankets. Animal pelts hung from curtain rods as if drying.

Benais nodded toward a straight-backed wooden chair set against a blanket-covered window. He still had not said a word. I sat down on the chair and folded my hands clumsily in front of me, trying to control the claustrophobic fear that was rising in my throat. He moved a few articles of clothing from another chair and pulled it up across from me. He sat down carefully and pulled himself closer until our knees almost touched. He still had not looked at me.

I glanced furtively around the room. Every surface was covered with animal skins or piles of porcupine quills and feathers. There were buckets of water with hides soaking in them, and the sink was full of dishes. Skulls of various animals hung on metal hooks and stared down at me from shelves. The kitchen table — if, indeed, it could even be called a kitchen — had boxes of cold cereal sitting open next to a jar of instant coffee. The whole place felt less like a man's home than an animal's cave.

Benais took the package of Prince Albert from his pocket and poured some into a cigarette paper. He rolled it into a clumsy cylinder using the two remaining fingers on his hand, pulled a few strands of stray tobacco out of its ends with his teeth, and lit it with a drugstore lighter he had tied around his neck with a leather thong.

He nodded slightly toward me as he inhaled deeply in order to get the tobacco burning. His eyes were intense and piercing — like small black seeds that seemed to absorb all light.

"Ozhaawashko-binesiikwe," he said at last. "I know her." They were the first words he had spoken in English, and just hearing them gave me a great feeling of relief. "What do you want?"

I didn't know whether to pour out the entire story or say as little as possible. "She helped me find out about a little girl for a friend of mine. She said you might be able to help me find out more."

He nodded, as if this was enough information for now.

He reached across the table and took a braid of what I assumed was sage from a cigar box that was balanced on a pile of skins and paper. He pulled a stick match from a pile on the table and lit it carefully. I noticed that he did not use his lighter. He blew slightly on the sage until it glowed, then moved it slowly back and forth through the air in front of him. The acrid smell filled the room and burnt my eyes.

He said a few words, then placed the sage in an abalone shell and returned to his cigarette. Everything was done slowly, with attention to every detail and movement.

I sat uncomfortably in the looming silence. I realized that other than the swirling smoke, there was no movement in the house — no clock, no small electrical diodes blinking on the fronts of computers, not even the faint hum of an electrical appliance in one of the other rooms. It was an almost unnerving stillness, made all the more stultifying by the closeness of the surroundings and the blanket-covered windows that shut out all the sounds and movements from outside.

Benais continued smoking. His gestures had a hypnotic slowness about them, and I wished for all the world that I could run out the door and go back to the comfortable rhythms and movements of my car driving down the highway. But there was no way to leave. All I could do was sit in the sepulchral half-light and watch the orange glow of Benais's cigarette ash grow strong, then weak, as he inhaled and exhaled.

The overwhelming silence was interrupted momentarily by the honking of geese flying overhead outside the house. Benais stopped his smoking and looked up. He tapped me several times on the knee to get my attention.

"*Nikag*," he said, pointing at the ceiling. "Geese. They love to say their name: *Nikag. Nikag.*" The folds around his dark eyes crinkled. The way he said *nikag* was a near approximation of the sound the winging birds were making.

He stubbed his cigarette out in a butt-filled tuna can on his table. "Do you know *bineshii?*" he asked.

I shook my head nervously. I had no idea who or what *bineshii* was.

"I heard the robin this morning,' he said. "*Mino-giizhigod. Geget igo noongom.* It's going to be a beautiful day."

He crinkled his eyes again and gave a small smile that revealed a few blackened stubs of teeth. He drew one final time on his cigarette and snuffed it out on the end of the table.

"I knew you were coming," he said. He lifted his hand slowly and made a gesture of tapping with his index finger. "*Baapaase. Baapaase.* The woodpecker. *Baapaase* told me."

Other than the few cryptic comments about birds and animals, Benais made no effort to communicate. We sat in heavy silence for what seemed like twenty minutes until, abruptly, he stood up and walked toward the door. He gestured for me to follow. I was relieved to be returning to the open air, where I wouldn't feel like the walls and ceiling were closing in on me.

Benais walked slowly down the wooden steps and across the clearing toward the forest. His steps were steady and he used no support.

Ahead of us I could see the faint presence of a path where the forest began, about the width of a trail made by a deer. I looked around nervously for any sign of the bear I had seen when I drove in.

The path wound through a thicket of birch and pine. Every step I made seemed to result in a crack or a crunch, while Benais's steps, in his old worn moccasins, were noiseless.

Some frogs croaked in a pond in the distance.

"The frogs. You hear them?" he said. "They're thanking the

rain. *Gimiwan. Gimiwan.* They're thanking the rain for coming last night and giving them babies. Giving them water where they can lay their eggs."

He made a sound back to the frogs and continued down the path.

I fell in behind him, again trying to keep my steps as noiseless as possible. His dark eyes were cast downward, but his head was constantly moving to hear the sounds around him. Whenever he heard a sound he would stop and listen, sometimes chortling a bit, sometimes saying something in Ojibwe.

At one point he reached down and touched a plant, not picking it but almost caressing it. "This will make your heart strong," he said. "You boil it. Drink it for a week." He touched the plant again and said something under his breath.

We continued along the path at this deliberate pace. Benais could not go more than a few steps without stopping to attend to a sound or a plant or a shaft of light. He seemed almost indifferent to my presence, as if I was but one more piece of the natural world through which he was passing — of no more or no less interest to him than an insect or a plant.

After a short time we came to another small clearing. Like the clearing around his house, this was swept clean. The perimeter had been carefully ringed with cuttings of cedar boughs. In the middle was a single log, laid on its side.

"Sit," he said, pointing to the log. He took out his tobacco and sprinkled it on the ground in front of him, then took a seat on the other end of the log from me.

"You may ask me now," he said. He kept his eyes focused on the ground in front of him.

This was the moment I had been waiting for, but now that it had arrived I was unsure how to begin. My thoughts seemed chatty and excessive. "There was a young girl," I said, trying to slow my speech to match his measured cadences. "She was the sister of a friend of mine. A Lakota man. He is old, near dying. I do not know that he has not already passed. His sister disappeared from the boarding schools many years ago. He asked me to help find her."

"And what does this have to do with Ozhaawashko-binesii-kwe?" he asked, "The woman you call Mary Johnson?"

"Mary went to school with her."

"Mmm," he said, revealing nothing.

"The girl was taken away from that school," I continued. "She was taken to a place that Mary said was for Indians with bad spirits. She said you knew about that place."

Benais tapped the ground with a stick he had picked up.

"Why did Ozhaawashko-binesiikwe not come here with you?" he asked.

"She, too, has passed."

"I did not know that."

"She had written a notebook," I continued. "Her grand-daughter gave it to me. It told me to come see you." I reached in the shoulder bag I was carrying. "I have it with me. Would you like to see it?"

Benais shook his head. "You read me where she says I should see you."

I untied the laces and opened the notebook to the last page. It was the first time I had actually looked at the writing. It was small and perfect — the hand of one schooled by nuns.

"*They took her to a place in South Dakota that was like a prison for Indians with bad spirits.*" I read. "*I did not believe they would take a little girl there, but that's what I heard.*

"*If you get this book there is a person I want you to go see. His name is Benais. I have heard he was in that place for Indians with bad spirits. I have never talked to him about it. I did not want to make it come alive again for him by making him talk about it. I think he knew that little girl Sarah.*"

Benais ran his hand slowly and deliberately through his shock of white hair. "I hear her in those words. I do not know the name Sarah."

He stood up and proceeded farther down the trail. "Walk a bit," he said. We walked slowly for almost five minutes before he spoke again.

"Yes, there was such a place," he said. "I was in it as a child. I do not know if I know the young girl you speak of. We were kept apart, the boys and girls.

"I will tell you what I remember. I will tell you only what I have seen with my eyes. It is not good to speak of things you have not seen. What I will tell you are the things that I saw."

His manner was formal, almost archaic; there was a singsong, dreamy character to his speaking, as if what he was saying had been practiced and learned and now was only being recited from memory, not thought or created as he spoke. I wanted to get everything right for Dan, so I slipped my hand in my pocket and clicked on my old cassette recorder.

"This place was the country of the Dakota people. In the place of the long grass, before the dry country. It was on a hill near a small town, a white town. It stood apart. It had windows piled three high." He made a gesture with his hands to indicate three stories in height. "It was made of stone. Red stone. There were bars on the windows and shades to keep out the light. Inside was dark and full of black dust that burned the lungs and hurt the eyes.

"There were only Indians there. They were from many tribes. They were chained to iron beds and made to walk around in the black dust. Clouds would rise up from our feet as we stepped in it."

He stopped and sprinkled some more tobacco on the ground before continuing.

"The windows would not open. The Indians there were very sad and full of pain. Some had been touched by a bad spirit.

Some had angered the Indians who worked for the whites. Some had refused to go the Christian way or had done nothing wrong. White people in white-people clothes would sometimes come and walk through the halls and look at us. We had to eat food that was not good for Indian people. Many of us became sick.

"There was a man there called Dr. Hummer. He did things to people. Sometimes he would put people in cold water. There were some women who screamed all the time. He gave them things to drink that made them quiet."

"Why were you there?" I asked. I hoped I would not insult him by interrupting.

"I am telling you this because you ask. Our family was not liked on the reservation. We were very powerful. My grandfather was teaching me the old ways. I was learning the ceremonies. They took me away to silence my grandfather. They wanted to be sure the old ways would die with him.

"They sent me to a school to learn Christian, but I would not learn their ways. I tried to practice our ceremonies. I showed other boys. They became angry and punished me. But their whips and belts did not hurt me.

"They took me to this place you speak of. I was there until it was closed down. When they were closing it there were many white men in dark suits walking around. There was much confusion. They were sending us to new places. I just walked away. I had twelve years of life at that time."

"Can I ask you about the girl?" I said. "The sister of my friend? To see if you knew her?"

Benais nodded.

"She was very young," I said, again trying to match the cadences and mannerisms of his language with my own. "Maybe seven. She could not speak. She had been sick and she had no hearing. I was told she had a beautiful face and round eyes. She loved to play with dolls. Her name was Sarah."

Benais thought for a moment. "I remember her," he said. "Yes. She was among the sad ones. She wore a white dress made dark from the black dust. Her hair was cut round. She made dolls from scraps. She carried them everywhere."

"That's her," I said.

"I did not know her name. I am glad to know it. It is good to be able to remember a person by name. She left before I did. We had almost the same years. I would see her walking. I would see her outside, where we were sent to play. She was always alone. There was a tall fence, taller than a man, made out of metal so we would not run away. She would go to that fence and look. There were hills far in the distance. She was always looking at the hills. She had a strong sadness.

"I do not know about her life. We boys could not go to the girls' side. I do not know what happened on that side. On our side, some people were chained to beds at night. I do not know if that happened to her. There were no lights at night. If you did not have one of the white pots you would have to empty yourself in your own bed. You would hear people screaming. The windows all had metal covers. It was hard to breathe.

"I remember a boy chained to a hot pipe. The other end of the chain was around his leg. He slept on a mattress on the floor. In the toilet room there would be people sitting on the floor eating from metal trays. These are things I remember. It may have been the same on the girls' side. I do not know."

He paused for a moment, as if trying to remember more.

"That is enough," he said abruptly.

I wanted him to continue but dared not ask. He had already been far more forthcoming than I expected. He took the stick he had been carrying and tapped at the ground.

"Come," he said. The edge of twilight was darkening the horizon.

We walked together through the path toward the trailer.

Though it was irrational, I was still nervous about the bear I had seen. I was almost afraid even to think about it, because I was convinced Benais could tell what I was feeling. But he paid no attention, walking silently in front of me with his eyes down and his hands clasped behind him.

I followed closely behind him, listening to the crunch and crack of the brush as I walked. The sounds of the birds and the frogs and the wind in the trees seemed louder than I remembered. In a way I had never experienced before, I felt observed and known by forces I could not name or understand.

CHAPTER SIX

"He Is Measuring Your Fear"

*B*enais built a small fire outside his house using birch bark and twigs from a pile he kept by the side of the door. He dragged two white plastic lawn chairs from the side of the trailer and gestured for me to sit. He took a corncob pipe from his pocket and filled it with the Prince Albert I had given him, using the same, precise gestures he had used for rolling the cigarette and sweeping the ground. It became obvious that he had certain places on his land that he used for certain activities. This was a sitting and conversing place.

Once in the chair with the fire started and his pipe lit, he began to open more to me. It was a slow unfolding, done at its own pace and in its own time. For the first time I could tell that his attention was more on me than on his surroundings, though he constantly turned his head or paused his conversation at the presence of sounds.

"You are not Ojibwe," he said.

"No."

"You are not Lakota."

"No, not that, either."

His eyes crinkled. "No teepee creepers?" he said. His lips pulled back in a grin that revealed his small, black stubs of teeth. It was a surprising bit of humor, and unlike any comment he had made before.

"Not that I know of," I said. "I had some grandpas with questionable habits."

"Ah, yes. So did I." He smiled an inward smile, as if the humor, like everything else, was private.

"Why do you try to help this man you talk about?"

"I'm a writer. He saw some books I did with students on the Red Lake Reservation. He had stories he wanted me to tell."

"Then you are a teacher."

"No, I was. Just for a while."

He nodded and fell silent. He was doing what the Indians I knew called "looking at the landscape" — walking a path around me both intellectually and spiritually to get a feel for the man at the center.

"And why do you come to me now? Why now that Ozhaawashko-binesiikwe has walked on?"

I chose my words carefully.

"I'd been having dreams. Mary — Ozhaawashko-binesiikwe — was in them. So was the little girl. Her Lakota name was Zintkala Zi — Yellow Bird. I thought I should go see Mary again."

"And she was no longer living."

"No."

Benais nodded. "Dreams are messages," he said. "They let your spirit journey without your body."

He reached up and brushed his cheek lightly with the back of his fingers. He kept his fingers cupped, moving them as a whole, like a man wearing mittens. It was as if his was more a paw than a hand.

"I must think about this," he said. "I will make some coffee."

It was the first gesture of hospitality he had made, and I wanted to take advantage of it. I quickly reached into my shoulder bag and pulled out the can of Folgers.

"I brought this for you," I said.

Again, his eyes crinkled and his blackened teeth shone. "Coffee is good. I will get some water."

He shuffled off into the house and returned with a dented metal saucepan filled with water that he placed on the edge of the fire. He gestured me to give him the coffee can, then poured some of the ground coffee directly into the water.

"Why was this young girl, this girl you call Yellow Bird, in the place you speak of?"

"They said she could communicate with animals."

He brushed his cheek once more with the edge of his fingers. "That would not seem to be a bad thing," he said.

"They thought so. They thought she was communicating with spirits, I guess."

"That, too, would not seem to be a bad thing."

The water had rapidly come to a boil, and the coffee grounds were roiling about on the bubbling surface. Benais took two tin cups from a box near his chair and filled them each with the boiling, muddy liquid.

"I think about your people and the four-leggeds," he said. "Some of them you take into your houses and give them human names. Others frighten you and you kill them. You put their heads on walls.

"This is hard for me to understand. The Creator placed the four-leggeds here before he placed us here. They have knowledge to share with us. Why would we be frightened of them?"

I thought of the bear I had seen at the edge of the forest when I drove in and how unnerved I had become.

"I don't know," I said. "I guess we're just not familiar with them. We live apart from them now. We don't get to know them."

"You know that our people take our clans from them. From all the different living creatures."

·"Yes," I said, recalling what I had learned about the Ojibwe clan system at Red Lake.

"I am of the Bear clan. We are the medicine people, the guardians. Ozhaawashko-binesiikwe was of the bird people. They are the spiritual ones. They fly high and look down upon us and give us guidance. The crane people, the loon people, they are the leaders, because when they speak all stop to listen. These learnings came from the long-ago people. They told us that each clan would have a special knowledge. When each clan shares its knowledge the people stay in balance. Much of that is lost now."

He sipped at his silty coffee. His eyes shone black in the firelight.

"It is good to listen to the animals," he continued. "They have much to teach us."

He stirred the coffee with a crooked finger, pushing the silt to the side.

"After I left that place of the black dust I went with my grandparents into the woods. There were many of us who did not want to live the white way. That is where I learned to listen to the animals. I am still listening."

He threw the remaining liquid from his cup onto the ground.

"Come," he said. "I want to show you something."

He stood up and walked toward my car. "We will take your car. I will show you where to go."

He positioned himself in the front seat and gestured toward the woods behind the trailer. "There," he said, pointing to an opening into the forest. "Go there."

I was concerned about the growing twilight and driving on unfamiliar trails in the darkness but could not deny his request.

"There was a bear over there when I drove in," I said, trying to be as offhand as possible.

"Yes. *Makoons*," he said. "He is gone now," as if this was explanation enough.

I drove the car through a narrow opening in the trees. The sky was rapidly emptying of light. The chorus of birds had receded, and the day had quieted. The path was a dark tunnel crisscrossed with shadows.

"Do not turn on your lights," Benais said.

The path cut straight through a long stand of tamarack and birch that crowded to the edge of the car. After about a hundred yards it opened onto a broad meadow that gradually descended into a deep valley at least a mile in extent. The whole world was slowly descending into a shadowy darkness.

Without the headlights it was hard to see, but all across the meadow and the valley I could make out solid forms standing in silence. At first I thought they were more bears, but as their shapes became clearer, I realized they were bison. There must have been more than a hundred of them.

"*Bishiki*," Benais said. "I have brought them here. They wanted to come home. Go. Drive to them."

I pushed on cautiously into the open field. There was a faint vehicle path I could follow — used, I guessed, to bring feed to the animals when the snows came. The great shaggy beasts shifted slowly in the shadows, then, one by one, turned and began walking down toward the trail. Soon the hills and field were alive with movement. The animals were coming en masse toward the car.

Benais seemed unconcerned.

"I bring them gifts," he said. He was rummaging in his pockets as he spoke.

"They were driven from here many years ago," he said. "But they remember."

"How did you get them?" I asked. The buffalo were moving in closer.

"People from the West gave them to us as a gift. Lakota. Like your friend. That is why I am showing them to you. They are sacred to your friend's people."

The beasts were closing in around the car. They moved placidly, encircling the vehicle, uttering low snorts and shaking their heads from side to side. Their eyes were dark and blank. They had a dark musk about them. Their heads were as big as oil drums.

"It is good to be around them," Benais said. "They carry a strong peace."

He removed some kind of grain ball from his pocket, rolled down his window, and held the ball toward one of the animals. The buffalo came up close — its head filled the entire car window — and enfolded the food in its large, green tongue. The others pushed up, bumping against the car with heavy thuds. There was an impenetrable emptiness to their gaze.

"Go more," Benais said.

The buffalo jumped aside with astonishing grace as I inched the car forward. Some raised their tails and pawed the ground while emitting low snorts.

"That one," Benais said, pointing to a huge animal with a great shaggy mane standing far back from the group. "That one has some cruelty. The others will not let it come near."

The animal stared at me from the hillside.

"He's new," Benais said. "He has earned no trust. He has been brought here from the land of your friend. He will be tested."

Even though I was in the relative safety of my car, I was filled with anxiety at the presence of the huge animals. Far from seeming peaceful, they emanated something darkly elemental. I pushed my way slowly through the herd. The buffalo followed along, tossing their heads from side to side. Their eyes were like pools, without expression, without bottoms. They snorted and grunted as they moved around and jostled the vehicle.

"They move in groups," Benais said. "They do not leave their land. That is why I brought them here. I had a dream that they were crying for this land. They were here once, before they were driven west."

"Do they stay?"

"There are those who know. They do not try to leave. The others we kill and use for food."

The solitary bull was staring down at me from a shadowy hillside. He moved along with the moving car, always keeping pace, but always at a distance.

"We do not know these animals, not like the Lakota and Cheyenne. For us it is the animals of our clans. They are our teachers. They show us how to live. My family lived far to the west, where the trees open to the prairies. We knew many of the Lakota and Dakota. I saw their respect for *bishiki*. I wanted to know what gave them such respect."

"Have you learned it?"

He moved his head slightly. "I am learning it."

He took another piece of food from his shirt and threw it out the window. The buffalo moved toward it, pushing against one another.

"They have much to teach about how to live. They let the female lead in search of food and water. They will take in a child that is lost. They circle around their weak, keeping them always at the center. They face danger rather than turning away from it. They will stand close together to hold up one who is wounded. They know what we are thinking."

The phrase sent a chill through me. The idea that the buffalo could know my thoughts touched something deep and dark in my imagination, especially because of the bull staring down on me from the hillside.

I thought back to the time in the Dakota grasslands with Dan when we had crouched motionless as what I thought were bushes and boulders on a distant hillside began to move and reveal themselves as buffalo. I had questioned Dan about how, with his bad eye and dimming sight, he had been able to see them. "I didn't see them," he said. "They showed themselves to me."

Now Benais was telling me almost the same thing in different words.

"How do you know that they can read our thoughts?" I asked.

"They don't read them. They know them. They have knowledge," he said, as if this was sufficient explanation.

I stared through the windshield at the dark mass of animals with their slow, patient movements and placid, empty gazes.

The strange bull was still on the hillside, staring down at me.

"That bull," I said. "He seems to be looking at me."

"He is measuring your fear," Benais said. "He is testing you."

The huge beasts kept milling around the car, waiting for Benais to give them more of the grain balls.

"Come," he said. "You have seen enough."

I shifted the car into gear and pushed slowly through the herd. It was not clear to me who had seen enough — me, Benais, or the lone bull standing motionless on the hillside in the darkness.

CHAPTER SEVEN

THE PLACE OF BLACK SOOT

*B*enais had no more to say. I could tell by his disengagement that he had told me all he felt I needed to know, or, at least, all he had been willing to share.

I shook his hand and thanked him for his time, then set off back down the path toward the road around the lake. The autumn sky was alive with stars, but the trees on the narrow path shielded them from me and left me driving in almost total blackness.

It seemed a betrayal to turn on my lights, but eventually I had no choice. Nonetheless, I felt a sense of shame as the bright swath of illumination cut through the trunks of the trees and the dark edges of the forest.

I was feeling more disquieted than I could ever remember. The eerie coincidence of Mary's death and the sound in the night; the discovery of the place of black dust; the brooding presence of the buffalo and the bear on the edge of the woods all swirled before me and left me deeply agitated.

And then there was Benais himself. I had never met anyone so impenetrable. He was affable enough but somehow unreachable, as if more animal than human. I could not free myself of the vision of him walking noiselessly across the ground, with that great shock of white hair and that dark and inward gaze, stopping to speak to birds and animals in a language they seemed to understand. I felt as if I had come close to something deep and elemental, something I should not engage or touch.

I drove on into the forest night, consumed with my thoughts. For the first time in weeks, I had almost forgotten about the dreams.

I spent the night on the side of the road in my car, wrapped in a sleeping bag. I was too tired to drive, and the memories of the bears at the Dumpster and the bear in Benais's yard kept me from setting up camp outside. Whether due to exhaustion or something else, the dreams did not pursue me, and I awoke refreshed and filled with the hopefulness of the growing morning light.

Though the previous night's agitation had receded, the responsibility to Dan had become even greater in my mind. I was not sure he was still alive, though I assumed someone would have contacted me if he had passed. But if he was still alive, this new information about Yellow Bird and the asylum was something I was convinced he should know. I thought of what Mary had said in her notebook: it was not for her or for me to decide what Dan should carry and what he should lay on the ground.

Of primary importance was getting the notebook to him. Mary, through Donna, had entrusted it to me. I was the messenger, and I did not take that lightly. But before I visited Dan, I needed to find out more about this place of the black dust, if it really existed. Mary had specifically instructed me to talk to

Benais, and Benais's only experience with Yellow Bird had been their common incarceration in this mysterious institution. She had obviously wanted me to know about this place and to share this knowledge with Dan. I did not want to speak falsely. I wanted to learn about this place for myself.

Yet Benais's description of the institution did not give me much to work with. All I had been able to glean was that it was in eastern South Dakota — "before the dry country," as Benais had put it; that it had been on the top of a hill near a "white" town; and that it had been like a prison for Indians with bad spirits. The conditions he described spoke of some kind of bedlam, or asylum. There were echoes of the Indian boarding schools in the involuntary incarceration and separation of the men and women, but clearly this had not been a place for children or for teaching. It had been something far more sinister. What concerned me was that I had never heard of it. I did not consider myself an authority on Indian history, but I knew about most major events and institutions, and in all my time and travels I had never heard mention of a place like the one Benais described.

I was obsessed with following the trail, but I was a long way out in the forests where cell phone signals didn't reach. So I drove back to the reservation trading post, bought a phone card, and made a few quick calls from the pay phone on the wall outside. It didn't take much to get some sketchy information, and when I got it, a chill ran through my body.

A woman in the South Dakota historical society put it to me matter-of-factly. "Oh, yes, I know what you're talking about," she said. "It was called the Hiawatha Asylum for Insane Indians." It had been built in the small town of Canton, southeast of Sioux Falls, in the early 1900s to house Indians with mental disorders. It had, indeed, been an imposing brick building set on a hill and had received inmates from many reservations around the country, though most seemed to come from the Dakotas, Minnesota, and Nebraska.

"Beyond that, we don't have much information on it," the woman said. "It was shut down in 1933. It's not there anymore. It was torn down sometime in the fifties."

She gave me a few other insignificant facts and apologized for her lack of information. "There just isn't much in the historical record about it," she said. "I've always been curious about it myself. I hope you have some luck."

I hung up the phone and walked back to the car. I didn't know which was more disturbing — that a place with such a name and a purpose had actually existed or that there was almost no information on it in the historical society of the very state where it had been located. Perhaps it had been small and historically insignificant. But it was not insignificant to those who had been incarcerated there, or to their families. I couldn't help but feel that this was one of those bits of American history that we had simply chosen to bury — like the Sand Creek or Gnadenhutten massacres — in our efforts to create an uplifting narrative of the conquest and development of our country.

I headed back toward home convinced that I had stumbled on one of America's dark, forgotten secrets. How much of it should be brought into the light and placed before an infirm old man was something I had not yet decided.

Peeling back the first layer of silence proved relatively easy. With the assistance of the Internet, some helpful tribal historians, and the excellent collection of Indian materials at the local university, I was able to piece together a rough picture of the institution that Benais had called the "place of the black dust."

It had indeed been named the Hiawatha Asylum for Insane

Indians — an unintentionally macabre reference to Henry Wadsworth Longfellow's mythical hero who gave up his land and culture to welcome the coming of the white man. The asylum indeed had been built in Canton, South Dakota, just across the border from southern Minnesota, as part of a maneuver by a local politician to bring jobs and money to their tiny rural enclave. Claiming that Indians were not well served by mainstream institutions — themselves horrible places at the time — the senator had been able to convince officials in Washington that a small South Dakota farming town with a population of under a thousand was the ideal place to "treat" Indians, because it was centrally located to tribes where the incidence of "insanity" was rampant and growing.

The building itself was completed in 1901 and by late 1902 had begun accepting Indian patients, who were sent there for reasons ranging from epilepsy to alcoholism to opposing the practices of elected tribal officials and Christian missionaries.

Everything that Benais had remembered was borne out by the research. The building was set high on a hill. It was built of red pressed brick and was surrounded by a seven-foot fence. The patients were kept inside in darkened rooms that were filled with soot from the coal furnace heating the building.

There were references to the overflowing chamber pots he had mentioned, as well as to an unbearable stench. The story of the small boy chained to the pipe was corroborated. Perhaps more disturbing was a reference to a ten-year-old boy who had been kept in a straitjacket for three years. I could not do the math to work things out, but it was possible that it had been Benais himself.

The overall effect of the materials, recorded so matter-of-factly, was as chilling as reading German records of concentration camps: factual data on inmates, catalogs of purported pathologies, and collections of data that reduced unspeakable human suffering to numbers and lists and institutional protocols.

What upset me the most was thinking of a man like Benais —

and I was sure there were others like him — for whom the natural world was everything being kept in dark rooms with padlocked doors and air choked with coal dust and the stench of feces. It was small wonder that the records showed inmates becoming violent and uncontrollable, or hanging themselves, as one man did, while a room away from him heavily drugged inmates were staring uncomprehendingly at a movie that was being shown to keep them pacified.

The man named Doctor Hummer whom Benais had mentioned was, indeed, real. He seemed to be the dark force behind the entire enterprise. He had been the veritable dictator of the institution and had committed people only on the hearsay of tribal officials, many of whom used the asylum as a way to rid themselves of undesirables or political opponents. He used no medical standards for admission other than his own observation, often making diagnoses like "idiocy" and "psychosis with organic brain disease," all because people refused to comply with requests that would violate their cultural beliefs and practices.

Because there were no standards for admission and no medical treatment once a patient was incarcerated, there was no possibility of getting well and no possibility of getting out. Being committed was essentially a life sentence. It was, in every sense of the word, a warehouse for undesirables — unscrutinized, unregulated, and, as the historical record indicated, unremembered.

As I sat at the table in the tribal archive, poring over the material, I shuddered at the thought that children like Benais and Yellow Bird had been incarcerated in a place like this. There had been inmates younger than ten and as old as eighty-four. If a child was born in the institution — and there appeared to have been children conceived there through either rape or inmate cohabitation — it was assumed that the insanity was passed down genetically, so those children were doomed to a lifetime of institutional confinement, if, indeed, they were allowed to live at all.

It seemed cruel beyond measure that children like Benais could be sent to an institution because their parents had practiced the old ways or that people with epilepsy or retardation, or who spoke with a slur because of a stroke, could be taken away from the families and communities that had always prided themselves on caring for all of their people, and be locked up for life. Yet this is what the records showed.

Little Yellow Bird, a child who had lost her hearing because of smallpox and was unable to understand or to speak clearly, had been locked up in this place because she spoke to dolls and had a connection with animals that had unnerved the priests and nuns in the boarding school.

What was most disconcerting was the absolute absence of any documentation by the inmates themselves. Many were illiterate, unable to speak English, either mentally deficient or driven to the point of physical or mental breakdown by the horrors of the asylum, and their helplessness was underscored by their silence. There were letters by family members trying to get information about their relatives and ancestors who had been incarcerated there, but always these letters had been intercepted by officials who wrote back bland administrative letters indicating that there was no information available or that the individual had died. There were no voices of the dead.

It was the dead, and their silence, that finally drove me to a decision. The records indicated that there had been a field of unmarked graves just outside the asylum. When the building had been torn down, the gravesite remained. The city of Canton, not wishing to waste prime hilltop property, had established a golf course on the site of the asylum. The field of unmarked graves was allowed to remain, unmarked and unremembered, between the third and fourth fairways.

In the succeeding years, one man, a Lakota journalist named Harold Iron Shield, had waged a lonely battle to get a monument placed at the site of the graves. His attempts had not been appreciated by the citizens of Canton, but in the end, he had succeeded in getting a small metal plaque listing the names of the dead placed on the site.

As I read this man's lonely struggle to honor those who had been buried without ceremony on this site, something came over me. I thought of my father and mother, buried in that soulless government cemetery where thousands of identical white stones marched in military cadence over acres of indifferent ground, and of Mary's caring and intimate burial site where she lay with her brothers and sisters and ancestors on a piece of earth where she had spent her childhood and where her family had made offerings and given thanks for the bounty the earth had given them.

The haunting words of Chief Joseph, the great Nez Perce leader and one of my heroes, rose up in me: "A man who does not love his father's grave is worse than a wild animal." How many of these fathers and mothers, and even little children, had been buried in this ground that was neither loved nor remembered?

As much for myself as for them and for Dan, I felt I needed to visit Canton and stand on this earth where the unremembered dead had been buried, to bear witness to their suffering and pay tribute to their lives. Perhaps in the process I could find someone who could fill in the blanks about life inside the asylum so I would have more information to share with Dan when I saw him. But even if no details came from the visit, I would be helping in some small way to hallow the ground where a little girl I had come to know and love had been locked in an institution for the simple crime of having skin of a different color and believing in spiritual powers that did not conform to the Christian norm.

Filled with a new resolve, I picked up the file folders, thick with random articles and documents and uncataloged notes, and prepared to carry them back to the tribal archivist. As I stood up, one of the folders fell open, spilling its contents onto the floor.

Among the jumble of scattered papers I noticed a brightly hued postcard. It was an old colorized image from the 1920s, showing the asylum in its early days. The photo had been taken from in front of, and slightly below, the main building, and showed a stately, monolithic red-brick structure with a green roof and a central porch sticking out beyond the patient wings like the prow of a ship.

It seemed benign, stolid, and reflective of a cultural confidence that stood in absolute contrast to the horrifying actions that had taken place inside. But it was not the cruel visual irony that struck me. It was the fact that the building, though presented in bright artificial postcard colors, was almost identical to the ghostly image of the dark looming structure that stood in silent brooding witness behind the figure of Yellow Bird in the dream I was trying so hard to escape.

CHAPTER EIGHT

THE WOMAN IN PEARLS

*T*he city of Canton was a six-hour journey from my home in northern Minnesota. On the map it was little more than a tiny dot in rural farm country, nestled in the corner where the states of Minnesota, South Dakota, Iowa, and Nebraska converge. The atlas legend said it had a population of 3,110. It seemed a strangely isolated and insignificant setting for so imposing a structure as the multistoried brick building I had seen in the postcard image.

My intention was simple: I would drive to the town, spend maybe a day or two seeking out information about the asylum, then return home to plan a trip out to visit Dan. I did not want too much time to elapse before my visit out to Lakota country, since I wasn't even sure that Dan was still alive. Yet I didn't want to contact anyone at the rez until the information I had was as complete as possible. The old man, if he was still alive, was surely infirm and fragile. I needed to share whatever I discovered in a clear and complete manner, doing honor to Mary's instructions while providing him the best, most compassionate picture I could of the life his little sister had led.

I drove into Canton from the east, preferring, as I always did, to stay off the freeways and see as much of the countryside as possible. As I passed through the rich farm fields of the Big Sioux River valley, I could easily imagine the old Norwegian settlers coming over the hills in their oxcarts and wagons, lifting a handful of this rich, black earth and saying, "Yes, this is where we will stop. This is where we will stay." It was country that would yield to the plow and reward hard work — exactly the kind of country that God-fearing people escaping from old-world poverty were seeking.

The words *gracious* and *bucolic* kept coming to mind. The hills were gentle, the river cut through the bottom lands in slow, unhurried curves, and the forest of deciduous trees that lined the river valley beckoned with protective leafy canopies that spoke of Sunday-afternoon picnics and evening summer strolls.

I knew from past experience that this was all an illusion, and that once you rose out of the river valleys onto the surrounding prairies, this was flat, featureless country that was raked by cold winter winds and beset in the summer by locusts and tornadoes and violent thunderstorms. But in the lazy, early autumn heat, as I drove along the river bottom, all that seemed a thousand miles away.

I continued down the curving two-lane blacktop road feeling an overwhelming sense of midwestern peace. This was the kind of America people imagined in the most nostalgic corners of their dreams, with families sitting in lawn chairs at the local baseball field, watching their children and grandchildren play Little League baseball games, then gathering at the local drive-in to share stories and cherry Cokes with friends and neighbors who had grown up together and who all knew each other's names. With each passing mile it became harder and harder to imagine this as the site of a brutal institution that imprisoned people in a soot-filled hell.

I had intended to go directly to the asylum. But before leaving home, on a hunch, I had made a call to several nursing homes in the area in search of someone who might have had some personal experience with the asylum. I knew from my time doing oral histories that often residents in these homes had stories and memories ignored by history books. Since the Hiawatha Asylum had been in existence until 1933, and many of the people who had been employed there had been locals, my thought was that there might be some people still alive who either had seen the asylum in operation or had heard stories from neighbors or relatives who had worked there.

As it turned out, I was right. Though most of the nursing homes I called had few staff people who had even heard about the asylum, one institution in a town not far from Canton mentioned that they had a resident named Edith who had referred to it once or twice in conversation.

After discussing it with her, they had informed me that she was willing to meet with me. Her grandma, she had said, had worked in the asylum and had often talked to her about the place.

I had set a time to visit her, but owing to some unforeseen detours and slowdowns behind lumbering harvest machines that blocked the entire width of the two-lane rural roads, I was now running so late that I would have no time to stop at the asylum before our scheduled meeting.

I looked longingly at the highway signs telling me that Canton was only a few miles away, then turned north toward the flat alluvial farm country that led to the small town where I knew Edith would be waiting.

The nursing home was a long, low-slung one-story brick building set on the edge of a cornfield a few miles outside town. It was

the kind of place you would hope to live in if you needed to go
to a nursing home — a quiet, intimate building, almost more
like a motel or a small grade school, with walkways and benches
and garden areas where the residents could go outside to pass the
hours.

As I stepped from my car into the warm September wind, a
man of about eighty, with his pants hitched high above his waist,
greeted me from a bench outside the front entrance.

"Nice day," he said.

"Air like apple wine," I answered.

He drew once on the cigarette he was smoking before snuffing
it out in an urn filled with about fifty other cigarette butts. "Getting near harvesttime. Should be a good year."

I nodded in agreement, though I knew nothing about farming.

He pointed to the sky. "Got to watch for the rain," he said.
"I lost a lot of crops by waiting too long. Used to try to leave
them until the moisture content was thirteen, fourteen percent.
Big risk, though."

"Timing's everything," I said, pretending I knew what he was
talking about.

Through the windows I could see people sitting alone in their
rooms staring at flickering images on small television screens.

"You farm?" he asked.

I rubbed my hand over my chin. "The only thing I can grow
is a beard."

The man chuckled and patted the bench next to him.

"Here. Sit down a bit," he said. "If you got the time."

I imagined him coming out to this same bench every day,
surveying the sky and assaying the weather, waiting for someone
to come by so he could convince them to sit awhile to discuss the
fields and the crops that had been so much a part of his life.

"Love to, but I've got to meet someone," I said.

"Well, you get a minute, you come on back." He lit up

another cigarette and stared off into the morning. He had heard that answer before.

I pushed through the glass door and into the lobby. Five elderly women were sitting in wheelchairs on either side of the hallway. It was obvious this was where they stationed themselves every morning after breakfast.

"She's in the lunchroom," one of them said.

"Excuse me?"

"Edith. She's in the lunchroom," the woman continued. "She's expecting you."

"I didn't know I was a celebrity."

"Oh, it's a small place," the woman said. "Word gets around."

The other women smiled up at me. Their hair was freshly done and they were dressed in proper clothes, as if waiting for someone to come to take them out for the day. The hallway smelled of lavender and disinfectant.

The receptionist at the desk signed me in, then directed me down the hall to the lunchroom area. A few ancient men were sitting hunched over in chairs by the windows, and two women were working a jigsaw puzzle on a long Formica table at the end of the room. In the middle of the room, seated in a wheelchair, was a tiny woman of about ninety wearing pressed khaki pants, tan espadrilles, and a shiny green polyester blouse. Her cheeks were heavily rouged and powdered, and her thin white hair had recently been set and done with a light peach rinse. Around her neck hung a necklace of heavy costume pearls. She smiled brightly as I walked into the room.

"Are you Edith?" I asked.

"Yes," she said. "You're the gentleman who's come to talk to me?"

"Yes. I'm Kent Nerburn. The woman on the phone said you knew something about the Hiawatha Asylum."

"I'm glad you've come to see me. I don't get many visitors."

She began to say more, then noticed that several of the women from the lobby had rolled themselves over to the door to see what was happening.

"Could we go somewhere else to talk?" she said.

"Wherever you're most comfortable," I said.

"I was hoping maybe we could go out somewhere for coffee," she said. I looked down at her hands. She had her purse in her lap.

"Sounds great to me. Is there a place nearby you like to go?"

Her face lit up. "Why, there's a nice little café in Canton," she said. "Or at least there used to be. They have great baked goods. My walker's by the door. We can pick it up on the way out. If you give me a hand in getting up, I can get around just fine."

I signed Edith out, then pushed her down the hall toward the door. The women in the wheelchairs smiled as we passed. Edith hardly looked at them.

The man with the cigarette was still sitting on the bench staring out at the fields. "Good day, Clarence," Edith said to him in a formal, stilted manner. I imagined she might once have been a small-town schoolteacher.

"No rain yet," he said. "Clouds building, though."

"Just another one of the busybodies," Edith said, shaking her head, as we left Clarence behind and wheeled toward the car. "The place is full of them."

"So, you don't get along with the other residents?" I asked.

"Oh, I get along just fine. I just keep my distance, that's all. It doesn't pay to get too close. We all just die anyway."

Her hard edge was off-putting, and I was beginning to wonder if I had made a mistake in arranging a meeting with her. But I was already this far into the encounter, so it seemed best just to follow it out to the end.

Edith was light as a bird and well able to move herself around once she was helped to her feet, so getting her into the car was easy. Her right hand had a rhythmic, palsied shake, but otherwise she was strong and able.

I put her wheelchair in the trunk and headed toward Canton. I was excited to finally get to the town where the asylum had been. Edith kept watch over the surrounding countryside. Her eyes gleamed as she surveyed the passing fields. "Things have changed so much," she said. "I don't get out very often anymore."

"No children? Grandchildren?"

"They've all moved away. Pittsburgh. The East Coast. They try to make it back at Christmas. They have their own lives." Now that she was outside the confines of the nursing home, her voice had lost its hard edge.

Every half mile or so a modern well-kept split-entry house sat on a lot that had been carved out of the surrounding cornfields.

"You know, this used to all be crops," she said. "We all worked together. It was a good time."

"You were raised around here?"

"Yes. In Canton."

"Was it a good place to grow up?"

"Oh, yes, it was wonderful," she said. "Everything was so beautiful. Canton was the most exciting place in the world to a little girl, with all the beautiful buildings and all the stores up and down Main Street. I remember when my dad would take us to the courthouse. I thought it was the most amazing building I had ever seen. We used to watch the clock on the tower move and thought this must be just what Europe is like."

She looked over at me. "Do you think we could drive by and look at it?"

"Absolutely," I said. I was anxious to hear her stories about the asylum, but it seemed only right to let her enjoy the ride and wander at leisure through her memories.

The country road and fields were gradually giving way to a

small enclave of tree-lined residential streets as we dropped down into the river valley and the town of Canton. The tower of the courthouse could be seen rising in the distance. I turned at the earliest opportunity and headed in its direction.

As we drove by the stately tan-brick building set back on its spacious green lawn, Edith pointed up at the tower. "See, that's the clock," she said. "Just like when I was little."

We drove slowly up and down the streets. Her eyes shone with excitement and nostalgia.

It was obvious that Canton had once been a prosperous town. There were gracious red-brick residences with wraparound porches and intricate architectural details, and, even now, long past the town's heyday, there was a tidiness to the homes and neighborhoods.

After we finished our drive through the residential area, we headed down the main street. It still had well-preserved two- and three-story brick buildings that spoke of a wealthy merchant and banking class that had taken great pride in the community it had created. The whole town had a midwestern brick solidity that was quite different from the dusty, wide-street small towns of the West, or the hardscrabble huddling rural enclaves of my own north country. Though many of the buildings were now vacant or converted into smaller stores, it had the feeling of a town that had shrunk to fit the scale of the times, not a town that was dying. The ghost of its gracious past was everywhere.

"Where was the asylum located?" I asked.

"Oh, it was out of town to the east a little ways," Edith said. "Out by the golf course. Maybe we can drive by it after we get some coffee."

"Sounds good to me," I said. "I was hoping you'd be willing to show me the site."

We passed down a street with a number of small storefront

businesses. "There it is," she said, pointing to a small café. I pulled up to the curb in impatient anticipation. I was a cup of coffee and a leisurely conversation away from an encounter with land that had shaped a little girl's life and haunted the darkest corners of my dreams.

CHAPTER NINE

"We Didn't Know
Any Better"

The café was typical of rural midwestern America, with booths along the sides and tables in the center, and a menu featuring specials like "hot turkey sandwich with mashed potatoes and vegetable and roll" written in Magic Marker on a whiteboard above the cash register.

A few solitary old men sat sipping cups of coffee, and several businessmen were engaged in animated discussions over some figures on a yellow legal pad. At one of the center tables a family was just finishing off plates of fried chicken, meatloaf, and some kind of tuna salad sandwich on white toast. They were waiting for a little girl of about five who was happily digging out the last vestiges of an ice cream sundae from a tulip-shaped dish, and putting the spoon in her mouth upside down, like a sucker.

Edith smiled at them as we went past. They all smiled back. The whole place had an air of small-town friendliness.

I helped her into a booth. "This place is famous for its cake," she said. "You should try some."

"I just ate," I lied. "But you get whatever you want." I wanted this to be a special outing for Edith, but I was anxious to get to the site of the asylum.

Almost before we were seated, a clean-faced young blonde girl came over and stood before us with a pencil poised over her note-pad. She was bright-eyed and innocent — no more than eighteen — and had on a pink waitress apron and gleaming white tennis shoes with white anklet socks.

"Should I get you menus? Or do you know what you want?" she smiled.

"Coffee's fine for me," I said.

Edith looked up at her with anticipation. "Do you have cake?"

"Our special today is devil's food," the girl said. "It was just baked this morning."

Edith clasped her hands together. "Oh, good. I'd like a piece of that. And coffee." I could hardly believe how different she seemed from the distant, severe woman I had picked up at the nursing home.

I was pleased to see her having such a good time. It was evident that this was a big event for her, maybe the biggest in weeks or months. I was almost ashamed to have to darken it by discussing the asylum. But she had told the staff she was willing to talk, so I had to hope that conversing about it would not put a damper on the obvious pleasure she was feeling at being out of the confines of the nursing home.

"So, you knew something about the asylum?" I said when the waitress left.

Edith was looking at the cheap dime-store pictures of windmills and pastoral scenes that hung on the wall above each booth. She seemed almost not to hear me.

"I think those are some of the same pictures that were here before," she said.

It felt inappropriate to push her, so I sat quietly while she surveyed her surroundings. Nothing escaped her notice. She pointed out the print of an old man praying over a loaf of bread, the framed first dollar that the restaurant had ever earned, and the salt and pepper shaker collection that sat on a shelf behind the cash register.

"Those were all here when I used to come here," she said, as if their presence somehow connected her lost past with her lonely present. When she caught a glimpse of her reflection in the window across the room she stopped talking and dug in her purse and pulled out a white handkerchief and touched it against the corner of her lips.

"I guess I didn't get my makeup on right," she apologized. In the bright light of the café her red lipstick and heavily powdered cheeks seemed overdone. My heart went out to her in her almost childlike excitement. I suddenly wanted this to be a significant occasion for her, a bit of celebration and festivity in her otherwise colorless life. The asylum could wait. It had been waiting for more than a hundred years.

"Your hair looks very nice," I said.

"You think so? I thought the hairdresser used too much rinse. She's new. The regular woman comes tomorrow. But I wanted to get it done this morning before we went out."

"Well, I think it looks very pretty," I said. She blushed a bit and touched the side of her hair with her tiny wrinkled hand. It was obvious she didn't receive compliments anymore.

I was ready to resign myself to the tiny festivity of the outing when she said, out of nowhere, "You know, my grandma worked there."

The abruptness of the comment caught me off guard. "Where?"

"The asylum. Hiawatha. She worked there for years. That's what you wanted to talk about, isn't it?"

"Well, yes, it is. But I'm just enjoying the company."

She made a coquettish little flip of the hand. "Oh, you're too kind," she said. "But I'm happy to tell you about it. This is such a treat for me."

"Well, if you don't mind."

"No, no, that's quite all right. I like talking about my grandmother. No one much asks about her. She was such an interesting woman. I remember her very well and the stories she told."

"I'd love to hear some of them."

Edith adjusted herself in her seat and gave a perky little turn of her head. "Well, then, I'll tell you some."

The family at the nearby table was just getting up to leave. The little girl had chocolate syrup and ice cream all around her mouth, and her young mother was wetting a napkin and using the edge of it to clean the girl's face. As the family walked by us, Edith reached out toward the little girl — an almost involuntary gesture filled with yearning and love. The girl pulled back and grabbed at her mother's leg.

The mother smiled down at Edith. "She's kind of shy sometimes," she said.

"Oh, that's all right," Edith responded. "She's such a cute girl."

"Say 'thank you,' to the nice woman, Tiffany," the mother said.

Tiffany cast her eyes downward and murmured a polite thank-you. Edith watched them as they walked out the door.

"Wasn't that little girl just darling?" she said.

"Absolutely."

"I miss children so much," she said. "They never come to the nursing home unless they're with their families, and then they're very shy. Old people scare them, I guess."

I shrugged and smiled. It was not a discussion I felt like entering.

She reached across and touched me on the sleeve. "You're about the youngest person I get to see, other than the staff girls."

"And I've got more than half the tread worn off my tires."

The comment delighted her. She let out a surprised laugh and touched my sleeve. "Now, where was I?"

"You were telling me about your grandma."

"Oh, yes. My grandma. She was a Trondseth. Inger Trondseth. She was born in the old country. Near Stavanger. She and her husband came over when she was in her twenties. She didn't speak very much English. I remember her always standing really tall and straight, with her hair pulled back in a bun. She always wore a white long-sleeved blouse, even in the summer. It always looked like it had just come out of the laundry. We girls used to laugh behind her back and say that her hair and her blouse were the same color." She giggled again at the memory of the old joke.

"Lots of people were scared of her because she didn't smile much. I guess that was just her way. But, really, she was so nice. She used to come in and check our hands before bed to see if they were clean and tell us to be sure to say our prayers. 'You don't want to talk to Jesus with dirty hands,' she said. Then she'd give us little pieces of candy. She always told us to keep quiet. 'Quick. Go brush your teeth when you finish it. If your mother finds out, she'll be very angry with me.'

"Even today I make sure I wash my hands right before bedtime. That's why I was reaching for that little girl. She still had a speck of chocolate on the side of her cheek. Just force of habit, I guess."

"But no candy now," I said.

"No." She leaned over toward me, as if telling me a secret. "But sometimes I keep some in my drawer, just to have a little treat before I go to sleep."

"Grandma would be proud," I said.

"That's what I think," she answered. "But I never let the aides know."

"So, how'd your grandma end up working at Hiawatha?" Now that we had gotten to the subject, I wanted to keep the conversation on track.

"She went to work there after Grandpa died. Most women didn't work in those days. They just stayed at home. But Grandma had trained to be a nurse in the old country before she and Grandpa came here. After he died she didn't want to just sit around. She said a woman could do anything a man could do, sometimes better. So she went up to the asylum and they hired her. She didn't get to be a nurse, but I think it helped her with the patients."

"What did she do there? Was she an aide?"

"I don't know what they called it. She worked in the wards, mostly. I know she worked in the kitchen for a while, but that got her really upset."

"Why was that?"

"She thought the food they fed the people was awful. Grandma was a very proud person. She believed you should always try to make people a good meal, even if you didn't have much. That's how she had been raised.

"It upset her that they made such terrible meals for the patients. She used to talk about something they called a meat and carrot stew. She said it was just fat and bones and water. 'How can they call that meat and carrot stew?' she said 'There's no meat, no carrots, not even broth. Just water. No one should have to eat like that. No wonder those poor people are sick all the time.' The cook got angry at her and told her it was none of her business. Grandma was very outspoken."

"Didn't she speak up about it?"

"You mean, like tell the director? I don't think so.

"That was another thing. She didn't like the director at all. She said he was from somewhere back East and thought everyone out here was a yokel. He was always bragging about all the money he saved, while the patients didn't even have decent food or clothes. He would never listen to anyone, no matter what they said. She said he treated the staff like they were his personal servants."

"Was that Doctor Hummer?" I asked.

"I don't know his name. She just called him 'the director.' She said he kept things for himself and his family that were supposed to go to the patients. His wife would come to the pantry and take most of the sugar, so they couldn't do any baking. She took the washcloths and the towels, too. They were supposed to have towels for everyone, but Grandma said they only had eight towels for all thirty-two patients in her ward. The director used more towels and washcloths just for his family than they had for all the patients in the asylum.

"I think that really bothered Grandma — the selfishness and the dirt. She really believed it was important to be clean. 'If cleanliness is next to godliness,' she said, 'how can we bring these people close to God if we can't even keep them clean?' "

"So the place was really dirty?" I asked.

"Grandma said it was awful. They used old coal furnaces for heating, and there was something wrong with the ventilation, so in the winter everything got covered with soot. Some mornings she would come in and the soot was so thick that you could see the footprints of the patients on the floor. They'd walk around in this soot and then get in their beds and the bedding would be so filthy that she couldn't even get it clean.

"And that director would only let them turn on the hot water three days a week, so even if they tried to wash the bedding they couldn't get it clean. They had to bathe people in cold water. And since they didn't have enough dishes for everyone, when the hot water was off they just fed people off dirty dishes and made them share forks and spoons."

I was struck by how closely this corresponded with what Benais had said, especially the part about the soot.

"It sounds like a terrible place."

She shook her head in disgust. "And it looked so nice from the outside."

"I've seen pictures," I said.

"So you know. Everyone in town was so proud to have such a beautiful and important building in Canton. But Grandma said that inside it was just terrible. The windows all had bars on them and were sealed shut, so the air was stale and dirty. Most of the patients used chamber pots and there wasn't enough staff to empty them, so the place smelled awful. Sometimes the chamber pots would sit for days before being emptied. Grandma told me of one woman who used to kick and scream, so the director made them chain her to her bed and just leave her there. She couldn't get up, so she just soiled herself and they left her in it until her bed was filled with maggots."

Her palsied hand trembled violently as she became more upset, so she hid it below the edge of the table.

"It was so hard for Grandma," she said. "She liked the Indian people. She said they reminded her of the Sami people back in her homeland. She used to spend summers up near Lapland, and the Sami people would give her rides on their reindeer. She said they had a lot of the same beliefs.

"In fact, the only time I ever saw her get really angry was one time when a man came from the University in Vermillion to do some kind of study of the Indians. He wrote that some of the Indians in there were Catholic and some of them were Protestant and some didn't have any religion at all. Grandma got very upset and told him that they did too have a religion, and that just because it wasn't the same as his religion it didn't mean it wasn't a religion.

"The man got angry with her and said that he was a professor and that it wasn't her place to tell him what to think. She just told him that he could think what he wanted, but that as long as she was there, no one was going to say that these people didn't have a religion. She said that just because he was a professor didn't mean he knew everything. I think she got in trouble for talking back to him that way.

"I know it bothered her that a lot of the people in the asylum didn't belong there. She said they were so sad. Some of them were the only ones from their tribe so they couldn't talk to anyone else. Lots of them just sat on chairs and stared. Lots of them cried all the time. The director would bring visitors from out of town and show the people off like animals in a zoo. It was so cruel."

I could feel her mood darkening. When the waitress came and placed the cake on the table in front of her, she didn't even look at it.

"Grandma said they didn't have any clothes. They would have old patched things with holes in them. Some of them just wandered the halls in hospital gowns with nothing under them. There was one boy they chained naked to a mattress and just left him there. People were crying and screaming all the time."

Here, too, was corroboration of Benais's dark memories.

"'Oh, the chains,' she used to say," Edith continued. "'The chains and the locks.' They had these wrist cuffs that they put on the people, then chained them to their beds. Wrist cuffs and ankle cuffs. They would leave them there for days. Sometimes they couldn't even find the keys and they'd just leave the people there."

She lifted her face toward me. Her eyes were moist and her rouge was streaked with tears. "Why would they do that, Mr. Nerburn? Why would they treat people like that?"

I was saddened by her descent into these dark memories. The coffee stop had started on such a festive note. "A bad man? A bad system?" I said. "I don't know. Lack of understanding of Indian people?"

"Grandma said many of them weren't even sick at all. There

were soldiers who had fought in the Great War and come back with shell shock and they would lock them up and say they were insane. These were men who had fought for our country. The people didn't have toothbrushes or toothpaste. They didn't get any dental care. These were people who were used to being outside, and here they were locked up all fall and winter in a place with filthy air and filth in the hallways. Couldn't they at least have put some pictures on the wall?"

Her memories were flooding out now, brutal and without shape or focus. "There was a baby born there to one of the women, Grandma said. They tried to keep the men and women apart, but sometimes it happened. They didn't even give that baby a name. They just kept it there because they said if the parents were insane then the baby would be insane. Grandma said it died before it got too old.

"She said the director made them wash one woman in a bath filled with creosote. They put mercury on the head of one woman to get rid of some disease and it was so thick the aides had to scrape it off her pillow with a knife. How could people do that?"

I kept my eyes down, hoping that none of the other patrons were overhearing.

"I remember the day they found that woman with the maggots. That night was the only time I ever saw Grandma cry, except for when Grandpa died. She just went to her room and shut the door. We could hear her sobbing. She didn't come out until morning."

Edith's tears were flowing freely now.

"She said the night shift was the worst. She hated the night shift. The director wouldn't let them have the lights on because he wanted to save money, so they had to do their rounds with lanterns. They couldn't even use the lights in the bathrooms. Sometimes, if they heard something wrong in one of the wards, they couldn't even open the padlocks to get in because it was so dark. After it rained, they would be stepping in puddles on the floor, because the roof leaked. Just think of those poor people with no shoes wandering around in the dark halls stepping in puddles of wet ashes and soot."

She sniffed several times to try to compose herself. I handed her a couple of napkins to dry her eyes.

"I'm sorry. I've never talked about this to anyone before. I feel so ashamed at what we did to those poor people. I used to go up there and stand outside the fence and look at them just wandering around on the grounds.

"I remember one time in the summer, there was a woman lying outside on a blanket. The aides came out and told her to get up and go inside. She wouldn't do it, so they just grabbed the corners of the blanket and bumped her up the stairs. I don't think she could even understand them.

"Sometimes we kids would hear screaming and moaning from inside the building, like animal cries. We would dare each other to go up close to the fence and to reach in and try to touch one of the inmates. Then we'd go hide and tell stories about what we would do if we were ever caught inside there at night.

"Oh, we were so awful. But Indians were frightening to us, Mr. Nerburn. They were dark and spoke funny, and we had all heard stories about murders and scalpings. They weren't even like people to us. We didn't even think of them as people."

She reached across the table again and put her frail, shaking hand on my arm.

"Were we wrong, Mr. Nerburn? Were we wrong? We didn't know any better. We were just little kids. We didn't mean any harm."

I hated that she kept asking me to respond. But I had elicited this, and it was up to me to bring it to a gentle conclusion.

I put my hand on top of hers. "No, you weren't wrong," I said. "What you did was wrong, but you didn't know any better. You weren't trying to be cruel."

"No," she said. "We weren't trying to be cruel, but we were cruel."

"Kids do cruel things. They all do. We all did. We only know what our parents tell us, and we don't understand people who are different from us. You were just doing what was natural for the time."

She kept her tiny hand on my arm, as if trying to convince me of the importance of what she was saying. "But those were real people. People who had been taken away from their families. There was even a hill out back of the town where the families would come and camp to wait for someone to get out. But nobody ever got out. They couldn't. The only way was to escape or die. Lots of times those families would end up taking the body of their grandma or grandpa home to be buried. They never even got to see them alive."

I wanted to move her away from the horrors of the asylum in a more hopeful direction. "There must have been some who escaped?" I said.

"How could they? They didn't speak English, most of them, and they were miles away their own tribes. If someone saw them wandering around they'd just go tell the director and he'd have someone capture them and take them back."

"It sounds more like a prison than a hospital," I said.

"It was. That's what Grandma said, too. She said if there was no way to get well, there was no way to get out. And that director was the one who decided if people got well, and he didn't believe people could get well. He just kept them there until they died."

The tears were beginning to well up in her eyes again. I gave up trying to direct the conversation and just let things flow where they would.

"Grandma said the people were made insane by civilization. She said their minds were primitive and couldn't handle all the knowledge of civilization. So they had to be kept there as protection. She said that even though they were good people with their own good religion, they were like little children. I don't know why she thought that way. She was an intelligent woman."

"Many people thought that way back then," I said.

"Still, it was so wrong. So, so wrong." She tightened her tiny hand on my sleeve.

She squeezed my arm with her fingers. "Grandma wasn't a bad person, Mr. Nerburn. I want you to know that. She loved those people. She was just trying to do what she thought was right."

"I'm sure she was," I said. "And I'm sure she helped a lot of the people there. She did more good than people who didn't work with them, because she tried. Sometimes that's all we can do, is try." I didn't want to begin sermonizing, but I wanted to bring this conversation to a close.

"The cake is waiting for you," I said. "It looks good, just like you said. Shall we just change the subject and enjoy our meal?"

Edith took out her handkerchief and dabbed her eyes. "No, I don't think I want to eat now. Maybe we can take it with us. I'm ready to go."

I felt terrible for having opened this dark corner of her memories. I had learned more about the asylum — maybe more than I wanted to know. But it had come at a cost, and I wasn't sure the cost had been worth it.

I paid the waitress and had her box up the cake. She smiled warmly as she took it away. She obviously was used to dealing with old people and understood on some level what had taken place. I left her a good tip and helped Edith out of the booth. The waitress held the door for us as Edith made her way in her walker, sniffling, back toward the car.

"Do you want to stop at a store or something?" I said. "Get some groceries or treats?" I didn't want our outing to end this way.

"No." she answered. "I want to go up and see the asylum. I want to go back there. I want to do it in memory of Grandma and all those poor people."

CHAPTER TEN

UNQUIET GROUND

*T*he site of the asylum was just east of town. It wasn't far out — maybe a mile or two. Edith sat straight and silent in her seat, dabbing occasionally at her eyes with her handkerchief. She was slowly regaining her composure.

"There it is," she said, pointing off to the left as the road opened into the broad river valley. All I could see was a sign for a hospital and a golf course and a curving drive leading up a green manicured hill. "It was up there," she continued. "Up where the hospital is. They tore down everything. There's another road up about a quarter mile. Take that one."

We continued down the two-lane highway to the next road. On a pull-off just across from the gravel road leading up the hill were two historical markers mounted on metal poles. They were handsome black-patinated bronze plaques shaped like heraldic shields with raised gold lettering. I expected at least one of them to offer some information about the asylum. But one commemorated the Canton ski hill and a sixty-foot ski jump that had once been situated on the far side of the river. The other memorialized Augustana College, which had operated a campus in Canton for a number of years from the late 1800s to the middle of the twentieth century. There was no mention anywhere of the asylum. I could imagine the inmates staring out of the soot-covered windows in the winter at the ski jumpers launching themselves off the wooden jump far across the river valley.

"No sign?" I said.

"Canton never wanted to talk much about the asylum," Edith said. "Not after it was closed. There was a big fuss when they tried to shut it down because of all the jobs that were lost. But once it was gone, people just kind of stopped talking about it."

She pointed again toward the gravel road. "Just drive up there."

I drove across the highway and proceeded up the hill. When we reached the top Edith held up her hand. "Stop," she said. "This is the place." She pointed to a grassy area surrounded by a split-rail fence several fairways over, about a hundred yards off the road. "I think that's the graveyard. It's where they buried the patients who died if no one came to get their bodies. Some Indian man made a big to-do about it a few years ago. So they put up a plaque and that fence. I guess golfers were hitting off the graves and the Indians wanted that stopped."

"Harold Iron Shield?" I asked.

"I don't know. The town wasn't very happy about it, I know. There were Indians marching up and down Main Street. People said they were radicals."

"It doesn't seem too radical to try to keep people from playing golf on top of your grandma's grave," I said.

"Well, a lot of people thought it was a big to-do about nothing. 'Just leave the past alone' was their philosophy. They figured the Indians just have to get over it."

"The dead don't always pass easily," I said. "The earth remembers."

"Now you're sounding like an Indian."

"Maybe it's rubbed off."

It suddenly occurred to her that she hadn't asked about my purpose for the visit.

"Say, you aren't an Indian, are you?" she asked. "You know, a lot of them don't look like Indians anymore."

"No. No Indian in me. Just white-bread American."

"Then why are you interested in this?"

"I have a friend. He's Lakota. His little sister was in the place for a while, as I understand it. I just wanted to see it and learn about it so I could tell him something about it when I see him."

She put her hand over her mouth. "When would she have been in there?" she asked.

"I don't know. Maybe the late twenties. I was going to ask if your grandma had ever mentioned a little girl in there. One who always wore a white dress."

Edith's hand was shaking. "I might have seen her," she said. "I had forgotten all about the little girl."

I sat upright in my seat. "Tell me," I said. "This could be really important."

"I don't know anything, really," she said. "Grandma never talked about the patients except the bad things that happened to them. She said it was bad enough that they had to be there without people gossiping about them. Like I said, she kept a lot of things to herself."

"But the little girl. You said you might have seen her."

"Yes. They put up a swing set and a seesaw in the front yard inside the fence. Sometimes we would see the Indians swinging on it. There was one little girl who always had on a dirty white dress. She used to come out by herself and swing, back and forth, kicking her legs way up high. She was always singing."

I felt a pang of excitement. "Do you remember what she looked like?"

"No, except that she had her hair cut around her head like a bowl. And she was always singing, always swinging and singing in that dingy white dress. She had a pretty voice. I used to stare at her from behind the bushes, because I didn't want her to see me."

"Why?"

"I don't know, really. Because she was little, like me, maybe? Maybe I thought she would want to be my friend if she saw me."

"It doesn't matter," I said. "I'm happy you told me. Would you like to go over to the cemetery, or whatever that is?"

Edith opened her car door. "Yes, I'm sure it's the cemetery. We should go see."

The September heat had taken on a late-summer edge. The temperature had moved well into the eighties and the air was thick and humid. A few golfers could be seen in the distance taking practice swings on one of the tees. "Let's take the wheelchair instead of the walker," I said. "We'll get across the fairways quicker."

Edith agreed, so I took her chair from the trunk and helped her get situated in it. She took a big green straw hat from her bag and placed it on her head.

The grass was freshly mowed, but the pushing was still difficult. Edith's wheelchair had been made for pavement and sidewalks, not uneven fairways and rough.

Despite the growing heat, I was struck by the pastoral beauty of the setting — long, green fairways flanked by tall deciduous trees, all overlooking a sweeping river valley.

"It's really a beautiful setting," I said.

"Oh, yes," Edith responded. "The asylum was quite a beautiful place. There was a big white barn and walkways and all kinds of trees and shrubbery and gardens. It was almost like a park. That's why our town was so proud of it. If it hadn't been for the metal fence around it and the big metal gate, it might have seemed like some fine school or hospital."

"Appearances can be deceiving."

"I don't think they were trying to deceive anyone. I think that's the way they wanted it. Not everyone was a bad person, Mr. Nerburn. They wanted the Indians to have a beautiful place to live where they could sit outside in the summer and work in the gardens and on the farm. It was only the fence and the arch with the words Hiawatha Asylum — that, and the people wandering around — that made it seem so frightening."

"Ah, yes, another arch," I said.

"What do you mean?" she asked.

"It was something the government did to make a point to the Indians. They'd mark something off with a fence and put an arch with its name over it, so the people entering would know that they were now entering the world of white authority. Fences and rules — that's what white government meant to most Indians."

"Well, I suppose it could be looked at that way. But to us it was just a way of keeping the patients in. We would see them walking around, just staring at the ground, or just sitting and looking into the distance. It was like they were the living dead. We were scared to death of them."

We made our way slowly across the fairways toward the split-rail fence. "Where was the building?" I asked. "Was it near that cemetery?"

Edith pointed past the fenced enclosure up toward the site of the new hospital at the top of the hill. "It was over there," she said. "Where the hospital is. We didn't even know the cemetery existed. There was nothing to mark the graves until that Indian man made all the fuss."

I looked out over the Big Sioux River valley. The trees were just beginning to take on the rich colors of autumn. It was hard to associate this parklike setting with the horrors of the asylum, but I knew all too well from my work with the boarding schools that a large part of the philosophy of social control was to build imposing, intimidating structures that reinforced the dominance of the American government and culture. And, as Edith had mentioned, some social reformers truly believed that creating a peaceful, tranquil setting was a way to help Native people adapt to the complexities of modern civilization. It was all part of their philosophical contention that Indians were like children, with undeveloped brains that could easily go awry if subjected to too much stimulation or new information.

I would have liked to talk to Edith more about community attitudes toward the asylum and its inmates, but it was clear that for her this journey was more personal than sociological or political. This quiet stop at the cemetery that had been so much a part of her childhood was the last gift I could give her before leaving her to her solitary life at the nursing home. I would let her revisit her memories in the way that gave her the most peace. I had already received more from her than I could have reasonably hoped.

The fence that marked off the cemetery was a simple affair framing in a rough rectangle of about 200 by 150 feet. The ends of some of the rails had fallen out of the posts and were lying on the ground, giving the enclosure a feeling of disrepair.

I wheeled Edith through an opening in the fence and headed toward a plaque on a low, concrete base in the middle of the fenced-off area. Pushing her was becoming increasingly difficult, and I realized that I was trying to shove her across ground made uneven by the settling of dozens of unmarked graves.

The thought made me recoil. I did not like to step on human graves. But this whole grassy area was pocked with the ghostly depressions, and there was no way to get to the plaque without crossing this stretch of ground.

I said nothing to Edith but pushed her as gently as I could

toward the marker. If she had any of the same feelings of violation, she did not let on. Her hands were folded on her lap and her
eyes were focused straight ahead. Her necklace of costume pearls
clicked and clattered as we moved.

We made it to the area in front of the plaque and paused there
amid the bird chatter and the buzzing of insects. A small rabbit
lifted its head and ran in front of us, and squirrels jumped from
branch to branch in the trees above us. Periodically, the peace of
the setting was interrupted by the hollow *thwok* of a golfer hitting
a tee shot on a distant fairway.

Edith reached in her purse and put on some heavy glasses.
"Wheel me as close as you can," she said. "I want to read the names."

I pushed her to the very edge of the low concrete plinth on
which the plaque was fastened. It was a crude memorial formed of
cheap, granular concrete that was chipping around the edges. The
plaque, which was made of bronze or some other cast metal, had a
heading that read, simply, "Names of Indians buried in Hiawatha
Asylum cemetery." I could not help but notice that the full name
of the asylum — the Hiawatha Asylum for Insane Indians — was
nowhere to be seen.

Beneath the heading were three columns of names of those
who had been buried in this fenced-off enclosure. They represented many different tribes and language groups. Names such as
Long Time Owl Woman, John Coal on Fire, Kay Ge Gah Aush
Eak, and James Chief Crow were interspersed with more Europe-
anized names such as Jessie Hallock and Baptiste Gingras. I made
a quick estimate while Edith was staring at the plaque. There
appeared to be more than a hundred names.

While I was counting, Edith let out a short gasp.

"Is something wrong?" I said.

She had her hand over her mouth. "No. No. It was just kind
of a shock to see the name Edith. I never thought of it as an Indian

name." She pointed to the name Edith Standing Bear. "It just kind of brings it home to see someone with the same name as mine."

"Real people with real lives," I said. "Mothers and daughters and fathers and sons. That's what makes it so upsetting."

She continued to read.

"Oh, dear," she said.

"What?"

"Baby Ruth Enas Pah. Baby Caldwell." She put her hand over her mouth again. "Grandma never talked about the babies other than that one." I could see she was starting to cry again. "Oh, the things Grandma must have seen that she kept inside."

"And the things the Indian people keep inside," I said. I didn't want to minimize her grandmother's suffering, but the hard truth was that it must have been nothing compared to the suffering the mothers had felt as their infants had been taken from them and buried unremembered in this potter's field far from their homelands and the caring, grieving hands of family and friends.

I left Edith alone with her thoughts in front of the plaque and walked over to the fence to reinsert some of the fallen rails into the upright posts. A man in an electric golf cart came rolling over and stopped next to me.

"Can I help you?" he said. There was an edge to his voice.

"I'm just putting back some of the fallen rails."

"Are you part of some group, or something?"

"An army of one."

I nodded toward Edith. "Her grandmother used to work here."

The sight of an elderly white woman sitting in a wheelchair quieted his suspicions.

"Yeah, there's some Indians buried here, if I remember correctly," he said.

"Over a hundred. They died in an asylum over there," I said. "It was a sad place."

"I suppose," he said. "Well, I'm glad those days are past. At least they've got the casinos now."

I continued walking around the perimeter of the fence reinserting the rails in the posts. The man watched me closely for a while, then turned his cart and headed back toward his foursome. I could see Edith leaning over close to the plaque. When I got back to her, she was crying softly.

"Are you okay?" I asked.

"Oh, I don't know. I was just looking at these names. I counted them all. There are a hundred and twenty-one. Then I started thinking about the little girl on the swing, then I remembered the little girl in the restaurant and how she had her whole family with her, and I thought of the little children buried in here, and I just got sad. I guess I'm just an old lady. I cry too easily."

I put my hand on her shoulder. "It's too bad more people didn't cry for these folks," I said. "Maybe something would have been done."

Edith pushed herself backward. "We just didn't know. We just didn't know. The people I grew up with, they were good people. But we just didn't know."

In the distance, the man in the golf cart had rejoined his friends and had just finished his tee shot. We could hear their filtered laughter as they got into their golf carts. I turned Edith around and headed her back toward the car. As we reached the roadway, I looked back over the field of ghostly depressions inside the fenced enclosure. In the distance the men in the golf carts were laughing loudly.

"At least they have the casinos now," I said under my breath.

"What?" Edith said. "I'm a little hard of hearing."

"Oh, nothing," I said. "I was just talking to myself."

CHAPTER ELEVEN

HAUNTED WITH GHOSTS

I dropped Edith back at the nursing home. The man with the high pants was still sitting on the bench next to the cigarette butt receptacle.

"You missed lunch," he said. "Meatloaf and diced carrots."

I pushed Edith through the door, past the women, who had resumed their posts on either side of the entryway. They smiled at her as we passed. She straightened her back and stared straight ahead.

"You can leave me here," she said as we passed the lunchroom. The hunched-over men were still asleep in their chairs, and several of the ladies were back at work on the jigsaw puzzle. I had been intending to give Edith a hug, but before I could do so she stuck her hand toward me in a decidedly formal manner. Taking her cue, I reached my hand out and took hers in my grasp.

"Thank you for the morning," I said. "This has been a real pleasure."

"I hope I've been of some assistance," she said. Her manner had once again become formal and distant.

I squeezed her hand once more in an attempt to convey my appreciation. She accepted the squeeze without reciprocating, then pulled her hand away.

"Good-bye now," she said. She turned her face away from me and stared into the lunchroom. The women from the hallway had wheeled themselves over to watch. I hesitated for a moment, then walked toward the door. Out of the corner of my eye I could see Edith sitting upright in her chair with her hands in her lap, holding the Styrofoam box containing the piece of devil's food cake. She would not look at me.

My visit with Edith had upset me more than I had realized. The overwhelming loneliness of the nursing home, the revelations about the asylum, and the unsettling disjunction between the lush golf course and the horrors of the forgotten institution weighed heavily on me. But it was the hollows of the sunken graves that had bothered me the most. Even in the tranquil and bucolic setting of the golf course, those graves had an unearthly quiet about them. It seemed like any encounter with Indian reality was destined to be haunted with ghosts.

The humid haze of midafternoon was just beginning to dull the edges of the day. I drove along the country roads, past the fields of ripening corn, wondering what to do next.

Edith had confirmed everything I had feared and had left me with an indelible image that would not give me rest: a young girl in a dingy white dress, trapped behind a chain-link fence, swinging alone and singing softly while men and women walked lifelessly back and forth behind her in the shadow of a great brick building they would never be allowed to leave.

I had come to Canton to seek clarity, and now I had no clear idea how to proceed. Did I want to share this image with Dan? Did I want him to hear about children chained to steam pipes or left naked on bare mattresses? Did I want him to hear about people locked in dark rooms with overflowing chamber pots while soot drifted down on them, burning their eyes and filling their lungs? Had that little girl on the swing even been Yellow Bird?

All I knew for certain was that the presence of Yellow Bird lived on the edges of many people's memories, and that Mary, in death, had charged me with a responsibility I could not evade or deny.

I looked over at the deer-hide packet on the seat next to me. I had taken to carrying it with me everywhere, partly out of fear that I would lose it, and partly because it had become almost a living presence in my life. In that deerskin was Mary's voice, Mary's words, Mary's message. It challenged me with its silent presence. I needed to return home to let all this settle.

It was a long drive — almost four hundred miles — but it was still manageable if I got on the road quickly. Very likely I would end up napping in my car outside some truck stop at two a.m. until I was alert enough to keep driving, but I had done that before. I just wanted to be in my own house, my own bed, surrounded by my own life.

Once back in the car it was apparent that the day and the humidity had taken their toll on me. I was already nodding off as I drove. There was no chance I could make the journey without falling asleep at the wheel. So I decided to spend the night in Canton, then head home in the morning.

Due to my son's chiding about my getting old and soft, I had purchased an odd combination cot-tent contraption that allowed me to sleep outside comfortably while keeping my old bones off the ground. Though it was heavy and clumsy and difficult to set up, I had taken to carrying it with me in the car whenever I set out on one of my "little trips" into the Dakotas or the Minnesota north woods. And, much as my son had predicted, it had opened the world of camping to me in a way I had almost forgotten.

I was preparing to find a small park or local campground where I could set it up when the weather turned ominous. The sky began roiling and the air became heavy and oppressive. A fierce prairie thunderstorm was rolling in. With no interest in fighting with the cot contraption and no need to prove anything, I found a cheap motel room and settled in amid the smell of mold and stale liquor.

It proved to be a good decision. The storm was indeed fierce and violent, with cracks of ear-splitting lightning followed by explosions of thunder that shook the windows and rattled the lamp shades. With each lightning crack the lights in the room flickered, and the sky outside exploded in a flash of blinding illumination. I kept thinking of the golf course and the depressions in the ground, and of little Yellow Bird huddled in her lonely bed at the asylum during storms like this, unsure if they were messages from the thunder beings, as her grandparents had taught her, or punishments from the Christian God, as she had learned from the priests and nuns in the boarding school.

I'm not sure if sleep ever really came. Though the dream no longer haunted me every night, it came with enough frequency that I seldom gave myself over to deep rest. And the events of the day, combined with the possibility of the dream's arrival, left me tossing and thrashing on the sagging mattress. I lay listening to the raging and lashing outside my window, while my mind raced and my emotions tumbled out of control.

I must have gotten up and walked around the room ten times during the night, trying to separate thoughts from presentiments, and memories from imagination. A little girl on a swing. Dan. Edith in her wheelchair. Benais shuffling slowly along the forest path. Buffalo moving like shadows among the trees. By morning I was emotionally and physically exhausted.

I opened the door and peered out into the growing daylight. The storm had passed, but the air was filled with a heavy wetness. The day was going to pick up where the previous one had left off — a humid, oppressive scorcher with air so heavy that you can hardly catch a breath and each step becomes a sweat-laden labor.

I was anxious to get on the road, but before leaving I needed to address two bits of unfinished business. I went to the local variety store and purchased a pack of Prince Albert tobacco, a bouquet of flowers, and a box of chocolates.

"Wrap them up nicely," I said to the girl at the checkout counter. "They're kind of a belated Mother's Day present." She nodded seriously, then went into the back room and put the flowers in a vase and wrapped the white box of chocolates with a wide purple ribbon. Then I drove up to the nursing home and went in to find Edith.

The woman sitting at the desk looked up at me from her book of crossword puzzles. It was the same woman who had been on duty when I had brought Edith back from our outing. She had a hard expression on her face.

"I'd like to see Edith again," I said.

The woman's manner was curt. "She's in bed. She's been there ever since you left. She's been very upset. We couldn't even get her up for breakfast." There was no attempt to hide the accusation in her voice.

I was tempted to try to explain, but there was no point. Her jaw was set; her eyes were cold.

"Just give her these," I said, placing the box of candy and the bouquet of daisies and daffodils on the counter.

"She's not allowed to have chocolate," she said, pushing the box of candies back toward me. She took the flowers brusquely

and set them on the floor behind the desk, indicating by her manner that there was little likelihood Edith would ever see them.

"Sometimes it's hard to revisit the past," I said in a feeble
effort to justify myself.

"Sometimes the past just needs to be left alone," she said, and
went back to her crossword puzzle.

I picked up the chocolates and walked out past the man in the
high-water pants who had assumed his morning post staring into
the sky and the distant fields.

"Hell of a storm," he said.

"Set back the harvest, I'll bet."

He smiled broadly at my apparent interest.

"At least a week. Unless we get some real heat. You staying for
lunch?"

"No, got to get going."

"Smelled like pot roast," he said. "They do a good job of it."

"Take a bite for me," I said. "I've got a long drive."

He nodded once and turned back toward the fields. I left him
alone and vigilant, staring emptily out into the heavy, colorless
sky, threw the box of chocolates in the trunk, and headed back
on the country roads toward the golf course. Everything was con-
spiring to make me feel melancholy. Edith, the nursing home,
the thoughts of little Yellow Bird, the old man and his vigil — all
echoed with loneliness and isolation. I needed to invest the visit
with something more, something of significance — to make an
offering, an acknowledgment — to somehow do honor to this
unquiet ground. That, after all, was the reason I had come.

I drove up the gravel road that skirted the golf course and
parked in the same spot where Edith and I had parked the day
before. The golf course was empty and silent. Mist was rising from
the fairways as they dried in the morning heat.

The split-rail fence stood benignly in the distance, shrouded in the ground fog. The plaque on the crumbling cement plinth glinted in the sun.

I walked slowly across the fairways toward the monument. When I reached the fence, I took out the package of Prince Albert and sprinkled the tobacco over the graves, one by one, as best as I could find them — a pinch on each spot of sunken earth, along with a silent prayer. All around me the mist rose from the graves like specters. Then I walked to the stone and read off each name on the plaque in a quiet whisper. When I finished, I placed the last of the tobacco on the plaque.

As I prepared to leave, a breath of wind rose up from the west. It rustled the tobacco, then, in a single rush, grabbed it and scattered it across the phantom graves.

Perhaps it was the sleepless night, perhaps it was the memory of Donna finding a message in the swirling wind that had lifted the tobacco off the small platform in front of her Grandma's spirit lodge, perhaps it was just the buildup of guilt I felt over avoiding the hard call to tell Dan about the notebook.

But seeing that gust of wind take the tobacco and sprinkle it like a benediction over the forgotten graves made a claim on me that I could not deny. As much as I wanted to be home and in the security and comfort of my own bed, I could not avoid the fact that an old man whose little sister had been incarcerated on the very land where I was now standing, was sitting alone — if, indeed, he was even alive — while I held in my hands the very document that would fill in the story that for eighty years had torn a hole in his heart.

It was time to call out west, to find out if Dan was still alive, and if so, to bring the notebook to him without delay. Anything else was simply an act of selfishness and cowardice.

Part Two

INTO THE WEST

CHAPTER TWELVE

THE LAKOTA TWO-STEP

*T*he prelude to the message on the answering machine was interminable — about forty-five seconds of repetitive powwow music before the thundering basso profondo of Jumbo's voice came on. "I ain't here," it grunted. "Leave a message." I started to identify myself when the machine shut off abruptly and a high-pitched voice cut in, "Who's this?"

I recognized the nasal tones of Shitty, Jumbo's "business associate" in the operation of the filthy repair garage Jumbo ran on the outskirts of the reservation town where Dan lived. Shitty was the Jack Spratt in black welfare glasses to Jumbo's ponderous four-hundred-pound slow-moving presence. I was never quite sure what Shitty's role was at the garage other than to keep Jumbo company, but the two of them were clearly close friends.

Jumbo had worked on my old truck during my first visit to Dan's almost a dozen years earlier, and his was the only phone number on the reservation that I had committed to memory.

I was not excited about talking to Shitty, but under the circumstances, he was the best I could hope for.

"Shitty," I said. "It's Nerburn. The guy who helped Dan find his sister."

I sensed a dim brightening in the presence on the other end of the line.

"Jumbo ain't here," he said.

"That's okay. Listen, do you know if Dan's still alive?"

Shitty thought for a while. "He ain't dead," he answered.

It wasn't a ringing endorsement of Dan's health, but it was enough to send a great wave of relief through me.

"When will Jumbo be back?" I asked.

"Can't say. He's at a powwow with Grover and Wenonah."

The news took away some of the elation I had felt on hearing that Dan was alive. It was actually Grover or Wenonah I wanted to contact, and I had hoped Jumbo could connect me to them. As much as I wanted to respect Mary's request that I bring the notebook to Dan, I was not sure that even she had understood the dark realities of the institution where little Yellow Bird had been sent, or the full implications of what that knowledge would do to a man of Dan's age and health.

Wenonah, Dan's granddaughter, and Grover, his best friend, would know his physical and mental state better than anyone. Together they would be able to sort out the information I was bearing and decide how much of it the old man should hear. Now they, too, were unavailable.

"So, where's this powwow?" I asked.

"Don't know. Somewhere up near Standing Rock."

The information gave me faint hope. The Standing Rock Reservation was a six-hour drive northwest from Canton. Since powwows were community events, someone would surely be able to direct me to the site where it was being held. With luck, I could intercept Wenonah and Grover and share the notebook with them and get their advice before heading out to see Dan.

"Do you know how long they'll be up there?" I asked.

"Couple days, at least," Shitty said. "They left yesterday."

I thanked him for his help and got off the phone. I set my course toward Standing Rock and drove off into the growing morning sun.

Now that I was sure Dan was alive and I had made the hard decision to travel out to see him, the pall that had settled over my spirit was lifting. I had not realized how much of my darkness had been a product of my avoiding the encounter with Dan. Now that I was moving toward some sort of resolution, the heaviness in my heart was finding release.

The drive across the border into the Dakotas buoyed my spirits even further. I always had a feeling of expansiveness when I broke free of the heavy richness of the American Midwest into the high bright skies and broad spaces of the West, and even now, with the dark memories of Canton and Edith's loneliness so close to the surface, that same release of spirit was taking place. Mile by mile I could feel my shoulders relax and the tightness in my chest disappear.

By the time I had completed the three-hour journey to the banks of the broad, languid Missouri River, the somber feelings that had overwhelmed me at Canton had almost completely dissipated. I turned north and drove breezily along the banks of the river as it wound its slow, serpentine course through the rolling, golden landscape. Rows of tiny whitecaps marched in rhythmic unity down the wide, flat, waterway, while billows of clouds moved placidly through the blue prairie sky.

I would find Grover and Wenonah, they would relieve me of the burden of deciding what to do with the notebook and how much to share with Dan, and I could turn this journey into a long-overdue visit to an old man who had become as much father to me as friend. A day I had been dreading had turned into a day to savor. Like the landscape itself, I was once again opening myself to the capacity to dream.

Shitty's vague instructions proved adequate. A few handwritten posters nailed to utility poles announced the existence of the pow-wow, and the steady stream of cars and old vans heading north from the reservation gave me all the directions I needed. By mid-afternoon I had arrived at the dirt path leading back to the pow-wow site.

I was not too concerned about locating Grover and Wenonah. The powwow grounds were small and intimate, set in a field surrounded by a grove of trees. Everyone would be gathered around the powwow ring talking to friends or sitting beneath the surrounding arbor in lawn chairs, watching the dancers and listening to the drummers. Besides, Shitty had said that Grover had taken his '71 Buick, and I knew the car well. Unless Grover had changed his habits since the last time I had seen him, the car would be polished to within an inch of its pea-green automotive life and would stand out from the various vans and rez-mobiles like a shiny dime in a pile of pennies.

Finding Grover turned out to be even easier than I had expected. As luck would have it, I spotted his car coming toward me as I drove up the path toward the powwow parking area. He was slouched back in his seat with one hand on the top of his steering wheel and the other hanging out the window, tapping a rhythm on the side panel of his car. His face was obscured by a broad-brimmed white cowboy hat cocked forward on his head, and a cigarette dangled from his mouth, giving him the air of some kind of lowrider geriatric juvenile delinquent.

I waved wildly out of the window to get his attention, but he seemed not to notice. I didn't want to honk, because it seemed disrespectful to the singing and dancing that were going on in the ring.

"Grover, Grover," I yelled as our two cars approached each other. I blinked my lights several times, to no avail. Finally, as we were almost nose to nose, I faked a swerve toward him. This caught his attention and he leaned forward in his seat and squinted in my direction.

A glimmer of recognition crossed his face. He drove up alongside me and stared strangely at me.

"Nerburn?" he said through his window.

"Hey, Grover."

"Well, I'll be damned," he said. "What brings you out here?"

This was no time or place to get involved in a serious conversation about the notebook, so I just joined in the banter. "I missed you," I said. "A guy can only go so long without seeing your smiling face." He gave a little snort and snuffed out his cigarette in a Mountain Dew can he had propped on his dashboard.

Cars were lining up behind us. Someone shouted from his car window and one or two people, less concerned with propriety than I, leaned on their horns.

"We should pull over," I said.

"Nah, just follow me. I'm turning out here. Got to pick up Jumbo. He's camped out in the field. We can talk there. It's good to see you."

I was pleased to receive such an affable greeting from Grover. I had never felt that he really liked me, and this was a measure of warmth beyond what I had expected. It was a good start for what I knew would be a serious conversation.

I swung my car around and followed him as he bumped his way through the field surrounding the arbor.

As at most powwows, cars were parked in haphazard formation and tents were set up randomly throughout the area, leaving only a small trail through the prairie grass for vehicles to come and go.

Grover wound his way through the cars and tents toward the far end of the field where it backed up against the grove of trees. Families were cooking meals on Coleman stoves, and elderly women were braiding the hair of young girls who were preparing to enter the powwow ring to begin their dances. Between several parked cars two young women in matching blue-and-white jingle dresses were practicing dance steps. One old man wearing only his leggings and breechcloth sat on the hood of his car smoking a cigarette. He waved at Grover as we passed.

As we got through the field and approached the edge of the woods, I saw a single blue-and-white dome tent set off by itself. On the ground next to it a huge figure was lying spread-eagle. From the massive protuberance of the belly, almost mimicking the shape of the tent itself, I guessed it had to be Jumbo.

Grover parked a short distance from the tent, and I did likewise.

"Is that Jumbo?" I said as we met between our cars.

"The one and only."

"He looks dead."

"Dead-tired, maybe. He did the Grand Entry. Wore him out. He's not in great shape."

"I didn't know he was a dancer."

"Just started. Trying to lose weight. Reclaim his tradition."

"How's it working?"

Grover pulled a pack of cigarettes out from the pocket of his pearl-buttoned cowboy shirt.

"The tradition? Not so bad. The weight? Not so much."

Jumbo had on full powwow regalia, with knee-high deerskin moccasins rimmed with bells and deer toe rattles. Lying there on his back with his feather bustle propped on his heaving belly, he looked like an expiring turkey.

Jumbo was deep in a thunderous sleep. His breathing was something between a grunt and a snore, punctuated by an occasional snort. His mouth was open so wide you could have stuck a grapefruit into it.

"Why's he camped over here all by himself?" I asked.

Grover looked out from under the brim of his hat. "You ever sleep near Jumbo? Stuff goes on you don't even want to know about."

While we were talking, two men walked past and paused next to us. "Jesus, he was hoofing it," one of them said to Grover. "The whole ground was shaking."

"Lakota two-step," Grover said. "He's been doing it for years. Two steps to the refrigerator, two steps back to the couch."

The men laughed heartily and continued on their way.

I stared at the astonishing sight of Jumbo splayed out on the ground. It was hard to imagine a four-hundred-pound man dancing, but Jumbo had surprised me before.

I could see that this was not the time for any serious discussion about Dan or the information I was carrying, so I just settled in to enjoy the camaraderie and festivities.

It was clear from Jumbo's regalia that he took his newfound passion seriously. Aside from the knee-high moccasins with their bells and rattles and intricate beading, he had on a pair of buckskin leggings that must have cost half a dozen deer their lives, a blousy calico shirt decorated with multicolored ribbons, and two heavily beaded wristbands that went almost up to his elbows. Beneath the feather bustle he was holding on his chest, a bone breastplate heaved up and down as he breathed. A variety of pelts and bracelets and anklets festooned various other parts of his body. Most astonishing of all was a real wolf or coyote headdress that lay on the ground next to him like a disemboweled carcass waiting for the taxidermist.

I didn't want to seem disrespectful, because I knew that

powwow regalia had sacred significance to many dancers, and I had seen some of the most serious-minded and traditional elders pull younger dancers aside and berate them for cavalier and unearned use of eagle feathers and other articles of spiritual significance. But Jumbo had always seemed anything but traditional. I would have been less surprised to see him dancing with a string of pipe wrenches hanging from his belt than with an animal headdress on his head.

"Did Jumbo earn that headdress?" I asked Grover.

"Yeah," Grover answered. "Did a valve job on John Sixkiller's pickup."

"I mean, aren't you supposed to get your regalia from doing something of significance to earn it?"

"Maybe it was a tough valve job."

"God, you haven't changed, have you?" I said.

He gave me a wry smile. "You think I should have?"

He walked back and opened the rear door of his Buick. "Jumbo's trying," he said. "Sometimes when you're trying to get back into traditional stuff, it's hard to know where to begin. Jumbo just kind of decided to begin everywhere."

He flicked his cigarette onto the ground and stepped on it with the toe of his boot.

"We can talk more about it later. But right now we've got to get him into the car. We've got to go to town. Get some supplies."

"Can't we just wake him up?"

He stared at me from under the brim of his hat like a professor staring over the top of his spectacles. "You want to try to wake him up?"

I looked over at the heaving, snoring lump of a man.

"Probably not."

Grover walked over and gently lifted the feather bustle from Jumbo's grasp and held it toward me. "Here. Take this and tickle the end of his nose with one of the feathers. Look out. He might thrash."

"Why don't you do it?"

He just smiled and forced the bustle into my hands.

I moved up cautiously and stood behind Jumbo's head. Carefully, I lowered the bustle and brushed his nose with the end of a feather. He let out a dark, rumbling sound and flung his arm across his face.

"That's a good start," Grover said. "Do it again."

"He's quick," I said.

"Like a snapping turtle. Do it again."

I lowered the bustle again and brushed it back and forth across Jumbo's nose. He emitted some kind of gargling roar and sat up with a start, rubbing his nose with the sleeve of his dirty shirt. "What the fuck?" he rumbled.

"Time for lunch," Grover said.

Apparently those were the magic words. Jumbo rolled himself over and worked his way onto his hands and knees. His rattles clattered and his bells jingled. He pushed himself upward with much grunting and wheezing. I reached out to give him a hand. His eyes focused and he broke into a great jack-o'-lantern grin.

"Jesus, it's Nerburn," he said.

"Hey, Jumbo," I said. "Good to see you. Come on. I'll help you up."

I grabbed his hand and did my best to serve as a counterweight as he hauled himself upward. The smell of sweat from his pow-wow outfit — especially the animal skin headdress — was overwhelming. I sensed it had not been properly cleaned or tanned before being turned into a piece of regalia.

"Why don't we just make a sandwich," Jumbo said. "I got another grand entry later."

"Can't," Grover said. "Wenonah's got all the food. She took off early. She was worried about the old man."

The news of Wenonah's departure came as a mild blow. I was counting on her to be the final arbiter of what should be shared with Dan. Now I had to rely on Grover. But at least he could give me some preliminary guidance.

Jumbo gave a great gaping yawn and lumbered over to the open rear door of Grover's car.

"Here. Bring his headdress," Grover said, handing me the long, grey pelt with the animal head at the top. "Don't want someone stealing it." It was wet with sweat and smelled like a decaying carcass.

I carried it gingerly to the car and placed it next to Jumbo, who had already slid in and was spread out, wheezing, across the entire rear seat.

"You might as well come along," Grover said. "Unless you got some little hoochie you're meeting here."

"You're the hoochie I'm meeting," I said. "I told you."

I pushed a few cigarette packs and Little Debbie wrappers into the center of the passenger seat and took my place next to Grover. Jumbo was heaving and rasping behind me. The smell from his regalia was overwhelming.

"You got my clothes?" he wheezed. He was still winded and barely able to talk.

Grover shifted the car into gear and moved slowly back through the wiregrass. "They're in that garbage bag next to you," he said. "You can change while we're driving."

Jumbo reached over and grabbed a green plastic garbage bag that was lodged against the door. He pulled halfheartedly at some piece of clothing it contained, then fell back against the seat. "Not much room back here," he gasped. "Don't think I can change."

"You better give it a try," Grover said. "It's getting pretty ripe in here."

Jumbo muttered something and dropped his head back. His breathing had already begun to even out.

"I think he's falling asleep," I said.

Grover pulled out another cigarette. "Reclaiming your tradition can wear a guy out."

We navigated through the grass field onto the dirt path that led to the paved road, then turned onto the main highway, which curved along the edge of the Missouri.

"Maybe we could stop at a gas station and let him change in the restroom?" I offered.

Grover shook his head. "White gas stations in Indian country all got 'Out of Order' signs on their toilets. Don't want 'skins taking free shits."

He looked in his rear-view mirror. Jumbo was spread out across the seat, snoring like a buffalo bull.

"Just open another window," he said. "There's a town across the river. We'll get some sage or sweetgrass there to cover the smell."

It seemed like an odd solution, and far from the ceremonial usages of the herbs to which I was accustomed. But the smell inside the car was almost unbearable, and I was willing to consider anything that would offer us some relief.

"I'm surprised you even let him in your car," I said. "I remember you as kind of picky."

Grover ran his hand over the shiny green upholstery. "Virgin vinyl," he said. "Cleans up easy with water and Lysol. Besides, Jumbo's my friend. Got to help him out."

He turned onto the bridge, and the car hummed and whined its way across the metal bridge deck to the east side of the Missouri.

"Really, what brings you out here?" he said. "The old man's been asking about you."

"So he's doing okay?" I said, dodging the question with a question of my own. I was still not quite ready to share the story of Edith and Benais.

"I wouldn't say okay. He spends most of his time in bed. Gets to the store now and then. But he has a hard time walking. Can't keep his balance. He's about ready to be plowed under."

The tone in his voice belied the flippancy of his words. He obviously was saddened by the old man's deterioration. It saddened me, too, and made me realize even more how selfish I had been to procrastinate so long in getting the notebook to the old man.

"That's too bad," I said.

"Yeah," he responded. "He's just winding down. Old leaf falling off the tree, and all that."

I expected a little more interrogation about the reason for my visit, but I was saved by a huge blubber and wheeze from the backseat, followed by a long, liquid, rancid belch.

Grover wrinkled his nose and shook his head. "Man, that's rough," he said. "We got to do something."

CHAPTER THIRTEEN

THE EAGLE MAN VERSUS THE *WICHASHA WAKAN*

*W*e wheeled onto the main street of the small riverfront town and crept along at about ten miles an hour. Grover kept his eyes on the shops as we passed.

"I remember seeing it when I came through here before," he said. "Some kind of hippie bead place. Those places always have candles and sage and a bunch of phony herbs."

"Maybe they went out of business?" I offered.

"Places like that don't have any business to go out of," he said. "Just some old druggies who come out here to go Native. It doesn't take much to keep them going. Besides, there's always tourists coming through who want to buy Indian stuff but don't have the guts to talk to real Indians."

The car moved like a great green lizard past the low brick storefronts that stretched for a few blocks before the road opened out into the great emptiness of the prairies. The dry wind coming in through the windows blew the scent of Jumbo into every corner of the car.

"Maybe we should just run him through a car wash," I suggested.

"Nah. It's too rough on the feathers. This is better. Keep looking."

We had almost reached the end of the main street when Grover slammed on his brakes and cut sharply onto a side street. I fell hard against the window. Jumbo let out a gargling grunt.

"There," Grover said, pointing to a small storefront with a striped awning overhang and the words *Native and Shamanic Arts* printed on a sign over the door. "That's what I was looking for."

The shop window was filled with dream catchers and Tibetan prayer flags and cheap turtle-shell rattles. "They'll have something," he said.

"I'll come in with you," I said. I had no interest in staying in the car with Jumbo and his regalia, even with the windows rolled down.

"Good idea," Grover said. "You might find some nice turquoise jewelry for your hoochie."

He adjusted his cowboy hat, cinched up his string tie, and stepped from the car. He still had the rolling, bowlegged gate of a sailor, but the years and arthritis had taken their toll. He now walked with a severe limp.

He stopped for a moment in front of the "No Smoking" sign in the corner of the window, then flicked his cigarette into the street and walked through the door, making sure to hold his last breath of smoke so he could exhale it inside.

The shop was dark and smelled of incense. Faux Native flute music floated ethereally from some unseen speakers. A thin attractive white woman in her late forties, wearing a peasant blouse and a dozen strands of silver jewelry, was seated comfortably behind the counter. She had a ring on every finger and was paging through a book on the Tarot.

She smiled warmly when we came in. She had the fading good looks of someone who had kept herself in shape at great expense, but now, despite her best efforts, was starting to get stringy and tight. Her long salt-and-pepper hair, still full and rich, was held loosely in back by a silver-and-turquoise barrette. She looked more like someone who should be running a yoga studio in Taos than the proprietor of an unlikely boutique in a small South Dakota town.

"Good morning," she said in a voice both mellifluous and welcoming. I could detect just the hint of a German accent.

"Morning," I responded.

Grover was nosing his way around the counters. He made no effort to acknowledge her greeting.

"Are you looking for anything in particular?" she asked.

I waited for Grover to answer, but still he said nothing.

"Just browsing," I said. "Thank you."

The woman smiled graciously and turned back to her Tarot book. "Well, if I can be of assistance, just let me know."

Grover was looking at a small red object decorated with buckskin and feathers. His face was almost entirely obscured by the brim of his hat.

"What's this?" he said gruffly.

The woman looked up.

"Oh, that's a sacred prayer pipe," she answered. "It's used by Native Americans to offer prayers at the first light of day." It was obvious that she didn't recognize Grover as an Indian.

I could see Grover's back stiffen. He made a low grunt and stuck his finger in the bowl and pulled on the feathers.

"I can give you a very good price on it," she said. "It's the end of the season." She was eyeing Grover closely, unsure if she was about to make a sale or simply watching someone manhandle her goods.

Grover put the pipe to his mouth and sucked hard on the stem. The woman winced. I tried to figure out what he was up to, but his face was still hidden in shadow beneath his cowboy hat.

He grunted several times, then put the pipe back down and walked to the rear of the store to the display of herbs. It was large, stretching across almost the entire back wall. There were bundles of sage bound with pieces of rawhide, sheaves of sweetgrass wrapped in plastic, and various braids of medicinal herbs hanging from hooks on either side of the display.

Grover picked up a bundle and sniffed it.

"That's a traditional Indian love bundle. Lavender and sage," the woman said, now fully alert and concerned. "The sage cleanses negative energy and the lavender produces a feeling of peace. Many people give it as a housewarming gift or use it as a blessing. I've heard that the Native people use it as an aphrodisiac."

Grover held it up, rolled it over in his hands, then put it down and picked up another.

I could see that the woman was becoming increasingly uncomfortable. Grover was doing the same thing I remembered my students at Red Lake doing when they went into a white-owned store: handling everything and saying nothing, just to upset the proprietor.

He walked over to the edge of the wall display and took down one of the braids of sweetgrass. He held it by both ends and examined it carefully, making a few guttural "umms" and "unhhs." Then, in a single motion he took off his cowboy hat and turned to face the woman.

"Where'd this come from?" he said in his heaviest Indian patois.

The shock in the woman's expression was palpable. Seen full face, even with his close-cropped grey crew cut, Grover's Indian features were undeniable. He had on one of his darkest, most threatening scowls.

"We get it from a company back East," she stammered. Her eyes had widened and her voice had gotten tight. "They're very respectful. They have a medicine man who blesses everything before they send it to us. I believe he's Cherokee."

"This Cherokee medicine man. His name's eagle-something, isn't it?" Grover said.

"Why, yes," the woman replied, hoping that she had made some kind of cultural connection. "Eagle from the Light. It's in their literature."

Grover took the braid and held it out in front of him. He uttered a few words in Lakota, then turned back to the woman. "How well do you know this eagle fellow?"

"Well, I've never actually met him," she said. "I think there's a picture of him in their promotional material. Would you like me to find it? He blesses everything before they send it out. They're very respectful. They do everything in the traditional manner."

Grover appeared not to be listening. He lifted the braid high in front of him and rotated it in the light. He peered at it for what seemed to be an overly long period of time, then held it toward me.

"Do you see?" he said.

I cast him a confused glance. He glared at me and kicked my foot hard with the toe of his boot.

"Do you see?" he repeated.

"Yes," I answered, unsure of what else to say.

He held the braid out toward the woman. "It is right-braided," he intoned, adopting a stilted, faux Indian formalism — what he had in the past called "tom-tom talk." "See how the first piece of grass goes on top of the second?"

The woman, too, was completely confused. But Grover's

obvious Indian heritage and serious manner commanded assent. She examined it closely and nodded.

"It should not be that way," he said. He held the braid up and rotated it again. "All things must move in the direction of the sun. This goes against the sun. That is not good."

The woman was pulling nervously on one of her turquoise rings, unsure of what she was confronting. "The supplier assures us they're authentic," she said, trying hard to counter Grover's disapproval.

Grover was paying no attention. "*Wasichu*, go out and get the *Wichasha Wakan.*"

I looked at him, wide-eyed.

"The holy man. I believe he's almost finished his prayers. Tell him to come silently and not to speak. Make sure he brings the sacred animal skin."

He turned the braid over again in his hand. "This is not good," he repeated.

I remained by the counter. His actions were so over-the-top that I could not tell if he was joking or serious. He shot me a steely glance. "The *Wichasha Wakan*. Get him now."

The shopkeeper's eyes were darting back and forth between the two of us. Grover nodded emphatically toward the entrance. I smiled weakly at the worried woman, then hurried out the door and up the block to the car.

Jumbo was still snoring in the backseat. His mouth was open and his head was flopped back.

"Jumbo. Wake up," I said. "Grover wants to see you."

Jumbo grunted several times and shifted positions slightly. His sweaty powwow outfit made a flatulent sound as it moved across the vinyl of the Buick's rear seat.

"Hurry up," I said. "He wants you in the store."

Jumbo opened his eyes and squinted several times. "Jesus," he said.

"Come on. He wants you to go in and pretend you're a holy man. It's something about some braids of sweetgrass."

"Shit," Jumbo muttered.

"He wants you to wear your headdress. And he wants you to keep quiet."

Jumbo hoisted himself upward and swung his feet heavily onto the ground. The bells on his leggings jingled, and the deer hoof rattles clattered like castanets. He pulled himself upright by holding on to the door, positioned the headdress on his head, then started slowly down the sidewalk. The air in his wake had a sepulchral stench.

"What store?" he asked.

"That one with all the Indian stuff in the window," I said, pointing toward the striped awning.

He grunted and lumbered toward the door, jingling and clacking like a team of Clydesdales.

"I'll tell him you're coming," I said, hurrying ahead. I was more than a little apprehensive about what was going to take place.

I pushed my way into the store while Jumbo remained outside adjusting his pants. Grover was standing at the back with the woman. He was still holding the braid of sweetgrass.

"Where's the *Wichasha Wakan*?" he asked.

"He's outside," I said. "Preparing."

"Good." He turned to the woman. "This is a very powerful medicine man. Fifth generation. From the coyote clan. You know the coyote clan, right?"

The woman nodded uncertainly.

"He'll know what to do."

The woman nodded again. Her eyes were wide and frightened.

As we were talking, the hulking figure of Jumbo passed in front of the store window. There was much jingling and clattering, and a huge shadow appeared in the doorway. Grover picked up his hat and held it against his chest while bowing his head, then started chanting softly under his breath.

It took a few seconds for the full force of Jumbo's presence to take effect. Slowly, the fetid odor from his clothing and headdress made its way to the back of the shop. The woman blanched and leaned backward against the counter.

"The coyote people live among the animals," Grover said. "They do not smell like you and me."

Grover began intoning something in Lakota. Jumbo lumbered slowly in our direction, wheezing and muttering. With the coyote headdress on he appeared to be about seven feet tall.

Grover took one of the braids of sweetgrass and held it out to Jumbo, as if in offering.

Jumbo took the sweetgrass in his huge hand and stared at it uncomprehendingly. Grover kept up a running commentary in Lakota. Whether Jumbo understood him, or even if he was saying anything at all, I had no idea.

"It is not braided sunwise," Grover said in his stilted cigar-store Indian patois.

Jumbo started to say something. Grover shook his head to silence him.

"We must speak of this outside," he said. He nodded toward the sweetgrass. "Away from the presence."

He took the braid from Jumbo and handed it to me carefully, like a man holding something on a platter. "Do not touch the ends," he said. Then he took Jumbo by the elbow and guided him toward the door.

The two of them jingled and rattled their way out into the sunlight, leaving the woman and me standing together uncomfortably in front of the rack of herbs and boughs and bundles. I had no idea what Grover was doing and no idea if the woman's discomfort was a result of Grover's ominous manner or an actual fear that she might be in violation of some sacred protocol.

"I don't understand a lot of the things they do," I said. "But I have to respect their ways." The woman smiled weakly. The ethereal tones of the Indian flute music on the CD rose and fell in the background.

After a few seconds Grover and Jumbo returned. They walked directly past the woman and me and headed toward the back wall.

"They must be destroyed," Jumbo said. His voice was low and ponderous.

The woman blinked several times.

"He knows this eagle man," Grover said, inclining his head toward Jumbo, who nodded in return. "The Cherokee have among them some with dark spirits. He thinks that perhaps the eagle man is cursing the grasses sent to Lakota country."

"But most of my customers are white," she protested.

"It does not matter what earth suit you wear," Grover said. "Medicine knows no color. You would not want such medicine in the house of any of the four races."

"Perhaps I can send it back?" she said. "Find a local Lakota supplier?" It was obvious she was desperate.

Grover shook his head. "That would be good," he said. "But it is too late" — he waved his hand across the wall display of sage and lavender and cedar and sweetgrass — "for this."

"They must be destroyed," Jumbo intoned again.

The woman kept looking toward the door hoping that another customer would come in to save her from whatever was taking place. I thought for a second she might bolt and call the police.

Grover walked over and stood in front of the display. "Is there a back alley?" he said.

"There's a vacant lot out there," she said, pointing hesitantly toward an India-print cotton curtain that hung on a wooden rod over a back doorway.

"Get them now," he said to Jumbo.

Jumbo pushed past her and pulled the entire display of herbs

and grasses to his chest. She started forward toward them protectively, then shrank back as she thought better of it.

"You gather the rest of them," Grover said to me as he and
Jumbo pushed through the curtain. "Do not leave any behind."

I gathered up the remaining sheaves and bundles and stray
braids and stalks that had fallen to the floor.

"I'm sorry," I said. "I have to do what they say."

"But they've been blessed by a Native American," she repeated,
as if trying to negotiate with the one white man who might understand her situation. "They assure us it is done with the utmost
respect."

"This is not for me to say," I shrugged. I felt sorry for her and
wanted to say something to put her at ease, but I was caught in the
middle of a situation that was way beyond my control.

We could see the light streaming though the open back door
and hear the rhythmic clacking of rattles and the jingling of bells.
A pungent, overwhelming smell of perfumed herbs and grasses
mixed with the musk of decaying animal came wafting through
the curtain.

The woman looked desperately at me. "I have to bring these
out," I said apologetically. I could see she was near tears. I pushed
through the curtain with the remaining braids and bundles. The
woman followed closely behind.

Outside, in the bright sunlight of the late morning, Grover
and Jumbo had built a crackling fire of the braids and bundles
and sheaves. The smoke swirled upward in a grey, sinuous cloud.
Grover was continuing to chant in his Indian patois. Jumbo was
shaking a turtle rattle and circling the fire in an elephantine toe-
heel dance.

Grover looked at us and shook his head somberly, as if to caution us not to disturb the ceremony that was taking place. The
acrid smoke of the burning herbs burnt my eyes and nostrils.

"You must place the rest of it in now," he said to me.

I quickly placed the remaining sheaves and bundles on the fire and covered my eyes against the searing smoke.

He nodded toward Jumbo. "The *Wichasha Wakan* must now stand where the smoke is strongest. He must take as much of this eagle man's dark medicine as he can."

Jumbo moved slowly around to the far side of the fire and stood directly in the line of the blowing smoke. His huge bulk formed a barrier to the prairie wind, causing the roiling, acrid smoke to rush toward him, almost engulfing him in a cloud of perfumed haze.

He coughed several times. "Shit," he sputtered, and put his hands over his eyes.

"This is not easy for him," Grover said to the woman.

I was convinced that Grover was taking things too far. I was certain that in the bright glare of daylight Grover and Jumbo would be seen for what they were and that the woman would run for the police. It was a small town, and two Indians and a white man in a '70s-vintage Buick would be easily spotted, and probably not dealt with in the kindest fashion. I could foresee thirty days in a county jail and a thousand-dollar fine, which I knew would land on me to pay.

"Do you not think that we have perhaps done enough?" I said to Grover, hoping that he would catch the edge in my voice.

Grover saw the hard look in my eye. He matched it with an equally hard look, then slowly he broke into a wicked grin.

"Perhaps you are right," he said. "I believe that the *Wichasha Wakan* has absorbed most of the eagle man's bad medicine."

Jumbo stood motionless, choking and gasping. He was almost obscured by the huge cloud of smoke from the fire.

"You must let this burn out now," Grover said to the woman. "Allow none to remain unburned."

She was standing at my side, staring at the smoldering pile of inventory on the ground before us.

"It is normal to give gifts to a medicine man who performs such ceremonies for you," he continued. I glared at him with all the disapproval I could muster. He was taking things way too far. He gave me just the slightest edge of a smile.

"But it is also not good to take from people without return," he said, turning to the woman. "We Native people know this, for your people have been taking from us without return since your arrival on our land. It is part of our tradition to pay fairly for what is taken. So before we leave, our *wasichu* friend here" — he nodded in my direction — "will pay you for your goods. It may not be full value, but it will be a sign of our respect for what you have allowed us to take from you. And we will tell our brothers and sisters that yours is a good place for Native people to come because they are treated with honor and respect." He put his hands together as if praying, and bowed slightly in her direction.

"Come now," he said to Jumbo. "We will leave it to our *wasichu* friend to make things right." He nodded to me, then took Jumbo by the arm and led him down the alley. Jumbo had his hands over his eyes, trying to rub them free of the burning effects of the smoke. His coyote war bonnet was hanging askew on his head.

"Treat this woman with generosity," he said to me as he left. "She has been good to allow us to undo the harm of the eagle man. Give her all you have, for she has given us all she has." He raised his hand toward me, as if in benediction, and spoke some words in Lakota, then proceeded down the alley.

I looked at the woman with the most impassive face I could muster. I was caught between rage at what Grover had perpetrated and fear that the woman had finally seen through the bizarre charade Grover had performed and was about to call the police. I did not believe that anyone could fall for what I had just witnessed, but Grover was both threatening and convincing when he assumed that dark demeanor, so it was not impossible that someone who did not know him might be taken in by the strange performance.

Jumbo and Grover had almost reached the end of the alley. We watched them as they turned the corner, then I opened my billfold and riffled through my cash — 127 dollars. I did not want to leave her with credit card information, and I didn't want to seem penurious. I just wanted to get out of town without being arrested.

I surreptitiously slipped a twenty into my pocket and handed the rest to her. She looked at the money and hesitated. "I don't know if I should take this," she said.

"No. Go ahead," I said. "Use it to buy new herbs from the Lakota people. I'm sure it will make my friends happy and you will be helping to honor the old ways. Just say nothing to anyone else about this."

She stared at the bills for a moment, then folded them over and put them in the pocket of her skirt. "I'll do that," she said. "Thank them for teaching me."

I smiled and took her hands in mine. "You have done a good thing," I said, and hurried down the alley.

Grover's car was idling at the corner. He was leaned back in his seat choking with laughter. Jumbo was hunched over in the rear seat, still rubbing his eyes. The inside of the car smelled like a bonfire laced with sweat, dead animal, and perfume.

"That was really pushing it," I said, as I slipped into the passenger seat.

"Fixed the problem, didn't it?" Grover said.

"On my dime."

"You got a lot of dimes."

"Not as many as you might think."

"Hope you have enough left to buy dinner. The *Wichasha Wakan* worked up a pretty good appetite doing that ceremony."

Jumbo was still coughing and sniffling in the backseat. "Just get us out of town," I said. "The *Wichasha Wakan* can eat when we put some miles behind us. Nobody could have bought that story. I don't know how you got away with it. The woman might be calling the police right now."

Grover burst out laughing again. "She's not calling any police. She's probably just happy the *Wichasha Wakan* didn't curse her store."

He was laughing so hard he could hardly drive. I had never seen him take so much pleasure in one of his tricks. "Did you see her face when Jumbo walked in?" he choked.

"I saw her face when I gave her a hundred bucks."

"Worth every penny."

"That's easy for you to say."

Grover was almost gasping. "Christ, the 'eagle man,'" he said.

"That's another thing," I said. "How'd you know the guy was named eagle-something?"

"Law of averages. With phony medicine men it's always eagle-something or wolf-something. With a woman it's always summer dawn or raven or something to do with rain. I just made a guess. You don't want your sage blessed by fieldmouse man or gopher man."

"Well, I thought it was a little unnecessary," I said, perturbed as much by his malicious enjoyment as by the scene itself. "She seemed like a decent sort. You knew she sold sage and sweetgrass. Why didn't you just buy it and get out of there?"

"I was going to, but then she started talking about the pipe. You don't joke about *Chanupa*, and you don't put *sacred* and *money* in the same sentence."

"Then why didn't you have Jumbo gather up the pipes and destroy them rather than all the herbs?"

"They were just Chinese crap. I saw a sticker on the bottom. But that's not the point. *Chanupa* is our sacred connection with the Creator. White people shouldn't even be talking about them. They sure as hell shouldn't be selling Chinese knockoffs of them. We don't sell plastic crucifixes at our powwows." He spit a long stream of tobacco-laden saliva out the window. "You make money off Indians, sometimes you've got to pay.

"Besides," he said, nodding toward the backseat and starting to laugh again. "Breaking the pipes wouldn't have had the same cleansing effect." Jumbo was coughing and snorting and rubbing his blazing-red eyes. The car smelled like a perfumed forest fire.

Grover shoved the car into gear and headed back across the bridge toward the west. No cars were following us, and the hills had taken on a quiet, golden glow.

He wrinkled up his nose and sniffed several times. "Open your window, Nerburn," he said. "The *Wichasha Wakan* absorbed a lot of bad medicine."

CHAPTER FOURTEEN

A STRONG HEART TO SERVE

I was even less inclined to talk to Grover about the notebook and the asylum after the fiasco with the shop owner. His obvious pleasure at making the woman uncomfortable and his willingness to use Jumbo as a foil had put me off. After seeing the pain and sadness in Edith's face, and experiencing the almost mystical depth of Benais's understanding, I found Grover's behavior callow and insensitive. I had no desire to share anything even remotely heartfelt with him.

I knew I would eventually have to get his opinion on the notebook and the asylum. But for now I just wanted to keep my distance while I sorted things out. It was Dan who mattered most. Grover was just a gatekeeper, and right now, I didn't appreciate the way he was minding the gate.

We crossed the Missouri and turned north along the winding road that hugged the water's edge. Grover smoked and joked while Jumbo sat hunched over in the backseat dabbing his eyes with the edge of his dancing shirt.

"I'll drop you back at the powwow grounds," Grover said. "Since you're going out to see the old man anyway, Jumbo can ride with you. I got a stop to make. We'll meet up on the Rosebud later tonight." He made a vaguely obscene poking gesture with his right forefinger. "Or tomorrow morning."

Once back at the powwow grounds Grover parked his Buick next to Jumbo's tent and polished its dashboard with a handkerchief in preparation for his journey to whatever mysterious stop he had in mind. I sat on the hood of my car and stared off toward the dance arbor while Jumbo went off into the woods to change his clothes.

Even though I was feeling sympathetic toward Jumbo for the way Grover had used him, I wasn't sure I was up for three hundred miles of his company. He had always been pleasant enough, though his conversations tended toward the monosyllabic and always seemed focused on machines or food. I couldn't imagine spending the rest of the afternoon with him. And despite some fresh clothes and the dousing of smoke he had taken behind the shaman woman's store, he still smelled like a cross between a barnyard and a charnel house.

As I was musing, he emerged from the bushes carrying his leggings, headdress, ribbon shirt, and moccasins. He had on stained sweatpants, laceless high-top tennis shoes, and a dirty white T-shirt with the slogan Powered by Frybread, stretched over his belly like a tent. He was chewing on a large chunk of meat he must have kept sequestered for emergencies such as this.

Grover leaned out his car window and gestured me over like a man about to share a secret. "Two words," he said. "Casino buffet. You remember that, and you'll do fine."

He waved jauntily and rumbled slowly out through the field

of grasses, leaving the smell of cigarette smoke and cheap drug-store cologne floating in the air behind him.

Jumbo was busy taking down his tent and gathering his regalia. "I guess you're riding with me, Jumbo," I said.

"I can do that," he said. "I was thinking I'd get to dance again."

"I guess Grover's got business."

"Yeah," he said wistfully.

I opened the trunk so he could pack his gear away. I didn't want it inside the car, especially the animal pelt. He placed the objects gently next to my own bags and sleeping gear, and adjusted them with slow, careful gestures. There was a surprising delicacy to his actions.

"Where'd you get all your regalia?" I said in an effort to establish some rapport.

He grinned a gaping smile of pride. "Lot of it belonged to my grandpa," he said, sliding into the passenger seat. "The bustle and stuff. The headdress was a gift."

The car settled and creaked as he adjusted himself and struggled to pull the seatbelt across his ponderous belly.

"Too short," he said. Even fully extended, there was a gap of about a foot between the hasp and the buckle.

"I'll be careful," I said.

The lingering smell of herbs and sweat filled the car, but it was not oppressive. The conflagration had done its job, and with the headdress packed away in the trunk, the worst offender had been eliminated. Still, I was not at all comfortable with the situation. I knew almost nothing about Jumbo other than that he ran a squalid repair shop and seemed to be an earnest and good-hearted fellow. He and I had probably exchanged no more than twenty sentences over the years. I had no idea how, or if, to engage him in conversation. I knew most Indians were comfortable being quiet, but six hours of silence with this hulking, toothless man seemed excessive.

We drove without talking for almost fifty miles. Though Jumbo seemed comfortable enough with the situation, I was feeling the heavy weight of the silence between us. He was like some huge elemental force — as much beast as man. He wheezed and rattled as he breathed, causing dark, rumbling sounds to emanate from deep in his chest. And the way he pulled on the chunk of meat with his few remaining teeth seemed almost Paleolithic. Eventually, I decided I had to initiate a conversation.

"Does it bother you when Grover does stuff like make you pretend to be a holy man?" I asked, as casually as I could. It was the subject that was at the front of my mind at the moment.

"Don't bother me," he answered.

"I thought it was kind of cruel," I continued. "Tricking that woman and making you stand in the smoke of the fire."

Jumbo furrowed his brow. "Wasn't cruel. He was protecting the people."

"How was that protecting the people?" I persisted, though I knew I was taking a chance by forcing the issue. One lesson I had learned over the years is that you don't get between Indian people, even when they have strong disagreements between themselves.

But Jumbo seemed to take no offense. He fell silent and breathed heavily through his nostrils. I was sure I had invaded private territory or pushed too hard, when suddenly he reached his hands out in front of him and made a large, round gesture.

"It's like the powwow ring," he said, forming his words slowly. "You shouldn't go in there unless you're invited. That woman was trying get inside our ways. She wasn't invited. Grover was trying to teach her."

It was the most expansive comment I had ever heard him make.

"I never thought of it that way," I said, hoping to keep him talking.

"Grover has *wayounihan*."

"*Wayounihan?*"

"A warrior spirit. He helps people. He protects us. He never asks for nothing. Sometimes you got to do hard things. Sometimes you don't have any friends."

He sat silently, as if deciding whether to say more.

"He's my friend, though," he said softly. "It felt good to help him."

There was a softness in his manner that I had never seen before.

"You did a good job," I said.

He cast his eyes down. "I tried my best."

This was far and away the longest conversation Jumbo and I had ever shared. I smiled inwardly as we rode through the lyrical, rolling landscape toward the burnished golden hills.

Before long, the dips and swales induced an almost hypnotic reverie and peace.

"Beautiful country," I said, almost to myself.

"Kind of like the sound a flute makes," Jumbo said.

The comment caught me off guard. "What?"

He reached his huge hand out over the dashboard and traced the outlines of the rolling landscape, like a conductor giving a pace to an orchestra.

"The way a flute sounds, all up and down without stopping."

I looked at him in surprise.

"I ain't never learned to play the flute," he continued. "I done some drumming, though. Drums are more like thunder." He kept his eyes averted, as if embarrassed to be sharing so much of his thoughts. "Sometimes, when I dance, I try to be like thunder."

The words were so unexpected that I hardly knew what to say.

"I didn't know you thought about things like that," I said.

"I ain't stupid," he replied.

"I didn't think you were," I lied.

"I just don't talk much." He paused for a second as if deciding whether to say more. "I ain't like a white man. I don't talk when I ain't got nothing to say."

"Yeah, that's one of our problems," I said.

"Animals don't talk much and nobody thinks they're stupid," he continued.

It was a strange comment, poignant and revealing — an almost plaintive justification for his taciturn manner. I wanted to keep him talking.

"You like animals?" I said.

"I learn a lot from animals. My grandpa said that the Creator uses animals for teachers. He puts a special power in every animal so we can learn from it by watching. We watch the animals to know how to live."

I was filled with a sudden shame for the assumptions I had made about this huge man. Though his words were simple, his thoughts were deep.

"You learned a lot from your grandpa?"

He nodded again.

"Would you tell me about him?" I asked. I suddenly wanted to know more about the man hidden inside the body that was the butt of so many jokes.

I could see the turmoil on his face as he struggled with whether or not to open up to a white man.

"Well," he said after a moment's pause, "I guess I could tell you a little."

He took a deep breath and began slowly. "Grandpa was a medicine man. Lots of people came to him. I used to listen when he talked. He said I'd learn more by listening than by talking."

"A lesson we should all learn."

Jumbo nodded. "I went everywhere with him. I wanted to be a medicine man like him. But he said I couldn't. He said a medicine man had to be hard, that I wouldn't be good at dealing with the spirits. Sometimes you have to fight them, he said. He said I wasn't a fighter."

"More a lover, eh?"

He kept his eyes down and nodded his head slightly, as if the acknowledgment was embarrassing to him.

"One time he gave me a little *shunka* — a little puppy — to see how I raised it," he said. "I carried it around with me and talked to it all the time. He asked me if I would let him be killed for ceremony to help the people. I told him, 'No. I want you to find another *shunka*.' I thought he would be mad at me. He just smiled. He said that was good, and now he knew my heart."

"So you got to keep the pup?"

"For a while. Then someone shot him." From within the heavy folds and jowls I could see a tiny glisten of moisture near his eyes. He turned his face toward the window. "They didn't have to do that."

The gentleness in the man's soul was a revelation. I felt ashamed at myself for the glib way I had dismissed him for years, taking his huge size and lumbering manner for slowness, even stupidity.

"That dog was my best friend," he said.

"Dogs are about the best friend you can have," I said.

"They don't care that I'm fat," he said softly.

The poignancy of the comment tore at my heart. "Big body, big heart," I said.

"I like to help people," he responded. He had decided to open up to me. "That's what my grandpa said I should do. He said I could serve my people by helping. He said I was humble and that was good." His kept his eyes down, as if embarrassed by even this slightest hint of self-praise.

Eventually, after a long pause, he spoke again. "My grandpa said there were four things a Lakota boy has to learn." He lifted his hand and started counting on his stubby fingers, slowly enumerating the values his grandfather had taught him, as if repeating them by rote. "He has to learn to give. He has to learn to respect. He has to learn to be brave. He has to learn to be wise. Grandpa said the Creator gave us all one gift stronger than the others. He said we had to find which one we had, then use it to help our people. He said we had to learn it and follow it our whole life."

"And you found giving?"

He nodded. "*Wacantognaka*. Being generous."

"How'd you find it?"

He shifted slightly in his seat. "I could tell you a story," he said.

"Would you?"

He waited a second before speaking.

"I could do that. I got this older brother, Odell. He was strong, like Grover. He had a warrior spirit. I used to follow him everywhere. He had a pet wolf. That wolf lived on the ridge way out behind our house. There were some babies and a mother wolf, too.

"Odell had raised that wolf from just little. It never bothered nobody. Odell would bring food up there, parts of a cow or buffalo. That wolf never took anything it didn't need. It would just take a bit, then drag the rest back to its family.

"I told my grandpa this. 'That's how wolf is,' he said. 'He doesn't ask for anything and always takes care of his family.'

" 'I'd like to be like that,' I said.

"My grandpa smiled at me and put his hand on my shoulder. 'That's more Odell's way,' he said. He told me to have patience and he would help me find a path.

"I was just little, like seven. It was right after my little dog got killed. Grandpa held ceremony every night. People always came to him. Sometimes he sent me to get water, just like I did for the grandmas. He said that was what a boy did to become a man, because it was hard and it was important.

"I would bring him buckets of water from the well or the

creek when the well wasn't working. He would use it on the stones in the sweat, or give it to people to drink. 'This is water my little grandson brought,' he'd say. 'He has a strong heart to serve.'

"He wanted me to hear it. He was putting me in front of the community, giving me something to live up to.

"One day I said to him, 'It makes me proud to hear you say these things, Grandpa. But I can't just bring water my whole life. What should I do to help the people?' I still wanted to be a medicine man. I wanted to be strong like the wolf.

"He put his hand on my shoulder. I liked it when he did that. 'You come to my house tonight and I will give you something,' he said.

"That night I went to his house. He went into his back room and came out with a leather bag. It had ribbons all over it. 'Here,' he said. 'Take this home. You look in it when you get home. When you are done you come see me.'

"'What am I supposed to do when I open it, Grandpa?' I asked.

"'You just go home and open it,' he said.

"I ran home fast across the field. I wanted to see what was in the bag. When I got home I opened it. It was all full of bones.

"I didn't know what I should do. I thought they might have spirit power. I put them out on the table. I was nervous. I left them there for a whole week. I didn't know what he wanted. Then one day I just had the thought that I should try to put them together. I felt like they were talking to me and they were saying they wanted to be together. I took the bones and put them all connected to each other the way that I thought they should be. It just came to me.

"When I got them all together I went to my grandfather and said, 'I took the bones and I did something.'

"He said, 'Let me see.'

"We went back to my house. I showed him all the bones, laid out.

"Grandpa put his hand on my shoulder. 'Do you know what that is?' he asked.

" 'Its back legs bend forward,' I said. 'It doesn't have hooves. It has a skull like a wolf but it's small. I think it's a young wolf or a dog.'

" 'Tell me about the wolf and the dog,' he said.

" 'The wolf is strong,' I said. 'It's my favorite animal. It only takes what it needs. It is good to its family, just like you taught. It always watches everything.'

" 'And the dog?'

" 'The dog is helpful. It has a good heart. It always is by the side of the people. It will give its life for the people.'

" 'Which one sounds like you?'

" 'I think the dog, Grandfather,' I said.

" 'You are right,' he said. 'Now, why did you put the bones together?'

" 'I don't know,' I told him. 'I saw them and I felt sad that they were all apart.'

" 'Did you have any vision?'

" 'No.'

" 'Did you hear any voice?'

" 'No.'

" 'Did anything come to help you put them back together?'

" 'No, I just did it. I wanted to help them.'

"He took the bones and put them back in the bag. Then he gave it to me. 'These are the bones of your little *shunka*, your little dog,' he said. 'The one that got shot. He gave his life for you. When he was alive he showed me your heart, because you did not want him to die, even for the people. Now that he is dead he has shown me your mind. You will help your people put things together. You will not ask what things mean; you will only think about how things work. You will teach the children. The animals will help you because they will know you and will not fear you. You will not take any money except what the people give you. If you do these things you will be an important man for our people.'

"I was so proud. I just sat there holding the bag with the bones of my little dog and thinking about how my grandpa had done all this just to give me a lesson.

"'I will do that, Grandfather,' I said. He died the next year."

Jumbo stared straight ahead. His jaw was set and his eyes were narrowed. I thought of his repair garage with its dripping hand-painted sign that read "Broke Car's and Stuff 'fixed,'" the benches full of dismantled toasters and old water pumps, his patient efforts to teach the children how to repair their bicycles, and the almost reverential way they had led me to his garage that time years ago when my car had broken down, knowing that he alone could help get a lost *wasichu* back on the road.

"I think your grandpa would be proud," I said.

"I still talk to him some, ask him for help."

He fell silent for a while. I could see that he was thinking hard.

"Can you stop?" he said. "I got to get something out of the trunk."

I pulled to the side of the road and popped the latch for the trunk. Jumbo lumbered to the back of the car and rummaged around in his powwow gear. When he returned he was carrying a small pouch.

He opened it carefully and pulled out a small white bone. He held it over to me without looking at me.

"This is from my little dog," he said. "You can have it."

I took it gently and cradled it in my hand.

"*Pilamaya, cola,*" I said. "Thank you, friend." It was the only time in my life I had ever spoken the word *friend* to someone in Lakota.

CHAPTER FIFTEEN

"Your Silence Makes a Lot of Noise"

*W*e drove westward into the twilight glow. Jumbo's gift had overwhelmed me in its kindness and had filled the car with intimacy and peace. I held the bone gently in my hand as I drove, as if I had been entrusted with a sacred relic.

"I wanted you to have that," Jumbo said. He kept his eyes averted from mine. "Grandpa Dan says you had a strong heart for *shunka*. He says he tested you with Fatback the first time you were here and Fatback told him you were a good person."

The memory of Fatback made me smile. The old black Lab and I had spent many hours together in the back of Grover's Buick, she with her head on my lap and her back leg kicking as she whimpered and wheezed through some dog dream.

"She was a really good dog," I said. "I really loved her."

"Grandpa Dan knew it. Fatback loved you, too. He could see that." He fidgeted a bit, as if the word made him uncomfortable.

"You got a dog now?" he said hesitantly, as if by asking he might somehow be intruding on my privacy.

"Yeah. A sweet little yellow Lab named Lucie."

He kept his eyes down. "What's she like?"

"Really quiet. We got her from a pound. She seems sad a lot."

"Do you think maybe she got beat when she was little?"

"I don't know. If I move fast or say a harsh word, she gets scared. Maybe she just has a frightened spirit."

He chewed on this for a moment.

"Maybe she was sent to teach you to be gentle."

I smiled at the inference. "You might be right. A little more gentleness never hurt anyone."

He looked down and squeezed his hands together nervously. I had come to recognize this as the gesture he made when he wanted to speak of something important.

"I got something to ask you," he said after a long silence.

"Ask away."

He fidgeted a bit more before proceeding. "How come your church religion don't talk about animals?"

It was a matter-of-fact question and asked without rancor. But it took me aback.

"What do you mean?"

"That's something my grandpa asked," he said. "He said if I ever got to know a white man I should ask it. Grandpa said he listened to white preachers and they never talked about the animals except a bad snake that had the devil inside it. He said he couldn't trust those preachers, because, for us, the animals were good. They came to us with the Creator's knowledge. They were the way the Creator gave us teachings."

This was the second time Jumbo had brought up the subject of animals as teachers.

I did a quick inventory of my cursory biblical knowledge and realized that the only animals I could think of in the Bible were indeed the snake in the Garden of Eden, the donkey Jesus rode on into Jerusalem, and the pigs that were filled with demons and ran into a lake. I was sure there were more, but they didn't play a central role in my memory. And they certainly didn't play the role of teachers.

"Grandpa thought your preachers probably didn't prepare themselves," Jumbo went on, "so the animals never visited them. He said that was because your preachers were always talking so they didn't have time to listen. Animals don't come to people who are always talking. That's why I don't talk much. I want the animals to come to me. So I always try to sit and listen."

He leaned back in the seat and closed his eyes. It was obvious he had said more than he'd intended. "I'm gonna take a nap now. If you see somewhere to eat, it would be okay if we stopped there. I'm getting kind of hungry."

We rode on into the growing twilight. The tar strips beat a hypnotic rhythm beneath us as the lonely asphalt highway cut a meandering line through the treeless hills toward the horizon.

It was a peaceful, almost empty landscape. Every few miles a gravel road would cut off from the main highway, and a small house could be seen sitting alone and isolated far up in the hills. Here and there a rusted car body sat solitary in a field, or a broken farm windmill rose above the landscape on its spindly, triangular stilts. But mostly it was just earth and sky and the thin ribbon of roadway coursing like a fierce, dark river through the great, unpopulated land.

I was pleased that Jumbo had fallen asleep. I needed to be alone with my thoughts. I had seldom had a day filled with so many emotions. From the old woman in the nursing home, to the ghostly presence of the asylum graves, to Grover's cruel trick on the woman and Jumbo's inestimable gift and personal revelations, I felt I had traveled half a lifetime's journey in just a few hours.

I was almost falling asleep myself when the jangle of a cell phone shocked me into awareness. It was coming from somewhere on Jumbo.

"Jumbo," I said, jostling him with my elbow. "Your cell phone is ringing."

He snorted and coughed and jerked his head upright. He fumbled a bit in the leather pouch he had hung on his belt and pulled out a tiny black phone. He flipped it open and held it up to his ear. It looked like a postage stamp in his huge mitt of a hand.

"Yeah?" he said.

I could hear the edges of a raspy voice on the other end.

Jumbo listened intently, then said, "Okay," and hung up.

"That was Grover," he said. "He's in Mission. He wants us to meet him on the corner by the stoplight. He said he needs to talk to you alone."

It was a curious request, and I could see no reason for it. I flipped my road atlas open and tried to identify our location. Mission was in the center of the Rosebud Reservation. We were about twenty miles away as the crow flies.

"We should be there in less than a half hour," I said.

Jumbo rubbed his hands together nervously. "Since Grover wants to talk to you alone, you think you could drop me at the Subway? It's right on the edge of town. I could walk to the stoplight when I'm done."

"You don't have to walk anywhere," I said. "I'll drop you wherever you want and buy you whatever you want, then pick you up. It's the least I can do for you."

"Subway's good," he said. "They usually have specials." He licked his lips involuntarily. "Yeah. Subway's good."

Soon the few lights of the town of Mission began to give off a dim glow on the horizon. Evening was descending, and the small reservation town was like a tiny pool of human habitation in the great growing duskiness of the high plains twilight.

I left Jumbo at the Subway with my last twenty dollars and instructions to keep the change.

He wedged himself out of the seat and moved quickly toward the light of the restaurant, like a moth toward a flame.

"I'll be back in about half an hour," I said.

"Don't hurry," he grinned over his shoulder. "I'm pretty hungry."

I found Grover where he had said he would be, sitting on a con-crete berm in front of a small boarded-up blue-and-yellow shack on the apron of an abandoned gas station just past the town's stoplight. Apparently someone had once hoped to use the shack to start a coffee stand but had given up on the idea. Weeds grew knee-high through the cracks in the concrete, and white plastic trash bags had piled up outside the door. Beer cans and pop bot-tles were strewn across the ground.

He waved as I drove up. He had a smirk on his face and looked freshly washed. He pointed to a handwritten sign with faded let-ters that said "Espresso."

"Thought I'd surprise you with a capistrino," he said. "I guess the rez just wasn't ready for your kind of coffee."

He took a pack of Camels out of his shirt pocket and removed a cigarette with his teeth. He lit a stick match by slashing it across the thigh of his jeans, then cupped his hand around the flame and drew on the cigarette until the smoke enveloped his face.

"Sit down, take a load off," he said. I was curious about his request to talk to me alone, but I decided I would let him take the lead.

I slid onto the berm next to him. "You take care of your busi-ness?" I asked.

He stared down his nose at me. "I always take care of my business." The smell of his cheap cologne was overwhelming.

"Where's Jumbo?" he asked.

"I dropped him at the Subway on the edge of town."

He nodded his approval. "That'll keep him busy for a while."

"It'll keep Subway busy for a while," I said. "He's really a pretty interesting guy."

Grover held his hands out, palms up, and shrugged. "I told you. White people see an Indian, they think he's stupid. They see a fat Indian, they think he's really stupid. Jumbo's got a hard mountain to climb."

"I guess I misjudged him."

"You misjudge a lot of things. Comes with the territory."

He spit a long string of saliva into the night. "So," he said. "What are you doing out here, really?"

"Just a visit," I said. I had almost decided to skip Grover entirely and wait until I saw Wenonah before sharing the story of the notebook and the asylum.

"You ain't ever made 'just a visit' before."

"There's always a first time."

"Yeah, well, this ain't it. What's going on?"

"Nothing. I'm fine," I said.

He shook his head in disgust at the obviousness of my lie, then sat back and stared at me while I drew patterns in the dust with a stick. I could feel his gaze boring into me.

"You don't do quiet very well, Nerburn," he said. "Your silence makes a lot of noise."

"I'm just thinking," I said.

"Well, your thinking makes a lot of noise, then. You got something on your mind, you should man up and say it."

I made one last effort to move the conversation away from the notebook.

"I guess I'm just still bothered," I said. "The way you treated

Jumbo and that woman in the shop really put me off. It seemed cruel and unnecessary."

He pulled out another cigarette and lit it with the same practiced gesture. "Cruel, maybe. Unnecessary, no. She needed to be schooled."

"But Jumbo? Making fun of him in that way?"

He blew a long stream of smoke into the thin, evening air.

"Listen," he said. "Jumbo and I go back a long ways. People have been making fun of him for so damn long that he doesn't even feel the hurt anymore. But I wasn't making fun of him. I was letting him help me. He understood that. He knew we were protecting our people."

"By making sport of a white woman?"

"I told you. I wasn't making sport of her. I was schooling her. She was messing in places she didn't belong. Sweetgrass, sage, cedar — those are our sacred medicines. It was all a game for her."

He shook his head in undisguised contempt. "Christ. 'Housewarming gifts,' 'Indian love bundles.' She wants an Indian love bundle, I'll give her an Indian love bundle."

He walked slowly to the edge of the crumbling concrete apron. The heels of his cowboy boots clicked hollowly in the night.

"I got no apologies to make for messing with that woman. Your people took damn near everything we got. Now you're coming for our spirituality. If I've got to knock some stringy old hippie woman around to protect what we got left, I got no problem with that."

"You're a hard man, Grover," I said.

"And you're a soft man, Nerburn. You think being nice is the same as being good."

"They're close cousins, I would think," I answered.

"Well, you would think wrong. 'Nice' is about wanting people to like you. 'Good' is about doing what you're supposed to do, even if nobody likes you. When you're worried about being liked, it gives people too much power over you. They can lead you around like a dog chasing a bone. All they got to do is withhold their approval, and you'll piss down your leg to make them like you. You're an easy mark. That's one of the reasons I've never quite trusted you."

"I'm not quite that easy," I said.

He spit a thin, wicked stream of tobacco and saliva across the pavement.

"You'd be surprised."

The conversation was taking a strange course. I was trying as best I could to keep the subject away from the notebook, and Grover, if he had a reason for wanting to see me alone, was making no effort to make that reason known.

We sat in awkward silence for a few moments until Grover stood up abruptly and walked toward his car.

"Come on," he said. "We need to go for a ride."

"I don't need to go for a ride," I said. "I've been riding all day."

"I'm not asking you, I'm telling you. We need to go for a ride."

He continued across the pavement. There was a strange purposefulness to his manner.

"What about Jumbo?" I said.

"How much did you give him?"

"Twenty bucks."

"He's fine, then. Come on."

He slid into the front seat of his car, reached over, and flipped the passenger door open. Hesitantly, I took my place in the seat next to him.

"Where are we going?" I asked.

"To have a talk."

"But we were having a talk."

"We were just bullshitting. I mean a real talk. You may not be man enough to say what's on your mind. But I am. We got a few things to get straight."

CHAPTER SIXTEEN

PRIESTS AND PELICANS

*W*e drove north from town along a dark highway. The twilight glow had faded and the stars had begun to come out. The ghost of a moon was just beginning to show itself over the bald Dakota hills.

My curiosity was great, but I knew better than to question Grover further. I had learned long ago not to push him on issues of importance, and whatever was on his mind seemed to be such an issue.

After a few miles of silent travel, he slowed the Buick and turned onto a dirt path. We rattled across a cattle grate and veered down a rutted trail toward a shadowy stand of trees. The car bounced and scraped along the dried mud ridges.

The silence and increasing isolation were beginning to concern me. "So, what's up?" I asked, trying to sound as casual as I could.

"I got some things to say to you," he said, "and you got some things to say to me."

"And we couldn't say them back at the gas station?"

He shook his head and kept his eyes on the path. "Nope."

The trail had deteriorated into two weedy parallel ruts. Small ground animals scurried through the grass in front of us, illuminated by the weak cones of Grover's headlights.

We passed through a stand of gnarled, stunted oaks and low brush before coming to a stop in a clearing at the edge of a tiny, torpid stream. It looked like the kind of place kids came for late-night drinking parties or to park with their girlfriends. Beer cans and used condoms littered the ground.

"So this is where we needed to go to talk?" I asked.

"Yep."

"Is there something special about this place?" I said as he stopped the car and shut off the lights. I was losing my veneer of nonchalance.

"Will be."

He stepped out of the car and limped over to the clearing by the edge of the creek and began gathering twigs. "Get some wood," he said.

I did as he instructed, picking up pieces of deadfall from beneath the oaks. He formed the wood into a precise teepee and lit it with a single match. In a few minutes a small fire was glowing and crackling in the growing darkness.

Grover pointed to a stump on the other side of the fire. "Sit down," he said.

He got down on his knees, took a foil pouch out of his back pocket, and fashioned a small pyramid of what looked to be tobacco on the ground between the two of us. His actions were focused and meticulous. He was speaking under his breath in Lakota.

He took a second substance from his shirt pocket, added it

to the pile, then extracted a burning twig from the fire and lit the small mound with the flame, all the while continuing his low incantation. The sweet smell of tobacco and sage rose into the night.

When he had the mound burning well, he settled back and nodded toward the smoldering pyramid. "You know what this is?" he said.

"Tobacco? Sage?"

"You know what it means?"

"You're calling on the Creator."

"That's right. It means it's time to stop the bullshitting. Both of us. It's time to speak the truth."

He touched his chest and thrust his hand forward, palm out, like he was throwing his heart to me. "This is man to man. There must be nothing clouding our hearts as we speak."

It was rare for Grover to stop joking. Whatever was on his mind was something he did not take lightly. I returned the gesture, hoping I was doing the correct thing.

"Now I want you to listen to me," he said. He spoke slowly and precisely. "I don't know what you're doing out here. But I know it's something, and before we leave you're going to tell me what it is. Agreed?"

I started to answer, but he interrupted. "Careful, now. No bullshit. Agreed?" He pointed at the tobacco smoke streaming its way into the sky.

"Agreed," I said, reluctantly.

"Good," he said. "But first, I've got to talk. Now, this ain't easy for me and I don't like it. But the old man made me promise that if I saw you again, I would take away the shadow on the ground between us. He said the people who had come together around his life should not hold anger against each other. He said he wanted this all cleared up before he passed. I gave him my word, and I don't break my word."

"So that's why you brought us out here?"

"That's right. I want to honor the old man's wishes, and I want it to be done in the Creator's sky, not in some parking lot next to some fucking stoplight."

He blew on the glowing pile of tobacco and sage until a thin ribbon of smoke rose sinuously into the air. "Now, I'm going to talk first. If you've got something you want to know or something to say, you stop me and go ahead and say it. But mostly, I'm going to talk and you're going to listen. It's going to take me a while, but I need to lay this out on the ground before us. Then when I'm done, you're going to place what you have on the ground between us. Understand?"

"Yes," I said.

He pointed toward the pile of smoldering herbs and followed the rising smoke with his finger until it pointed to the sky. "Remember, the Creator is listening."

He sprinkled some tobacco across the ground in front of him, like a man sowing seed, then straightened his back.

"You think I don't like you much," he began.

"That's fair," I said.

"And you don't like me much."

"I respect you, but I don't like some of your ways."

"Good," he said. "You're talking straight. That's what I like."

He sprinkled some more tobacco on the earth in front of him. "You remember when you first came out to the rez?"

"Like it was yesterday."

"Well, so do I. That was a hard time for me. One more white man on our doorstep, all full of 'help the Indian' and wide-eyed bullshit, come out to visit an old man I honored like a father."

"I only came because Wenonah asked me. You knew that."

"Yeah, I knew that. But I still didn't like it. Neither did she."

"Then why did she call me?"

"Because her grandpa told her to. When an elder tells you to do something, you do it.

"We both thought the old man was making a big mistake. He didn't know you. We didn't know you. Nobody knew you. It's not the Indian way to take a white man on trust. No Indian ever got hurt by doubting a *wasichu*. We learned our ways from the animals. We like to watch for a long time before coming close.

"But the old man, he doesn't see things that way. He thinks everything's a message. A bird flies over, it's a message. A dog barks twice while it's facing the east, it's a message. He'd been looking for someone to tell his story, and when he saw those Red Road books you did with the kids at Red Lake, then he saw that Fatback liked you and heard that you were about the same age as his boy who got killed, he thought it was a direct call from the Creator. He was ready to trust you with his life."

He spit into the fire.

"Well, Wenonah and I weren't. We don't agree on a lot, but we'd both take a bullet for the old man. When we saw how much he trusted you, we got worried. So I said, 'Let's rough this white boy up a bit. See if we can chase him home.'

"Well, I tried. I knocked you around pretty good. Figured you'd be out of here in a couple of days. But you stuck around. You kept coming back and trying to help the old man. You and that damn tape recorder. Pretty soon we realized you really liked him. It didn't matter that he was an Indian. You liked him as a man."

"He reminded me a little of my father," I said.

"Whatever it took," Grover went on. "Thing was, you stayed. You stayed and you didn't push. You respected him. You respected the job he wanted you to do. You respected the distance between our people and yours. You had patience and you kept your mouth shut."

"I was a guest. I didn't want to go where I wasn't invited."

"And it was a good thing you didn't. It helped me learn to respect you. But I still didn't trust you. There was something about you that didn't add up. Most white people who come out to the rez, they're easy to figure. They start poking around, asking all sorts of things, want to get close real fast. 'Take me to ceremony. Can I do a sweat? Can you give me an Indian name? How do I earn an eagle feather?' They bring a box of used clothes and think that gives them the right to stick their nose in everywhere. Or else they come out here all Native with ponytails and Great Spirit talk, claiming they were an Indian in a past life or that they had a Cherokee grandmother.

"You weren't like that. You were a little bit whiny, but other than that you stayed inside yourself. I couldn't get a read on you. It was like you were all full of respect, but there was just this whiff about you like maybe you thought you were better than we were. Like you were slumming it when you came out to hang with the 'skins. It almost felt like you were some kind of anthropologist — that you were watching us more than trying to be with us. That really had me watching. Then, when I got to know you, I realized we had a bigger problem. You weren't hanging back out of respect or even curiosity. You were afraid."

The comment shocked me. "What do you mean, afraid? Afraid of what?"

"You didn't want to piss anybody off."

"So what's wrong with that?"

"It was the way you were doing it. You were afraid to stand up. You always backpedaled whenever someone got after you, agreeing with things you didn't believe just so they didn't get mad. I'd say the damnedest stuff just to piss you off. Tear into white people. Tear into you. And you'd always back up, even when you knew that what I was saying wasn't fair.

"That's not a sign of respect, that's a sign of fear. It's the exact opposite of respect. It said you didn't even respect me enough to tell the truth. And it sure as hell didn't give me confidence that you were the one to do the old man's story.

"I knew people were going to be angry at the old man's words. They were going to be angry at what he said, angry that he let a white man write it, angry at a whole bunch of things. They were going to try to find him and try to get on him and they were going to jump on you for the way you did things and try to get you to cave in and tell them things you shouldn't reveal. I was worried you'd roll over when things got tough. I didn't think you could handle it."

"Well, it's been ten years now. Do you still feel that way?"

"A little. Like, take that hippie jewelry lady today. She's ripping off our spirituality and selling it for love bundles. That's wrong and you know it. But you wouldn't stand up. You could have talked straight with her. You're a white man; she would have listened to you. But you just stood there doing the nice guy soft shoe, telling her things were okay. You were more worried about her getting upset than protecting our ways.

"Suppose she'd been selling communion wafers for cheese crackers at cocktail parties? Would you have rolled over and played dead then? Sometimes wrong is wrong, and being nice just lets the wrong grow stronger."

He stood up and stretched his back.

"Remember years ago when I told you that sometimes you've got to do what you're supposed to do, not what you want to do? Lots of your 'nice' stuff isn't about doing what you're supposed to do, even though you think it is. It's really just about staying out of the line of fire. You follow me?"

"I follow you, but I'm not sure I agree with you."

"Well, trust me. A man can't see the shape of his own house when he's standing in it. I'm just trying to level with you."

"Okay," I said. "I understand what you're saying. I just don't know why you're saying it. What does this have to do with taking away the shadow between us?"

"I'm trying to explain why I'm always rough on you. Why I don't trust you around the old man."

He rubbed his chin, as if thinking. "But this is a two-way street. That's how the old man wants it. So now I'm going to level with you about who I am. As far as I'm concerned it's none of your damn business, and I don't like doing it. But the old man wants the shadow gone, so I'm going to do it for him. Maybe it will help you figure a few things out."

He flicked the cigarette end over end toward the stream. The ash hissed once, flared up, and disappeared into the darkness. He exhaled the smoke slowly, as if giving long thought to what he was about to say.

"To do this, I've got to go back a bit. I've been thinking about this the whole drive, and this is the way I think you've got to know it. I've got to go back before the white man tore up our world, back before my time. You need to listen and try to keep your ears open. Don't do one of those white-man things where you're not really listening but just waiting for your chance to talk."

I nodded my assent.

"Okay," he said. "This is for the old man." He sprinkled more sage and sweetgrass on the fire.

"In the old days — what the elders call 'the long-ago days' — the whole community worked together. Everyone watched out for everyone else. They'd look at the kids, see which ones were the leaders, which ones talked to the animals, which ones hung around the old folks.

"They'd all watch and they'd see where our gifts were and they'd try to guide us. They'd set us with someone who could teach us, help us walk our path. Or maybe they'd wait until we'd done *hanbleceya* and see what vision we brought back, then give us a name we had to live up to. Everything was done in front of the whole community, so everyone would know who we were, how we could be raised to serve the people.

"When the white man came and started putting us in the boarding schools, everything changed. They didn't want us to think about the people, they wanted us to think about ourselves. 'You got to get yourself into heaven,' they said. 'Don't listen to the elders, don't follow the old ways. Those are the ways of the devil,' they told us.

"They took away the names we had been given and all the power that went with them. They cut our hair, changed our clothes, stole our tongues, broke our hearts. They taught us to hate who we were and where we'd come from. Pretty soon we didn't know what to believe or who we should be.

"You get a couple of generations of that, and everything starts to fall apart. The kids don't trust the old people, the old people can't relate to the kids. The people don't know the language of the animals, they don't know the traditional medicines or the traditional ceremonies. They're ashamed to talk about the old ways and they don't believe in the new ones. They're lost and they got nothing.

"That's how things were getting by the time I was born. Life had really fallen apart. People were drinking. Families weren't staying together. Hell, people even forgot what a family was. The white churches and government had ripped the hearts out of us. The women were being raised by them damn nuns in their pelican suits and old white men with yellow teeth instead of by the grandmas. Men were having their whole reason for living taken away by a government that wouldn't let them speak their own language or practice their own religion or teach their children the old ways.

"No work, no way to support your family, no nothing. Just sit around with your hands out waiting for the white man to give you enough to make it until the next time he comes around to give you more. Or else go off, cut your hair, get shoes for your feet and shoes for your horses until damn near nobody's feet ever touches the earth anymore, and pretend you're a white man. Our lives were nothing but shame.

"That's how my parents were. My dad just sat around. My mom lived in the bottle. They'd fight and beat each other up, then the old man would take off and be gone for weeks. When he was sober he was a good man, but he didn't know how to be a father. My mom was the same. She'd never had a chance to learn from the grandmas. She'd been raised by the pelican nuns and they didn't know a damn thing about being mothers. All they knew was Jesus, Jesus, Jesus and some Virgin Mary, another lady in a pelican suit. The only time my parents ever touched me was to hit me, 'cause that's the only time they ever got touched when they were kids. They were just passing on what they had learned.

"It wasn't easy and I didn't like it. But I didn't think anything of it. That's just the way it was. I'd get up and my mom would be passed out from drinking all night and my dad would be gone. I'd try to make myself some breakfast but there was nothing to eat. I'd go to my auntie's to get something to eat and my uncles would be sitting there feeding my little cousin beer in his baby bottle and watching and laughing.

"One day someone found me outside digging in the garbage, trying to scrape some food out of some tin cans. I didn't have any shoes on. There was snow on the ground. They took me away, put me in one of them boarding schools. I was eight years old."

He inhaled deeply and stared off into the night. I could see how hard this was for him. He stood up, walked to the edge of the creek, then turned around and walked back. He took two more deep breaths to compose himself before continuing.

"From then on," he said, "that was all I knew — little boy wearing an army uniform being told what to do by old white men with stinking breath and women in bird suits who hit you with rulers. I'd write letters to my mom, telling her to come and get me, then wait to get something back. Just a little boy, going down every day to see if his momma had sent him a letter. And every day, nothing. I cried myself to sleep every night thinking she was dead.

"It turns out the school never sent them. They never sent anyone's letters. They thought we might be saying something bad against the school. The only time they ever sent letters was when it was to say, 'Your boy died from smallpox last night,' or something like that. Then the parents would come and pick up the body. We'd see them through the window, all crying and taking the body away, and we'd all jump back in our beds and cover our heads and try to pray to that Jesus that he wouldn't let us die alone away from our families.

"That's the way it was the whole time I was growing up. I was never hugged. I was never held. I never had ceremonies done for me, never was taught the old ways, never went on *hanbleceya*, never was taught how to be a father or a man. I was told that if I didn't believe in some guy in a desert I was going to burn forever in a fire that never went out."

He held his cigarette out and shook it toward me. "One time one of the priests thought I wasn't praying hard enough. So he grabbed my hand and burnt it with a cigarette. Ground it right in. He said, 'See how that feels? If you don't pray right you're going to a place where your whole body feels like that forever.' God, I wanted to cry, but I wasn't going to let that son of a bitch see any tears coming out of me."

Grover stared at his palm. "Sometimes I think I can still see the scar where that holy bastard burned me."

He flicked his cigarette away, as if by tossing it into the darkness he could toss the memory along with it. The ash threw off sparks as it spun into the night. "I learned early on that the world wasn't going to look out for me, Nerburn. So I learned to be strong, not to need anybody. I learned to follow orders. I learned to be brave."

He stood up again and gazed off into the star-filled sky.

"They talked about Jesus and love in that school, Nerburn. Well, there was a lot of Jesus, but there wasn't no love. There was only rules. They had those Ten Commandments pasted up all around, with all that stuff about 'covet' this and 'covet' that. I didn't even know what the hell they were talking about. All I knew was that being good wasn't about doing the right thing, it was about not doing the wrong thing. And it sure as hell wasn't about finding your gifts and serving the people, like it had been in the old days. It was about following the rules.

"And if you were bad. If you didn't follow the rules..." He leaned forward and spit into the fire. It hissed and steamed. "Tsst. You fry in the hot place."

"That's how it was for me as a little boy, Nerburn. Every day. I was scared of dying. I was scared of being beat. I was scared of burning up in the Christian god's fire. I was scared of dying in a white man's bed surrounded by the bird women and the men with the yellow teeth.

"I was scared and lonely, and I didn't know who I was. I didn't know who I was supposed to be. But I knew what I was supposed to do. I was supposed to follow the rules.

"So that's what I did. That's all that I did. I didn't say nothing. I didn't do nothing. I didn't smile. I didn't cry. All I did was keep my mouth shut and follow the rules.

"When I was sixteen I ran away to join the service. I figured being a soldier was about being strong and following rules, and I knew I was damn good at that. But I wanted to get as far away from the rez as I could, so instead of joining the army like most of the 'skins, I joined the navy. I figured being on a ship in the ocean was as far away from those bastard priests as you can get.

"I was a hell of a sailor, I'll tell you. Cleanest uniform. Best behavior. Never stepped out of line. Finally, I was getting a chance to practice the old ways. I was getting a chance to be a warrior. At least, that's what I wanted to think.

"But I knew in my heart I was only half a warrior. I was acting tough and strong, but that ain't the same as being a warrior. A real warrior serves the people. A real warrior protects the weak. A real warrior helps the elders.

"I was serving the country, but the country didn't mean a damn thing to me. The land, yeah. The country, no. As far as the people — my people — I wasn't there for them. I was just doing what I learned in boarding school — being hard and following rules."

He paused to see if I was listening. "You with me?" he said.

"Yes," I answered. I was stunned. He had never been this open with me.

"Okay. When I got out I knocked around a lot. Got heavy into the bottle, lived on the streets. Finally, a 'skin down on skid row grabbed me by the collar. We were down under a bridge sharing a bottle. He was older than me, maybe forty, forty-five, but he looked like he was a hundred. He had these rotten yellow eyes and his nose looked like a goddamn purple gourd.

"He pushed me against a wall and breathed a mouthful of rot on me and said, 'You get the hell out of here. Stop feeling sorry for yourself and get back to your rez and start doing something for your people.'

"He pointed to his face and said, 'Another year on the bottle and you're going to look like this. Then you're going to die, just like me, lying in your own piss and shit under a white man's bridge.'

"That 'skin changed my life. Maybe he was sent by the Creator to teach me. Maybe I was just ready. But I left the next day, hitchhiked back to the rez, all stinking and messed up, ashamed as hell, scared as hell. I didn't know what I was going to do. Didn't know where to go. All I knew was I had to come home.

"It took me three days. I was out of money, out of food. I was sitting by the side of the road, just inside the rez line, hungry as hell, strung out with the dry heaves, feeling sorry for myself. I see this car in the distance. An old truck. The guy stops for me and says, 'Where you going?'

"I said, 'I got nowhere to go.'

"He says, 'Now you do. You're coming to my house. Get in the truck.' It was the old man.

"He took me home, gave me a bed, never asked me a damn thing, let me stay there like I was one of his own. I stayed there for two years, living with his family, drying out. Him and his wife and their boy. Those were the best years of my life. I ate at their table, helped him with his chores, helped him teach his boy. It was the closest thing I'd ever known to family in my life."

His voice trailed off and he stared into the glowing embers. I watched the emotions pass across his face as the creek moved noiselessly behind him.

"I got just a little more to say, then I'm going to shut up. I don't like telling this stuff to a white man. But the old man wants the shadow gone."

He threw some more tobacco onto the smoldering ashes and spoke silently in Lakota for a moment, touching his fingers to his lips as he spoke.

"How much you know about the old man and his family?"

"I know he married some white woman from back East and they had a boy who got killed in a car accident." Danelle, Dan's granddaughter, had revealed this to me years earlier on my first visit to the rez.

Grover nodded. "I'm going to tell you a little more now."

He touched his fingers to his lips again and began.

"The old man, he had a hell of a family. It was small — just him and his wife and their little boy. He was so damn proud. He'd been hurt by the boarding schools, too. Just like me and all the others. But there was still something left in his heart. It wasn't all dried up, like mine. He was trying to bring himself back to the traditions. He never hit anyone. He never raised his voice in anger. There was no drinking, no cursing. He treated his wife with respect and tried to teach his boy the old ways, bringing him to ceremony, talking to him in Lakota, having him sit with the elders."

Grover poked a stick into the fire and watched the embers flare up and catch a moment of flame. "He loved that family more than anything. He was one of the good ones, trying to reclaim what had been beat out of us." He jabbed the fire violently with the stick. "But then he lost it. That wife of his tore it up."

He looked up at me. "What do you know about that wife?"

"Danelle told me a little, that she was a social worker or something."

"That's right," Grover said. "A *wasichu* woman from tree country. Come out here to save the 'skins, make herself feel good. Or maybe bag herself a buck."

He spit hard into the fire. I could see that the mere thought of Dan's wife made him angry. He wouldn't even call her by name.

"It was back in the forties. The big war was just starting. The Germans were killing everybody. Everyone wanted to go fight — 'skins especially. It was the only place where you still got to be a warrior. Plus, it was a paycheck and three squares. So everyone wanted to go.

"The old man, he tried to enlist. But they wouldn't take him. He's got this bad eye from getting hit by an arrow when he was playing around as a kid. Couldn't see out of it. They said he wasn't fit to serve with that eye. This hurt him really bad. Shamed him.

"Hell, back in the old times, when we fought with other tribes or against the soldiers, everyone picked up a gun. A bad eye didn't stop anybody. I remember the elders telling us the story of one guy who lost his feet in a snowstorm as a kid. Got left outside; froze 'em up. They turned all black, had to cut them off. When the warriors went into battle he went right along with them, rolling off the horse and dragging himself along by his hands. Fought alongside everyone else. Now here's the US Army saying the old man can't join because he can't see out of one eye. Saying he's not good enough to be a warrior. Made him feel ashamed and worthless."

Grover stirred the flames until sparks jumped up into the night sky.

"So, anyway, here he is, pretty much the only young man on the rez, good-looking as hell except for that eye, sad as anything because he can't go and fight. That white woman had come out here a couple years before for some missionary thing. She saw him all sad, not able to go fight. Grabbed him like a mother grabbing a little boy. Was going to make him feel all right."

"She made him feel all right, all right. Long blonde hair. Pretty as hell." He drew an hourglass shape in the air with his hands. "Damn, she'd have made anyone feel all right."

Grover gave a wan smile. "He must have made her feel all right, too. They went and got married. Did it in the white man's way, in a church. Had that boy, Bobby. The old man was so proud of that kid. Took him everywhere with him. He was going to get to raise up a son, do it right, teach him the old ways. Give him the things he'd never had. But then that *wasichu* wife lost hold — spaces too big, life on the rez too strange. One day he woke up and she was gone. She'd grabbed the boy, gone back East, killed the family. It tore the heart right out of him.

"The old man started drinking. He was going down fast. He told me it got so bad he was going to put a rifle in his mouth and finish things off. Then, just about the time he hit bottom, his boy come back. He couldn't take it back East in *wasichu* country. The same things that drove his mother crazy out here were the things he missed.

"The old man held *wopila* for him. Put him up before the whole community. He was so damn happy. Then the boy got killed. Car accident. Or so they said. Him and his wife. Left those two little girls, Wenonah and Danelle."

An image of my own son, hundreds of miles away, flashed through my mind. "I can't imagine losing a son," I said.

"Neither could he. That's what put him over the edge. He went back to the bottle. Sat all day, staring. Wouldn't talk. Wouldn't shave. Wouldn't even go to sweat. I'd come over and sit with him and he wouldn't even look at me. The only ones who could get half a smile out of him were the two girls, and even they couldn't get near him. It was like all the stuff inside him was eating him up. And when it finished eating his body, it started in on his spirit."

He fell silent, as if the memory had taken him to a dark place. Then he grabbed a few more twigs and threw them on the fire. It flared and flamed and filled the night with a blast of orange light.

"I'm going to show you something now," he said. "I want you to understand this."

Slowly, he undid the pearl buttons on his cowboy shirt and sloughed the shirt off his shoulders. In the glow of the fire a line of crude parallel welts about an inch long, like caterpillars crawling under his skin, could be seen along both sides of his chest and across his back.

"You know what these are?" he said.

"Sundance piercings?" I said.

"Damn straight. Tied to that tree for four days. No water. No food. You know why I did it? Not to show off. Not to prove I was strong. Not to get into any white man's heaven or to follow any white man's rules. I did it for the old man, after his wife left and his son died. I wanted the spirits to look down on him and heal his heart. I wanted to show him that someone would stand by him, even though everyone else was leaving him. He came out and sat there and watched me. All four days. A hundred degrees, and him sick with a wounded heart. Watched me, gave me the power to go on. That was his gift to me."

"These" — he pointed to the scars — "these were my gifts to him."

He pulled his shirt back over his shoulders, as if uncomfortable drawing such attention to himself.

"Since then I've stayed by his side, doing what I can to keep his spirit strong." He pointed at me with the stick. "And making sure that no damn do-gooder *wasichu* come out here to help the 'skins ever gets the chance to rip out his heart again."

CHAPTER SEVENTEEN

No Bullshit

I sat in stunned silence. His openness had shocked me, and his message to me had been unequivocal.

I stared across the fire at his worn, lined face and dark, intelligent eyes flickering in the shadows of the dancing flames and thought of the wounds, both psychological and physical, that he had endured — the childhood abuse, the loneliness of the boarding schools, the spiritual confusion and anger of his wanderings in an uncaring white society. For the first time, I truly understood that he had been tempered by life in a way I could never comprehend.

His life had been pared to a knife edge of readiness and vigilance, and all that mattered to him now were self-control and unflagging service to his people, which meant devoting his life with absolute rigor to protecting the culture of his ancestors and serving an old man whose only remaining dream was to share his people's ways and belief with a world that had largely forgotten they existed. What I perceived as virtues in my life — gentleness and kindness — "being nice," as he put it — were as foreign to him as his personal privations and private sufferings were to me.

I kept thinking of those caterpillar-like scars on his chest and back. I had known of the sundance practice of piercing your flesh with eagle bones and attaching yourself by leather thongs to the sacred cottonwood tree, but I had never seen its effects up close, nor had I understood on any visceral level the true degree of suffering that participants endured. Now, in a single moment, all that had changed. Those parallel scarifications on Grover's chest and back spoke of something close to torture. Suddenly, his chiding me as soft and his constant questioning of my suitability to pass on Dan's stories made perfect sense.

I looked across the fire at his sinewy forearms with their fading tattoos and fading muscles, and imagined him dancing in the deathly heat of a Dakota summer — the leather thongs piercing his chest and the thongs through the flesh on his back attached to buffalo skulls as he dragged them through the dust during the four-day dance. And the old man, broken in spirit, sitting under the sundance arbor meeting Grover's eyes with his, communicating a wordless gratitude for the suffering that his friend was enduring on his behalf.

"Thanks for sharing all this with me, Grover," I said.

He nodded his acknowledgment. "The old man wants the shadow gone. I do what the old man wants."

"You really love that old guy, don't you?" I said, taking a chance at an unwarranted intimacy.

He poked the fire with the end of a stick. "That ain't a word I use. Let's just say that growing up made me hard; the old man made me good. That ain't something I forget. We'll leave it at that."

We sat silently under the star-filled sky, letting the weight of his confession find its place in our hearts. He made a few final passes with the tobacco on the ground in front of him, then got down on his knees and blew on the small mound of tobacco and sage between us.

"Okay," he said, handing the pouch of tobacco and sage across to me. "I've talked. Now you. Why are you out here, really?"

Though I had pretty much decided not to tell him about the old woman and the notebook, I now felt I had no choice. This was for Dan, not for me, or even for Grover. I took some tobacco from the pouch and spread it on the ground before me, as I had seen him do.

Grover uttered a low "hnn, hnn." He pulled some of the smoke from the small pyre of tobacco and sage and bathed himself in it with a ritual cupped-hand gesture, then nodded for me to do the same.

"No bullshit now," he said.

"No," I said. "No bullshit."

I took a deep breath and began. "You're right. This isn't just a casual visit. I came to talk to Dan. I found out something more about his little sister."

Grover's neck tensed and his eyes narrowed. "What kind of something more?"

"A kind of a troubling more. You remember the old woman I visited who had been in the boarding school with her as a child?"

"The *Shinnob*, right?" he said, using the slang for the Anishinaabe, or Ojibwe people.

"Yeah. Mary Johnson. The one who lived up by the Canadian border. Well, I went to visit her again."

"Why'd you do that?" Grover said. There was an edge in his voice.

"I'd been having dreams."

"Lots of people have dreams," he said.

"Not like these," I said. "They weren't like ordinary dreams. It was like they were brighter, closer to reality or something."

Grover muttered something under his breath. "Keep talking."

"They came every night. And they were always the same. I've never had that happen before. And Mary and Yellow Bird were both in them. But Mary was old, like in real life, and Yellow Bird was just a little girl, like in the photo Dan had of her. She had on that same white dress. Yellow Bird kept gesturing to me, like she wanted me to follow. It was like — I don't know — like she was trying to pull me right inside her life."

Grover kept his head down, with his hands steepled over his mouth, as if he was thinking.

"I couldn't sleep. It felt like she wanted to grab me or touch me. Then I'd wake up. It scared the hell out of me."

"Go on," he said.

"I kept telling myself they were just guilt for not having gone back to visit Mary, not telling her what we had found out about Yellow Bird. But every night? It didn't make any sense. Then one night there was this thunderclap. Just when Mary's face was looking at me. At least it sounded like a thunderclap. But no one else heard it. My dog didn't even move. I thought I was going crazy."

Grover flexed his fingers and cracked his knuckles. His cheek muscles tightened and loosened.

"That's when I had to go see her," I continued. "I felt like I had to. I didn't know what else to do."

I was like a child pleading his case to a parent for his misbehavior. "I just wanted those dreams to go away. I figured if she was in them and was reaching for me they had to have something to do with her."

Grover nodded and looked down, as if trying to absorb the import of the words. "And what did you find out when you visited her?"

"It turned out she had died. The same night I heard that thunderclap."

Grover stood up and walked to the edge of the clearing. He blew a long, low whistle through his lips.

"So, if she died, why are you out here?" he said without looking at me.

"Her granddaughter was still alive. She was living in Mary's trailer. She said there were a lot of things her grandma hadn't told me about Yellow Bird. She said her grandma hadn't trusted me at the time because I was a white man. But after I left she had felt bad. She felt there were other things Dan should know. She said she had wanted me to come back so she could tell them to me. She wanted me to pass them along to him."

"Like what kind of things? Did the granddaughter tell you?"

"You remember how Mary told me that Yellow Bird had covered her ears and started shouting 'horse' in Lakota when they went by a field where horses had died a bunch of years before?"

"I remember."

"She said this kind of thing happened a lot. Like there was a place by the school — a swampy kind of field — where there'd been a big battle a hundred years ago or so. Ojibwe and the Sioux. Lots of folks had been killed, mostly Sioux. One time the nuns were walking Yellow Bird and the other kids by this place on the way back to school. Little Yellow Bird started singing. They couldn't shut her up. Mary didn't know what she was singing because she couldn't understand Lakota. Later some of the Lakota kids said she was singing a death song."

Just recounting the story made the hair on the back of my neck stand on end.

Grover was still facing away from me. He flipped his cigarette into the darkness. It landed in the stream, spit and hissed, and disappeared into the night.

"So, anything else?"

"She kept hearing voices, talking to people who weren't there. Birds would come land on her hand. The kids said she could talk to the animals. The school people got really upset with her. They said they couldn't keep her anymore, that there was something wrong with her."

Grover was rocking on his heels and staring into the star-filled night. His breathing was short and tight. "You're wading in deep waters," he said.

"I know. That's why I'm here. But there's more. And this is the hard part, the stuff I don't know if Dan should know. They sent Yellow Bird to a place in a little town called Canton. Way over by the Minnesota border, a couple of hundred miles from here. I was just over there. It was called the Hiawatha Asylum for Insane Indians. It was a terrible place. They chained people to their beds, made them live in their own shit."

Grover was pacing along the edge of the creek and speaking quietly under his breath.

"What were some of the other things she did?" he asked. He did not look back at me.

I thought maybe he hadn't understood me. "Grover, didn't you hear me?" I said. "Yellow Bird was sent to an asylum, locked up like a prisoner. Bars on the windows, the place choking in coal smoke. They chained people up and tied them to their beds. Fed them slop. Made them sleep in their own shit."

"What else do you remember about what she did?" he asked, as if the information about the asylum was irrelevant.

I couldn't believe his indifference to the revelations. "I don't remember," I said, trying to suppress my irritation.

"Try. This is important."

"Jeez, I don't know. There was something about crying when a doll was thrown in a fire. It's like she thought the doll was real. I just don't remember. But it's all in a notebook. Mary wrote it all down. I'm supposed to give it to Dan. That's why I came looking for you. To see if you and Wenonah thought it was something Dan should see."

Grover whirled on me. "There's a notebook? Where is it?" he said.

"It's in my car."

"In your car? Jesus. Why didn't you tell me?"

He knelt down quickly and squeezed the small pyre of herbs into ashes and placed them in his pocket. "Put the fire out," he said. "Kick dirt on it. Take a piss on it. I don't care. Just get it out and meet me back at the car. I need to see that notebook."

He stood up and hobbled back to the car, shaking his head and cursing under his breath.

I quickly smothered the fire with sand and ran after him. He had already started the engine and shifted the car into gear. "Do you think Dan should know about the asylum?" I asked. I was still confused by his seeming indifference to the little girl's plight.

Grover was already bouncing down the path at a breakneck pace. "We'll deal with that when we get to it," he said. "Right now I want to see that notebook."

"Jesus, Grover," I said, letting my exasperation overflow. "That asylum sounded like some kind of hell. I can't believe you're so unconcerned."

"I didn't say I'm unconcerned. I'm just not surprised. This is Indian country. Little girls got raped in boarding schools and had their babies burned in stoves. Kids died every day. Smallpox. Being left outside in winter. I'm sure Yellow Bird had a terrible life. It would surprise me if she didn't. And, yeah, we're going to have to tell the old man. But there's something bigger going on here. Something you don't understand."

"Well, then let me in on it."

He shook his head and squealed the car around a curve. "You'll figure it out soon enough," he said. "Right now I just want to see that notebook."

He drove with a fierce urgency, lighting and discarding cigarette after cigarette, tossing them out into the night, until we
topped a hill and saw the lights of Mission stretched out like a
string of pearls before us on the darkened prairie. He gunned his
Buick, dropped into town, wheeled down the side streets, and
came to a stop right behind my Toyota.

"Go get it," he said. "Shit, I can't believe you just left it in
the car."

I unlocked my trunk and grabbed the deer-hide folder. I
wasn't sure whether to feel embarrassed or angry. Grover was
already halfway to the abandoned station building, holding his
hand out behind him like a relay runner waiting for a baton. He
took the folder and pushed his way through the piles of two-by-
fours and old plywood to an orange junk-covered Formica table
next to a shattered window.

"You go get Jumbo," he said. "I need some time alone with
this."

I left him sitting in the derelict gas station, lighting match
after match and staring at the open notebook. I could see his lips
moving as I drove off. I could not tell if he was reading out loud,
cursing me, or saying some kind of prayer.

Jumbo was standing outside the Subway holding two wrapped
sub sandwiches about as long as baseball bats. He seemed unper-
turbed by the length of time I'd been away.

"They were having a special," he said. "I got four for the price
of two."

I didn't bother asking him where the other two were.

He settled heavily into the car. "Thanks for buying these for
me," he said. He held a few coins out in his huge, greasy hand.

"There ain't much change left. You were gone kind of a long time. But you can have some of these other subs if you want."

"Thanks," I said. I hadn't eaten all day and was famished.

He placed one of the sandwiches on the dashboard and peeled back the wrapping on the other. A strange combination of odors filled the car.

"Tuna and baloney," he said. "I invented it myself. You could have it all, or we could share."

"Thanks," I said. "Why don't you eat it. You can save the other one for Grover. It could be your gift to him for taking you to the powwow."

"You sure? I got two."

"I'm sure," I said as I dug morosely into a bag of leathery beef jerky that I kept in the storage pocket of the driver's door.

I was tempted to ask Jumbo if he knew what might have made Grover so upset at the information about Yellow Bird. But that would have entailed explaining the whole situation to him, and I had neither the will nor the interest to do that. So I held my peace and hurried back to the abandoned station.

Grover was still sitting inside the station as we drove up. I could see matches flare and go out as he kept lighting them to read Mary's tight, precise script in the notebook.

"You stay here," I said to Jumbo. "I'll tell him you've got something for him."

Jumbo nodded. He was already finished with the sub. There were smudges of mayonnaise on the edge of his mouth, and he was nervously fingering the edge of the wrapper of the remaining sandwich.

Grover was reading the final page of the notebook when I approached him. He looked up at me with a hard, emotionless expression.

"You're messing in things you don't understand," he said.

"I know," I answered.

"No, you don't."

He sat quietly for a few moments, then lit a final cigarette. His manner was coiled and tense.

He slammed the notebook shut and put it under his arm. "We need to talk to Wenonah," he said. "This is way above my pay grade."

I was shocked by Grover's tense behavior. He was usually calm and taciturn — a model of self-control and quiet vigilance. Now his breathing was fast and his movements sharp. He kept sucking violently on his cigarette and blowing smoke out in short, staccato breaths.

"Jumbo's in the car," I ventured. "He bought you a sandwich."

"I don't need a sandwich," he said, grinding the butt of his cigarette harshly under the toe of his boot. "I need time to think. You take him home. I'm going on by myself." He stood up and shoved the notebook under his arm. "Meet me at the old man's house in the morning. Don't come too early. I need time to show this to Wenonah."

Without so much as a nod or a good-bye he hobbled over to his car, turned the key, and roared off down the road. I had never seen him drive so fast in all the time I had known him.

I headed back to my car with a tightness in my chest. Grover's uncharacteristically nervous behavior and enigmatic comment about being involved in something bigger than I understood had set me on edge.

I had been feeling uneasy ever since I had first experienced the dream about Mary and Yellow Bird. But except for moments of late-night panic, I had been able to keep it in some kind of perspective. But the cascade of events — the thunderclap, Benais's otherworldly strangeness, the ghost of the asylum, and the haunting depressions of the rows of unmarked graves — had now filled me with a vague and constant dread. I felt like a man swimming in dark waters who sees shadowy forms moving below him but is unable to get back to shore.

Jumbo was happily tapping out a powwow beat on the dashboard as I returned to the car.

"So Grover doesn't want a sub?" he asked.

"No, he said he wanted to do some thinking."

"More for us," Jumbo grinned.

"More for you," I answered. "Tuna with baloney's not my thing. Grover said I should take you home, then meet him at Dan's in the morning."

"You can stay with me at the shop if you want," Jumbo said. "Shitty's at his girlfriend's. You can have his mattress."

The prospect of Jumbo's company was appealing. But I remembered what Grover had said about why Jumbo's tent was set apart from the others at the powwow. And the vision of a grease-stained blanketless mattress shoved in a corner amid a pile of used oil filters and old rags with Shitty's sweat and God knows what else ground into it was too much to overcome. I didn't even dare contemplate the thought of him sharing that mattress with his girlfriend.

"No, I think I'll camp somewhere," I said. "I need a little time to think, too."

Jumbo shrugged and unwrapped the last sub and bit heavily into it with his two incisors. They hung like yellow fangs on the edges of his dark cave of a mouth. "Kind of hard to chew," he grinned. "Got to find the sweet spot."

"You stay with it," I said. "I'm sure you'll find it."

We drove silently through the star-drenched night back toward his reservation. The only sound other than the hum of the tires on the pavement was the occasional grunting and the tearing of a piece of bread as Jumbo ripped off another chunk of sandwich by clamping it in his incisors and pulling at it with both hands.

Eventually he fell asleep, and I was left alone with my thoughts. I tried to occupy myself by tuning in the scratchy AM radio signals that cut across the empty night air from faraway cities like Denver and Tulsa. But the events of the day kept coming into my mind. I was glad to have handed the notebook over to Grover but unsure of what it portended. In my confused state, I wondered if I had violated some unspoken trust or spiritual command by not delivering it into Dan's hands myself.

It was well past midnight when we arrived at Jumbo's shop. The dark building hulked like an abandoned freighter in the flat emptiness of the prairie. Unidentifiable chunks of metal and oil drums lay half buried in the surrounding weeds.

I nudged Jumbo with my elbow. He grunted once or twice and fumbled his way into consciousness.

"You're home," I said.

"Gotta get my stuff," he mumbled as he pushed his way up from his seat. He stumbled around to the trunk of the car and carefully removed his powwow regalia, then reached out his huge tuna-scented hand for me to shake.

"Friends," he said.

"Friends," I answered, taking his hand in my own.

"Sure you don't want to stay?"

"Nope. Thanks for the offer, though."

"I wouldn't mind going with you to see Grandpa Dan tomorrow," he said. "Why don't you come by for breakfast and get me?"

"I'd like that," I said. "See you in the morning."

He wiped his hands on the front of his T-shirt and walked into the darkened building. I waited outside for a while, just out of habit, to make sure he got in safely.

After about five minutes I gave up and drove off. No lights had come on anywhere.

CHAPTER EIGHTEEN

"I'm a Really Good Dog"

I crunched my way out onto the main road and headed for the border of the reservation. I didn't know where I intended to stay, but I knew that most of the small nonreservation towns in the Dakotas had public parks that permitted camping. Many of them even had showers and wash-up areas. I figured if I got lucky and could stay awake long enough to get there, one of those would be a perfect spot to bed down for the night and try to get my thoughts and feelings under control.

An hour of so of driving brought me to exactly what I had been looking for: a small, sleepy farm town with a single main street and a few residential side streets trickling off into the prairie, and a municipal park with a welcoming sign that said "Overnight Camping Permitted. Please Leave $3 in the Box."

I drove around until I found an ATM machine on the side of a local bank, withdrew enough to pay for camping and a few more days on the road, then pulled into the park among the teeter-totters and swing sets, and set up my cot tent by the illumination of my headlights. It was almost two in the morning.

Within minutes I was asleep. It seemed half a lifetime ago that I had left Canton and driven west into the Dakotas, and I doubt that even the hard ground could have kept me from settling into an almost catatonic slumber.

The dim predawn light had just begun to crease the edges of the sky when I heard the sound. At first I thought it was the dream, returned to haunt me once again. But I soon realized that it was a rustling, that it was very real, and that it was very near. Thoughts of robbers and murderers and rattlesnakes raced through my mind. But there was something more focused about this sound. It was rhythmic and stationary and devoid of furtiveness.

I quietly unzipped the covering on the cot and stuck my head out. The sound was directly beneath me. I took one of my work boots and held it at the ready as a weapon should I have to strike at something. But even as I moved, the rhythmic sound continued, as if my presence was irrelevant.

I cautiously looked under the cot. Some kind of large animal was stationed there, engaged in licking its front paw.

I quickly pulled my head back in. In the dim light it was impossible to make out what it was. But my movement had been enough to startle it, and it let out a loud, deep-throated bark. The realization that it was a dog did little to calm my nerves. It was obviously very large and it had, for reasons unknown, chosen to station itself directly beneath my cot.

Warily, I lifted my boot into striking position and whispered, "Hi, good dog." I was still not convinced it was not a wolf or a coyote or some distant wild relative of the dog that had retained the capacity to bark, and I had no interest in engaging in hand-to-hand combat with something that had teeth as long as my little finger.

"Hey, dog," I said again.

The shape made a weak "ruff" of acknowledgment, followed by a swishing sound that I thought might be the wagging of a tail.

I grabbed a piece of beef jerky from the pack I had taken into the cot with me and threw it a few feet away in the grass.

The shadow crawled out, stood up, and hopped on three legs toward the jerky.

It was clearly a dog, it was clearly injured, and it was clearly very hungry. The realization set me at ease.

"Hey, good fella," I said again.

The dog wolfed down the jerky and turned to face me. It was a sad-eyed old hound whose ancestry included ample parts Labrador and shepherd. He had a snow-white muzzle, one floppy ear with a chunk bitten out of it, and a badly injured front paw. His fur was a wiry grey-brown that was matted with dirt. He was quivering so badly that his whole back end shook.

"Come here," I said. "I won't hurt you." I stuck out my hand, palm up, in a gesture of friendship. The dog shied back, uncertain whether to respond or run.

"Come on," I said.

The dog took a step toward me, uncertain and afraid. Then, after a moment's hesitation, he turned and limped off to the edge of the park, where he stood, looking back at me, with his rear legs quivering and his tail between its legs.

I took out another piece of jerky and threw it as far in his direction as I could. The dog hopped over to it, keeping his head down, grabbed it quickly, and limped back to the perimeter of the park. When he had finished eating the chunk, he put his head low between his front paws, wagged his tail, and stared at me. I took another chunk and threw it, this time not so far away from me.

The dog limped over to it, and the scene was repeated.

We did this several times, with each toss landing closer and closer to the cot, until the dog was coming to within a few feet of my hand. The morning light had begun to creep over the barren hills sufficiently that I could see he was wearing a collar. There was a piece of manila card attached to it with a twist wire, like the kind of tag used to identify something in a repair shop.

"Come on," I said. "Let me see that. Maybe I can get you home."

I took the last piece of jerky I had and held it out. The dog moved toward it, then shied back. He barked once, as if to let me know that I should throw it in his direction.

I shook my head. "No, if you want this, you have to come over to me."

Cautiously, the dog advanced. He came close to my hand, and I gingerly patted him on the head and slipped my other hand under his collar. I held the jerky tight while he nibbled at the edges of it — he was very demure and didn't snap or lunge. I let him pull at the jerky while I slowly pulled the tag around to where I could read it. It was dirty and rumpled, but the writing was still legible. It appeared to be in a young girl's hand:

> My name is Festus.
> I'm a really good dog.
> My owner can't keep me anymore.
> Please don't let me die.

I spent the next hour trying to get Festus to trust me. His fur was ratty and his ribs pushed out against his skin. His left front paw was badly swollen. He had big soulful hazel eyes that seemed to carry an apology in their very depths, and his ragged, bitten ear flopped helplessly to the side. He watched me from a safe distance and followed my movements closely as I got dressed and folded up my cot.

I went over to a spigot on the side of the small shower building and turned the water on slightly. When I had retreated to an adequate distance, Festus limped over and lapped thirstily at the puddle that was forming at the base. He must have lapped and slurped for almost two minutes before stepping back and staring up at me with frightened, hopeful eyes.

"No more," I said.

He wagged his tail several times and let out a short bark. I could tell he was hungry and hoping for more jerky.

"Okay," I said. "You wait here."

I hurried back to my car and drove the block onto the main street of the town. It was probably no more than seven in the morning, but the one grocery store and meat market in town had just opened its doors, and the proprietor was out sweeping the sidewalk.

He was a man in his fifties with a short crew cut and large jowls. He was wearing a white butcher's apron.

"Morning," I said.

He looked up and nodded.

"I spent the night in your park. It's a nice little town you've got."

He glanced at my license plate to see if it was from a state that he felt was trustworthy, and finding Minnesota acceptable, said, "Pretty quiet. We like it that way."

I couldn't tell if there was a message in the comment, or if it was simply the standard response he gave to the rare out-of-towner who managed to wander far enough from the main highways to end up at his store.

"There's an old dog out there," I said. "It seems lost. Is there a humane society in town or somewhere nearby?"

"Pierre. Mitchell. Maybe Chamberlain. None here."

"How about a vet?"

"Pierre. Mitchell. Maybe Chamberlain."

"How about the other direction?"

"Rapid, probably. There are probably others. Lot of people leave strays along here. Hunters. Indians. Dump them off by the highway."

"What happens to them?"

"Someone picks them up. Or they die. In the winter lots of them freeze to death."

I found his callousness distasteful.

"It's a good dog. Someone wrote a little note on its collar, saying they couldn't keep him. Looked like a girl's writing. Its name is Festus."

"Someone will probably find it," he said. His disinterest was palpable.

I decided to ignore him and address the issue myself.

"Do you sell dog food here? And peroxide?"

"If it's sold in this town, you'll find it here."

I left him to his sweeping and went into the store. It was dark and decrepit, with dim lighting and old off-white wooden shelves that were poorly stocked. I wandered up and down the three aisles looking for what I needed to doctor Festus.

When I finished my shopping the man came in and went behind the cash register. He pushed my bag of dog food, pack of sweet rolls, box of Q-tips, bottle of peroxide, and pack of needles to the far end of the counter, keying in the price of each as he went.

"I don't mean to sound like I don't give a damn," he said as he placed my purchases in a brown paper bag. "But this is a quiet town. We got enough problems of our own. No one out there is trying to solve ours, and we aren't about to solve theirs."

"I'm not trying to cause problems," I said. "I'm just trying to help an old injured dog."

"Well, good luck to you on that," he said, obviously unconcerned.

I picked up the bag, went out to my car, and drove back down the main street past the boarded-up storefronts and empty lots to the park with the sign and the pump and the empty children's playground.

Festus was sitting right where I had left him. He was holding his injured paw up as if in a gesture of offering or pleading or hope.

Festus proved to be a very good patient. He lay quietly on his side while I lanced the swollen paw and cleaned it out with the Q-tip and peroxide. When I finished, he wagged his tail several times, laid his head on my lap, and licked my hand.

"Good work," I said. "How about some breakfast?"

I reached under the backseat of the car and pulled out an old Styrofoam tray left over from some long-forgotten take-out meal and filled it with dog food. I was feeling vaguely guilty about my intention to abandon this sweet dog to an uncertain fate, but I could see no other choice. I was hundreds of miles from my home, I needed to get to Jumbo's early in the morning, and the unsympathetic store owner had indicated that there were no humane societies or dog pounds within a reasonable driving distance.

I salved my conscience with the thought that since we were in a park and not near the highway, the person who had dropped Festus off probably lived nearby and was just down on her luck. Perhaps, with his paw repaired and a bag of dog food by his side, his owner would return or someone else would pick him up. He was clearly a very good dog who liked people and wanted to please.

"You eat as much as you want, Festus," I said. "I'm going to take a shower." Festus looked up from his ravenous chewing on the heap of kibble and wagged his tail earnestly. He was obviously happy to hear someone call him by name.

I left him wolfing down his food and went off to shower in the little concrete-block building.

When I returned, the plate was empty and Festus was nowhere in sight. I felt a momentary twinge of sadness, but it was more than made up for by a deep sense of relief. Now that Festus had eaten and could put weight on his paw, he had probably gone off to someplace where he knew someone or felt more at home.

I bagged up the tent cot and dragged it over to the car. I had left the back door open while I had gone to shower. In the rear seat, lying flat on his stomach with his head on his paws, was Festus. He thumped his tail twice and stared up at me with doleful, expectant eyes. Dangling from his neck, at just the angle to make it impossible to miss, was the manila card with the message "Please don't let me die."

Reluctantly, I set off back down the road toward the rez. It seemed as if the universe had spoken. I was now the caretaker of a worn-out old dog with a chunk out of its ear and the strangely Roman or rural name of Festus. It was one more element to add to the increasingly strange and complex set of circumstances in which I found myself.

I chewed on a sweet roll and looked at Festus in the rear-view mirror. He was sitting upright in the backseat, with his tongue hanging out the side of his mouth and a broad dog smile on his face.

"Not what I had in mind," I said. He let out a blubbery wheeze and settled in for the ride.

Festus rapidly showed himself to be a good passenger and a trouble-free guest. He lay splayed out across the entire length of the rear seat. Periodically he would get up and lick at my hand when I draped it over the back of the driver's seat — perhaps in hopes of getting some residue from the sweet roll — and I'd scruff his head in return. When he felt the need for air he would nose at the glass and I'd open the rear window. He'd stand on the armrest on his one good paw and stick his head out with a big dog grin on his face and his ears pinned back like airplane wings in the wind.

Had it not been for the burden of finding him a home, I might have enjoyed his company. He took my mind off the disconcerting conversation I had shared with Grover the previous evening and the far more significant burden of bringing the news of the notebook to Dan. He seemed interested in the world around him and was unusually responsive to the mention of his name. He had a kind, thoughtful manner — though a bit tragic, especially when he lay on his stomach with his head between his outstretched legs and his soulful eyes staring up at me, as if in hopeful anticipation. I imagined he still carried the wounds of being abandoned and, in some dog way, wondered what he had done to deserve such a fate.

I had no idea what to do with him. He was definitely an impediment to the task at hand. I knew I couldn't keep him — I already had a dog of my own at home. I was not going to abandon him, and I was not likely to see someone standing on the side of the road with a sign that said "Dog Wanted."

I think in the back of my mind I had already determined that I would have to take him with me to the rez. Grover was waiting for me, and I had neither the time nor the energy to invest in finding him a suitable home before I got there. I knew I could not just drop him off on the side of the highway; abandoned dogs on any reservation quickly meet a sad and unsavory fate. I had to hope that someone — Jumbo, Wenonah, Grover, or one of their friends — might find him appealing and be willing to offer him a home. Dan was the perfect potential owner, but he already had little Bronson and was unlikely at his age to want to add another dog to his household.

"Want to be a rez dog, Festus?" I asked. Festus, ever alive to the mention of his name, thumped his tail and licked my hand.

"I'm guessing that's a yes," I said. "You just be on your best behavior. We'll try to find you a new owner." Festus wagged some more and stuck his head back out the window. Strings of spittle flew off his jowls as he smiled into the wind.

By the time we arrived at Jumbo's, Festus had taken full ownership of the entire backseat. He nuzzled my hand with his nose and licked my hand when he wanted attention. A happy dog smile and winning manner had almost completely replaced the doleful eyes that had greeted me when he had first crawled out from under my cot. He was obviously smart as a whip and a bit of an operator, well able to size up a situation and the people around him.

"You played me pretty well," I said. "If I didn't know better I'd say you wrote that note around your neck yourself."

Festus, pleased that he again was being addressed, made two short barks of acknowledgment and pushed against my hand with the top of his nose.

In the bright light of morning, Jumbo's garage seemed even more decrepit than it had in the dark. I remembered it from my last visit as a white 1930s-era concrete block structure with two sagging multipanel garage doors. The whitewash was now almost entirely worn off, leaving the building a blotchy, dingy grey. One of the service doors was permanently wedged open, held up by a long, rusted pole. The other was detached entirely from the garage and just propped against its frame to give the illusion of being a functional door. The plate-glass window on the small office area, which before had been merely filthy, was now rendered completely opaque by grime and was rent on a diagonal by a giant crack that had been hastily patched over with random pieces of duct tape.

The old hand-painted black-and-white sign with its strange punctuation and dripping letters still stood out in front, weathered into near unreadability by the high plains wind: "Broke Car's and Stuff 'fixed.' Not running 'ok' Jumbo."

Various transmissions and greasy car parts lay on the side of the building amid the patchy wiregrass, along with a pile of rusted bicycle frames, a broken shopping cart, and a few fifty-five-gallon drums leaking some dark, viscous fluid. Gas cans, fenders, and a stack of rotting car tires completed the tableau.

Jumbo was sitting on a huge tractor tire inside the open door of the one service bay. He was barely visible inside the dark interior except for his white laceless high-tops and his filthy, torn T-shirt. He was eating cereal from an orange plastic mixing bowl with a huge serving spoon that he held like a man gripping a stick. Just off to his right was a dented metal tool chest with a loaf of white bread and a large slab of unidentifiable grey meat sitting on its top.

He waved the spoon happily at me as I drove up.

"Ready for breakfast?" he asked. "Got Wheaties, but you got to eat them with water." He held the orange mixing bowl and spoon toward me. "You can use these. I'm done with them."

"That's okay," I said. "I had some sweet rolls before I got here. There's still a couple more in the car, if you want them."

He grunted his approval and turned his attention to the chunk of grey meat. It was the size of a shoebox and had a greenish tint to it. He pulled a hacksaw from the metal tool chest, cut off a slab about the thickness of a small phone book, and slapped it between two slices of white bread.

"You should give it a try," he said. "Jimmy Sixkiller left it. I ain't sure what it is, but it ain't bad," he grinned.

"I'm fine. Enjoy," I said.

From the backseat Festus rose up and began sniffing the air. Jumbo peered over at him from behind his slab of sandwich.

"Where'd that dog come from?" he asked.

"Someone abandoned him. He was in the park where I slept."

"He looks pretty old."

"He's got a few miles on him."

Jumbo pushed himself off the tire and walked over to the car. He stuck his head close to Festus's and squinted at the old dog's face. "Yeah, he's old," he said. "What's that thing on his neck?"

"It's a tag. Go ahead and read it."

Jumbo took a step back.

"I ain't much for reading," he said. "You could read it to me."

"Sure," I said, quickly coming to his rescue.

I read him the short, plaintive message. When I finished he looked up at me with a pained expression.

"You ain't gonna let this Festus die, are you?" he asked.

"Nope. Wouldn't let that happen."

Jumbo stuck his face back in the window to within a few inches of the old dog's muzzle. Festus sniffed at him once, then licked him full across the lips.

"This Festus is hungry," Jumbo said.

"You think? I just fed him."

"I can tell that kind of thing," Jumbo grinned.

He took the remainder of his slab sandwich and handed it through the window to the grizzled dog.

Festus took it gently between his teeth. He kept his injured paw in the air as he tried to turn around on the narrow car seat.

"He's hurt, too," Jumbo said.

"I know. He had an infected paw. I cleaned it out."

"Let me see."

He opened the door and grunted something to Festus. Festus limped gingerly off the seat with the sandwich in his mouth and stepped carefully onto the ground.

Jumbo spoke to him briefly in Lakota.

Festus sat down and dutifully held his paw up as if he understood exactly what Jumbo was saying.

Jumbo dropped heavily onto one knee and began examining Festus's paw like a physician.

"I got some Indian medicine inside. It'll help this here paw. Come on, Nerburn, help me up."

I grabbed his huge toad of a hand and, using my feet as a fulcrum, leaned backward until he slowly regained his footing. He lumbered into the darkened garage and began rattling cans and bottles. When he emerged, he was carrying a coffee can with a thick paste in it. "This'll do it," he said.

He uttered a few more words in Lakota, and Festus skulked over to him with his head low. He was still holding the sandwich fragment in his teeth.

"I'd say he's an Indian dog," Jumbo grinned. "Except he eats too slow."

He took two fingers of the paste and applied it to Festus's paw with surprising delicacy.

"That's good, Festus," he said. "You're going to be okay now." Festus wagged his tail, as if he understood, and dropped the sandwich at Jumbo's feet, like an offering.

"This is a good dog," Jumbo said again.

"I know. He's a really good dog."

He paused a bit before speaking again.

"What you going to do with him?"

"I thought of giving him to Dan," I said. "But he's got Bronson."

Jumbo cast his eyes at the ground. "Bronson walked on," he said.

"What? I thought he really liked the old man."

"Died. He was never quite right. Got some kind of cough."

The news shocked me. Bronson had been a winning little terrier mix, riddled with mange, that Dan had picked up at a store where we had stopped during our journey in search of Dan's little sister. The little dog had taken to Dan like a lost child, and Dan had reciprocated.

In some way, little Bronson had been a replacement for Fatback, the old swaybacked black Lab that had been Dan's closest companion when I had first come out to visit him almost a dozen years earlier. Dan had even speculated that Fatback had sent Bronson to him as a replacement.

I could still close my eyes and see Dan and little Bronson curled up together on top of the covers of a dirty old motel room bed where we had stayed, both fast asleep, with Bronson nestled against the old man's chest and the old man cuddling him in his arms like a baby. It saddened me to think that he was gone. It was just one more loss in an old man's life that had been filled with losses.

"Didn't they take him to a vet?" I asked.

Jumbo kept his eyes on the ground. "Ain't even people docs here. I tried to fix him up, but he just couldn't make it."

I could hear the sadness in his voice as he talked about the tragic little dog and his failed efforts to save its life.

I looked down at Festus. He was lying at Jumbo's feet. His head was on his paws and he was looking up at Jumbo with something close to adoration.

"Since Bronson's gone, you think the old man would like Festus?" I asked.

Jumbo shook his head. "Grover and Wenonah won't let him have another dog. They say it will make it harder for him to cross to the other side. I already talked to them about it."

"Maybe it would make his last days on this side easier," I said.

"That's what I think," Jumbo answered. "But Grover and Wenonah say it won't." His eyes were still downcast. "We got to do what they say."

He stood quietly for a few minutes flexing his fingers nervously. After a long pause he spoke very softly, keeping his eyes down.

"I wouldn't mind taking this here Festus," he said. "Unless you got someone else who should have him." Festus was licking the edge of Jumbo's big toe that was sticking out through a tear in the edge of his right tennis shoe.

"Well," I said. "He really seems to like you."

"I like him, too."

"Well, then, you should have him."

Jumbo lifted his face and looked at me with a huge, grateful grin.

"I could bring him to visit Grandpa Dan every day," he said.

"Yeah, you could do that."

His smile broadened even further and he bent forward and held his arms out to the ragged old dog.

"Come here, you Festus," he said.

Festus lifted himself up on three legs and leaned his head against the thigh of the huge man looming over him.

In a single swoop, and with a mighty grunt, Jumbo reached down and lifted the old dog into his arms and held him on his back like a baby. Festus didn't squirm or scramble or try to escape, but just lay there looking adoringly at Jumbo's florid face. Jumbo reached over with his free hand and took the remaining slab of meat from the tool chest and placed it between his lips. He leaned toward Festus, who reached up with his grey muzzle and delicately took the slab of meat like a baby bird taking a worm from its mother.

"Yeah. This Festus is a good dog," he said, turning toward me with a look of almost tragic appreciation. "A really good dog. *Pilamaya*. Let's go show him to Grandpa Dan."

CHAPTER NINETEEN

A RESPECT BIGGER THAN FRIENDSHIP

I had no idea what to expect as we drove up to Dan's house. Jumbo and Festus sat in the backseat staring at each other like high school lovers, while I drove nervously onto the white clay path that snaked its way back through the tall grass to Dan's ramshackle clapboard house.

In the years since I'd last been there the path had deteriorated to the point where it was little more than a bone-jarring swath of washboard clay and gravel bisected in numerous places by great suspension-destroying foot-deep diagonal fissures, making it perilous to cross at any speed more than a crawl. I marveled at the fact that Grover would drive up here in his precious Buick.

I navigated the gullies cautiously, listening to the creaks and groans of my car's aging suspension as the wheels dropped into the trenches. Jumbo grunted at each jar and jolt.

Grover and Wenonah were sitting on the cracked wooden stoop of Dan's house as we approached. They watched impassively while I inched my way toward them through the ruts in the drive. Neither moved or made any effort at offering a greeting.

"I wonder where Dan is?" I said to Jumbo. "Isn't he usually out taking in the sun by this time of day?"

"He's been kind of sick," Jumbo said. "He mostly stays in his bed. That's why I like to come to visit him. I think he's going to like seeing this here Festus." Festus laid his head on Jumbo's shoulder and licked at his cheek at the mention of his name.

Even at a distance I could see that Wenonah had aged. Her long black hair was streaked with grey. Her face, always round and full, had turned jowly and soft, though her piercing dark eyes retained a fierce vigilance and intelligence. She wore a pair of stretch sweatpants and an oversized grey T-shirt that made her look as square and sturdy as a tree trunk. Grover, as always, looked dapper and freshly showered. He was wearing a long-sleeved checked cowboy shirt buttoned at the wrists and collar, with fake pearl buttons and yoked pockets. A cigarette was stuck in the band of his cowboy hat, and patches of talcum powder were splotched around the bottom of his neck. The notebook was laid out flat on Wenonah's lap.

I kept hoping for some sort of greeting or wave of recognition, but none was forthcoming. Instead, they both sat stock-still, Grover cleaning his nails with his buck knife and Wenonah following our progress with her eyes as I drove into the middle of the yard and parked.

"This isn't much of a greeting," I said to Jumbo.

"Probably just sitting," he responded. "I do that a lot myself. You should go up and say hi."

"You coming up with me?" I asked.

"Nah. I'll wait here with this Festus for a while," he said. He smiled at the dog and rubbed its head. "We're getting kind of tight." Festus flapped his tail and looked at Jumbo with wide, soulful eyes.

I stepped from the car and approached with a false nonchalance.

"Hi, Wenonah," I said, reaching out my hand in greeting. "It's good to see you."

She took my fingers in a soft, lifeless grip. "Hello, Nerburn," she said. Her greeting, like her handshake, was without feeling. I scanned her face and posture for some further hint of her attitude, but there was none.

Grover grabbed his mug of coffee and stood up. "I'll go check in with Jumbo," he said. It was obvious that he and Wenonah had determined that this was a conversation she and I needed to have alone.

I watched him walk toward the car, feeling the heavy weight of Wenonah's silence.

"So, you've read the notebook?" I asked with forced brightness.

"Yes," she said.

"What do you think?"

She made no response.

"I probably shouldn't have gone to visit the old woman," I continued, trying to justify my actions in the face of her apparent disapproval.

"You did what you had to," she said. The flatness in her tone was unnerving.

We sat in an uncomfortable silence while I cast about for something to say. I was bracing for what I expected to be a harsh dressing-down for having gotten involved in something that was none of my business when I heard a sniffle. I glanced over and noticed that there was moisture around Wenonah's eyes.

"Is everything okay?" I asked. I had a momentary sense of panic that something bad had happened to Dan in the course of the night.

Wenonah's lips quivered slightly. Slowly, her air of indifference dissolved. "I never thought there would be anything like this," she said, her voice cracking. She clutched the notebook to her chest like a child holding a rag doll.

"I'm sorry," I said. "The old woman wanted me to bring it to him. I had to respect her wishes."

Wenonah shook her head. "It's not the notebook," she said.

"Then what is it?" I asked. "The asylum? Did Grover tell you about it?"

She shook her head again and dabbed at her eyes with the edge of her sweatshirt. I waited quietly while she composed herself.

"Grover said you'd been having dreams," she said softly.

"Yes," I said.

"Tell me about them."

I started to tell her about the thunderclap and the visit to Mary, but she held up her hand. "No, I just want to hear about the dreams," she said. "What's in them. Everything you can remember."

"Well," I began. "They are always the same. Yellow Bird is facing me, looking at me. She has this little bowl haircut. She never says anything, just stares. Her eyes aren't really warm or cold. They seem almost empty. She has on this white dress, kind of plain, and some heavy black shoes. She never smiles. She always seems brooding and serious, almost like she's accusing me of something."

"Anything else?"

"She has a doll. It doesn't seem important, though."

"Everything's important," she said. "Try to remember." She ran her hands nervously over the deer-hide cover of the notebook.

"Mary's face. The old Ojibwe lady. It's lined. Kindly. I feel kind of like she's bringing me Yellow Bird. Presenting her to me. They're in front of this big building."

I avoided telling her that the building looked like the pictures I had seen of the Canton asylum. I would let that all unfold in its own time.

"Then Yellow Bird starts to walk away. She walks off into a field. She keeps gesturing for me to follow. There are these humps, like haystacks. She's looking at me. I remember her eyes."

Wenonah bit her lip and stared off into the distance. "You say she wore a white dress?"

"Yes, kind of like a First Communion dress from those old boarding school photos."

"And she carried a little doll."

I nodded.

"And her hair was cut into a bowl cut."

"Yes."

She paused for a moment and stared off over the hills.

"Oh, Nerburn," she said. "This is so much bigger than you know."

As we were speaking, Grover came hobbling back across the yard. "What's with that dog, Nerburn?" he said. "Jumbo said you picked him up on the road somewhere."

"He was sleeping under my cot when I woke up. He's a stray."

"It takes one to know one," Grover said. "Jumbo said you were thinking of giving him to the old man. Good thing you changed your mind. He don't need that kind of pull." He rubbed his hand on his pants leg. "Christ, he's wiry. Like petting a porcupine."

Then, turning to Wenonah, he asked, "Did you tell him?"

She shook her head. "We'll let him see for himself. It's better that way."

I assumed they were talking about Dan's fragile condition. "Come on," Wenonah said. "It's time to wake Grandpa."

She stood and walked up the steps.

Grover stayed behind me, as if pinning me between them so I could not escape.

The feel of the house had changed radically since my last visit. There had once been an air of disheveled festivity about it, with people coming and going and the TV blaring; now it felt sepulchral and desolate. Cheap curtains had been hung over the windows, leaving the single living area bathed in a sickly half-light.

The same decrepit furniture was still there, but it felt unused. The cushions on the old, sagging wooden-armed motel couch had split open, allowing the stuffing to spill out, and the kitchen table, once the scene of late-night laughter-filled poker games, was piled high with shoeboxes full of magazine clippings and miscellaneous objects. The whole place had the air of a house where someone was living out his last days. A thin layer of dust covered everything.

Wenonah flicked on the fluorescent light over the kitchen table. Its single exposed tube blinked several times, then buzzed into life.

I looked at the piles of boxes and clippings. "I see he's still a collector," I said, trying to inject a little levity into the situation.

She smiled wanly. "Packrat's more like it. He keeps what he ought to throw away and throws away what he ought to keep."

She squared the edges of a stack of magazines on the table as she passed by, while Grover bent down and broke off a piece of loose linoleum that looked like it might cause the old man to trip if he caught his toe on it. I caught a glimpse of *To Walk the Red Road*, the oral history book I had done with the Red Lake students those many years ago, on a small table in the far corner. It was a grim reminder of better, more vibrant days when Dan and I had first met.

"How weak is he?" I asked.

Wenonah nodded toward the closed bedroom door. "You'll see. But first I want to explain something to you."

"Tell me," I said.

"You consider yourself my grandpa's friend."

"Yes."

"And he considers you his friend, too. But he's still an elder. And now he's getting ready to pass. You're still acting like a white person, being all familiar and treating him like you're his equal. You're not his equal. He's an elder. Do you understand me?"

The comment stung. "Have I been too familiar?" I asked. "I haven't tried to be."

"You think your friendship opens every door. It doesn't. It just gives you the right to be in his presence. He'll decide what to say and what not to say. You need to just let him talk.

"When you go in there to visit with him, you just remember where you are and who he is. It's okay to joke when you see him. He expects that of you. He likes it. But when it's time to give him the book, you are a messenger, not a friend. Do you understand?"

I nodded my assent.

"Do you have some tobacco?" she asked.

I reached in my pocket and pulled out the pack of Prince Albert I kept at the ready.

"Just give it to him before you hand him the notebook," Wenonah said.

She started toward the bedroom door, then stopped as if she had just remembered something. "Another thing," she said. "Don't leave until he tells you to. You should never leave before an elder. They will tell you when you can go, or they will leave first. Leaving first is like serving yourself first. No one will ever say anything, but they will notice."

"I'm sorry," I said.

"Don't be sorry," she said. "Just do things right. You have something he needs to see. You are a messenger from an old woman to an old man. That is a great honor. Think of her. Think of him. Think of what you are passing."

Throughout the conversation Grover had been uncharacteristically quiet. He drew placidly on his cigarette, occasionally nodding assent to what Wenonah said.

"You get all that, Nerburn?" he said. "This is what you've been training for."

"I didn't know I've been in training."

"Everything is training."

I was taken aback by the implied accusations in Wenonah's short lecture. I had always tried to be respectful of Dan's status, though perhaps, as she said, I been presumptuous of his friendship — a white man's error. But what struck me in her manner was how significant she felt it was that I follow the proper protocol. Clearly, this encounter and the delivery of the notebook had more significance even than I had imagined.

"We're going back in there now," Wenonah said. "We're going to wake him up. You need to get this book to him, but you don't just hand it to him. We'll get him ready to talk, then we're going to leave. You give him the book when you think it's right. Don't be all 'white-man impatient' to get to the business part of things. Remember. Your respect has to be bigger than your friendship.

"And remember the tobacco," she continued. "This is not about you."

She handed the notebook to me, handling it carefully, as if it was an object of great price. "It's about this. Give it to him in the Indian way, and don't give it to him until the time is right."

"How will I know when that is?" I asked.

"You'll know. He's old and he's tired, but he's no fool. He'll know you're here for something."

"Just like always," Grover added dryly.

"Now," Wenonah said. "Grover and I are going to get him up. You stay out of things while we do it. Then we're going to leave. It will just be the two of you. We have something to do. You just be respectful and let him lead the conversation. He'll get where he has to go."

She nodded to Grover, who walked over to the closed bedroom door and knocked several times.

"Hey, old man," he said.

There was no answer.

He knocked again, keeping the sound soft so as not to wake Dan too abruptly.

Hearing nothing, he pushed the door open a crack. The single window in the bedroom must have been covered with a curtain or a blanket, because the room was even darker than the rest of the house.

Through the crack in the open door I could see Dan lying on his side on a blue-and-white striped mattress on a metal bed frame. There was no bedding, just a rumpled bundle of blankets and old clothes pushed down toward the foot of the bed. He was wearing a pair of khaki pants and a sleeveless ribbed laborer's T-shirt and was breathing heavily.

Grover stepped over the threshold and gestured for me to follow. The temperature in the room must have been 110 degrees.

"Hey, old man," he repeated. "Look what I found down at the trading post."

Dan lifted his head a few inches and stared in my direction. His eyes were filmy and opaque. Grover nodded for me to respond.

"Hi, Dan. It's Nerburn," I said.

Dan pushed himself up on one arm and looked around, as if he was unsure of where he was. "Nerburn? Do you live around here?" Wenonah glanced at me, as if to say, "See, this is how it is."

Dan groaned several times and tried to push himself upright, but he was too weak. Wenonah stepped over quickly and grabbed him under the elbow to help him into a sitting position.

"Nerburn's come to see you," she said. "He lives in Minnesota."

"Minnesota? That's *Shinnob* country," Dan said, as if trying to situate himself in the conscious world. "They're the woods people. The secret ones. You never know what they're thinking."

I stood quietly in the background while Dan looked around the darkened room in confusion. I could sense his struggle to recognize me.

"You remember me, Dan," I said softly. "The Red Road books? Fatback's old friend?"

He squinted hard, as if to bring me into focus. "Nerburn? What? Oh, yeah. Yeah. I remember you. Sure. Nerburn. You're the book writer. Yeah, sure. You helped me find out what happened to my little sister. Come on in. Come on in."

He gestured shakily toward a wooden chair propped up against the wall. "Sit down." His chest was heaving.

I had expected him to be weak, but it was a shock to see him this confused and disoriented. His body, too, was a shock. His long hair was a ratted, grey mess. His skin was almost falling off his bones: just stringy, wrinkled flesh strung flaccidly over a skeleton. There was no muscle anywhere. It was a miracle he could even hold himself upright.

I moved toward the chair as he had instructed, but it was covered with clothes. "Just throw them on the floor," he said.

"Don't you do it, Nerburn," Wenonah said from the kitchen. "He can't pick them up, and I don't want to."

Dan shook his head several times as if trying to clear his thoughts. "If they would have built me a house with big closets like a white man," he said, "then I wouldn't have to throw my stuff on the floor."

"You don't need closets," Wenonah said. "You only wear one shirt, anyway."

The two of them went back and forth like this for a few minutes. Grover stood back, saying nothing. I took his cue and did the same. I gradually realized that Wenonah was trying to orient Dan by bantering with him. With each riposte his comments became more lucid and on point.

"I'm opening the window," Grover said, finally. "I didn't come here for a sweat."

He pulled down a tattered blanket that had been covering the window and an explosion of blinding high plains morning light filled the room.

"Jesus Christ," Dan said, putting his forearm over his eyes.

"That's how they say he comes," Grover cracked. "In a blaze of light."

He pushed the bottom half of the window upward and propped it open with a shoe placed on end. A blast of dry, hot air wafted in.

"Now, isn't that better, old man?" he said.

Dan was still blinking and covering his eyes.

Wenonah came in from the kitchen carrying a tray with a glass of orange juice and a piece of white bread and jam. She went to the chipped dresser on the far side of the room, opened a string of amber plastic pill bottles, and began separating out a collection of small white and pink pills.

She handed about ten pills to Dan, along with the glass of juice. He took them in his gnarled hand and shoved them in his mouth, following them up with a swig of the juice.

He made a face like a man having a sensitive body part squeezed, then leaned back on his elbows and breathed out heartily.

"Like swallowing a handful of stones," he said. "Those things supposed to kill me or keep me alive?"

"The doctor said he couldn't kill you if he tried," Wenonah answered.

"Well, he's giving it a damn good shot. They should be treating me like an elder instead of an old man."

"An elder remembers to pull up his zipper," Grover said, nodding at Dan's pants.

Dan looked down at the open fly of his stained khakis and made a feeble effort to grasp the zipper and pull it upward.

"You'd better get that, old man," Grover said. "You don't want to scare the kids."

"Aw, hell," Dan growled. "There ain't nothing left to see."

"That's what's scary," Grover said.

It was a pleasure to watch Grover and Wenonah maneuver the old man into awareness. If they were apprehensive about Dan's response to the notebook and its revelations, they gave no indication by their conversation or actions.

Wenonah shoved me slightly to make me step forward.

"We're leaving now, Grandpa," she said. "Nerburn wants to talk to you." She made one final gesture to me to proceed slowly, then she and Grover left the room.

I heard the screen door slam, followed by the sound of car doors closing and the telltale rumble of Grover's car moving slowly down the path.

Dan was now almost fully alert and present. He reached over and swept the clothes off the chair onto the floor. "Nerburn, Nerburn," he said. "Sit down." He rolled his shoulders several times in an effort to loosen them up.

"Damn, Grover and Wenonah, just yanking me up like that. They treat me like a damn kid."

He ran his crooked fingers through his stringy hair. "If I'd have known you were coming I'd have made myself pretty," he said, flashing me a wry smile. The smile changed quickly to a wince as some joint sent a shot of pain through his body. He rotated his shoulder as if to free it up in its socket. "You got an oil can?" he said.

"WD-40. Out in the car. It's kind of messy, though."

"Yeah, they do it to me every morning," he continued. "They come banging in here, making me get up like there's something I got to do. They don't understand nothing about being old."

"Grover's no spring chicken himself," I said.

"Nah, he's still got a little fuel in the tank. I'm talking *old* old, where everything hurts and nothing works. Here, look at this." He tried to lift his feeble bony arm up at the elbow. He was only able to get it about six inches from his side.

"That's it," he said. "That's all the further she goes. Now, that's old. Grover, he's got a little hitch in his giddyap, but he goes where he wants, does what he wants. I only go where my body lets me, and that ain't very damn far."

He flapped his hand in the direction of the kitchen. "Hand me that milk over there on the cupboard," he said. "Them pills ain't going south fast enough."

I reached over and grabbed a carton of milk that was sitting on the ledge. Even at arm's length I could smell that it was curdled and spoiled.

"Seems like it's been sitting out for a while," I said.

"Aged, we call it," he said. "Now give it to me."

He took the carton and moved it shakily toward his lips. Little bits of curdled milk dripped down the sides of his mouth as he took gulp after gulp from the quart carton.

"There they go." He wiped his mouth with the back of his hand.

He shook his finger at me in his old familiar gesture of admonishment. "See, this is how it is. When you're just regular old, like Grover, you still wake up thinking something's going to happen. You don't know what it is, but something's going to happen. You're part of the world and all the things going on.

"When you get *old* old, like me, you know nothing's going to happen. Your life ain't no bigger than the shape of your day. You got to make yourself care about stuff. The little kids come to see you, but they don't really like you. Your own kids come to visit, but they have their own life. You go visit other old people, all you do is talk about the old times or all the things that hurt or what the hell is wrong with young people these days.

"It makes you tired, I tell you. Ornery, too. You spend a lot of time going down all the paths of your life, wondering what you did and what the hell it means. You think of all the places you went one way when you could have gone another, all the cards you left on the table. It can be damn lonely, I tell you."

I was surprised at how quickly he had returned to full awareness. And it was comforting to hear him launch into one of his old, familiar diatribes, though it was disconcerting to hear the melancholic edge to his comments. I was torn between a warm feeling of nostalgia for the way he was embracing my presence and sadness at the uncharacteristic hint of self-pity that seemed to have crept into his thoughts. It raised an almost visceral apprehension in me about how the revelations in the notebook might affect him. But Wenonah's insistence that we show it to him, and her admonition about letting him lead the conversation, still echoed in my ears. I stayed quiet and let him take the conversation where he would.

He took another sip of milk.

"It's better for us Indians than for you white folks, though. At least our young ones still think of us as elders. They know they're supposed to listen to us, even if they don't want to. We see them doing something wrong, we give them a hard eye and it stops them. Some of them even ask to learn what we know. They got a sense of their tradition. They know that we got closer touch with some of the old ways.

"Your old folks, they're shoved off into some warehouse to die, where everything smells like piss and death. I seen those places. I had a friend in one of them. I went to visit him once. The only difference between him and being dead was that he hadn't died yet. Christ — tubes, machines. All those nurses coming around to feel his wrist. What? They couldn't tell if he was alive by looking at him? I got the hell out of there as quick as I could."

He took another swig from the carton. "I tell you, you ain't getting me into one of them places. Let me lie here and listen to the birds and the sounds. One day I'll go into my bed and won't wake up. If I feel it coming I'll wait until nighttime, then go outside, stare up in the sky. That's what I'd like. To take the long walk under *Wanagi Tachanku* — that river of stars. Make the journey in the steps of the ancestors."

He slowly pushed himself up to a standing position by grabbing onto the arms of his walker.

"I can help you, Dan," I said, jumping to his assistance.

He flapped his hand at me again. "Sit down," he ordered. "You got to let me do some things, even if they don't seem like much."

He moved slowly toward his coffeepot, shuffling his feet and clumping the walker along the floor. I could see why Grover had pulled up the chunk of linoleum; even the smallest obstacle could cause Dan to trip and fall.

He grabbed the handle of the pot and took a mug from the counter. His hand was shaking so badly that I thought he would spill the coffee all over himself. He poured half a cup of weak, watery brown liquid and tottered back to me.

"Here, I'm going to give you some coffee now, and I don't want to hear nothing about any expresso stuff. You're on the rez, you drink rez coffee. If it ain't strong enough for you, you just drink some more." He held the carton of curdled milk toward me. "Milk? I remember you like it that way."

"No, thanks," I said. "Black is fine."

"Suit yourself." He downed the last of the lumpy milk and threw the carton into the sink.

"You know, there's some good to being old, too," he continued. "We got no more part to play in the small things of life, so we can pay attention to the big voices. Sometimes you can even cross over. You can meet the ancestors, talk to them, hear what they have to say. You can bring that back if people will listen to you."

"You ever cross over?" I asked.

"More and more every day."

"You learn things?"

"Hell, yes."

"And do folks listen to what you bring back?"

"A little. Not enough. It ain't like the old days."

He clumped back into the bedroom and made his way over to an old, chipped nightstand that stood by the side of the bed. There were only two pictures on it — one, which I had seen before, was a photo of his son when he had graduated from Haskell Indian College in Oklahoma, and the other, stuck in the edge of the frame of the larger photo, was a small, fading snapshot that appeared to be Dan with little Charles Bronson on his lap.

"Is that Bronson?" I asked.

"Yeah. Some white kid took it down by the trading post. Nice kid. Real respectful. Asked before he did it. You remember Bronson?"

"I was there when you got him in that store, remember? Jumbo told me he passed."

A shadow crossed Dan's face. He sucked his lips in tight. "Yeah, little fellow never got his strength back."

"He was a good dog," I said.

"He was a hell of a dog," Dan corrected. "Smart. Real smart."

He took the photo from the edge of the frame and reached it across to me.

He dropped himself heavily into his wheelchair and pushed himself over next to me so we could look at the photo together.

"Yeah. Real smart, that Bronson," he said. "Old Fatback, she could only do things one way. It was a good way. All full of heart. But Bronson, he'd look at me, then go do something to make me feel better. Sometimes he'd pull at my socks. Sometimes he'd get a ball and bring it onto my bed. If I was having a bad day, he'd come up and nuzzle my chin, make me laugh. He was always thinking, always operating. He was smart as hell, that Bronson. You ever had a dog like that, Nerburn?"

"Yeah, I had an old shepherd once," I said. "A mixed blood,

you'd call him. He was sly. If I wouldn't let him in one door, he'd go to another. He even figured out how to push the door handle with his nose to let himself out. When people came over, he'd go right up to them and put his paw on their knee and cock his head, acting real cute, trying to make them his friend. Then at dinner he'd hit up all those folks for food. He made out real well that way."

"Sounds like some 'skins I know," Dan laughed.

As he stared at the faded photo his eyes took on a faraway gaze. "Yeah, *shunka's* special," he said, using the Lakota word for *dog*. "One of the Creator's best gifts. Our best friends of all the four-leggeds. Knew a 'skin from back East who said his people had a story about how in the long-ago time the humans came into the forest and the Creator asked all the animals what they were going to do with them. All the other animals said they'd kill them, tear them up. But *shunka* said that he wanted to help the humans because they were weak and helpless except for their brains. He said he'd be their companion, help them hunt, warn them about danger, carry their stuff. So Creator gave *shunka* a special place with us humans. He's still got that special place."

"That's a good story, Dan," I said.

"True story," he said. "True in the heart. Yeah, I wish more people would think about that. These days, folks on the rez don't respect *shunka*. Just leave him out. Tie them up on chains too short. They talk about reclaiming the old ways, then treat *shunka* like that." He shook his finger at me. "I can tell the real ones," he said. "The ones who still got the tradition. They treat *shunka* right."

He shifted in his char. "I think about *shunka* a lot," he said. "About how the Creator made them our best friends. Do you ever think about that?"

"I feel it, but I never really give it much thought," I said.

"You should," he responded, leaning forward and pushing

himself into a fully upright position. "You have to always think about every part of creation, about what it was put there for. If you don't pay attention to that stuff, you just live like the dead." He was once again the teacher, bringing knowledge to a willing student.

"Now, think about *shunka*. They're all different, right? Some barking like hell to make you nervous. Some just lying around. Some always got to be doing something. Some out on patrol or following you around. All different. So why do we all like our dogs the same if they're all different?"

"I don't know."

He wagged his finger at me.

"Because they all give us love in the same way. They all have the gift of an open heart. It ain't about what they do, it's about what they give. You follow me?"

I smiled and nodded. Once again, even in his infirmity, the old man was thinking and preaching.

"*Shunka* doesn't know I'm old," he continued. "*Shunka* doesn't know I'm ugly as hell. *Shunka* doesn't know if I'm a 'skin or a *wasichu*. *Shunka* doesn't care."

"You're right," I said.

He reached across and slapped me on the knee. "Of course I'm right," he said. "I'm too damn old to waste time thinking things that are wrong. But once they know us, they go to work for us. Remember how I said Fatback followed my spirit and kept it company, but Bronson tried to lift my spirit to a good place? That's different things. We got the dogs who help with the chores and the dogs who keep us safe. But no matter what they do, they're by our side. We should learn from them, Nerburn. They teach us about being faithful. They teach us about friendship."

He leaned closer to me. "You think much about friendship, Nerburn?"

"Yes, as a matter of fact, I do."

"Well, here's what you need to think. Friendship is the strongest bond, because there's nothing making you do it. There's no common blood, like with brothers and sisters. There's nothing you need from it, not like a man and a woman getting together. There you got that thing drawing you."

He gave a coy smile, as if going back to a warm place in his memories.

"Friendship is something you give, like a gift," Dan said, "without thinking of anything in return. In true friendship there's nothing selfish at the heart. That's why my friends matter to me. I would die for my friends, Nerburn. They would die for me."

A fleeting image of Grover's sundance scars passed through my mind.

"Now, your people, I ain't so sure," he went on. "Whenever I meet a *wasichu*, I think, 'What's he trying to get from me?' You folks always seem to be trying to get something from each other. You don't watch *shunka* enough. If you did you'd understand friendship better."

He reached over and slipped the photo back into the corner of the frame with his son, then turned and looked me straight in the eye.

"You ain't here to get something from me, are you?"

CHAPTER TWENTY

Eyes without Light

$\mathcal{I}$t took me a minute to recover from the ambush.

"Uh, no," I said. "I'm here to give you something."

"Good," he said, rubbing his hands together and licking his lips. "That's good. I like gifts. Puts a little excitement in my day. What is it?" He leaned toward me with a look of almost childlike expectation on his face.

It was just as Wenonah had predicted — Dan had offered me the perfect moment to bring out the notebook. I reached into my pocket for the tobacco, then stopped. Dan's innocent delight at the prospect of a gift held me back. The dark truths of Mary's words seemed too harsh and unsettling. Though I was probably making a mistake, I couldn't bring myself to place them before him just yet. I decided to let him bask in the lightness of the moment for a bit longer. Another opportunity, perhaps even more appropriate, would present itself soon enough.

"It's a visitor," I said, recovering quickly. His talk about dogs had given me an idea. "A special one."

"I like visitors, too. Where is he?" he said. Then he flashed me a sly smile. "Or maybe it's a she."

"No, sorry, it's a he," I said. "Someone I just met."

"Well, get him in here."

I had a moment's doubt and hesitation. I knew that Lakota traditionally did not bring dogs into their houses — that, except for certain small dogs like Bronson, there were actually cultural proscriptions against it. But I remembered that I had once asked Dan about it and he had said, "Aw, the hell with that stuff. I'll bring a goddamn elephant into my house if I want to. It's my house and I'll say who can be a guest and who can't." That, and his wistful comments about *shunkas*, made me think that Festus would be welcome in his home.

I went to the door and whistled to Jumbo, who was sitting under a spindly, almost leafless tree, feeding pieces of the grey meat to Festus. He had tied a filthy old sock around Festus's sore foot and fastened it to his leg with duct tape.

I gestured him into the house, then hurried back to the bedroom and positioned myself in the corner to watch Dan's response to Festus.

Dan leaned forward in anticipation as Jumbo clumped up the steps and filled the doorway like a huge shadow. For a moment I couldn't make out what was happening, then I realized Jumbo was carrying Festus, cradling him in his arms like an infant.

"Hau, Grandfather," Jumbo said. He had a broad grin on his round, grimy face.

Dan leaned even further forward and squinted at the looming figure with the dog in his arms.

"Well, I'll be damned," he said. "What the hell is that?"

Jumbo stepped in sheepishly. "This here's Festus, grandfather."

"Fest what?"

"My new dog, Festus. I didn't name him."

Dan rubbed his hands together and let out a little cackle of anticipation. "Put him down. I want to see him."

Jumbo placed Festus on the floor. The old dog looked around and licked his lips nervously. Dan leaned forward in his chair and made the familiar tsukking sound he used to call dogs. Festus moved slowly toward him, wagging his tail sheepishly and keeping his head low. The paw with the sock flopped as he walked.

"Well, I'll be," Dan said. "Festus. That's a hell of a name. Festus." He kept shaking his head and laughing softly, as if it was the strangest name he'd ever heard.

Festus lifted his wounded paw for Dan to shake. "Looks like this here Festus lost three of his socks," Dan chortled. Festus, hearing his name spoken over and over, licked the old man's hand.

Dan massaged the inside of each of Festus's ears with his knuckles, then spoke authoritatively to the old dog in Lakota. Festus cocked his head and stared at the old man. He appeared for all the world to be listening and understanding.

Dan tsukked several more times in a different rhythm and patted his hand on the mattress, and Festus scrabbled clumsily onto the bed, scuttling and pushing with his back legs to make his way up. He moved in close to Dan and sat there by his side, looking nervous and proud, as if he had been elevated to a status he neither understood nor deserved.

Dan tsukked again and said a few words. Festus lay down and put his head on his paws.

"This Festus is a good dog," he said.

I stood in the background, amazed. Festus had settled down next to Dan as if the old man had raised him from a pup.

Dan scruffed Festus on the head several more times and spoke to him intimately, like a grandparent speaking to a grandchild. Festus rolled over onto his side and put his head against Dan's thigh.

"See, Nerburn," Dan said. "I told you *shunka* don't care that I'm old and ugly. 'Course, he ain't much of a looker himself."

Festus thumped his tail several times, raising small clouds of dust from the mattress.

"Damn," Dan said. "I sure miss having a *shunka*. But Wenonah don't like it." He shook his head in disgust. "Treats me like a baby."

"I'll bring this here Festus to see you every day, Grandfather," Jumbo said. "He can be your dog at my house."

"I'd like that, Jumbo," Dan said. "I'd like that a lot."

Dan looked up at me and smiled. "This is a good gift, Nerburn," he said. "A real good gift."

I did not feel I could wait any longer. "There's something else I have to give you, Dan," I said hesitantly.

"More gifts," he said, licking his lips theatrically. "I like that. What is it?"

I reached into my pocket and took out the pouch of Prince Albert. My hands literally shook as I held it toward him. "I'd like to offer this to you so you know that I'm speaking from the heart," I said. My efforts at formality seemed clumsy and artificial.

Dan immediately grasped the change in tone. "Hau," he said, taking the tobacco in both hands. "What is this other gift that you have brought?"

Jumbo cast his eyes toward the floor. Though he knew nothing of the notebook, he could sense the change in atmosphere.

"You remember that old woman I visited who had gone to boarding school with your little sister?"

Dan's expression darkened. "The *Shinnob*?" he said. "Yellow Bird's friend?"

"Mary."

"Yeah, I remember her."

"I went to see her again."

It was as if the temperature in the room had suddenly dropped thirty degrees. Dan's face grew hard and the mirth went out of his eyes.

I carefully removed the notebook from my shoulder bag and held it toward him.

"I'm supposed to bring this to you. It's from her."

Dan placed the tobacco on the bedside table and extended his hands, palms up, like a priest preparing to receive an alb from an altar boy. "Let me see it," he said.

"The knots on the laces are real small," I said. "I can undo them for you."

"Just give it to me," he said.

I placed the deer-hide case carefully on his outstretched hands. He closed his eyes and set it on his knees, then ran his hands slowly over the surface like a man reading Braille. He spoke something low in Lakota, all the while keeping his hands moving back and forth over the fur cover, as if in some kind of ritual incantation.

"Jumbo, get some sweetgrass," he said. "It's in the cupboard. Next to the soup. And that stone bowl on the counter."

Festus nudged in closer to Dan and sniffed at the deerskin cover.

Jumbo lumbered to the cupboard and returned with a bundle of green braided herbs. It looked much like the bundles he had grabbed from the shaman woman in the store, but he handled this one with a different sense of ceremony and importance.

He placed the sweetgrass in the stone bowl and lit it with a wooden match. The pungent smoke rose sinuously and filled the air around us. Dan reached over and pulled some of the smoke toward him with a cupped hand. Jumbo and I did the same.

"Now," Dan said, handing the deerskin to me. "Read it." His breathing had become shallow and tight.

I untied the laces and began reading the bound pages: *"My name is Mary Johnson. That's my English name. My Indian name is*

Ozhaawashko-binesiikwe. I knew your friend's little sister. I think she was a very good person."

"*Ahna,*" Dan said, as if in acknowledgment of Mary's voice. He closed his eyes and leaned his head back.

"*I want to tell you these things. I did not tell them all to you before.*"

I continued reading Mary's words, recounting Yellow Bird's loneliness and isolation, her punishment in the closet, her frantic cries at the burning of the other little girl's doll.

Dan sat motionless. I kept glancing at him for any sign of a response. But he was still as stone. There were moments when I thought I detected a slight twitch or tightening around his mouth, but they were impossible to read. Jumbo sat with his head down and his hands folded. Festus pressed tightly against Dan's hip.

When I got to the part about the dead horse field and the animals, Dan's hand tensed on Festus's back.

I kept reading: "*I only told you that one story. But there were lots more. There was the time she made a bird come to her hand and she said things to it and it said things back to her.*"

Dan raised his hand. "Stop," he said. "Stop." There was quiet anguish in his voice. "Leave me alone for a minute."

He shifted himself out of his chair and onto his bed. Without another word, he turned over and faced the wall.

I looked at Jumbo, who nodded toward the door.

Slowly, I closed the book and stood up as quietly as I could. Jumbo did the same.

We left the old man lying there and retreated to the kitchen. Festus remained pressed against Dan, looking doleful and concerned. The thin plume of smoke from the sweetgrass rose in the air, separating our world from his.

"What was that?" I whispered to Jumbo as we stood outside the bedroom door.

Jumbo had a strange look on his face. "That stuff about Yellow Bird. It's hard to explain."

"How do you mean? Try."

"Well, the way she looked. That stuff about the birds."

"Yeah, but he knew all that."

I was about to ask him more when the bedroom door opened. Dan emerged and leaned unsteadily against the door frame. His face had an expression I had never seen before.

"Why did you go see that woman, Nerburn?" he said.

"Uh, I'd been having dreams," I answered.

"Get back in here," he said.

He turned and made his way back to his bed, supporting himself at each step by holding on to pieces of furniture.

"Me and Festus will wait outside," Jumbo said. He put his fingers to his lips and whistled sharply. The old dog scrabbled off the bed and limped after him through the front door.

Dan gestured me toward the chair. "Tell me about those dreams."

I sat down and collected my thoughts. Carefully, I told him about Mary and Yellow Bird and the old building and Yellow Bird gesturing for me to follow. I explained how the dream was always the same, and how it kept coming back.

He nodded quietly and chewed on his bottom lip. "These are good things to know," he said. "But why exactly did you go visit her? What made you just one day decide to do it?"

I was hesitant about discussing the noise that had awakened me, but I owed him complete honesty. "There was one night," I said, "when it was like I heard a shout, right in the middle of the dream. I couldn't tell whether it was real or not."

"Everything's real," Dan said. "You know that."

"It scared me. No one else heard it."

"So you thought it was from that old woman?"

"I didn't know what to think. I just wanted the dream to stop."

"So that's when you went to see her?"

"Yes."

A small smile crept across Dan's face. "And when you got there, you found out the old woman had died, right?"

"How'd you know that?" I asked, shocked. I had not mentioned this.

He waved his hand dismissively. "And you found out it had happened the same night as the sound," he continued.

"Yes. How'd you know?" His knowledge frightened me.

He smiled again and closed his eyes. His face had taken on an expression of peace.

"I want you to read the rest of it now," he said.

I opened the notebook and read to the end, finishing with Mary's instruction that I go see Benais and her wish that this not give Dan a heavy spirit.

Dan exhaled, long and hard.

"So, did you go see him? This Benais?"

"Yes."

"What was he like?"

"He's hard to describe," I said. "He was about your age, maybe ninety. He was almost more like an animal than a person. His eyes didn't seem to have any light. I couldn't tell at all what he was thinking."

Dan leaned back, steepled his hands over the bridge of his nose, and smiled.

"One of the old ones," he said, almost more to himself than to me. Pieces were fitting together in Dan's brain, though none of it was making any sense to me.

He stood up and slowly made his way across the room using his walker. He stared out into the bright morning light. "The eyes," he said. "The eyes. That's the old ones. You white people use your eyes to talk. We Indian people stay back; we don't let our eyes show what we're thinking. With the old ones, the really old ones, like that Benais, they stay way back. You never see them. They just come out when they want to."

He turned and looked at me. "Did he ever let you see him?"

I thought for a minute and remembered his joke about teepee creepers.

"One time. There was a moment when he made a joke. Then his eyes lit up and he felt like a person."

Dan licked his lips and nodded again. "He wanted to see how you'd respond," he said. "He was trying to draw you out. That's how they work. They show things just to see what you do. Then they have knowledge."

He thumped into the kitchen in his walker, leaving me seated in my chair. When I tried to follow, he gestured me back. Through the door I could see him gathering some more herbs from the cupboard.

When he returned, he sprinkled some on the floor before us, then placed the rest in a large abalone shell. His hand shook badly as he struck the match.

When he had the herbs lit and smoking, he sucked in his cheeks and turned to me. "What did this Benais tell you?" he said.

"He'd seen your sister. He'd been in a place with her called the Hiawatha Asylum for Insane Indians."

Dan accepted the knowledge without surprise.

"What did he say about her?"

"That she spent her time by herself. That it was a terrible place where people were chained to their beds and made to sleep in their own waste. He didn't know her much. They kept the boys and girls apart."

Dan nodded, as if none of this shocked him. "Did he say anything about how she looked?"

Once again, Yellow Bird's appearance seemed more important than the horrible circumstances of her life. "She wore a white dress and had her hair in a bowl cut and she used to sing a lot."

Again, Dan nodded. "How'd he say he got out of that place, this Benais?" he asked.

"He said he just walked away when they shut it down."

"Just walked away," Dan said almost derisively. He smiled knowingly, as if something was becoming clear.

"The *Shinnobs* were our enemies," he said.

"I know," I answered. "I've studied the history."

"I'm not talking about history. I'm talking about power. Did he do anything else?"

"Yes, he took me out into a field. He's keeping buffalo. He said they used to live in his country, too. He said he got them because he wanted to bring them home. He wanted me to see them."

Dan's eyes began to twinkle. "Did he say why he wanted you to see them?"

"He said it was because your people, the Lakotas — he knew you were a Lakota — had given them to him. He wanted to show me."

Dan smiled softly.

"I like this Benais, Nerburn," he said.

"He wasn't showing you. That old one was calling me. He was just using you to make the call."

CHAPTER TWENTY-ONE

THE BIG LEAGUES

I was completely confused by the conversation. Dan seemed almost pleased by the information about Benais, and his interest in Yellow Bird's physical appearance was as confounding as Grover's and Wenonah's.

He leaned back quietly in his chair as if he were falling asleep.

"Are you okay, Dan?" I asked.

He nodded his head and ran his hands gently over the cover of Mary's notebook. We sat in silence as he closed his eyes and mouthed words under his breath.

Finally, I heard the rumbling of Grover's car coming up the path.

Dan slowly lifted his head. His eyes were still closed.

"You go out with them," he said.

"You're sure it's okay?" I asked, remembering Wenonah's admonition about never leaving before an elder unless you are specifically given permission to do so.

"Go," he said again, flapping his hand like someone shooing away a small animal. The smile on his face was almost beatific.

I left him stroking the cover of the book and stepped out onto the stoop. Jumbo was stationed there with his arm around Festus.

Grover had already parked the car and was limping his way toward us. Wenonah was rummaging around in the rear seat. She leaned in and lifted a small child onto the ground.

I let out an involuntary gasp. It was a little girl with a bowl haircut, wearing a white dress and black leather shoes. She looked exactly like the old picture of Dan's little sister that he had given me, and exactly like the image of the child standing by Mary in my dream. She was grasping a little burlap doll.

"Who's that?" I asked.

"That's Zi," Jumbo said.

"Zi?"

"Shantell. Donnie and Angie's girl."

I remembered Donnie and Angie and Shantell from my last visit to Dan's. Donnie was a shy, earnest young man who had been trying to teach himself stone carving, and I had shared a few tricks with him from my days as a wood-carver. Angie, hardly more than a girl herself, was a quiet young woman struggling with the challenges of a motherhood come too soon. They were the best of the younger generation — good young people trying to preserve their culture and live in harmony with the old ways while building a family in the difficult circumstances of reservation living. Shantell was their infant daughter.

I remembered Shantell because of the inordinate interest Dan had taken in her. She had been sickly and squalling, and her parents were at their wits' end. Dan had insisted there was something troubling her spirit — some unfinished business "on the other side," he'd said. The doctors had said it was only an ear infection, but Dan had been adamant. "This is not a white-man sickness," he'd said.

When I'd last seen them, Dan had given Shantell one of his little sister's dolls as well as his sister's Lakota name, Zintkala Zi — the Yellow Bird. Now, apparently, she was going by the name of Zi. I could not tell at this distance if the doll was the same one Dan had given her. I did know that it looked much like the doll little Yellow Bird was holding in the dream.

Festus, suddenly alert, stood up, limped down the steps, and hobbled over to the little girl as if he had been called. Zi saw him and made a sound. Instantly, Festus lay down. She made another sound and Festus stood up and went right to her side.

Grover saw my astonishment. "I told you there was more going on here than you understood," he said. "Now, just watch. She'll come in to see the old man. Don't say anything. Just let her pass."

The little girl walked resolutely up the steps, passed by us all without looking or speaking, pushed open the door, and went inside. Festus limped in behind her as if he was responsible for guarding her and could not let her out of his sight.

"My God, she looks just like the pictures of Dan's little sister," I said.

"Bingo," Grover said.

Through the door we could see Zi cross the kitchen and walk into Dan's bedroom. No one else, not even Wenonah or Grover, had entered his room without knocking, but the little girl pushed her way in without concern. No one said a word.

We could hear some vague conversation from inside the room. It was all in Lakota and spoken very low. Soon the two of them emerged together, with Zi holding Dan's hand. Dan was using a cane instead of a walker, and seemed to have regained both his strength and his sense of balance. Festus was following close behind.

"Give them room," Grover whispered. "And keep your mouth shut."

Dan and Zi came down the steps unaided, paying no attention to us as they passed. Festus scrabbled behind with the sock flopping on his paw. The three of them moved purposefully across the dusty front yard, with Dan supporting himself on his cane and Zi holding tightly onto his other hand.

Zi helped Dan settle into one of two white plastic chairs that were positioned at the base of the west-facing hill. Her manner was precise and competent, like that of a nurse or a hospital orderly. I could not believe I was watching the actions of a four-year-old child.

"What's going on?" I whispered to Jumbo.

"When she comes around, Grandpa Dan is different," he said. "He's the only one she really talks to."

"She doesn't even talk to her folks?"

"Just a little. Mostly she just sings."

Wenonah had walked over and taken a place next to us on the stoop. "She'll talk to animals, too, Nerburn," she said. "And dolls."

A shiver ran through me. "Like Dan's little sister talked to the dolls."

Grover chuckled again. "I told you this was way above my pay grade, Nerburn.

"There," he said, gesturing toward Zi with his cigarette. She had stepped away from Dan and was heading over to a small hillock. "Watch."

She walked into the knee-high grass and picked up a small rabbit that had been observing them from the edge of the hill. The animal made no attempt to struggle or escape. "She can do that with birds, too," Grover said. "It was the part in the notebook about Yellow Bird picking up birds that stopped me in my tracks."

I felt like I had entered an alternate universe. None of this seemed possible. I stared at the little girl in her white dress and black leather shoes. She seemed like something that had stepped out of an old tintype or a forgotten memory.

She carefully put the rabbit down in the grass and walked back toward Dan.

"Do her parents dress her like that on purpose?" I asked.

"They don't dress her," Wenonah said. "That's all she'll wear."

"And the haircut?"

"Her choice. One day she said she wanted it cut like that, and now she won't let them change it."

Grover flicked his ashes into the cuff of his jeans. "You're in the big leagues, now, Nerburn," he said.

We sat back in silence and stared at the old man and the young girl and the worn-out old dog. A few wisps of clouds had moved into the pale high plains sky, and a ribbon of white butterflies fluttered past on the warm morning breeze. Dan and Zi sat side by side on the two plastic lawn chairs facing out toward the hills. They were holding hands. Little Zi was singing.

"Come on," Grover said. "You've seen enough. Let's go inside and cook up some eggs."

"I'll stay here," I said.

He batted me on the shoulder. "Come on," he repeated. "They ain't going anywhere."

I could hardly pull myself away from the scene that was playing out before me. An incredible transformation seemed to have taken place. Zi seemed like the ancient one, and Dan was suddenly full of brightness and life.

Jumbo touched his tongue to his upper lip. The prospect of another breakfast had gotten his attention. "I'll get the groceries from the car," he said. He stood up with an uncharacteristic swiftness and made his way quickly toward the back of Grover's Buick.

"You should see him when we go to the buffet in Rapid," Grover said. "He gets across that parking lot faster than Jim Thorpe."

My eyes were still locked on the old man and the little girl.

They were swinging their hands back and forth like children on a playground.

I turned to Wenonah. "How long has it been this way?" I asked.

"Since the beginning," she said. "From the time Grandpa gave her the feather and the doll. None of us really understands."

"What do her parents think?"

"They don't ask questions. None of us do about things like this. You just trust the spirits. We all just accepted it. But that notebook, well, it changes things."

"How so?"

"Well, it ties things together. I think that's probably why that Mary contacted you. She wanted to help Grandpa. She knew he needed courage."

I was rapidly entering a world that was way beyond my understanding.

"Why? Courage for what?"

"Grandpa's been fighting with the doctors. They think something's wrong with Zi. They think she's got something where her brain doesn't work right. They want to put her on some medications. Grandpa says that this doesn't have anything to do with white-man medicine, that it has to do with the old ways. He doesn't want her to take that medicine. Donnie and Angie listen to Grandpa, but the welfare people say that if they won't give her those pills they could take her away and put her in a home."

"Can they do that?" I said.

Grover snorted. "They're the government. They can do what they want."

He lit another cigarette. "Same as the old days," he said. "If something's too Indian they got to kill it. These drugs, they're like the new boarding school. Knock the Indian right out of you. And if that don't work, they lock you up or ship you off to a white family. Good thing that asylum you were talking about ain't there anymore. They'd have her there in a heartbeat."

The prospect of the little girl being taken from her family shocked me. "So, are Donnie and Angie — are they thinking of doing it?" I asked. "Putting her on meds?"

"Not if Grandpa can help it," Wenonah said. "He has her come to visit him every day. He tells her the old stories and teaches her the old ways. When he sees her he just lights up. And she listens to him like she understands everything he says. I think that little girl is the reason he stays alive. But he's been getting worn down. I can see it. He sleeps all the time. Talks about crossing to the other side. I think he's been about ready to give up. But the words of that old lady in the notebook — they gave him new strength."

She nodded toward the old man. He was doing some little hand game with Zi, who was giggling in response.

"Look at him. I haven't seen him like this in weeks. It gave him faith that the old ways still have power, that it's the ancestors that are talking through little Zi and not some white-man disease. You brought him a message, Nerburn. He lives for messages."

She reached over and touched me on the arm. "You did a good thing."

"Thank you," I said. Wenonah seldom made physical contact. Her small touch was a great and unexpected gift.

I looked out at little Zi in her white dress and bowl haircut, holding the old man's hand and singing.

"This is just so hard for me to understand," I said.

Grover let out a small, derisive snort. "You're not supposed to understand it," he said. "You're supposed to accept it. You're in Indian country now."

He exhaled a long stream of smoke into the bright morning air. "There's a lot going on beneath the skin of creation, Nerburn. You've got to get used to that."

CHAPTER TWENTY-TWO

KICKED OUT OF THE CREATOR'S LIVING ROOM

*T*he day was heating up and the sun had moved past its zenith. I stared out at the burnished hills and the two small figures seated next to each other in the plastic chairs. Festus had flattened himself on the ground between them.

Many times before when I had come to the reservation I felt that I had left my own life behind. But this time I felt completely untethered; it was not merely a cultural shift I was experiencing, but an entire shift in spiritual perspective. Everything had meaning, but none of it was meaning that I could understand.

"Stop worrying about things," Grover said. "Thinking about this ain't going to help you figure it out. Let's go mess up them eggs."

The four of us moved inside out of the growing heat. Jumbo immediately went to the table and sat down in anticipation of another meal. Grover melted a heaping dollop of lard in an old cast-iron frying pan, then broke about a dozen eggs into it and began mixing them up with hamburger. He turned the propane stove on high, filling the house with noxious, acrid smoke.

"A little something I learned while living under the bridge," he said. "It ain't nothing you want to get used to, though."

"No danger of that," I said.

Through the window I could see Dan and Zi sitting and laughing in the merciless sun.

Grover sloshed the egg mixture around until it congealed, then slid a pile of the gelatinous mass onto my plate.

"Just a little," I said.

Grover paid no attention. "White man eats what he wants," he said. "Indian eats what he's got. This is what we got. If it starts coming back up, you just chase it back down with some coffee."

I smiled weakly and lifted a forkful of the concoction toward my mouth.

Jumbo was already plowing his way through a huge helping of the egg mash with a tablespoon. He watched me carefully as I pushed the yellow pool of eggs around my plate. "If you ain't going to eat yours, I could help you finish it," he said.

"Be my guest," I said. "Unless you think we should save some for the old man."

Wenonah looked up from where she was sweeping dust out of the corner of the room. "I'm trying to keep him alive, not kill him," she said.

Grover was wolfing down a heaping portion, pushing it onto his fork with his thumb. "Ketchup helps, Nerburn," he said.

I kept glancing out the window at the two figures sitting in the midday sun.

"You got to get off white man's time," Grover said. "You can't change nothing and you can't hurry nothing. They sometimes stay out there for hours."

"In this heat? It's got to be pushing ninety degrees," I said.

"What's a degree? That's white man's stuff. They're sitting in the Creator's living room. The old man will teach as long as she'll listen."

The sweat was already pouring off me. I couldn't imagine a ninety-year-old man staying out in these temperatures, or a four-year-old girl sitting quietly under the burning sun listening to an old man talk for hours on end.

"So, what's he teaching her?" I asked.

"Don't know. It ain't for me to ask. Probably the old knowledge. When an elder sees someone with the right spirit, he'll start teaching. If they're listening, he'll keep going. If they aren't, he'll shut it down. That little girl, she listens."

Zi had climbed off the plastic chair and was sitting next to Festus, stroking the old dog's ears. Both of them were looking up at the old man.

"You should be happy he's doing this, Nerburn," Grover continued. "Someone needs to save the old knowledge. You white guys are busy taking temperatures and figuring degrees, but you're not listening. Our old ones, they've been listening their whole lives. Their parents were listening before them. And their grandparents before them. They know the original teachings. They hear the earth crying for its life and they want to help. They're trying to pass on what they know before they walk on."

"Yes, but to a little girl?"

He shoved the last lump of eggs and burger onto his fork with his finger.

"People don't learn with their minds, Nerburn. They learn with their hearts. He's teaching her how to see, how to look at the world. How to listen to the voices you people can't even hear.

"Besides, she ain't just a little girl," he said through a mouthful of eggs. "She's got an old spirit. She's open to the old ways."

He nodded toward the two of them sitting in the yard.

"That is, if he can get to her before the doctors put her on them pills and turn her into a white man."

I was fascinated and confused. At first blush, the little girl seemed to be just a child afflicted with some degree of autism. But the uncanny link with the past pushed this into a realm far beyond the square corners of Western medicine.

Grover seemed to be reading my mind. "This is what you white people don't understand, Nerburn. You come out here with your pills and your machines and you think you got things figured out. When something doesn't fit you try to make it fit. It's the things that don't fit that matter. The things that fit, that's the Creator teaching. The things that don't fit, that's the Creator speaking. Little Zi doesn't fit, at least in your world. But she fits in ours. She's the Creator singing.

"I'm telling you, Nerburn, there's cracks in reality where something else comes in. You got to know the right way to open those cracks and you've got to honor them when they happen. That's what the old ways are about. Anyone can learn the lessons. But the old powers, that's something else."

He tapped the edge of his plate with his fork.

"This is science, Nerburn. Indian science. It's about how the world works, and how to be part of that world. But you guys are just too damn full of yourselves to listen."

He pushed himself back from the table and dabbed at his mouth with the edge of the tablecloth.

"You don't ever see your white scientists out here. Anthropologists, yeah. Writers like you. Do-gooders and tourists and spiritual gypsies. But no scientists. Elders like the old man, they've pretty much given up trying to teach you white guys what they know, even though they know the world needs it more than anything right now.

"You call their teachings 'legends' and 'superstitions,' put them in storybooks. You don't see them as knowledge. So they've got to find the young ones, the ones open to the old ways, and try to teach them. And they can't just be open; they've got to be humble. Like Zi."

He pointed to the window with his fork.

"He's opening her spirit. Preparing her. I don't know what he's saying to her, but I can tell you it ain't the kind of Great Spirit talk you white guys are always trying to get."

Wenonah glanced at us from the corner. She had stopped sweeping and was leaning on the end of her broom. Grover reached across and ran his finger around the edge of his plate one last time and lifted the last string of egg into his mouth.

"You white folks think our old ways are a game. The hippie white girls and the ponytail white boys, they listen to some phony medicine man somewhere and say, 'Oh, those Indians are so spiritual. I think I'm gonna go out on a reservation and get me some of that.'

"If they knew what they were messing with, they wouldn't be so quick about asking for it. They're not really looking for spirit power. They're just out cruising the spiritual supermarket. All they want is some spiritual tingle. Real spirit power isn't something you play with. It's something you get trained in, something you respect, something that can do you damage."

Wenonah had moved in closer and was listening intently.

"So, the old man's training her?" I asked.

"Nope, he can't. He can teach her, get her ready, but he can't train her. He has traditional knowledge; he doesn't have the old powers. But he grew up around them. He thinks his sister had them. And he thinks little Zi might have them. That's why he talks to her. He's preparing her, trying to get her ready before he crosses over. He's just trying to fill her up with what he has."

"Then what? When he passes?"

"Teachers show up when we need them. He's just playing his part."

"And you? Can you help? After he's gone?"

Grover let out a derisive laugh.

"I had all that stuff tore out of me as a kid. The board-ing schools did their job. Filled me up with a white man's brain. I never had the old teachers. I probably didn't have it in me anyway."

Wenonah was circling ever closer. It was clear that she was wary about the direction this conversation was taking.

"That's why my grandpa wouldn't teach me," Jumbo said. "He saw it wasn't for me. I had to accept it."

"But you're trying to go back to the old ways," I said, trying to be conciliatory. "Going to the powwows, trying to learn the language."

"That ain't the same. That stuff helps me learn the old ways, but it don't give me spirit power."

"Jumbo's right on," Grover added. "Powwows keep your In-dian heart strong. They're all full of good feeling and meeting old friends. They help you with the culture, help keep traditions alive. But they don't claim any power, not the kind I'm talking about.

"In the old days, the old ones — the ones with real power — they could do things you can't even imagine. They could reach into a person's body and take sickness out. They could talk to the animals. Some of them could lie down at night and go talk to someone hundreds of miles away."

Wenonah had moved over and was standing directly behind us. I could feel her presence like a weight.

"I remember when I was just little," Jumbo said, mopping at his plate with a soft slice of white bread. "There was this little girl out by our house — she had these spells. There was an old woman. I think she might have been my grandpa's cousin. She lived by herself, only talked to the animals. This little girl's dad, he called this old woman. She came over with her pipe, pointed it in all four directions, then up at the sky. I watched her. She made the dad hold the little girl down on his lap and that old woman sucked on the back of her neck. She sucked and sucked until something happened. Then she kind of like vomited and this little ball came out. It was black, all filled with blood. That little girl never had spells again."

Grover shrugged, as if this was common knowledge. "That's what I'm talking about. Normal white people think this is bullshit. They can't handle it. The only ones who believe it are the ones who think they're getting messages from the spirits or were Indians in a past life. And they get it all mixed up with new age bullshit and the phony shamans who sell them snake oil and ceremonies.

"Then pretty soon they get bored and they're off wearing white robes and going to Tibet. Or else they go back to California and start giving lessons or selling sweat lodges, saying they learned from some old medicine man."

He shook his head in disgust.

"It's a good thing, too. If they get in too deep they might never get out again. And it ain't no place you want to be unless you've had long training and got a strong spirit.

"Lots of 'skins, they aren't any better. Like who was that shaman woman's guy? Eagle man? He ain't got anything. He ain't been trained. If he did he wouldn't be selling things that shouldn't be sold. He's just trying to make a buck. And he's playing with fire. The people with real power, they don't say nothing. They don't sell nothing. They just watch and wait. Someday that eagle man's going to wake up and find himself staring right into the face of something he don't want to see."

Wenonah had had enough. "I think it's time for you two to be quiet," she said. "These are not things you should be talking about. And Nerburn, you should just stay away from this." She whisked my plate from the table in front of me and placed it in the sink. "In fact, I think it's time for you to go home."

I looked at her with astonishment. "Go home?" Her abrupt

change in attitude made no sense. A few minutes before she had been touching me on the arm and thanking me for the gift I had bought her grandfather. Now she was telling me it was time to leave.

I glanced over at Grover. His face had gone hard. Jumbo was looking down and pushing the remainder of the eggs around his plate with his spoon.

She spoke quickly to them in Lakota, directing what sounded like angry words toward Grover.

"I don't mean to offend you, Nerburn," she said, turning her attention back to me. "I think you've done a good thing. I'm sure Grandpa is pleased with you and thanks you for your gift. You've given him courage and connected him with knowledge he needed to have. But you've done enough. It's time for you to leave. This is not something you need to be involved in."

I was not sure how to respond. This was as forceful a dismissal as I had ever received. I had driven all this way and had barely gotten to spend any time with Dan. It seemed impolite, even disrespectful, to just get up and leave. I wanted to talk to him, to tell him more of what I had discovered. I still hadn't told him about the asylum or much about the visit to Mary. I hadn't even mentioned Edith and the graveyard. And I wanted to ask his advice about my dream. I needed his help and guidance.

But Wenonah was adamant. She stood motionless at the side of the table with her hands on her hips, staring down at the three of us.

"You mean, like right now?" I said.

"Like right now," she answered coldly. "Grandpa's very weak. When he's done sitting with Zi he'll have a bite to eat, then go back to bed. Sometimes he sleeps all the way until morning. I'll tell him you had to go. He might not even remember that you were here."

Grover seemed as shocked as I was. I knew that he and

Wenonah did not often see eye to eye on what was best for Dan. But even to him, this dismissal was totally unexpected.

"You done okay, Nerburn," he said, trying to soften the blow. It was obvious that he was deferring to Wenonah's judgment in the issue. "You took a weight off his heart."

Jumbo kept his eyes down and his hands folded. "I'll walk out to your car with you, Nerburn," he said. "I think I might have left some stuff in there."

We stood up to leave. It was as awkward a moment as I could remember.

"Okay," I said. "Well, I guess I'll be going now. I'll say goodbye to Dan on the way out."

"You just let him be," Wenonah said. "It was good of you to do this. Just leave the two of them alone." She glared at Grover and ushered me toward the door.

As I was picking up my shoulder bag we heard a heavy clumping on the steps. Through the screen door we could see Dan coming up the stairs, flanked by Zi and Festus.

He pushed his way in and stood in front of us, leaning on his cane and breathing hard. Zi stood beside him, holding his hand.

"I want to see that old man," he said. "That Benais. And I'm bringing Zi with me. I want him to meet her." He shook his gnarled finger in my direction. "And you, Nerburn. You're going to take us."

The silence in the room was almost palpable. We stood for what seemed like a minute until Wenonah stepped forward and spoke.

"No, Grandpa. You're not going anywhere. You're too old and sick. You'd never survive the trip."

Dan looked at her with a steely expression. "You have no say in this, Granddaughter," he said. "I am telling you what I am going to do."

His words had assumed a formality that he used only when speaking of something important. Wenonah stared back at him. I could see her inner turmoil as she struggled with his request. She knew she could not defy an elder, especially her own grandfather.

Finally she composed herself enough to speak. Her words, too, were spoken in a formal manner. "Grandfather," she said, "when Daddy died I promised I would care for you. I have devoted my life to you. And I will always do what you say. But I don't think it's good for you to do this."

Dan reached out his left hand and placed it on Wenonah's shoulder. His voice took on a fatherly tone.

"You're worried about me dying, Granddaugther," he said. "I know that. But death is of no concern to me. All of us must die. I measure my time now in sunrises. Why should I care if I see one more or less? I think there is a reason why the old woman reached out to Nerburn and sent me that notebook and why that old man, Benais, reached out to me. I think that reason is this little *wakanyeja* here." He smiled down at Zi, who looked up at him with huge, round, hopeful eyes.

Grover was standing in the corner staring directly at the old man.

"I think maybe you should talk to Odell," he said.

I leaned over close to Jumbo. "That's your brother, right?"

"Yeah. The one my grandpa trained. He can talk to the spirits."

Wenonah moved closer to Grover. "Yes, Grandfather," she said, as if grabbing on to the one ray of hope that might stop him from making a foolhardy journey. "Grover's right. You should talk to Odell. Ask him if this is a good idea."

Dan looked hard at Grover for a moment, then slowly let his gaze pass across each of us in the room.

"All right. I'll talk to Odell. But unless he says I shouldn't go, I'm going. And you, Nerburn. You are the one who brought me the message, so you are the one who's going to bring me there."

I nodded my agreement.

"We'll go see Odell tonight. Then we'll decide." He turned and shuffled toward the bedroom. "Now, I'm going to take a rest." Without another word he walked into the bedroom and shut the door.

I looked from Grover to Wenonah to Jumbo.

"You should have left while the getting was good, Nerburn," Grover said.

Wenonah was nervously twisting the edge of her sweatshirt. Festus sat motionless, licking some remnants of egg and burger off Jumbo's hand. Little Zi just stood there, staring at all of us with her huge brown eyes, as if she knew a secret nobody else could fathom.

CHAPTER TWENTY-THREE

WATCHER IN THE SHADOWS

*T*he afternoon passed slowly under the relentless Dakota sun. Dan stayed in his room with the door shut. Grover went to town to buy some groceries to bring to Odell as a gift. Wenonah occupied herself with sweeping and cleaning and arranging the inside of Dan's house.

Jumbo and Zi retreated to the dappled shade of the lone spindly tree that stood in the patchy dirt at the edge of the pathway to the road, and sat down in the dust with Festus between them. The three of them seemed to have established some kind of bond. Zi and Jumbo busied themselves with pulling burrs and foxtails from the old dog's fur and stroking his ragged flank. Festus stared up at them with something close to love.

I had nowhere to go and nothing to do, and I wanted to keep my distance from Wenonah, so I stationed myself on the front stoop and observed the goings-on of the giant man and the strange little girl as they petted and picked at the old dog's coat.

Once again, I was struck by the gentleness in Jumbo's manner. He brushed his hand across Festus's flank with the soft attentiveness of a mother caressing an infant. His huge sausage fingers stood in stark contrast to the tiny, probing fingers of Zi, who was seated across from him, undoing tangles in Festus's fur with an almost clinical efficiency.

Though Jumbo's hand moved in slow, calming rhythms and Zi's picking took place in small staccato bursts, there was obviously some wordless communication taking place between the two of them. Jumbo would stroke, then Zi would pick, then they would repeat the gestures in alternating measure.

Sometimes Zi would reach over and position Jumbo's hand in a certain place on Festus's flank. They were like musicians engaged in an intimate duet. Festus, oblivious to the wordless dialogue being played out on his back, thumped his tail and raised clouds of dust into the still noon air.

The heat on the unshaded wooden steps was rapidly becoming unbearable. I looked around for some place to escape. I could not go back in the house; I did not want to confront Wenonah. And sitting in my baking metal car, even with the windows open, would have been even worse than sitting in the unforgiving sun. The only place that offered any relief was the spindly tree at the edge of the yard, and its small patch of shade was already occupied by Festus, Jumbo, and Zi.

I was about to walk over and intrude on their privacy when Zi stood up and walked directly around Festus and sat down on Jumbo's lap. Her movements were stiff and purposeful, much as they had been when she and Dan had walked past us up the steps. Jumbo accepted her with a huge, enveloping presence and began stroking her hair with the same gentleness he had displayed when petting Festus's flank. He looked like nothing so much as a great protective Buddha offering comfort to a small child.

Festus pushed his wounded paw toward Jumbo's lap. Jumbo

took it in his hand and cradled it gently. Zi placed her hand on top of Jumbo's and began petting the wounded paw with tiny purposeful gestures.

They sat this way for a few minutes, engaged in this wordless conversation through the intermediary of the old dog until Zi stood up abruptly and walked to the short wiregrass at the edge of the path. Once again, she reached down and picked up a young rabbit. It appeared to be a tiny cottontail rather than one of the rangy prairie jackrabbits that populated the area.

The little rabbit remained stock-still as the young girl carried it back toward Jumbo with arms extended, as if in offering, and set it down in front of him. The rabbit quivered and shook but did not move, despite its proximity to Festus.

Jumbo reached down and petted it with soft, gentle strokes. After a few moments, Zi removed Jumbo's hand and lifted the rabbit in her own. She moved it close to her face and stared into its dark, liquid eyes before placing it back on the edge of the path, where it quickly disappeared into the brush. Then she returned and repositioned herself on Jumbo's lap and resumed her petting of Festus's flank.

I watched in amazement as the scene unfolded. What I was seeing was so intimate, so private, and so far from my own reality that I dared not intrude on it.

I turned toward the door, deciding that it was better to endure Wenonah's disapproval than to break into the intimate sharing that was taking place between Zi and Jumbo.

As I stood to climb the steps, I noticed a shadowy form peering out through the torn screen door from the darkness of the kitchen. It was Dan, standing quietly, saying nothing.

The sun was going down in a blaze of orange by the time we set out for Odell's. It outlined the distant hills in the color of fire, then slowly spent itself as we proceeded down the lonely reservation highway. By the time we had been on the road for half an hour, the first tiny diamonds of starlight were beginning to pierce the twilight sky.

Only Dan, Grover, and I were in the car. Wenonah had chosen to stay behind with Zi, promising to come later on her own. Jumbo, too, had decided to stay behind so he could be with Festus and Zi.

We drove without speaking. Dan had said nothing as we had gotten him into the backseat, and neither Grover nor I had chosen to intrude on his silence. He sat slumped over, seeming almost asleep.

I sat back and focused on the highway while Grover smoked cigarette after cigarette in the seat beside me. Behind us, Dan's breathing became heavy and rhythmic. Soon he began to snore.

"What's with this visit to Odell?" I asked.

"He's still got some touch with the old ways," Grover said. "People go to him for advice."

"Do you think there's any chance he'll tell Dan not to go?" I asked.

Grover shrugged. "That's what we're going to find out."

Odell's house was about an hour further into the rez backcountry on dusty gravel roads. By the time we drove up the rutted white clay pathway into his yard the world had faded into nightfall. All was now in darkness, save for a thin lambent glow over the backs of the western hills.

Odell's house was one more cheap government rectangle with peeling fiberboard siding and weathered plank steps. It was set back on a piece of dusty earth in the center of a wide field. About ten or twelve cars were parked helter-skelter in the surrounding area. Several outbuildings, including the small hump of a sweat lodge, were scattered across the field.

I could barely make out the shadowy images of figures sitting on cheap lawn chairs and leaning against the cars. Here and there the small orange glow of a cigarette would flare for a moment before settling back into the darkness.

"There's Odell," Grover said, pointing to a hulking man half illuminated in the light cascading through the door from the kitchen. He looked to be about forty, with a long black ponytail and a wisp of a Fu Manchu mustache. He must have been about six feet four; he had the barrel-chested presence of a man who had lived well and hard and had at his core a great physical strength, though his shirtless body had softened and his manner was quiet. He had a large homemade tattoo of the word *Lakota* in old English script arcing across his belly.

He was talking with an aged, arthritic woman in a housedress who was seated on an overstuffed couch that had been dragged into the yard sometime long in the past. White upholstery stuffing stuck out from its arms and seat cushions.

"That's Jumbo's mom," Grover said.

Several dogs lay in the shadows at the old woman's feet. A skinny orange cat walked across the top of the couch, then stepped tentatively onto her shoulder and rubbed his flank against her cheek in an attempt to get some attention.

"Park here. We'll get the old man in," Grover said. Dan had awakened and was sitting up looking around.

"Will Jumbo be here?" I asked. I wanted the security of Jumbo's friendly presence as I entered into this unfamiliar and vaguely uncomfortable environment. Grover shrugged. Dan remained silent.

We helped Dan get his footing and held his arms as we crossed the yard, picking our way among the overturned lawn chairs, plastic toys, and abandoned stuffed animals.

Odell kept his eyes on us as we approached. He stood, backlit in the doorway, commanding the space around him with his powerful frame. As we reached the steps he reached out and took the old man's hand in greeting.

Dan said something in Lakota, then added, "This is Nerburn." Odell nodded to me and extended a soft grip that was more an acknowledgment than a greeting. He kept his chin high and seemed almost indifferent to my presence. I could see why Jumbo had grown up in his shadow, yearning for his approval.

Dan said something to the old woman that made her chuckle. "There's some food inside," she said as the cat wound itself around her shoulders and rubbed against her cheek. "Make sure the new boy gets enough to eat."

It was an oddly solemn setting. I was used to joking and laughter at almost all Indian gatherings, even funerals. But here, despite the number of people lounging around, the yard was almost silent. A few low murmurs rose from the darkness, but the only other sound was the wind in the grasses and the playful growls of a group of dogs tussling in the dust at the rear of the house.

On the far side of the yard someone got up, climbed into a car, and fired it into life. It bumped backward over the rutted clay with its lights off until it got turned around and headed out toward the gravel road. I watched as the small cones of the headlights bounced down the path, turned onto the roadway, and disappeared over the hills into the darkness.

"Come on, Nerburn," Grover said. "Let's go eat. When someone on the rez offers you food, you damn well better accept it."

Dan stayed in the yard talking to Odell in Lakota.

Inside, a young woman with a pockmarked face was seated at a heavily gouged table piled high with magazines, boxes of crackers, and packages of sweet rolls and store-bought cookies. Other people sat quietly on chairs and couches around the room. Almost none of them were talking.

A large aluminum pot of stew was boiling on the stove. The

woman filled a chipped melamine bowl with the brown liquid and handed me a spoon.

"Better eat, Nerburn." Grover said. "And don't go walking outside with your food. When someone makes food under their roof you eat it under their roof."

The stew was gristly and greasy but filled with interesting herbs and spices. It was a welcome meal after a day of nothing more than Grover's egg mash and a few chunks of jerky.

"Why so quiet?" I whispered to Grover.

"They just finished ceremony," he said. "Odell leads a sweat every night."

Outside the cars were leaving, one by one. Through the window on the far side of the kitchen I could see the glowing embers of a dying fire next to the sweat lodge.

Before long, Dan and Odell made their way up the steps and into the room. Dan was chuckling and nodding his head.

"Tell them," he said.

Odell cracked a wide smile. Like Jumbo, he had no front teeth — only incisors, like fangs. "I seen him," Odell said. "That Benais. He's been coming around, checking things out. He told me he wants Grandfather here to come and see him, but he don't want him to come until there's snow on the ground."

"Tell them the rest," Dan said.

Odell grinned even wider. "I been feeling someone out there, so I thought I better see who it was. It was that Benais. So I checked him out, too. He's okay, for a *Shinnob*. He come in a good way. He come humble — as *mastincala*, the gentle one."

I leaned close to Grover so I could speak in a low whisper. "What's *mastincala*?" I asked.

Grover shook his head. "Rabbit," he said. "He's been coming as the rabbit to check us out."

Dan's face had a look of almost beatific peace.

CHAPTER TWENTY-FOUR

Two Worlds inside You

I remained at Odell's for about another hour. Jumbo and Wenonah never showed up, and Dan and Grover went off on their own to visit with friends, leaving me on the periphery of an event, where I felt as alien as I ever had in my life. Finally, Dan told me I could go because he and Grover had a ride home. Gratefully, I got in my car and headed off, bleary-eyed, to an outcropping of badlands a dozen miles away, where I set up my tent cot and prepared to bed down.

It was a brilliant, clear night. The Milky Way, the *Wanagi Tachanku* — what Dan called the "river of stars" — flowed silently across the ink-black sky. It was easy to imagine a soul traveling up to that great trail of the spirits before passing on to some unseen judgment beyond the reach of human comprehension.

Despite my exhaustion, sleep did not come easily. I was troubled and confused. For years I had traveled in Indian country

— the forestlands of the Ojibwe, the mountains and gorges of the Nez Perce, these high plains and badlands of the Lakota. But always before I had been able to carry my own world with me in my memory as a place of refuge when things got too confusing or alien.

But this time something was different. Country that before had always offered contemplative quiet now seemed to teem with voices and presences. Every rabbit that jumped, every bird that flew, felt like it was carrying a message. Winds, directions, even thoughts and dreams all were active forces, each issuing a caution or making a demand. Far from being a place of peace and contemplation, this great rolling unpopulated land had become a world of forces, seen and unseen, commanding constant vigilance and spiritual humility.

"I seen him. I been checking him out." Odell's words echoed in my ears. Dogs. Dreams. Little girls who seemed from another time. Rabbits as messengers. Old women who sucked illnesses out of people's necks.

"It's time for you to leave, Nerburn," Wenonah had said. Now, as the night folded over me and drew me in, her harsh words seemed more like a cautionary note than a dismissal.

I lay with my sleeping bag pulled up around me. In the distance, an owl called. I shuddered, remembering stories of owls as harbingers of death. Nothing was simple; nothing was benign. I wished for all the world to be back in my own home, where the world was a backdrop against which I lived my life, not a presence surrounding me, shaping me, laughing at me, warning me. But the choice was no longer mine: I had walked through a door, and the door had closed behind me.

For the first time in all my years in Indian country, I was truly afraid.

"You're slow today, Nerburn," Dan said as I drove up. "You must be getting old."

I had contemplated heading for home as soon as I had awakened. But I owed it to the old man to give him the time he wanted. Wenonah's comment that you never leave until an elder gives you permission weighed heavily on my mind. Until Dan gave me his blessing to leave, I needed to remain in his presence, respectfully offering him whatever he sought and deferring my own wishes to his.

My fondest hope was that I would drive into his yard, he would gesture me over to his steps and offer me a cup of coffee, and say, "Odell told me what I needed to know. Grover will drive me up to see that Benais when he gets a chance. You just go home to your wife and family." We'd sit together for a while, have a good chat about my dream, the asylum, his little sister, and the goings-on in his life, and I'd be back on the road by noon. But, in my heart of hearts, I knew that things were not going to be that simple.

I found him dressed and sitting on an old van seat in the dust in front of his house. He looked like a different person from the man Grover and Wenonah had lifted gently and cajoled into consciousness the morning before.

I remembered something my dad had said right before he'd passed. "When you don't have anything to live for, you just wait to die." Yesterday Dan had been waiting to die; today he was ready to live.

He had on his usual stained khaki pants and a faded long-sleeved plaid shirt that was torn at the elbows. He still wore his sheepskin-lined moccasins — more bedroom slippers than shoes — and no socks. His long white hair was pulled back and tied in a ponytail. He looked scrubbed and freshly washed.

I assumed Wenonah had come and gone. Even the most astonishing change of attitude could not have given him the power to dress and groom himself and get himself down the steps into the yard.

"Morning, Dan," I said.

"Where's that Festus?" he said. "Ain't nothing like a dog breathing in your face to get you started in the morning."

"He's probably back at Jumbo's," I said.

"Well, it ain't quite a girlfriend, but I guess it's the next best thing." He chortled at his own little joke.

I was too tired for banter. The night had been hard and my sleep fitful. I had been alert to every sound, nervous about every dark shape that flashed by me in the sky. The only saving grace was that once again the dream had not come.

"Sit down, sit down," Dan said, tapping the seat next to him. "What did you think about what Odell said last night?"

I looked out at the clump of grass where little Zi had reached down and picked up the rabbit and handed it to Jumbo.

"It's not my world, Dan," I said. "All I can do is watch and try to honor it as best I can."

"A rabbit," he cackled. "That old man's good. He sends a rabbit. He's got a sense of humor, that Benais." He gestured me closer. "You know what we call them *Shinnobs*?"

I shrugged noncommittally.

"Rabbit chokers," he laughed. "They call us the dog eaters, we call them the rabbit chokers. So he comes as a rabbit. He's sharp. Besides, he knows what the rabbit means — gentle, humble, don't hurt anyone. That was a message to me. I like this guy, Nerburn. I can't wait to go see him."

"That's what I want to talk to you about, Dan," I said. "He said not to come until the snow falls. That's a long time."

"What? You worried about dying before it happens?" He elbowed me in the ribs. He was in the best mood I had seen him since I had arrived on the reservation.

"I was wondering if you'd be okay with having Grover or

Wenonah take you?" I asked tentatively. "If it was okay with them. I could give them directions."

"Nope," he said. "You're taking me."

The answer was deflating but not surprising. "I kind of figured as much," I said. "But if it's all the same to you, I'd rather go sooner than later. I've got kind of a busy fall."

"Nope. He said to come when the snow falls, so we'll go when the snow falls."

My exhaustion had given me a short temper. "A rabbit said you should come when the snow falls," I said. "So we have to wait until then?"

As soon as I said it I wished I could take the words back. It was precisely the kind of disrespect that Wenonah had warned me about. But Dan seemed not to take offense. He cocked his head and looked at me sideways, as if trying to assess my seriousness.

"You don't believe Odell?" he said.

"I don't know Odell. I don't believe him or not believe him."

"Well, I believe him." He smiled slyly and punched me in the shoulder. "And rabbits ain't liars."

He pushed himself upright and hobbled to the corner of the house, where he unzipped his pants and urinated on the ground.

"There," he said, pulling up his zipper, "Now that the tank's empty, I'm ready to go. Let's swing out to Jumbo's. I want to see that Festus. I took kind of a shine to him. Besides, we ain't had time to talk. I got some things to say to you."

"Okay," I said. It just prolonged the visit, but at least we would get to spend a little private time together.

He hitched his way to the car, not even waiting for my assistance, and settled into the front seat. "One thing I got to say for you, Nerburn," he said. "You always got nice cars. No bungee cords. No duct tape. Real high-class. It'll be good to ride in this up to that Benais."

We drove down the empty highway toward Jumbo's, with

Dan chirping like a bird. He was full of stories and jokes and odd reminiscences. The dark presentiments that had haunted me the night before were gradually lifting with the morning haze.

"You don't believe that rabbit, do you?" Dan said.

"I don't normally take their advice on issues," I responded.

"I wouldn't expect you to," he said. "Your people never listen to the animals. You didn't take the advice of a snake in that Garden of Eden place in your Black Book, and look where it got you. You've been wandering around trying to make it up to the Creator ever since."

He chortled happily at his joke. "How many times I told you that you need to listen to all the voices?" He put his hands up to the side of his head and wiggled them like antennae picking up signals. "You got to open up your ears."

I smiled my acknowledgment but said nothing.

We rode quietly for a few miles. Out of the corner of my eye I could see him flexing his hands nervously. It was obvious that he had something on his mind.

"Nerburn," he said at last. "I got to talk to you more serious." His entire mood had changed. His voice was softer and his tone more subdued.

"Good, Dan," I said. "I was hoping for that."

"It's about that little girl. The one who come out to visit me yesterday. You know who she was?"

"Yes. Little Zintkala Zi. Donnie's and Angie's girl. You gave her the doll that had belonged to your sister last time I was out here."

Dan nodded. "That's right. Did you get a good look at her?"

"Yes. It was kind of a shock. She looked just like the pictures of your little sister."

"And did you see how she acted?"

"Yes."

Dan put his hand on my knee. "The Creator sent her to me.

Here I am getting ready to cross over, and the Creator sends me something like that. When I look in that little girl's eyes I see my little sister. She's the most important thing in the world to me."

"I can see that. And it looks like you're the most important thing in the world to her."

"But I'm worried for her. Really worried. They've got her surrounded — the docs, the social workers, the whole white world. They're after her. They think she's got a disease in her head."

He wrung his hands together and chewed his lower lip.

"I can't let them get her. This stuff about rabbits and spirits, I joke about it, but it ain't a joke. I can't explain it in your language. But there's powers out there. She understands them. They talk to her. You saw the way she lifted that rabbit. That's no disease. She has the old knowledge."

He reached across and grabbed me by the forearm. "I want you to listen to me. I know you don't want to be here. I can feel your spirit leaning away."

"You're right," I said. "This stuff scares me."

"It should scare you. But I need you to help me. I was afraid you weren't even going to come back this morning."

"I almost didn't. Wenonah wanted me to leave yesterday. She was pushing me out the door when you came up the steps with Festus and little Zi."

"That's because this stuff scares Wenonah, too. She doesn't like white people messing with it. That's why she wanted you gone. But there's good scared and there's bad scared, and you got good scared. Good scared is just respect turned inside out. You got respect, even though you joke like you don't."

"I try, Dan," I said.

"I know you do. That's why I talk to you. You stay humble, not thinking your white-man knowledge is better than our Indian knowledge."

He gripped my arm harder. "I got to get to this Benais. I knew when I first saw that little girl — when she was just a baby, doing all that fussing — that she had a troubled spirit. I knew she still had some unfinished business on the other side. That's why she cried all the time. I could see it in her eyes.

"Then when she got older I saw what that unfinished business was. She had to go get my little sister. She's bringing my little sister back to me. I can't let the white people take her away again."

His eyes were starting to moisten. He had never opened up to me like this before. "That notebook. It was a good thing you brought that to me. I needed it bad. It made my spirit strong, and my spirit's been getting weak.

"Your people, your schools, your language, they've been making me lose strength for the old ways. They're taking over the world, and the Creator's not stopping it and it's made me think that maybe they're right and I'm wrong. I hardly even dream in Lakota anymore."

He kept his eyes away from me, as if he couldn't bring himself to admit that he was saying these things to a white man.

"It hurts my heart when I feel myself becoming weak to the old ways. It dishonors the ancestors. But I get so tired. All us Indian people get tired. Your people are like a big bully come into our house knocking us down, over and over. Every time we stand up you knock us down again. You kill our language, you kill our traditional ways. You make fun of us in your movies and disrespect us with your sports teams. You put us in jail for practicing our ceremonies. You keep beating us down until we can't remember who we were and we don't know who we are and all we have is what you tell us we're supposed to be."

He took a deep breath. His exhalation was shaky, as if he were about to cry.

"What hurts me is that it was our open hearts that let this happen."

"How do you mean, Dan?" I said. I did not want to interrupt, but I wanted to understand.

He shook his head, as if responding to some inner struggle. "This is hard for me," he said. "I'm not used to saying this stuff to white people."

"I'm listening," I said. "It's a gift for me to hear these things."

He collected himself and continued. "You see, it's all about power. Not strength like you guys got, where you can beat up everybody else. I'm talking about real power — being in touch with the Creator. You understand me?"

"I think so."

His breathing was shallow. "Good. You've got to let me talk. I've got to get this out."

"See, we Indian people have always believed that the Creator gave power to those who followed his ways. You could tell if someone was favored by the Creator by what kind of power they had.

"In the old days, our people had lots of kinds of power. There was the power to heal, the power to know the future. Some people had power to understand the animals and the plants. Some had special power in battle. I know you don't believe this, and we have mostly lost those things, but in the old days, those powers were there. And we respected the people who had them.

"When your people came you brought a different kind of power. You had medicines that could heal sicknesses we didn't understand, you had guns that could kill with more strength than our bows and arrows, you had tubes that you could look through that would make far things look close. You had all kinds of power our people had never seen. We were amazed and we were humbled.

"When we asked you where it came from, you said the Creator gave it to you because you followed the way of the Black Book. We thought the Creator must favor you and your ways. So we started to open our hearts more to the Black Book's ways.

"At first it was easy. We knew the Creator hadn't given all his truth to one people, and much of what your Black Book taught made sense to us. We had known for a long time that there were men with great power among the tribes to the west of us who would fall to the ground and go into a death sleep for three days. They had no heartbeat; they got cold like stone.

"We know a dead person when we see one. These men were dead. But they came back to life after three days. And they brought messages from the spirit world. They had been to the other side.

"When the Black Robes came and talked about that Jesus being dead for three days, then coming back, we understood. It wasn't like it made our way false; it made our way stronger. It told us that the Creator was bringing the same truths to different people in different ways.

"Even the cross we understood, about Jesus being nailed to a tree and suffering for his people. We had our sundance where men were lashed to the sacred *Wagichun Wagi* — what you call the cottonwood tree — and suffered without food or water for the good of the people. When we heard about Jesus letting the men take him and nail him to that tree just like our sundancers let their skin be pierced with eagle bones, we thought, 'That man has a strong spirit for his people, just like our sundancers have strong spirits for the people.'

"We thought that maybe this Jesus got his power because the Creator looked down on him and said, 'Look at how strong that man's heart is for his people,' and he filled him up with spirit power.

"There were so many things like that. We were excited. We saw that our ways fit together with yours. We thought we could share the knowledge the Creator had given us in our ceremonies and teachings with the knowledge he had given you in your Black Book. We thought that together we could know more about the Creator's ways.

"But when we tried to tell you about our knowledge, you said that our way was wrong. You said that our way was not the same as the way of the Black Book, but that it came from a dark spirit. You said that the Creator only gave his knowledge to you. You told us that if we wanted that knowledge we had to turn our back on the old ways — the ways our ancestors had taught us — and only follow the way of the Black Book.

"We did not think the Creator was so stingy that he would only share his power with one people. But we respected your powers, so we listened. And when we listened, you set us on a path away from our old ways.

"It did not take many lifetimes to lose touch with those ways. You took away our language, and our connection with the plants and animals lives in our language. You moved us from our land, and we met the Creator in the land. Our way of thinking changed and we lost touch with the old power. Maybe we forgot, and it is still there. I only know that it's now only a ghost living inside me. It is like the echo of a sound I can no longer remember."

His hand was shaking badly and I thought he would be unable to continue. I started to say something to reassure him, but he motioned me to be quiet.

"Then along comes this little Zi," he continued. "She talks to the animals. She hears the voices in the land. She is like the old ones. It is like the Creator has given her a gift of knowledge and given me the gift of seeing her so that I will remember that knowledge. He knows that my heart was taken out of me when my little sister was stolen, so he sends that gift with the voice of my little sister. Can you understand this, Nerburn? Can you understand it at all?"

"I try, Dan. I really do."

"That's all I want," he said. "I want you to try. It's important." There was urgency in his voice.

"When little Zi began to grow," he continued, "and I could

see my sister in her eyes, it made my spirit leap. I was filled with the joy of the Creator. But then the doctors and the social workers came. They did tests. They took Zi to a hospital and put her in machines and put wires on her head. They said they had seen this before and they knew what was wrong with her and they knew what to do. They wanted to give her white-man medicine. They said her parents had to do what they said or they would take her away."

"Can they really do that?"

"We're Indians. They can do what they want."

"What did they say when you told them about the dress and the way she looked?"

"Why tell them those things? They'd just say it was old Indian superstitions.

"Her parents are young. They are afraid of the doctors. They don't know the old ways and they don't trust the new ways. I told them I had seen this, too. I told them not to listen, because the old ways were alive in their daughter, that their little girl had the old power, that their little daughter had a gift. I told them to let me teach her and not to give her white man's medicine.

"They listened to me, but they were scared. They're still scared. Now they bring her to see me. They let me teach her. But I don't have much time.

"Sometimes I lie in my bed and ask the Creator if I'm doing the right thing. Wouldn't that little girl be happier if I just let them take the Indian out of her? Give her the white-man medicines? She could have friends. She could live in the white-man way. She's so alone. And her parents are so scared.

"I was getting ready to give up. I was getting ready to give up for me. I was getting ready to give up for her. Then you come with that notebook and tell me about the old man who knew my little sister calling out to me. It gave me strength. I knew that the old voices were still speaking, that they wanted to be heard. I knew that they would give that child strength, too.

"This man — this Benais — will see the old ways in little Zi's eyes. He will see my little sister's spirit in her face. He can show her mother and father that there is nothing wrong with her, that what she has is good, not a sickness.

"I need to see him see her. I need it for her, so she knows she's not alone and that the ancestors are with her. I need it for her mom and dad so they can have courage and know that their daughter has a gift and not a disease. And I need it for me so..." he paused and breathed in deeply. "So I know I'm not just an old man holding on to something that's gone."

"No one thinks that, Dan," I said.

He turned his face from me.

"You're a good man, Nerburn, and you mean well," he said. "But you don't know what it's like to live with two worlds inside you."

CHAPTER TWENTY-FIVE

THE TREMENDOUS TONTO

I could feel Dan moving into a dark place. The lighthearted jaunt to visit Jumbo and Festus was becoming a journey into painful memories.

"You sure you want to talk about this, Dan?" I said.

But he wasn't listening. He sat silently, staring off into the hills.

As we approached the turn toward Grover's house, Dan flapped his hand distractedly.

"Go get him," he said.

I was relieved at the request. Though I had wanted time alone with Dan, we were moving into waters too deep for me to navigate alone. Grover would know far better than I how to deal with the old man's darkness.

It had been years since I had last visited Grover's house. I remembered it as an oasis of order and cleanliness in the midst of the general squalor of the reservation. But even my memory left me unprepared for the fastidiousness I encountered as we turned off the asphalt and drove up the hill to his home.

The pathway was smooth and raked; you could see where he had filled in the holes and fissures in the clay with gravel. The sides were marked with equally spaced white painted stones that led up to a parking slab where his old green Buick sat, perfectly centered, on a well-swept square of concrete. His trailer was as white and pristine as the stones, as if his little homestead had somehow found a way to defy the endless dust and wind and heat of the reservation sun. A huge satellite dish aimed up at the sky, and an American flag flapped on a pole above his house.

Grover was standing out front in jeans and cowboy boots and a preternaturally white T-shirt, holding a green garden hose that snaked out the front door from some faucet inside. He was dribbling a low stream of brackish water onto a bed of irises that were growing inside a frame made of railroad ties.

The splash of bright purple was a shock amid the relentless browns and tans and prairie greens of the reservation palette. It was obvious that Grover had imported these flowers to give color to the setting, and he tended them with care. He gave me a little salute as I drove up.

Though I wanted to blurt out my concerns about Dan's mood, I decided it was best to keep the tone light until he had a chance to look at Dan for himself.

"If you were a white man you'd have dug a canal from the Missouri to irrigate those things," I said as I stepped from the car.

He held up the hose and let the brown, foul-smelling water flow down over his hand. "If I was a white man I'd bottle this stuff and sell it as 'Indian ceremonial water.' I could get that eagle man to bless it. He probably needs the work now that he lost the shaman lady's account."

He handed me the hose and went back in the trailer to shut off the spigot. He emerged, drying his hands on a clean striped towel. "I thought you'd have hightailed it out of here by now. I figured that Odell and his rabbit scared hell out of you."

"Well, in fact, they did. But the old man wanted to go for a ride." I nodded toward the car where Dan sat motionless in the shadows. "He thought we should pick you up."

Grover looked over at the old man. "He must really like you, Nerburn," he said. "Ain't no one can get him to go anywhere these days."

"It's not me. He wants to see Festus."

Grover let out a sharp, brittle laugh. "I should have known," he said. "A dog. He'll hardly get out of bed to see his own kin, but he'll get up and go for a ride to see a dog."

He coiled up the hose into a perfect circle and hung it on a hook on the side of the trailer.

"How's he doing?" he asked.

"I don't like it. He's moved into a pretty dark place. He's talking about Zi and the old ways and everything that's been lost."

Grover nodded knowingly.

"That's what happens. You can't scratch the surface. There's too much pain underneath. It'll be good for him to see that dog, if it ain't keeled over yet. It looked pretty worn-out when I saw it. Where is it, anyway?"

"Jumbo's."

"Ah, good," he said. "I got something for Jumbo. Just a minute."

He went into the trailer and emerged a few moments later with a brown paper bag whose bottom was saturated with grease.

"Doris makes them at her house," Grover said, holding it out to me. "I picked one up last night on the way home. Figured it would feed me for a week. Like shooting an elk in the old days. It'll make a good snack for Jumbo."

I opened the paper bag and unwrapped a tinfoil-covered object about the size of a cantaloupe. Inside was an Indian taco made from a huge chunk of fry bread stuffed with hamburger, grated cheese, tomatoes, taco sauce, and a green substance that dripped down the sides and formed a pool in the bottom of the bag.

"A Tremendous Tonto. It's her own recipe. The green chili really fires it up. Jumbo loves them. Just stay upwind."

He repacked the Tremendous Tonto and wiped his hands on the bandana in his pocket. "Now, let's get that old man to that old dog."

We walked over to the car where Dan was still sitting morosely, lost in his thoughts.

"Leave him to me," Grover said.

"Hau, old man," he said, sliding into the rear seat.

Dan reached his hand over the seat back for Grover to shake. Grover took his fingers and held them in a gesture of friendship. "I thought the only thing that would get you out would be a new girlfriend, and Nerburn sure ain't it."

"Nerburn's taking me to Jumbo's," Dan said curtly. "Then when it snows we're going to that Benais." His tone was humorless and businesslike.

Grover pointed to the sky. "Well, it ain't going to be this afternoon," he said. "High of about 100 white-man degrees, I'd guess."

"I got time."

"You couldn't tell by me."

Dan tightened his jaw. "Benais said to come when the snow falls. That means he knows I'll be around then."

"Yeah, but Nerburn might not. Drinking all that capistrino and expresso could burn a hole right through him."

The comment brought a slight chuckle from Dan.

"You should teach him how to make reservation brew," Grover continued. "Comes out just about the way it goes in. Doesn't stick around long enough to do any damage." He laughed heartily at his joke and punched Dan on the shoulder.

Dan grunted noncomittally, but I could see a faint smile pass across his face.

"Come on, Nerburn," Grover said. "Let's get going. Even if you make it, that old Festus might not. Hell, Jumbo might even have rolled over on him in the middle of the night."

Dan snorted and shook his head. He tried to suppress a chuckle but couldn't.

I marveled at the deft way Grover had lifted Dan's spirits.

"Hi-yo, Silver," I said, and set off down the road toward Jumbo's. The hills were burnished in gold and the morning sky was a bright robin's-egg blue. It was shaping up to be a warm, beautiful autumn day.

I was looking forward to seeing Jumbo. No small part of this was because, despite Grover's efforts at levity, I was still bothered by Dan's anguished confession and the disconcerting events of the previous evening. Jumbo's garage seemed like a sanctuary of ordinariness and kindness amid the brooding darkness of events I could not understand.

"It will be good to see Jumbo," I said.

"Well, I'm glad you're starting to understand," Grover said. "Inside that sloppy body is a real Lakota man. He's humble. He speaks from the heart and always tells the truth.

"He has *waunsila* — compassion toward everything. He never turns to anger when people treat him wrong. He gives thanks to the Creator for everything he has.

"People are always making fun of him. But he never takes it hard, never fires back. All his life, all he's cared about is helping other people. Fixing bikes for kids, fixing cars for folks on the rez. If someone's got something broke, he fixes it. Never asks for anything more than what someone can pay. He doesn't even know it, but he lives in the old way. He's the best that we got."

Grover spit a wicked stream of saliva out the window. "He isn't all full of poison like me and half the other people on the rez. I wish I had half the strength he does."

Dan reached his hand over his shoulder as if in offering to Grover. Grover took it, like a child accepting the welcoming hand of an adult. "You do okay," Dan said. "We all have our gifts. Yours just have a sharp edge"

Grover spat out the window again. "I just wish more people saw Jumbo for what he was."

Though I said nothing, Grover's words cut deep. I felt ashamed for how long it had taken me to get past Jumbo's appearance and see the real heart of the man.

We wheeled around the corner and headed toward the decrepit shop at the end of the road. Even at a distance we could see Jumbo looming in front of it like a small mountain amid the car parts and barrels. He was surrounded by a gaggle of young boys who were leaning in like hospital interns as he hunched over a bicycle with a socket wrench in one hand and some other large greasy tool in the other. He performed some act of adjustment with the socket wrench, spun the rear wheel, and flipped the bike upright, all in one gesture. The boys let out a cheer.

One of the boys jumped on the bike and rode it in a circle, doing wheelies as he navigated the junk-strewn lot. The other boys chased after him, laughing.

"Where's that Festus?" Dan said.

Grover pointed to the far end of the lot, where a lone figure stood silently. It was little Zi in her white dress and black shoes. No one was paying any attention to her, and she was paying no attention to them. Festus was standing next to her with his head against her hip.

"What's Zi doing here?" I asked.

"Wenonah brought her over. She called Zi's mom and dad and told them we'd be coming by," Dan said. "They make sure I see her every day. She's just waiting."

Zi was standing with her hands at her side and her head facing slightly downward. For the first time I noticed that she was slightly pigeon-toed.

Jumbo wiped his hands on his pants and walked over to her as the boys ran off toward town. She held her arms out, and he lifted her up and put her on his shoulder, like some huge St. Christopher carrying the Christ child across a river. Festus paraded next to them with his head held high, as if proud of his association with two such important personages.

I tapped my horn and pulled into the lot. Jumbo saw us and broke into a grin. He walked over and bent down to the window, keeping Zi on his shoulder. He stuck his still-oily hand in the window and shook our hands one at a time.

It was the first time I had been able to get a close-up look at little Zi. Because of her somber manner I had not realized how cute she was. She had the face of a little elf and a way of pulling her chin to her chest that made her seem almost coquettish. Her hair had the fresh sheen of a raven's wing. But it was her huge, brown eyes that fascinated me. At a distance they had looked disengaged and indifferent, but up close they were dark, liquid pools that seemed to exude knowledge without giving out an ounce of light. She was like a wild animal, watching without revealing. It was one of the most unnerving looks I had ever seen in a child.

Dan pushed open the door and stepped out of the car without waiting for assistance. As Jumbo set Zi on the ground, she ran around to the old man and wrapped her arms around his leg. He stroked her hair and spoke softly to her in Lakota. She nodded, then took his hand, and together they walked across the dusty lot and sat down on an old tractor tire that was lying next to the door of Jumbo's shop.

Festus, who had been following close behind, wagged up to Dan and put his nose in the old man's lap. Dan took the dog's head in his hands and pressed Festus's forehead to his. Festus's wagging increased in intensity and he lifted his injured paw, still wrapped in a sock and duct-taped to his leg, for Dan to shake. With one arm around Zi, who had snuggled up against him, and the other holding the old dog's paw, Dan looked toward us and grinned. "If *Tunkashila* wanted to take me now, that would be fine," he said. "It don't get no better than this."

"I don't think he wants you yet," Grover said. "You've got to baste a little more."

Zi kept staring in my direction. At first I thought it was my imagination, but after a few minutes there was no mistaking her gaze for anything other than what it was: she was measuring me — though I had no idea for what — just as that buffalo bull had measured me on the hillside at Benais's home. She whispered something to Dan, then stood up and pulled several weeds from a patch near the tire. She walked purposefully in my direction and held them out to me in a stiff, formal gesture. She kept her eyes locked on mine.

"Why, thank you, Zi," I said as I accepted the strange bouquet. She measured me for another moment with that liquid, unreadable stare, then turned and walked back to Dan without saying a word. Festus, who had followed behind her, looked back at me with brown, doleful eyes, almost as if in apology. He seemed more human than she did.

"Well, the old man always said you were good to dogs and children," Grover said. "She must have decided you were okay."

Little Zi was staring at me again. I could make no sense of it. I was used to reading people's eyes and shades of expression for clues as to what was going on in their hearts and minds. But Zi's expression offered nothing. It was like a dark void that took everything in but sent nothing out. I felt as if I was being watched by some ancient presence rather than by a four-year-old child.

"Do you see the way she's looking at me?" I said.

"Get used to it," Grover answered. "That's how it is with the ones who have old spirits."

He swung himself out of the car and arched his back with his hands on his hips. "I should bring Jumbo his Tremendous Tonto," he said. "They get pretty gamey in this heat."

In the distance we could make out the faint rumble of an approaching vehicle. It had the deep-throated sound of a large truck or car with a faulty muffler.

"Donnie," Grover said, as the white four-door, four-wheel-drive pickup rolled around the corner. The truck drove to the center of the lot, lifting dust as it stopped. The driver's door opened, and Donnie, little Zi's father, stepped out.

He looked much the same as I remembered him. He had high cheekbones and narrow eyes — almost Asiatic — with a long black ponytail down the middle of his back and a quiet calm that you could sense even at a distance. He had filled out some, from a slender boy just moving into adulthood to a powerful, broad-shouldered young man, but he still had the air of humility and self-containment that had attracted me to him originally.

He walked around to the passenger door and opened it for Angie, his wife, who took his hand and stepped carefully onto the ground.

Angie, too, had changed. When I had last met her, my over-riding impression had been of a very young woman overwhelmed by the responsibilities of motherhood. Though she had hardly spoken, she had seemed wide-eyed and almost frantic. Now her round, youthful face had a look of inner satisfaction and peace. She was pregnant again, and she carried herself with the gentle delicacy of someone comfortable with the child inside her and protective of its health and well-being. She smiled at Donnie as she took his hand.

It was good to see the two of them together and looking happy. I recalled how Dan had admonished Donnie to stay with the mother of his child and to be a good father. Clearly, he had taken Dan's words to heart. His manner with Angie was both solicitous and caring.

"Did he ever get to the art school in Santa Fe?" I asked Grover. Donnie's fondest dream had been to attend the Institute of American Indian Arts in Santa Fe to study sculpture. I remembered vividly his struggles to create a memorial carving to his grandmother and his poignant comment about how he wanted to create art to help his people.

Grover tamped a cigarette on the back of his hand. "He gave it a try. But he didn't last. He couldn't afford to bring his family there, and they needed him at home. His old man had a stroke and there wasn't anyone to do the heavy lifting. So he came back."

He lit the cigarette and blew a long stream of smoke into the air.

"That's just the way it is around here. Most 'skins never make it off the rez. The family's got no money, so they've got to pool what they have. Life is hard and the strength of the young ones is needed. Some leave, but they usually come back. Donnie's just another one who got pulled back."

I was saddened to hear that this young man with so much promise had given up on his dream. "That's too bad. He had a lot of talent," I said.

"Still does," Grover continued. "And then there was Zi. He couldn't take her away from the family. She needed the grandmas, and the grandmas needed her."

"And the old man, too," I said, nodding toward Dan.

"And the old man, too."

"The joyful burden of family," I said.

"It ain't always joyful, but it's always family," Grover answered. "That's our way. Family, tribe, it's always been like that, always will be. But it ain't all bad. He got talking to some of the elders. They told him he should be careful about that art school. They said that it wasn't good to make things just to make them beautiful. They told him he was messing with power, that when you made an image of something it called the spirit world to pay attention. That got him thinking."

I was reminded of a story I had heard from a Nez Perce woman about how they beaded the backs of their cradle boards in blue because it was the color of the sky — "the color of forever," they called it — and placing the baby's head against it would call down the spirits to give the baby a long life. I mentioned it to Grover.

"It's kind of like that," he said. "But it's deeper."

He waved his hand across the horizon.

"This world here is just the spirit world taking form. When you make an image of something, you are asking the spirit world to come into that form. You're making a home for spirit power. That's no game. The elders told Donnie that if he really wanted to be a Creator for the people, he needed a lot more training." He tapped himself on the heart. "Here."

Donnie and Angie had walked over to the tire where Jumbo and Dan and Zi were sitting. Zi immediately stood up and took her father and mother by the hands, as if she had been waiting for them. Without saying a word, she led them toward Grover and me.

I was looking forward to talking with Donnie and Angie again but curious as to why little Zi was bringing them to us. Once again, she had her eyes locked on mine. She led her parents directly over to where we were leaning against the front fender of my car.

"Nerburn," Donnie said softly. He reached his hand out in greeting, keeping his eyes down.

"Donnie. Angie," I responded, shaking each of their hands in turn. "How's it going?"

Donnie had always been terse in his expression, and I expected nothing different. Angie, for her part, had hardly spoken at all in the short time I had spent with her. I picked up the conversation without waiting for a reply.

"Still carving?"

Donnie nodded. I could see he was uncomfortable.

Zi was tugging at her father's sleeve. He tried to ignore her, but she persisted. Finally, she reached her hand into the pouch on his black sweatshirt and pulled out a stone object about the size of a fist. Donnie looked down, almost embarrassed. Zi held it toward me. It was a carving of a buffalo.

I took it in my hands and smiled approvingly. "Yours?" I said.

Donnie nodded.

He had obviously improved his technique. The figure was round and full. He had established the shape before adding details, like the horns and hooves. In fact, the original shape of the stone dominated the image. It was almost as if he had found a stone that had the inherent shape of a buffalo and then had merely carved indentations to indicate the legs and horns and head. It was as much stone as it was image.

It reminded me of a large totem rock I had seen years ago in a roadside enclosure alongside Highway 2 in northern Montana. There, some ancient carver had seen the inchoate form of a buffalo in a large boulder and had chipped away the excess until the rough form of a head, a spine, and ribs had emerged. It evoked rather than described, and in a subtle, almost subconscious way, drew the viewer into an imaginative relationship with the form. Donnie's small carving of the buffalo did the same.

"It's really good," I said.

"I'm not working the same way anymore," Donnie answered, almost apologetically.

"I know. Grover told me." Grover was behind me, leaning against the car and staying out of the conversation. Over Donnie's shoulder I could see Dan and Jumbo sitting on the tire with Festus between them. Jumbo was eating something from his orange plastic mixing bowl. Festus was staring longingly at the bowl's contents.

"One of the elders is teaching me," Donnie continued. "He used to make pipes when he was young. He said I'm making homes for the spirits. He said I should wait for the image to come to me, then make what the spirits show me."

"Makes sense," I said. It was a different way of looking at art from the way I had been taught but very much in the indigenous tradition.

"He has me fasting," Donnie said. "He tells me to wait for a vision. He says I have to learn to open to the spirit world. He's teaching me how to prepare."

I was pleased to hear him refer to a teacher. It meant he was learning in the traditional fashion, at the feet of a master, though it appeared that his teacher was more focused on his spiritual development than his artistic development.

"The old ones never went to art school," he continued. "They listened to what the spirits told them. I'm not making things to sell. I'm making them to honor the Creator."

"That's why we're on earth," I said.

Donnie nodded his agreement.

This was the most expansive he had ever been with me, and I wanted to keep him talking. I looked down at the small buffalo carving in my hands. "Do you look for the stone first, or wait for the vision, then go out and find the stone?" I asked. It sounded academic as I said it, but I knew it was a question he would understand.

"My teacher has me prepare by fasting and doing sweats. Then he sends me out. He tells me to wait until a stone calls to me. He says I will know. He says the stones are the oldest. They have the oldest knowledge. Sometimes I bring Zi with me. She helps me choose."

Zi was looking intently at the carving in my hand.

"And this *tatanka*?" I said, using the Lakota word for buffalo, "did the image come to you while you were fasting?"

"No, this one was right in the stone. I saw it right away. It was like it had been lying there waiting for me. I just had to let it out."

"Where did you find it?" I asked. "Is there a special place you look for stones?"

I didn't mean to pry, but I could see that Donnie was hungry to talk. I guessed that not too many people asked him about his work.

"I found it on the mesa over there," he said, pointing to a large, flat-topped landform in the distance. "It was lying with the round ones that look at the sky."

I knew the Lakota stories about how the large improbably round rocks on the tops of table mesas were believed to have taken their form from looking at the shapes of the sun and moon.

"My teacher told me to go up there. He said that's where the stones speak the loudest. He said not to take any stones that were still partly in the ground, because they hadn't decided to come into our world yet." He pointed to the stone in my hands. "Zi saw this one. It was right where we were walking."

Zi had been listening closely. At the mention of her name, she pulled urgently on Donnie's sleeve until he bent over and put his head next to hers. She cupped her hand around her mouth and whispered something in his ear. He nodded and turned back to me.

"She says she didn't see it. It called out to her."

She pulled on his sleeve again. Again, he bent his head down to listen to her.

"She said it was singing."

This was a chance. Wenonah had said Zi would often sing but seldom speak to others.

"Can she sing what it was singing?"

Donnie looked down at her, waiting for her response.

She reached up and grabbed the carving from my hand, then began singing a strange, melodic tune. It was a song without words, almost more like a prayer or a chant. Her voice, though childlike, was strong and clear, as if it had been trained. Its tiny power made me shiver. Dan and Jumbo looked up, and Festus became suddenly alert.

The song continued, with little Zi shifting the buffalo image in her hands as she sang. The tune rose and fell as her hands moved over the grooves and hollows in the form. It was as if she was singing the buffalo into existence.

Then, abruptly, she stopped and turned back toward Dan and Jumbo and Festus. She carried the stone out in front of her, as if it were an object of veneration.

The rest of us looked at one another. Angie kept her face down and Donnie laughed nervously. Finally, Grover stood up straight, stretched his shoulders, and yawned.

"Well, no sense just standing around," he said. "I got some stuff to do." He reached through the car window and brought out the greasy bag containing the Tremendous Tonto. "Need to get this to Jumbo. Don't want his earth suit to get too loose."

CHAPTER TWENTY-SIX

Indian Science
and the Little Fellows

*W*e watched little Zi as she crossed the lot toward the two men and the dog. Jumbo and Dan moved apart slightly so she could take her place between them. Grover casually ambled his way over and dropped the bag with the Tremendous Tonto in the mixing bowl. Jumbo looked up, grinned, then dug into the bag like a child on Halloween. Festus's nose was close behind.

Donnie and Angie and I stood side by side, pretending to focus on the goings-on at the tire. But our silence was uncomfortable; we all knew that something — almost too much — had been revealed.

"I'm making it for her," Donnie said, nodding toward little Zi, who was holding the buffalo carving out in front of her. "But she doesn't know it."

"Oh, I think she knows," I said. "After all, it sang to her."

Donnie smiled slightly, unsure if I was being serious or just being patronizing.

Angie was fidgeting nervously. Never one to make her presence felt, she had always remained far in the background, letting Donnie do the talking. But now she was shifting slightly from one foot to the other as if she had something to say.

"It's good to see you, Angie," I said clumsily, trying to draw her into conversation.

She kept her glance averted; she would not look me in the eyes.

"Zi's a beautiful child," I said.

Still, she would say nothing. She remained silent for almost a minute. Finally, she spoke. Her voice was so quiet I could hardly make out her words.

"Mr. Nerburn," she said. "Wenonah told me that Grandpa Dan wants to take my daughter to see an Ojibwe man you met. She said he thinks he will understand her."

I wasn't sure if this was a question or a statement. But I wanted to put her mind at ease as best I could.

"Yes," I said. "He's a good man. Very powerful. He knew Grandpa Dan's little sister. It would be good for Zi to meet him."

She paused a long time before speaking again. When she spoke, her words were halting and tentative.

"Mr. Nerburn? You know white medicine. Do you think something is wrong with my daughter?"

"I don't know, Angie," I answered. "There's a lot that white medicine doesn't understand."

"Grandpa Dan says he understands her."

Again, she paused. "Do you think we should listen to the white doctors?"

"You should listen to everybody, but you should do what you think is right. She's your daughter. She doesn't belong to the doctors."

Angie turned away and spoke with her head down.

"She doesn't belong to us, either."

As if embarrassed that she had revealed so much, Angie cast her eyes on the ground and turned away. I knew it had taken a great deal of courage for her to speak up like that, especially to an older white man. I wanted to say something to comfort her. But I could think of nothing.

Donnie took her hand, and they walked quietly toward their truck. Neither of them looked at me.

They reminded me of so many parents I had known over the years who had watched helplessly as their child exhibited behavior that defied explanation, while doctors made wild guesses and speculative diagnoses. They were desperate for some answer, any answer.

But little Zi's behavior defied conventional diagnoses. It reached down to a taproot of cultural knowledge that went far below personal pathology. I felt helpless in its presence.

Even a month earlier I, too, might have cast about for some rational explanation for everything that was taking place. If people said they were hearing stones talk, I could write it off as exaggeration or fanciful projection. If dreams recurred, I could attribute them to unresolved psychological issues. If thunderclaps came that no one else heard, I could say it was just a quirk of circumstance that no one had happened to be listening when the sounds took place. Always there was an explanation. But not now. A bigger world had intruded, and I could no longer deny it.

Suddenly, I was filled with an overwhelming feeling of protectiveness toward Zi. I imagined her in an antiseptic examining room surrounded by men in white coats with machines and computer readouts, tapping on her knees and placing her in MRI machines.

How could I stand by idly while the medical establishment took a little girl who could talk to birds and pick up rabbits and reduce her to a pathology that could be addressed with drugs or therapy or placement in a different social environment? To do so would just be consigning her to the same anomic existence as the parents and grandparents who had the Indian beaten out of them in the boarding schools until nothing was left of them but shame and anger and the echoes of ghosts.

This little girl was hearing the actual voices, not just the echoes. However far this was beyond my understanding, I needed to do what I could to protect her. And I needed to do what I could to help this good young mother and father, not to mention an old man whom I loved and revered, come to peace about this strange and remarkable child who had, in Grover's words, taken on an earth suit and come to them from the spirit world.

I walked over to where Donnie and Angie were standing. "You're doing the right thing," I said. "Whatever it is, she's special, and that specialness needs to be protected, not taken out of her."

Donnie put his arm around Angie. Keeping her eyes down, she reached out her hand in a gentle handshake. "Thank you, Mr. Nerburn," she said. "That means a lot, coming from someone from your world."

It was a kind comment, and I appreciated it. But at that moment, my world seemed like a small and paltry place.

The sun had moved past its zenith, and the day was heating up. Though my stay had been short, it felt like it was time for me to take my leave. I had met with Dan, I had given him the notebook, Grover had made his peace with me according to Dan's instructions, and I had made a real friend in Jumbo. Everyone had done what they had felt called to do, and I knew the task that lay in front of me. I was ready to get back to my own home and my own world.

As if he could sense my intention to leave, Dan beckoned to me from across the lot.

"Nerburn," he said. "Nerburn. Come here."

Grover and Festus and Zi had wandered off toward the shade by Jumbo's shop. Dan was sitting alone in the hot midday sun.

Reluctantly, I walked over. He patted the tire next to him. "Sit down," he said.

Hesitantly, I sat down. "Good," he said. "We should have a little talk." He pulled out his old fisherman's cap and slipped on a pair of wraparound reflective sunglasses he had been carrying in his shirt pocket.

"You like them?" he said. "I just got them."

"Pretty sporty," I answered.

"Drives the girls crazy," he said. "You should give them a try. They sell them at the Dollar Store."

He gestured toward Zi, who was standing in the shade of Jumbo's shop, turning the buffalo rock in her hands while Festus buried his head in the orange mixing bowl in a desperate attempt to get at the remains of Jumbo's Tremendous Tonto.

"What do you make of my little friend?" he asked.

"I've never seen anyone like her," I said.

"That's because there ain't many like her. She hears the old voices."

From across the dusty lot I could hear Zi singing to the buffalo rock. The tiny melody cut like birdsong through the thin prairie air.

"It's like she's singing that little carving into existence," I said.

"She's just singing what she hears," Dan said. "All the stones sing. Your ears are just too full of noise to hear them."

My expression must have betrayed my skepticism.

"I've tried to tell you, Nerburn. This isn't your world. People like Zi don't fit in there. They make people from your world afraid.

"I saw that right away when I went with Donnie and Angie to

take Zi to the doctor. Those doctors were afraid of her. Their fear ran so deep that they didn't even know that it was fear. They called it 'studying her.' They said they wanted to help her, but really they were just afraid. She was a window to a place they couldn't understand. They wanted to shut that window, to use their medicine to make her forget that place. That way they could forget about it, too.

"That's wrong. She needs to remember it. She needs to remember it for herself, and she needs to remember it for our people. That is why I teach her; our people need to know that there are some among us who remember this place. That's why I want to take her to this Benais. I've prepared her as best I can. Now I want to bring her to one who also knows this place."

"And you're sure Benais does?" I said. "Just because of what I told you?"

"You have told me enough. That old woman called out to you. She sent you to Benais. Benais called out to me. I'm just following the voices."

"And I'm honored to help."

He gave me a little jab in the shoulder. "You didn't have a choice. That old woman would have come to you every night. That dream would have followed you forever." He looked at me with a devilish grin. "She might have had to blow your house down if the thunder beings hadn't gotten your attention."

This was the first time Dan had mentioned my dream.

"So you think the dream was real?" I said.

He held his hand up with his thumb and forefinger an inch apart. A small smile crept across his face. "Real for you is about this big," he said.

We sat in silence watching little Zi sing to the stone. She seemed to be in a world all her own.

Dan slipped off his sunglasses and gestured with them like a professor giving a lecture.

"Let me tell you why she's important, Nerburn," he said. "The young ones going to ceremonies, doing powwows — the ones like Jumbo — they're trying. They're doing their best to reach back toward the old ways. But they'll never get all the way there, because they are double-minded. They see the world through the eyes your schools and language have given them. They can't shut that out. They can try, but it will always be there.

"Someone like Zi, she isn't double-minded. She doesn't talk like you. She doesn't think like you. Her heart is pure. She was born with the old knowledge. She hears the old voices. That's why we have to protect her. She reminds us of the place we come from. She shows us who we were before your people made us who we are.

"Right now the other kids laugh at her or just leave her alone. They stay at a distance. But they know. They know."

He looked across at Zi. "Just watch her, Nerburn," he said. "Watch her close."

Zi had left Jumbo's side and was walking across the dusty lot in her strange, stiff fashion, with the buffalo rock held in front of her. Sometimes she would hear a sound and turn her ear toward it. Other times, for no apparent reason she would pause, look up, then move on. Sometimes she would speak a word or two before proceeding, as if talking to an unseen presence.

What gradually became evident as I watched her was that what had seemed strange and stilted when I had first seen her was really just a different way of taking in the world. Her pauses were different, her way of directing her attention was different, the way she used her senses was different. What struck me most was that much of her attention was focused not on objects but on the winds or the sun or the spaces around her. She was like an animal scanning the unseen, absorbing information from sources not available to me.

Festus had abandoned the mixing bowl and was right at her side, almost touching her. Without being told, he walked with her, paused with her, stood silently by while she surveyed the world through whatever distant lens she was using. He asked for no attention and needed no instruction. It was as if he was an extension of her in both his perception and his behavior. They moved and acted as one.

"That dog," Dan said. "He's part of this. He's a guardian. He was sent to watch over her." He tapped the ground with his walking stick. "The Creator sent him to you because he wanted to make sure that you came to see me again. He knew that your work wasn't done here, and that if he didn't do something, you'd just get back in your car and drive to your house. He knew if he sent you a dog you'd bring it out to see me. He likes to work on you with dogs, you know."

"I know," I said.

Dan punched me on the shoulder. "Creator's no fool," he said. "Now, I want you to listen to me a little more. I've been thinking about this for a long time. I think it's why the Creator wanted you out here. I think he's got some more stuff he wants you to help me say."

"I'm happy to do it," I said.

"I know you are. That's why I talk to you."

He took a deep breath — a habit I had learned to associate with the coming of a long talk or a complex explanation.

"You know, a whole lot of Indian folks don't want us to share our traditional knowledge with the white man. They think it is just one more thing that you'll take and turn into something you can sell. They say our spirituality is our gift from the Creator and that if we lose it we lose who we are."

"I tend to agree," I said.

"Well, I don't, not completely," he said. "I used to be really strong in this way. I still am. But I've come to think that the way we believe is different from what we believe. Do you follow me?"

"Not exactly."

He snorted heavily through his nostrils and shook his head slightly.

"The way we believe is the way we understand the world. What we believe is the special knowledge the Creator has given us. That special knowledge is none of your business. But the way we understand the world is something we should share. It's something your people need to hear."

He touched his hands to his chest. "See, your world starts with here" — he thrust his hands forward and extended them toward the horizon — "and goes out to there."

He reversed the gesture and pulled his hands back to his chest.

"Our world starts out there, and comes back to here.

"We are the small part, not the big part. Everything doesn't run through us. We know our mind is too small to hold the Creator's truth. So we just watch and listen and take everything in.

"We're trained this way from when we're just little babies. If we start talking all the time, our mother puts her hand to her lips and says, 'Shh, you got to listen.' She makes us take the world as a whole, not in pieces. Our little being gets full of feelings and sounds, not just a lot of words.

"Sometimes the grandmas take us out onto the hills, never say a word. They keep our arms wrapped tight in a blanket so we can't spend all our time playing with our hands or grabbing at things right in front of us. They know that you have to take in the big things, not just the small things. That way we learn to listen to the wind and the grass. We learn to see things that don't have any shape and hear things that don't have any sound."

"Like the way little Zi is listening," I said.

Dan smiled and held his hand up in approval. "Like the way

little Zi is listening. Our Dakotah brothers and sisters over your way in tree country used to hang their baby's cradle boards from tree branches so the baby would sway with the wind, just like it used to breathe with its mother's heartbeat. It made them connect the close and the far. You understand me?"

"Yes," I said.

"Well, I hope so," he said. "Because that's the key to our way of understanding the world, Nerburn. It's about learning connections. Everything is about connections. It's about seeing how everything fits with everything else."

He tapped my knee with his finger.

"Now, let's go back down the trail to that little baby, all wrapped up in a blanket carrier, going everywhere on its mother's back. That little baby is still close to its mother's heartbeat. It went from being inside the mother to being in the outside world without hurting its little spirit. It can still feel her heart beating, still feel her breathing. That's important. Why do you think the Creator made the mother's breasts so close to her heart? So her baby would feel her heart as it nursed. Her heart and her breath, the two steady sounds in life. It gave the baby peace and trust.

"And you know why they else they kept it wrapped tight in that little pouch? They kept it wrapped up so it would feel protected, just like it did when it was in its mother's womb. It didn't have the big shock of being thrown alone into the world."

He tapped my knee again. "Now that's our science. It's not taking things apart to see how they work. It's trying to take the pieces of the world and make them into a whole.

"Then, as that little baby grows," he continued, "and it goes around on its mother's back, it learns about life because it sees where the mother has been. Their heads are close — almost touching — so the mother can whisper things about what it is going to see. She can be its first teacher."

He reached up and punched me playfully on the shoulder.

"It's not like being pushed around in some little cart. All that does is get the baby ready to drive a car." He mimicked holding a steering wheel. "You must have been pushed around in one of those carts a hell of a lot." He let out a short flat laugh and slapped his knee at his own joke.

Across near a pile of transmissions, little Zi and Festus were sitting together in the dust. Zi was singing in her clear, tiny voice. Festus had his head on her lap. Dan looked over at them and smiled.

"You know where this all starts, Nerburn?" he said. "All this seeing of connections?"

"No," I said.

"It starts with Mother Earth and how she is alive for us. That's where the river of our understanding begins. You can't go around with a checklist, like 'this tree is alive, this rock's not alive.' You might as well look at a person's body and say, 'That elbow doesn't move, it must not be alive. That eye moves, it must alive.' If it's part of the body, it's part of life. For us, the earth is our mother's body. That's why we call her Mother Earth. Everything that's part of her, everything on her, is alive.

"We were all raised with that. We knew that you couldn't hurt part of our mother without hurting all of her. When we had to do something like cutting down a tree or killing an animal for food, we asked her permission in ceremonies and we gave thanks for her letting us do it.

"You guys never gave thanks for anything. You'd cut down a whole forest or dig up a whole mountain and never think anything of it. You just did whatever you wanted to make life better for you. That kind of thing causes trouble. Big trouble. It insults the Creator. It denies the connections.

"Let me ask you. If I stop the blood in your veins, are you going to be healthy?"

It was a rhetorical question, but I knew Dan liked to have me answer so he knew I was paying attention.

"No," I said.

"So, if you dam up the rivers, do you think the earth is going to be healthy?"

"Probably not."

"But if you think about the human first, you don't see that. 'What's one less mountain? There are lots more.' 'What's one less forest? We can go find another one.' 'Let's move this river over here. It isn't going to matter.' Well, it does matter, because everything's connected.

"And you don't have to think big, like rivers and mountains. Just look at the trees. They're more our size, easier to understand. The different trees grow together like friends. You go down in the river bottoms, you see the cottonwoods and the birches. They're together like friends. You go to a hill and find an oak and you think he's all by himself. But if you look close, he's standing with his arms over a bunch of little fellows so they can be protected while they grow.

"And what do we do? We cut down the oak, without thinking about the little fellows. Leave them without protection. They get cold, or they get too hot and die.

"We cut down all the trees on a hillside and say we'll plant some new ones. All their little friends are crying because they're going to die, too.

"You think this is all crazy Indian talk. I'm telling you, Nerburn, this is science. If *sisoka* — what you call the robin — builds its nest in sister cedar, and it brings seeds and berries to feed its babies, and some of those seeds and berries drop on the ground so they can grow, what happens if we cut down that that tree? *Sisoka* has no place to build a home, so she doesn't bring the seeds, so no seeds fall on the ground, so no new plants grow.

"Then the animals who eat those plants come, and there's no

plants, so they leave or maybe they die, and then they're wandering in some place where they don't belong.

"You've heard all the stories about how the old ones knew that the white men were coming before they actually got here. You know how our elders knew you white men were coming? They watched the birds and the animals. They said, 'Are there new birds that weren't here before? Are there new animals?'

"They knew that when there were too many new birds and animals, something was wrong. They knew these birds and animals were coming west because they were fleeing from the new humans who were filling up the land.

"It all has to do with watching and listening. I have a friend back in the tree country who says he can hardly go outside without crying. He says all the singing he heard from the birds and all the chatter he heard from the animals when he was young is gone. He says the white man has killed all of the Creator's music.

"That's what I'm talking about when I talk about connections. They aren't something we make up. They're there. And that's what worries me about your people and the way you understand the world. You think you can decide what connections matter. You can't.

"Nature has rules. Nature has laws. You think you can ignore the rules, or if you don't like them you can change them. That's what you did with us. If you made a law with us — you called them treaties — and it didn't work for you, you changed it. You said the old rules, the old laws, didn't apply anymore. You just made new ones.

"Well, that doesn't work with Mother Earth. She doesn't make deals. She doesn't change the rules. It takes fifteen minutes to cut down an oak tree and a hundred years to grow another one. Are you going to change that? If you kill all the animals are you going to go to Mother Earth and say, 'We made a mistake, give us another chance?'

"You don't get another chance.

"I'm telling you, when you can count the animals, you're getting near the end of your chances. We can count the eagles. We can count the buffalo. I've heard that in Africa they can count the tigers and the elephants.

"That's Mother Earth crying out. She's giving us a warning and she's begging for her life.

"Let me tell you, the way we're living, the earth would be a whole lot better off if we weren't here. I said it before — we're the least important, not the most important. Your Bible got it right when it said that the Creator made us last. The other two-leggeds, the four-leggeds, the things that crawl and the things that fly, they were all here before we were. They were given the knowledge that they needed to survive. They didn't need us. Not one of them.

"But when we came, we needed them all to survive. We still do. The plants and animals give us food and medicine. The trees give us wood for shelter. We're the naked animal. All we have is our hands and our brains. We need everything else to survive.

"So we ought to be helping Mother Earth and thanking her, not just taking from her. Instead we're just taking everything, using everything, thinking we got a right to everything and that we can fix everything if we get it wrong.

"Well, we can't fix everything. We can't make it all fit the shape of our own lives. Mother Earth thinks different than we do. She thinks in the Creator's time, not human time. She's got long patience, but she's got her laws.

"Here's what worries me, Nerburn. It's something your people don't seem to ever learn. There's going to come a day when things can't be fixed."

He swept his hand across the broad expanse of hills and sky before us. "And you know what? It's going to be a day just like today."

Dan sat back and exhaled heavily, like a man who had just laid down a burden and was pausing for a well-earned rest.

"I'm sorry to talk like this, Nerburn," he said. "It's not our way to tell other people what to think or how to live. But we all live on this earth together. The elders taught us that creation is like a drum. What is struck in one place is felt in every other. Your people hold the great stick and are beating the drum. But you are so busy hitting it that you do not feel what is happening in the rest of creation.

"But we Indian people feel it. We feel creation shaking and we know what it means. But you won't listen to us. You think our way is a savage way. Our way might be the old way, but it isn't the savage way. It's the way of knowing that understands that the earth is made of connections and that the rest of creation came first and that it is our task as humans to find our place among the things of the earth."

He adjusted his sunglasses and stared into the sun.

"It's like I told you. We see your anthropologists here on the rez. We see your church people. But we never see your scientists. But they're the ones who should be coming. They're the ones who need to know what we know.

"Our knowledge is long knowledge. Deep knowledge. It is one of the Creator's laws that we become strong in what we do over and over. If we do something for a lifetime, it will make us strong in that knowledge. If we do it for a hundred lifetimes, it will make our whole people strong in that knowledge.

"We Indian people have been listening and watching for hundreds of lifetimes. We understand the connections. We understand the relationships. It is who we are, it is how we live, it is how we think.

"That's why I have wanted you to stay around. We have this knowledge. But your people won't listen to us because they see us as the ones who lost. They see our traditional ways as primitive, like we need to be lifted up into civilization. They don't see our knowledge as real knowledge.

"You have a loud voice in your books. Maybe you can make your people listen. That's why it's important that you come along to Benais. If this Benais has the old knowledge, you will see it. Donnie and Angie will see it. We will all see it, and it will give us courage to speak up against the small world of the white man's mind. It will remind us that the power of things is not as strong as the power of spirit."

He pointed his crooked finger across the sun-baked lot at little Zi, who was turning the buffalo rock in her hands and singing. "That little girl, she already knows what we have to learn."

"What's that, Dan?" I asked.

"That when we sing to the stones, the stones sing back to us."

Dan adjusted his hat and settled into a long, comfortable Indian silence. With his eyes hidden behind the reflective sunglasses, it was impossible to tell if he was just thinking or if he had fallen off to sleep.

Eventually, I decided that I was just going to have to leave. Though Dan had not given me permission, it was obvious that he had said what he'd needed to say.

I stood up and moved carefully over to where Jumbo was sitting with Festus. Dan did not move a muscle.

"The old man's sleeping, Jumbo," I said. "So I'm going to get on the road. I've got a long drive."

Jumbo reached his hand up for me to shake. "Been good to see you, Nerburn," he said. His warmth was heartfelt.

"I wish I had something to give you," I said. I touched the pocket where I had placed the bone from his little dog. "After the gift you gave me."

He rubbed the top of Festus's head with his paw-like hand. Festus looked up with love in his eyes. "Ain't no need of that. You brought me this here Festus."

"I'm going to miss you, buddy," I said, crouching down and holding Festus's head close to mine. "But I think I found you a good home."

"I'll fatten him up," Jumbo said. "I'm good at that."

Festus wagged his tail earnestly and licked at my face.

"Remember to brush twice a day," I said.

While we were talking, little Zi came over and stood next to us. Our activity must have drawn her attention. She took Jumbo's right hand in her own and placed her other hand on Festus's back.

"You like to be connected by touch, don't you, Zi?" I said. She stared at me with her huge, expressionless eyes. I had no idea if she understood what I was saying.

Grover, sensing that I was about to leave, had awakened Dan, and the two of them were making their way across the dusty lot in their matching faux Ray-Bans — Dan supporting himself with his cane and Grover hitching along with his bowlegged sailor's gait.

"Getting ready to skedaddle, eh, Nerburn?" Dan said.

"As soon as you tell me I can go. One should never leave before he gets permission from an elder."

"Where'd you get that stuff? You been reading books?"

"Nope, been talking to rabbits."

He shooed me with the back of his hand. "Go on," he said. "That wife of yours might forget who you are."

"Maybe she already has," Grover said. "There's a lot of good-looking young bucks up there in *Shinnob* country where Nerburn comes from."

I waved to Angie and Donnie, who were sitting on the running board of the pickup. Donnie nodded and Angie waved shyly. We kept eye contact for a few moments, as if there was more we should say.

Finally, I started toward my car. I had only gotten a few steps when Dan's voice stopped me.

"Nerburn?" he said.

I turned to face him. He reached his hands into the air and wiggled his fingers in a pantomime of snow falling to the earth.

"I'll remember," I said.

He smiled and nodded.

I was almost to the car when his voice came again.

"Nerburn?"

"Yeah?"

He touched the brim of his fisherman's cap and gave me an impish grin.

"Sweet dreams."

"That's the only kind," I said.

Festus thumped his tail twice, and I headed off for the sanctuary of home.

Part Three

NORTHERN LIGHT

CHAPTER TWENTY-SEVEN

Roll Call of the Dead

*W*hatever else had transpired during my visit, something had caused the dreams to stop. I slept the sleep of the just, thankful for whatever had put my mind at peace.

I spent my days watching the sky like the old man in the nursing home. The languid haze of autumn took on a crisper edge as the days shortened and the nighttime winds began to rise. The waters of the lake by our home darkened, and geese moved with urgency through heavy, leaden skies. The seasons were turning; snow was in the air.

Then, on a Thursday, it happened. I went to bed listening to the gentle rhythm of leaves falling like soft rain on the roof and awoke to the holy silence of a snow-covered earth. Overnight, autumn's golden light had changed to icy greys and blues. What the Lakota called *waziya*, the giant of the north, had come.

"This is it," I said to Louise as the winds rattled the window-panes. "This one's going to stick." Outside, gusts of wind swirled and danced on the powdery snow. "It's time."

I picked up the phone and dialed Wenonah's number. There was a long pause before the signal kicked in, then a scratchy, distant, barely audible voice came on the line.

"Hello," it said. I could hardly tell if it was a man or woman.

"Wenonah?"

"Yes."

"This is Nerburn. The snow's come. Does he still want to go?"

"That's all he wants," she said. "It's all he talks about. He sits at the TV every day listening for weather reports from up your way."

"Well, he doesn't have to listen anymore. We got three, four inches last night, and it isn't going anywhere. It's got to be even heavier up north where Benais lives."

"Then I suppose you'll come and get them," she said. I could feel the resignation in her words.

"Them?"

"Donnie. Angie. They're coming along. And Grover and Jumbo. Little Zi. And that dog."

"I can't fit all of them in my car."

"No, but you can lead. Grandpa's been planning this since you left. He wants you to meet them at that asylum place you told him about. He wants to see it before he goes to Benais."

This was the first time anyone had shown any interest in the asylum in Canton. I was pleased that Dan wanted to visit the ground on which his little sister had walked, but I was nervous about the effect it might have on his emotional well-being. Still, it was not my decision to make. Like Wenonah, I had to accept that Dan was going to do things his way.

"I'll meet them there whenever they want," I said.

The asylum site was about halfway between our two homes,

and I had kept a bag packed in anticipation of the event. I was prepared to leave at any time.

"Well, I suggest you get started," Wenonah said. "Grandpa has had his bag packed for weeks. "

I smiled to think of the two of us, hundreds of miles apart, sitting in anticipation of the coming snows, with bags at the ready next to our respective doors.

"Tuesday afternoon?" I said. "One o'clock? Next to the roadside historical markers on highway eighteen just east of Canton?"

"He'll probably be there the day before."

"No Indian time, eh?"

"Just be there when you say," she said.

She hung up the phone abruptly, as if she couldn't wait to be rid of me and the entire affair.

The day dawned blue and magical on the morning of my departure. Winter had fallen in a single stroke, and the land was a rolling sea of white. The whole earth seemed to hold its breath at the sudden stillness.

I drove down my snow-covered driveway and headed south.

I was nervous about showing up at Benais's with so many people. I had not contacted him; indeed, I had no way to contact him. Dan had assured me that he would be expecting us and there was no cause to worry. But I had no way to confirm this. In the world I came from, psychic connections and visitations from rabbits did not constitute an invitation. But Dan had been adamant. "Do this my way," he said. "I told you, this is not your world."

I drove the four hundred miles from my house to Canton in a state of continuous agitation. Neither the soothing tones of classical music nor the diversions of talk radio could lighten my mood. I was like a man heading off to some dire medical test he could not avoid.

The snow cover gradually lessened as I made my way south. The whites and soft blues of the fresh winter gave way to the desiccated browns of late autumn, and the heavy darkness of the northern pine forests opened into the cold emptiness of fallow farm fields of broken cornstalks, patchy troughs of snow, and howling prairie winds.

The car shuddered in the gusts, pushing me around the road, and I wished for all the world that I had been more forceful with Dan either about making the journey earlier or not going at all. But now there was no way out; I had to see this through to the end.

By the time I arrived at Canton, the gales had picked up to the point where the small South Dakota town was little more than a forlorn, windswept prairie outpost. The single main street swirled with blowing snow from a fast-moving squall, and a layer of white powder covered the dun grasses and clumps of frozen leaves that had built up in the ditches during the final days of autumn.

I had made a difficult decision during the drive: though I knew it would be hard on Edith, I wanted Dan to meet her and hear her story. She was a link, though distant, between him and his little sister. Through her eyes and memory perhaps he could get a more intimate glimpse of the little girl in the white dress who had spent her days in that horrible asylum swinging by herself and singing.

But when I stopped at the nursing home to arrange the meeting, the same woman who had treated me with such disdain during my last visit informed me that Edith's family had taken her back East a month before. "She was failing," she said. "It started right after you were here." It was impossible to tell if she attributed that failing to my visit, and I did not want to ask.

I looked for the old man who had been keeping watch outside

the door, but he was nowhere to be seen. Harvesttime was done and it was too cold to be standing outside. Perhaps he too had moved or had been reduced by the cold weather to sitting in his room. Or perhaps he had come to the inevitable end that all nursing home residents meet. I walked out into the whipping winds feeling like an intruder who had brought some pernicious disease and needed to be exiled and forgotten.

With a heart full of loneliness and regret, I drove down to the side of the small rural highway at the base of the asylum site and parked in a pull-off by the two markers commemorating the sites of Augustana College and the now-dismantled ski jump across the river.

Trucks roared by on the roadway, shaking my car as they passed. I tried to read to pass the time but could not. The wind continued strong and brutal, coursing down the river valley, whistling and keening and whipping the branches of the leafless trees. I entertained the faint hope that perhaps Dan and the others had chosen not to come and that after a respectful wait I would be free to return home.

But as the clock on the dashboard reached 12:45, Donnie's huge pickup rumbled up beside me. I could see numerous heads in the cab — Donnie's, Dan's, Angie's, and Festus's in front; Grover's, Jumbo's and little Zi's in back. All of them were nearly obscured in a haze of blue cigarette smoke.

Donnie stepped out and walked over to my window. He was almost blown over by a gust of wind.

"Grandpa Dan wants to go to the asylum place alone," he said. "Just you and him and Zi. We'll go back and wait in that restaurant at the edge of town."

He hurriedly opened the door and helped Dan and Zi onto the ground. The wind nearly snapped the door off its hinges. Festus scrambled out behind them.

"Festus, too?" I said.

"He goes where she goes," he said. "He won't leave her side."

When the old dog saw me he wagged over to the car window and held up his paw. The sock was off his foot. I reached through the window and scruffed the top of his head. He licked my fingers and nuzzled my wrist.

"Good boy, Festus," I said. "I'll pet you more later. Now we've got to get going. This wind is rough." As if he had understood me, he scrabbled into the backseat next to Dan and little Zi, who had slid in while I was talking. Donnie strapped them both in, then got back in his truck and drove off toward town. Dan sat upright holding the forked stick that had apparently become his cane of choice. He thumped it several times on the floor of the car.

"Well, Nerburn," he said. "Time's come. Let's get on with it." He was wearing the same cheap nylon jacket with duct tape patches he had been wearing the last time we had traveled. It was barely adequate protection from the cutting prairie winds.

"You going to be warm enough?" I asked.

"A little wind never hurt anyone," he said. "Just the Creator breathing hard."

Zi had on a dirty pink snowsuit jacket that looked like it had been taken out of a Goodwill donation box. It was zipped to the neck, and her head was covered by a striped wool cap with sagging ear flaps. She had on long white leggings and her worn fleece-top snow boots appeared to be about two sizes too big. She looked like a Balkan refugee, but at least she was dressed for the weather.

"There's not much to see up there," I said over my shoulder to Dan, thinking of the wind and the cold.

"I ain't going up there to see," Dan said. "Let's get moving."

We drove up the gravel road along the edge of the golf course. In the distance I could make out the split-rail fence marking off the area of the graves.

"That's the cemetery," I said.

"She won't go in there," Dan said, nodding toward Zi. "She doesn't like graves."

"She won't know they're graves," I said. "There aren't any markers."

He clucked and shook his head. "She don't need markers."

I pulled several sheets of paper from the glove box and handed them across the seat to Dan. They were photocopies of pictures of the asylum that had been in the folder in the library. "I thought you might like to see what the place looked like before it was torn down," I said.

Dan squinted at the image of the colorized postcard of the asylum. It made the building look like a looming castle on the hilltop.

"Hard to imagine they'd build something like that out here on the prairies," I said.

Dan shook his head. "That's how they built stuff for Indians. Big, solid — scare the hell out of you. They wanted to remind us who was boss." It was the same thing I had tried to explain to Edith months before.

He flipped to another photo that showed the building through the metal fence surrounding the grounds. "Always a fence and a gate. They liked to mark things off, let us know where our world ended and theirs began. Once we walked through the gate we were part of their world. They never let us forget who was in charge."

I thought of the old abandoned boarding school we had visited years before when we had been searching for information about Yellow Bird. With its great, solid brick front it had felt intimidating even to me as I stood in front of it. And if it had been intimidating to me, how much more so would it have been to people who lived in light, movable lodges and small, humble dwellings. These huge brick buildings would have towered over the landscape with the same unquestionable authority as the cathedrals of medieval Europe. Dan was right: they were not just architectural creations; they were conscious implements of social control.

I stopped my car on the side of the gravel road. The fenced-in grave area was about a hundred yards to our left. We stepped out into the wind and made our way across the grass, just as Edith and I had done months earlier. But this time there were no lush, green fairways — only the dead, snow-dusted grasses and leafless wind-bent trees.

Dan held the collar of his jacket as he walked, while Zi walked stiffly at his side with her hat pulled down over her ears, holding his hand. I supported him as best I could.

It was just as Dan had said: Zi would not go inside the fence. She was very matter-of-fact about it — she simply stopped when we got to the entrance and stood still as Dan and I continued to the stone plinth with the engraved plaque. Festus remained with her.

Dan looked at the names and ran his fingers over them.

"Read them to me," he said.

"All of them?"

"They're all buried here, aren't they?"

I began the litany. I felt like an official reading off the names of the dead at some military ceremony. "Long Time Owl Woman. Juanita Castildo. Mary Fairchild." Dan listened carefully. Occasionally he would stop me and say, "I know that name."

The wind was raw, but Dan didn't seem inclined to hurry. He insisted that I read every name and give each a moment of reflective pause. There was no sadness in his demeanor, just a respectful quiet. He kept his head down as I read.

I kept glancing up to keep an eye on little Zi. She and Festus had left the edge of the fence and were wandering across the snow-skiffed grass toward the crest of the hill. I didn't want to stop the reading — it was obviously a moment of ceremonial solemnity for Dan — but I didn't want to let her get out of sight.

"Guy Crow Neck. John Big. A. Kennedy."

I finished reading the list of names and prepared to catch up to Festus and Zi. But Dan stopped me. He reached in his jacket and took out a buckskin scroll. Unwrapping it carefully, he removed what I assumed to be an eagle feather. He held the quill in his shaking hands and slowly touched the feather to each name, one at a time, each time lifting the feather high into the air and speaking something low in Lakota. One hundred and twenty-one times he did this. His actions were slow, laborious, respectful.

The ceremonial reserve with which he did this was touching. Only a few months before I had stood in this same spot with a woman, about the same age as Dan, who had been overcome with grief and remorse for the lives that had been so sadly wasted and forgotten at this dark institution. Now I was standing with a man whose very people had been in this place, yet he seemed resolved and almost at peace with the knowledge.

He rewrapped the eagle feather and placed it back in his jacket. "You help me outside the fence," he said. "Then just leave me be."

"In this wind?" I asked. "Are you steady enough?"

"If I fall, I fall on the ground where my sister walked. I'm fine."

I glanced up at Zi, who had wandered farther up the rise. Dan noticed my concern.

"Don't worry about her," he said. "That Festus will take care of her. I told you, he's a guardian."

I helped him through the opening in the fence and stepped back. I was hesitant to leave him. He grabbed the collar of his thin jacket and began walking in a large arc across the frozen grasses. He moved slowly but intently, passing his hand over the ground like a man sowing seed and saying something low under his breath. After making a complete circle around the fenced area, he stopped and faced up the rise in the direction of where the asylum building had been. Again he took out the feather and held it up in that direction.

Zi and Festus were far ahead of him, almost to the top of the rise. Zi had come to a complete stop and was standing in that strange fashion I had seen before, with her arms tight at her side, looking around and inclining her head as if listening for voices.

I pulled the old photo of the asylum building from my pocket. It was hard to keep it steady in the cutting wind, but from what I could tell, it looked as if Zi was standing in the exact spot where the asylum swing set had once stood.

CHAPTER TWENTY-EIGHT

A World of Other Laws

*O*nce Dan had finished his private homages, he insisted that we get on the road. We gathered the others from their plates of hamburgers and french fries at the café and headed north.

We had agreed to take the back roads — Dan did not like the speed of freeways, though the lonely rural highways were in many ways more treacherous in the wisping, swirling snow. Dan had insisted on riding with me but seemed disinclined to speak.

I was happy for the silence. I had once again been chastened by standing on that piece of earth where so many poor, helpless people had been interned for no reason other than the color of their skin and the difference of their ways. Apart from the paltry marker and a flimsy fence that a dedicated Indian man had forced the state to put up, these people had been forgotten as surely as the building that had housed them had been forgotten by the town. Once more, I was reminded that any encounter with Indian reality was destined to be haunted with ghosts.

Dan, too, seemed to have disappeared into his thoughts. He sat quietly in the passenger seat, staring out at the passing fields. I was curious why he had insisted that it be only the two of us: Donnie's pickup, though massive, was crowded to the point of discomfort with all the people who had been forced to fit inside its cab. We could easily have accommodated another passenger.

Still, this was Dan's world, not mine. I had long since learned not to ask questions unless they were something that needed an answer.

We had traveled about thirty miles before he spoke. "Why do you think they put people in that place, Nerburn?" he said.

"I don't know. Politics? Alcoholism? Refusing to give up the old ways? Maybe just to get rid of them."

"Yeah. But like my little sister?"

"I suppose she scared them. They didn't know what to do with her."

"Kind of like little Zi scares you, eh?"

The comment took me aback. I had not expected his thinking to go in this direction.

"I don't know. Maybe. I hope not."

"But she frightens you, right? All of this frightens you — Odell, Benais, Zi."

"Yes, I guess it does. It's not my world."

"No," he said, "That's not what frightens you. What frightens you is that it *is* your world. There's only one world. It's just how much of that world you're able to understand."

He put his hand on my arm in a warm, fatherly gesture. "This is what happens when someone loses their understanding. They get frightened and confused. We know about that. It's the same thing that happened to us when your people came into our country."

He pulled himself upright in his seat.

"Think about it. We had always lived around other people

who looked like us. We spoke different languages and did not always agree with each other, but we shared an understanding of the world. Then one day, we wake up and men are coming into our camps who have white skin, eyes like dead fish, and hair on their faces like dogs.

"They capture light in pieces of glass and turn it into fire. They give us bitter water to drink that makes our minds go crazy. They tell us there is a place we will go where we will burn in fire for all time unless we listen to them about a man far away who was nailed to a tree. They tell us our old ways come from evil spirits and we should close our ears to them, or we will be sent to that place of fire.

"Do you think this didn't frighten us? Do you think we weren't afraid when they made small marks on pieces of paper and said these marks could talk to people far away? That was no different for us than it is for you to hear Odell say that he traveled through the night to check Benais out. They are both impossible to our own ways of understanding, and they frighten us. Do you see what I mean?"

"Yes," I said. "But they're not the same. Writing is just a skill. The Odell and Benais thing defies the laws of physics."

"Ha," he said. "The laws of physics. That's just one kind of law. The Creator has many kinds of laws. Our people knew some of them. Your people knew others. It's just that your way won, and now you aren't paying any attention to the laws our people knew."

He tapped his finger on my arm. "Let me ask you, do you watch those Olympics on television?"

The comment was so bizarre it almost made me laugh.

"Yes, of course," I said.

"Well, so do I. Grover got me that satellite thing and I started watching those Olympics, and guys are jumping over bars higher than their heads. Have you ever seen that?"

"Yes."

"Can you do those things?"

"I can hardly jump at all."

"Well, do you think it's possible?"

"I know it's possible. I see them do it."

"Well, if you'd never seen someone jump over a bar as high as his head, and some Indian came and held his hand up there and said, 'We've got Indians who can jump over bars this high,' you would think it's impossible. You'd say it had to be a superstition or a lie, because it defies your laws of physics. Or at least the laws of gravity. Am I right?"

"Probably."

"Then when they did it, you'd say it must be a trick, right?"

"I suppose."

"Well, that's what you say about Odell and Benais. It's just Indians being superstitious or believing lies or falling for a trick.

"But what if it's not a trick, like the people who jump over bars as high as their head? What if there are laws that Indian people know? What if there is training that the old ones knew that let them do things you don't think are possible?

"Remember when I told you that one of the rules of the Creator is that whatever you do for an entire lifetime will give you knowledge? And that whatever a people does for a hundred lifetimes gives them deep knowledge?

"Our people have been studying the laws of creation for a hundred lifetimes. We have knowledge that your people can hardly even begin to understand.

"Odell has been trained since he was a little boy. He has been trained to listen to sounds you can't hear, to feel things you can't feel, to read signs that you don't understand. His grandpa saw that he had talent so he gave him training. Hard training. Training that has been passed down from the old ones. It isn't a joke, and it isn't superstition."

I sat quietly, listening respectfully as he talked. He cocked his head and stared at me. "You still don't believe me, do you?"

"I don't believe you or not believe you. I'm just listening, trying to understand."

Dan snorted and shook his head. "Let me try this a different way."

He pointed through the windshield at the heavy grey clouds blanketing the horizon. "What do you see when you look at that sky?"

"It looks like snow."

"That's what I see, too. Now, if a man from only sunny places looked at that sky, would he know it meant snow was coming? No, he would just see a dark, heavy sky. He wouldn't know what it meant and it would probably make him afraid. But you have been trained to know the connection between a dark sky and snow. You have been trained by living in the presence of that sky.

"Men like Odell and this Benais, they have been trained to look for connections you and I can't even imagine. Some of them are simple connections that everyone can understand, like if they catch a deer in the fall and it has no fat, it means there will be a mild winter, or if they see ravens circling they know there is food below.

"But some are deeper. Much deeper. Most of us don't know them anymore. And if we don't know them we can't use them. They're part of what we've lost since you took away our old ways and made us live as white men.

"But even if we can't use them ourselves, we accept that they exist. Do you know why a plane flies? Do you know how a sound comes through a radio? No, but you accept those things. If you had never seen a plane, and one flew over your head, you'd be terrified. If you'd spent your whole life in the woods, and someone came to you with a box and pushed a button and voices started coming through it, you'd think it was magic; you'd be afraid, you wouldn't know what to do.

"That's what's happening to you with Odell and Benais. You see them doing things you can't understand, and it makes you afraid. They're just planes flying over your head and radios playing voices from places you can't understand."

"Why are you telling me these things, Dan?" I said.

"I'm trying to explain to you why I think those people were in the asylum. Why they would put someone like my little sister there. It was all about fear. All about things people couldn't understand."

He adjusted himself in his seat. I could tell he was on the trail of something.

"Let me tell you about a friend of mine," he said. "She's really old now, maybe older than I am. She won't speak Lakota, even though she grew up speaking it. When the Christians came, she was taught that same stuff about how ours was the language of evil spirits and that she would go to that place of fire if the Creator heard her speaking it.

"It frightened her so much. She never learned good English, but she doesn't dare speak in her own tongue. She has lived almost ninety years hardly talking to anyone because she has been so afraid. The Christian way stole her tongue and filled her with fear. It stole her from her grandchildren and great-grandchildren because she could not speak with them. She got caught between two worlds.

"That's what I think probably happened to a lot of those people in that asylum place."

Dan steepled his hands in front of his nose, as if trying to collect his thoughts.

"Think about it. Your people had been among us for years when they built that place. We had seen your power. We had heard your teachings.

"So, suppose something happens to you that's bad. Maybe your child gets sick and can't get well. Maybe someone dies. The white world tells you it's because you still believe in the old ways and the Creator is punishing you. The old ones tell you it is because you believe in the white ways and the spirit world is angry with you.

"You get all upset, all confused, not knowing what to think. Maybe you drink. Maybe you walk around trying to talk to the spirits. Maybe you get so afraid that you can't talk at all.

"So they take you to that asylum place and chain you to a bed. Maybe they dunk you in cold water. Maybe they give you pills. I don't know what they do. But they call it helping you and they call it civilization. And all you are is afraid — afraid of the old ways, afraid of the new, afraid of a world you don't understand. Now, I'm not saying that's what happened to everybody. But I think it happened to some of them.

"Then there were people like my little sister. She wasn't afraid of them; they were afraid of her. The white people thought they had everything figured out, and along comes a little girl who can call birds down to her hand and can tell when horses died in a field. That scared the white people so bad they had to put her away. It was that simple."

"I think you're right, Dan," I said.

"I know I'm right, because they're trying to do the same thing to my little Zi. They can't understand her, so they'll fill her so full of drugs that she won't even remember the truths the Creator put in her. That's their new asylum — drugs. And you know what will happen? They'll tell her that the things she knows are just a disease of the mind; they'll make her so confused and frightened that she won't know what to do. They'll kill her spirit, Nerburn. They'll kill her little spirit."

He turned away and slipped on his sunglasses. He did not

want me to see his eyes. I sat silently while he composed himself. When he felt comfortable enough to continue, he spoke again.

"Right now that's what's happening to Angie and Donnie. They're caught between the white world and the red world, and they don't know which way to go, because both ways pull on the spirit. So they're confused and frightened, too.

"And that's why I wanted to ride with you, Nerburn. Just the two of us. I wanted to warn you. Most white people don't have to deal with this double world, because for them the old ways aren't real. But you've seen some things. You've heard some things. You've gone some places where you probably shouldn't have gone. Now you're starting to get frightened and confused, too.

"That's why Wenonah told you to go home. She wanted to get you away from this double world, so you wouldn't get lost in between the two. She's your real friend. It's me who wouldn't let you go. I figured since you were already in this, you might as well follow it all the way to the end.

"But you've got to be careful," he said. He took off his glasses and looked me in the eye. His face had regained its old twinkle.

"If you don't look out, pretty soon you'll start thinking that every rabbit is carrying a message or that you're supposed to bring every dog you find to my house."

We drove through the day and into the night. Once again we were in pine country, where the snows glistened brightly beneath a canopy of shimmering stars. Dan fell into a heavy sleep, waking only briefly when we stopped for a meal at a small roadside café tucked deep in the northern woods.

Much to my surprise, when it came time to stop for the night, Donnie pulled out a roll of bills bound by a red rubber band and peeled off enough to pay for rooms for everyone at a small log cabin motel. I tried to make him let me pay for myself, but he refused. "You've given us a gift by bringing that book to Dan. This is my gift to say thanks." It was a heartfelt gesture, and I was honored by his generosity.

It would be stretching the truth to say that I slept comfortably. Though I had my own room — something I had not expected — sleep was fitful and elusive. I tried to tell myself that it was a result of the full moon, but I knew it was simple apprehension at the coming meeting with Benais. I did not know what to expect. I was worried that Dan's hopes might be dashed, and I wasn't sure I even wanted to see Benais again.

I kept thinking of Dan's words — that Wenonah in her gruffness had merely been trying to protect me from a world that I should not enter. But Dan had called me to be a witness, and I was intent on honoring his request.

Outside the window, the sky had taken on an icy brightness. The moonlight reflecting off the fresh snow created a world of shifting shadows as the pines swayed silently in the nighttime breeze. I spent the night staring out at the shimmering landscape and the river of stars that flowed overhead. Shafts of northern lights had begun to dance on the horizon.

By morning, a light snow had begun to fall. The flakes sifted weightlessly down to the silent earth. The trees sparkled in the morning brightness like chandeliers of ice.

I stepped out of my room to get a full breath of clear morning air. Grover, already awake and dressed, was leaning against the wall of the unit next to me, smoking a cigarette.

"God, what a day," I said.

He nodded and smiled.

From inside one of the units a huge, thunderous rumble rose and fell with rhythmic precision.

"Is that Jumbo?" I asked.

Grover nodded. "I told you not to sleep near him." He lit

another cigarette and drew heavily on it. "And that ain't the only reason."

"Did you see the northern lights last night?" I asked.

"Yeah. Good sign. Good for the old man."

"How so?"

"What goes on above, goes on below. The night was speaking."

We stood side by side in the quiet, watching the flakes descend and our breath form clouds in the morning air.

"Grover, can I ask you something?"

"Sure. But you might not like the answer."

"Are you nervous about this visit to Benais?"

"Not really."

"I mean, messages from rabbits?"

"I told you, the old man thinks everything's a message. He's usually right."

"But what if he's not?"

"Just because his body's weak don't mean his spirit is. If nothing happens, nothing happens. He'll handle it. But he pays pretty close attention. He's pretty sure the Creator will speak. This little girl is the last walk on his journey, and he thinks the Creator wants him to walk on in peace."

"I hope he's right."

"You've got to have a little more faith. You think you were the only one up last night looking at that sky? The old man, he'd get up four, five times, take that walker of his, and head off from the bed. I figured he was just going to take a piss, but I'd open my eyes and he'd be there looking out that window at those lights, whispering something under his breath. Finally, I asked him what he was doing. '*Wanagi Wacipi*', he said. 'The dancing spirits. I'm thanking *Tunkashila*. They're dancing for Zi and my sister.'"

He stubbed his cigarette out under the toe of his boot. "It's going to be an interesting day."

Jumbo's rumbling had subsided and we could hear movement in the other units. Before long the doors opened and the others emerged from their rooms. Dan had on his fake Ray-Bans against the bright morning sun. The snow was letting up, and diamonds of crystal light flickered on its surface.

Jumbo emerged from his unit looking disheveled and greasy. "Damn small showers," he said.

Zi ran over to Jumbo and touched his hand. Then she went around to each of us, touching our hands in turn, almost as if playing tag or counting innocent coup. Festus, having peed on several trees and all four tires of both of our cars, was rolling in the fresh snow.

"So, who rides with whom?" I said. We still had a fair distance to go, and I was anxious to get on the road. The roads were hard-packed snow, but this was northwoods country and conditions could change.

"*Whom?*" Grover said. "I've been talking for seventy years, and I've never used that word. You white guys got a whole lot of words you don't need."

"Helped us write treaties you couldn't understand," I said.

"Did someone say Wheaties?" Jumbo said with a big grin as he came down the walkway. He was cleaning his ear with a washcloth.

Dan shook his head in astonishment.

"Jesus," he said. "Come on, let's go."

Angie came out of her unit carrying a cellophane bag of white-bread sandwiches. She handed them out one by one. I snuck a glance inside: baloney with a thick layer of butter and a splat of ketchup.

"Grover, you come with us," Dan said.

"We could take more," I said. "That truck's kind of crowded."

Dan glared at me. "It ain't crowded, it's friendly. We aren't like white people, riding around by ourselves in big cars. Grover rides with us. The rest go with Donnie."

I shrugged and carried my aviator bag toward the car. Festus followed along, obviously interested in the sandwich I was carrying. As we got behind the car where no one could see, I slipped it to him. He took it delicately from my hand and dropped it in the snow, where he held it with his paw and carefully removed the treasure of the baloney at its center.

"You're a little picky for a dog who was homeless in a park," I said. Festus wagged his tail and pulled at the slab of pink meat with his teeth. "Or maybe Jumbo's been teaching you manners."

The others were slowly making their way to the vehicles. Donnie was carrying Dan's battered leather suitcase, and the others pulled their nylon gym bags and dirty backpacks. Little Zi was dragging a pink-and-purple child's suitcase with cartoon figures on it.

Jumbo snuck up behind her and whisked her onto his shoulders. She let out a squeal and a giggle, dropped her suitcase, and grabbed him around the neck. It was the first time I had ever heard anything childlike come from her lips.

CHAPTER TWENTY-NINE

STOLEN WORDS

*T*he drive to Benais's house went slowly. The road was slicker than I thought it would be, with dangerous patches of black ice, and the snow fell in squalls and bursts, sometimes so obscuring the view ahead that I had to pull over until the sky cleared. I drank coffee from my thermos while Dan and Grover chewed on their baloney-and-butter sandwiches. We seldom were able to go much over twenty miles an hour.

We made our way north at this cautious pace until, at long last, the great lake came into view. "Looks like an ocean," Dan said. The snow whisked off its frozen edges, racing across the icy roadway in swirling gusts. Steam rose like spirits from the dark open waters far out from the shore.

Though he said nothing, Grover's attentiveness had increased. I could see his head moving rapidly from side to side, taking in the unfamiliar landscape.

It took us almost until midafternoon to make it to the north end of the lake. We had turned off from the shoreline and headed, into the deep pines, where the road was little more than a pathway through a dark wall of swaying, whispering giants. The snow had stopped, and the earth had settled into a heavy quiet.

Occasionally, great lumps of cottony snow dislodged from the overhanging branches and drifted earthward, like white birds settling gently to the earth.

I drove slowly up the roadway, marveling at the stillness. There were no sharp edges, no sounds anywhere. It was as if the sky had exhausted itself; the earth lay buried under a mantle of white.

Dan was transfixed. "Hell of a country," he said.

"Used to be ours," Grover said. "Before the white man pushed the *Shinnobs* out here from the East and they pushed us out to where we are now."

"That's one good thing the white man did, if you ask me," Dan said. "This country's too damn tight for me. It ain't healthy when so many trees get together. They keep too many secrets."

Through breaks in the pines we could see the sky turning a distant, melancholy lavender across the snow-drifted fields. A roseate glow limned the far horizon. The day was descending into an early dark.

Dan kept emitting low whistles of amazement at the silent beauty of the scene.

"Stop here," he said. "I want to get out in this."

I pulled to the side of the road, and we all stepped out. The quiet overwhelmed us. High above, almost lost in the growing darkness, the tops of the trees swayed soundlessly.

"Hell of a different quiet," Dan said, looking toward the stars. "Closes right in on you. Ain't like ours, all full of noise and distance."

Grover was paying no attention. He had walked over to the edge of the road and was staring through a break in the trees at a frozen meadow that stretched in unrelenting whiteness toward the horizon. In the fading lavender twilight the snow on the silent field seemed to glow.

One by one the winter stars began to appear — crystalline specks against a velvet-dark sky. Orion. The Big Dipper. The Pleiades. Then, the whole Milky Way, flowing across the sky like a silent river of light.

I breathed in deeply. The sharp winter air burned my nostrils. Dan was still staring upward. "Nope, ain't like our country," he said again. "This ain't sky silence, it's earth silence."

I was fascinated by his preoccupation with the unseen. Any non-Native person would have been commenting on the beauty of the forest or the magic of the sky. But Dan just stood, moving his head around like little Zi had done, taking in the enormity of the night.

"Helps me understand the *Shinnobs*," he said. "Secret," as if that was a key to something he had thought about over the years.

"Yep," he said. "Yep."

He turned and headed back to the car. "Come on. I'm ready to see that Benais."

Donnie had stopped in a pull-off about half a mile behind us and shut off his lights and engine. He knew the old man's ways and wanted to leave him undisturbed.

"It's kind of late to visit Benais," I said as we got in the car. "Don't you think we should wait until morning?" I had no desire to visit Benais's brooding compound in the dark, and no idea where we would be able to stay.

"Nope. We'll go there now," Dan said. There was no room for compromise in his tone.

With no other option, I continued through the dark tunnel of pines, watching the forest close in around the thin glow of my headlights.

It wasn't long before I caught sight of the single feather swaying from the mailbox, announcing the turnoff to Benais's. Once again, there were no tracks, either human or mechanical, indicating that anyone had entered or departed.

I turned down the trail leading back to his home. As I had expected, the shelter of the trees had blocked the full force of the wind and snow, leaving the path almost untouched. Driving was slow, and I knew from memory that the trail itself was little more than two ruts along uneven, seldom-traveled ground.

"Your car doing okay, Nerburn?" Grover said. "This is supposed to be your kind of country."

I managed a brittle smile. "I'm glad Donnie's behind us. At least he's got four-wheel drive."

"He ain't behind us," Dan said. "I told him to follow us to the drive to see where it was, then go back to town and buy some stuff to give to this Benais."

"There isn't any town, Dan," I said.

Dan waved me off. "Donnie will find something."

The loss of Donnie and Angie and Jumbo and Zi — not to mention the comfort of Festus — sent a shiver through me. I hadn't realized how much I was counting on their presence. Now, without them, it would be only three old Indian men and me. If I had felt lost and alien before, now I actually felt frightened.

The light coming through the trees had turned strange and unnatural. It was somehow brighter than it ought to be — as if the reflected lights of a distant city were casting an unearthly glow above the horizon. But there was no city nearby. Perhaps, I thought, the incredible brilliance of the winter stars was illuminating the earth in a way I had never seen.

I cut tracks through the trees until the dim lights of Benais's trailer came into view. Because of the blankets he kept over his windows, only a thin perimeter of light traced the outlines of squares against the dark, snow-covered mass.

"You sure this is okay?" I said to Dan.

"How many times are you going to ask me that?" Dan snapped. "I told you, he knows we're coming."

We pulled into the clearing. A large form, as big as a dog, rose up from a lump of something and winged off into the air. My lights strafed the lump as we turned. It was the fleshy carcass of a large animal with the rib bones exposed.

"Jesus, there's a half-eaten dead animal there. Whatever that flying thing was could carry you away."

"Eagle," Dan said. "Probably a deer carcass the old man puts out there to feed him."

A shaft of light cut forth from the trailer. The door opened and the silhouetted form of Benais peered out into the yard. He did not seem curious or concerned. He watched us for a moment, then turned, went back in, and shut the door.

"He didn't even acknowledge us," I said.

"What do you think that was?" Grover answered.

"It wasn't a greeting."

"We showed ourselves to him. He showed himself to us. What do you want, a banner and a band?"

Dan was surveying the landscape with a curious eye. The skulls hanging from the trees seemed to glow in the night.

"Get the pipe, Grover," Dan said. "Nerburn, you keep me from falling on my ass."

Grover took the buckskin-wrapped pipe from the bag next to him on the seat and handed it to Dan. I helped Dan out of his seat and supported him as he moved toward the trailer.

When we got up the steps Benais opened the door without waiting for us to knock. His face was as dark as a walnut beneath the shock of white hair, and his seed-black eyes glowed empty in the kerosene light.

I had not realized how small he was. He could not have stood more than five feet four or five. His tiny stature made him seem all the more animal-like.

He grinned at us, showing his stubs of teeth, and gestured Dan to enter. He pointed at Grover and me. "You two, you make a fire. There." He pointed to a fire ring near the carcass of the dead animal, then ushered Dan inside and shut the door. Grover and I were left standing on the wooden steps in the shapeless night.

"God, I think he really did know we were coming," I said. Grover shrugged and lit a cigarette.

"Now what?" I said.

"We make a fire."

Grover's eyes, as well as his outdoor skills, were better in the dark than mine. He found Benais's wood pile and set about building a sturdy fire. I did not want to be so near to what seemed to be the meal of animals and large predator birds, but we had no choice.

Grover did not seem concerned in the least. The memory of the bear would not leave me, and I wanted to tell Grover about it. But I was embarrassed by my fear and did not want to open myself to his taunting.

Before long the door to the trailer opened, and Dan made his way tentatively down the four steps, holding tightly onto the two-by-four railing.

"He wants to see you, Nerburn," he said. "Alone."

The command made my blood run cold. Why would a man I had met only once, who knew nothing about me, want to see me?

"What's he want?" I said in a voice too high and shrill.

"Didn't ask," Dan said. "He just said he wanted to talk to the white man. Alone."

I stood up and looked around, hoping for a reprieve.

Dan just whisked at me with his hand. "Get on up there," he said.

I climbed the stairs with my heart in my throat. When I got to the top, the door opened without my having to knock. Benais stood there in front of the wood stove with the kerosene lamps flickering behind him. The smell of sweat and smoke and animal hides filled the room. Birch-bark scrolls were tucked into crannies on the various shelves. Animal bones were spread out on the table.

The smile was gone from his face. He gestured me in with the flap of his hand and pointed me to a chair at his table. He shut the door behind us and took a seat across from me. The only sound was the wind blowing through his wood stove and the rattle of his low, uneven breathing.

"It is good that you brought these people," he said. "But when you were here before you had a machine that could steal my words."

The comment almost made my heart stop. Had Dan told him that I carry a tape recorder?

"Yes," I answered.

"Why did you have it?"

It took me a second to recover. "I wanted to be able to share what you told me with Dan when I saw him. I wanted to get it right."

Benais stood silently, looking at me with those lightless eyes.

"I don't think that's all," he said. "Tell me."

I could not lie to this man. His understanding came from a different place.

"Sometimes I write books," I said. "I try to bring the Indian world to the white people and to help Native people tell their story. The tape recorder — the machine you're talking about — helps me get it right."

"I am not a story," he said.

"I'm sorry," I said. "I should have asked."

"Do you have this machine with you now?"

I pulled the old tape recorder from my pocket.

"Make it steal words."

I pressed the record button and recited, "One-two-three, one-two-three." I felt foolish and ashamed.

He nodded. "Let me hear it."

I pushed the play button. The tinny sound of my recorded voice cut like a thin reed through the silence in the room.

He sat for a long time before speaking. Then he reached over and took a braid of sage from the table and lit it. He waved it around in the air between us.

"A man who would steal another's words is not to be trusted," he said. "You leave."

The abruptness of his command shocked me. "I'm sorry," I said again. "I should have asked."

He had already turned away and sat motionless. I waited for him to say more, but he remained silent.

I stepped out of the trailer into the frigid night air, shaking with shame and fright. I could hear the rise and fall of his rasping breath behind me.

Grover had built a roaring fire. The sparks rose and danced upward into the night sky. He was sitting with his back to me, whittling a stick. Dan was at the edge of the woods staring at a strange orange fog that rose from the horizon like a ghostly prairie fire.

I pulled up a log and sat down across from Grover.

"You look like you seen a ghost, Nerburn," he said.

"I screwed up," I said.

"That's nothing new. What'd you do?"

"Last time I was here I had my tape recorder on when Benais was talking. I didn't tell him. He knew about it."

Grover shook his head. "Now, that was really stupid. You don't mess with guys like this. He knows more about you than you know about yourself."

"He just told me I have to leave."

Grover inhaled deeply and called out to Dan. "Hey, old man, we got a problem."

Dan pulled up his zipper and walked gingerly through the snow back to the fire.

"What's up?"

"Nerburn had that damn tape recorder on last time he was here, and Benais knew it. Now he's told him to leave."

"Did you tell him I had it?" I asked Dan.

"No, I didn't tell him," Dan said. He whistled through his teeth and shook his finger at me. "You shouldn't have done that, Nerburn. He's not the same as me. I asked you to come and get my story. He didn't. You were a guest in his house. You were stealing his words."

"That's what he said. I was just trying to get them right so I could tell them to you exactly."

"You should have asked."

"I know that now."

Dan exhaled wearily, like a man faced with the task of getting a child out of trouble. "Let me talk to him," he said. He grabbed his walking stick and crunched through the snow and frozen leaves back up the trailer steps.

"*Aanin*," I heard him say at the door. Benais said something in response and Dan disappeared inside.

Grover poked the fire, sending sparks into the night. "For a guy that really wants to do the right thing, Nerburn, sometimes you sure do the wrong thing. What were you thinking?"

"I guess I figured since I was doing it for Dan it was okay. I mean, Dan lets me record him."

"So one old Indian's the same as another? Put a bag over their head and they're all the same?"

"I don't know. It was just stupid."

"It was more than stupid. It was wrong. You go into someone's house and steal money off their shelf, you know they aren't going to trust you. This old man's words are more valuable to him than all the money he has. They're the teachings that were handed down to him from his ancestors, and you think it's okay to steal them?"

"I told you, I wasn't thinking. Should I go up there and apologize?"

"It's too late. He doesn't care what you say, just what you did. Leave it lie. The old man will work it out." He spit into the fire. "Or else he won't."

I looked up at the sliver of light coming from around the edges of the blanket over the window in the trailer. My cheeks were burning with shame. I wished that I could take back what I had done and start over again. But even more than that, I was afraid of Benais with his seedlike eyes and his knowledge and his power. How did he know I had the tape recorder? How did he know we were coming? I wished I had never come into these woods and up to his house.

Grover and I sat across from each other, staring into the flames. The silence hung heavy between us. Far above, the sky was alive with an explosion of stars. The Milky Way wound sinuously across the great vault of the night; the North Star shone like a beacon in the purple darkness.

"I feel like just getting up and leaving," I said.

"He might send a rabbit to find you," Grover said.

"I never screwed up this bad before," I said.

Grover just shrugged.

Overhead, a night bird shrieked.

"*Cetan,*" Grover said, turning his attention to the sound. "Hawk. Hunting."

"Do you suppose he'll come down for this?" I said, nodding toward the carcass next to us.

"Nah, *cetan* likes to hunt on his own. He don't like leftovers."

I stared at the dark margins of the clearing with its thick forest of trees, wondering how I could get out of this place. Suddenly I felt a presence moving around the edges of the forest.

I looked at Grover. He had lit a cigarette and was staring placidly into the fire.

"I think there's something out there, Grover," I said. I kept thinking of the bear I had seen in this clearing the last time I had been here.

"There's lots of things out there," he said. "You just aren't used to being watched."

I glanced around, all my senses on alert. I didn't want to seem childish, but something was moving through the trees around us. Fear gripped me in a way I had seldom felt before.

"There's something out there," I said again.

"If it's something that wanted to get you it would already have got you," he said. He gestured casually toward the sky and the darkness. "This is their time. You're in their house now."

Branches snapped. The snow crunched. It was definitely not just wind and winter sounds. I could feel a living presence.

I stood up and turned toward the woods. A massive shadow was moving slowly among the trees, grunting and snorting.

"Grover," I said. "Look. There's really something out there."

He turned casually and stared into the darkness.

"Ah, *tatanka*," he said. "Just like home."

My eyes focused, given a frame of reference by Grover's comment. He was right. It was the shadowy form of a huge buffalo.

A shiver ran through me. It was the buffalo bull, the outcast, the one who had been watching me from the hillside during my last visit. There was no doubt; he had the same malevolent presence, the same dark vigilance. He was moving slowly through the trees, just beyond the clearing. He was alone and silent.

"I know that bull," I said to Grover. My voice was thin and tight.

"He wants to know something," Grover said, as if this was the most natural thing in the world. "He's watching close."

I wanted to get up and run, but there was nowhere to go.

Just then, the door to Benais's trailer opened and a shaft of light cut into the darkness. Benais was standing in the door, silhouetted against the light.

"You," he rasped, nodding toward me. "You come."

I looked to Grover. He gave no response. "You. *Waabishkii-wed.* Come now."

I knew the Ojibwe word for white man. Clearly, he was talking to me.

I glanced at the shadowy form moving slowly in the forest, then at Benais — a shadow himself — standing in the doorway. If there had been a way to leave, I would have jumped up and bolted. I was trapped between two dark presences, and I was not sure which one frightened me more.

Benais reentered his home and shut the door.

I looked again at Grover. I was desperate for some help. He nodded his head toward the trailer. The buffalo bull was rustling in the woods, no more than fifty feet from me.

With no way to escape, I stood and climbed up the trailer steps.

I peered in cautiously. Dan was sitting at the table. Benais was in his old, torn armchair. The *Chanupa* — Dan's pipestone pipe — was carefully disassembled and set next to the bones. The two men had obviously been smoking together.

Benais pointed to a spot on the edge of an old trunk and gestured for me to sit down.

Dan did not acknowledge me. His wrinkled face wore a placid, grandfatherly smile, and his one white eye gleamed emptily in the dim light. Benais stared intently at me, showing neither anger nor warmth.

Without waiting for me to get seated or situated, he began

to speak. "You are a boy pretending to be a man. But *Mishoomis* here says your heart is good. He says you only stole words from me because you were too much of a coward to ask for them. He says you have taken words from him before and that you do not use them for harm. He says you use them to help and that white people listen to you and that you are careful with the words you take.

"That makes me trust you with my words. But it does not make me respect you. You have acted like a child. You can stay, but you must sit outside the circle."

"Thank you, sir," I said, sounding like a child being given a reprieve from a punishment he had earned and deserved.

"You go now," Benais said, brushing me out with his hand. Dan remained impassive and silent.

I stepped back into the star-filled darkness. Grover was still sitting by the fire. I could not hear or see the buffalo bull. I no longer cared why Dan had brought me here or what he thought I would witness. I was right on the edge of getting in my car and driving away. I didn't care about the shame and disapproval. I just wanted to go home and forget this Indian world forever.

Just then a small insistent sound rose in the distance. It was hard and mechanical, a low drone. It had to be Donnie and the others, returning from town.

A great wave of relief washed across me. The young couple and Jumbo represented something human to me, far more than Grover in his distant warrior righteousness. And in a way that was almost embarrassing, my desire to just put my arms around Festus's neck and feel a dog's unqualified love was almost overwhelming.

The lights of the approaching truck strafed the tops of the trees. Soon the beams of the two headlights broke through the forest and the truck rumbled into the clearing. The throb of the diesel engine, far from seeming intrusive, gave the silence a reassuring shape, and I almost ran toward it as it came to a halt.

Grover paid no attention. He was sitting quietly, with his elbows on his knees, staring into the fire, drawing on his cigarette.

Donnie shut off the engine and cut the lights, casting the world once again into darkness. The door opened, the dome light went on, and the small ding of a security bell broke the sudden silence.

One by one, the riders stepped out. Donnie helped Angie from the passenger seat, and Jumbo dislodged himself from the rear and lifted little Zi onto the ground. He was wearing a huge brown animal-skin coat that made him look like the bear I had seen the last time I had been in these woods. Festus scrabbled out of the seat and fell on his side as he stumbled after little Zi. It was all I could do to keep from running up to them and hugging them all.

Jumbo glanced around at the dark forest. "Jesus," he said. "I'm glad I don't live in the woods." Zi walked toward the fire and Grover. She radiated a strange confidence, as if she had been here before.

I glanced around for the buffalo bull, worried for Zi's safety. But the woods were quiet except for the whispering of the night winds and the occasional sound of some small animal moving among the pine boughs. The lump of the dismembered carcass sat silent, slowly covering over with drifting snow.

Zi was almost to the fire when she stopped and looked around. It was as if she had heard something or received some message. Without a moment's hesitation she turned, walked over, and put her arms around me as I sat on the log. She put her head against my chest and held me tight. It was the most unexpected and welcome gesture I had ever received.

She looked up at me with her brown, liquid eyes and took my hand in hers. I almost wanted to cry, I was so relieved and

comforted. How a small girl, so vulnerable and in need of protection herself, could offer such comfort to a grown man in this
great overwhelming darkness was beyond my comprehension. I
thought of Benais's comment during my previous visit when the
buffalo bull had shadowed my movements. "He is measuring your
fear," he'd said. In some incomprehensible way, this little girl, too,
had measured my fear and was trying to offer me comfort.

I put my arms around her and held her closely. The warmth
of her little body evoked the memory of my own children hugging
me tightly when they were young — a comforting sense that life
was as it should be and that all was right with the world.

Her embrace was a refuge from the enveloping night. Tears
welled up in my eyes. She started to sing in a tiny, singsong voice.
It was the same wordless tune she had been singing as she held the
buffalo rock her father had been carving.

Quietly, Jumbo came over and sat down beside me. He, too,
sensed my loneliness and fright. Festus followed behind and lay
his head on my lap.

Donnie and Angie said nothing but watched from a distance.

High above, the northern lights began to flow and dance.

CHAPTER THIRTY

THE NIGHT OF THE DANCING GHOSTS

"*H*ey, Nerburn," Donnie said in quiet greeting. It was as if he, too, was humbled by the power of the surroundings. Grover had left the fire and walked to the edge of the clearing where Dan had been staring at the orange ground fog. We could see his silhouette and the glowing ash of his cigarette as he looked up at the moving sky.

Without Dan or Grover nearby, the rest of us seemed like children gathered around a fire in the great northern night. The lights in the sky were taking on strange unearthly colors and beginning to flow like liquid down to the horizon.

"I never been in a place like this, Nerburn," Donnie said softly. "Is this what it's like where you live?"

"A little," I said. "But not this much." Angie stood close to him, hugging his arm.

Zi left my side and walked around the fire to Jumbo. She brushed her hand against the hands of her mother and father as she passed, making a little cooing sound. Jumbo was watching the growing cascade of lights that spilled down from the heavens. They were now dancing in all directions, changing from purple to phosphorescent green and back again.

I had seen northern lights before, but nothing like this. Still, I was not able to give myself fully to the spectacle; the memory of the buffalo bull, who moments ago had passed not more than fifty feet from where we were sitting, kept drawing my thoughts back to the earth. His dark presence had filled me with an unshakeable fear.

Angie moved closer to me. She still held tight to Donnie's arm. "What's this Mr. Benais like?" she asked. Her thoughts, quite understandably, were more on her daughter than the movements of the sky.

"He seems very wise," I said, trying to keep my voice even and steady. I did not want to visit my own emotional turmoil on this young woman who was obviously apprehensive, if not downright frightened, about the world we had entered.

Angie persisted. "Grandpa Dan said this man will understand Zi. He said he will show us that she's not sick."

"If that's what Grandpa Dan says, we should trust him," I answered with more calm than confidence.

She looked at little Zi sitting next to Jumbo and Festus. "I just want my little girl to be happy," she said softly. She seemed like a lost and desperate child.

I put my hand on her shoulder. "That's what we all want. For our kids to be happy. If Dan thinks this will help, it's good that we're here. I don't think anyone loves her more than he does."

"But he doesn't know this man," she said, almost plaintively.

"Maybe he does. There are different ways of knowing."

She touched her growing belly. "I just want them to be happy and healthy. I don't care how. I just want them to be happy and healthy."

I kept glancing over her shoulder, trying to keep my focus on her while scanning the shapeless forest for the buffalo. The memory of his presence would not leave me.

Donnie was staring at the sky. The lights were now shooting upward from the horizon and flowing in all directions.

"Jesus," Jumbo kept muttering as he watched the moving colors.

"It's the spirits dancing," Donnie said. "That's what my teacher says."

"My grandpa, too," Jumbo added.

We huddled together around the fire, looking upward as the sky overhead became a profusion of shifting lights and colors that silhouetted the dark trees and made the snow-covered ground come alive with a phosphorescent glow.

Little Zi stood up and took Jumbo's huge hand and led him to the edge of the clearing. Festus followed at their side. I was reassured by his presence. If the buffalo bull approached, Festus would let them know.

Just at that moment the door to the trailer opened and Dan and Benais emerged. They were talking in low tones and laughing together like old friends. It was the first time I had seen such humanity in Benais.

They came across the yard slowly. Dan was leaning on his forked stick, speaking in Lakota. Benais was answering in Ojibwe. I had no idea how or if they understood each other, or what they were saying. In the unnatural light the shadows they cast on the snow were twice as long as the men themselves.

They came to the edge of the fire and stood side by side, the bond of their common age far greater than the cultural differences that divided them. I had been worried that the long-standing enmity between the Ojibwe and the Lakota would form a barrier between the two men, but they seemed more like brothers than adversaries or men looking at each other from opposite sides of a cultural divide.

They sat down across the fire from us. Benais reached his small gnarled paw of a hand out for me to shake. "I feel no hardness toward you," he said. "*Mishoomis* has explained you and why you do the things you do."

His approval sent a wave of relief through me.

"It was a mistake. I was doing it to assist Dan," I said.

"You must not speak of it again," Benais said. "I have laid it on the ground. You must too."

He crinkled his eyes slightly, in what appeared to be a smile.

He turned toward Dan. "Who are these people you have brought with you?" he said. It was less a question than a request for introductions.

"They are the parents of the young girl I have spoken of," Dan said.

Benais reached out and took both of their hands in his own.

"It is good that you are here. I have been told that you have fear for your daughter," he said to Angie.

"Yes, Grandfather," Angie responded.

"Why do you have this fear?"

"She's different."

"And why would that cause you fear?" He was opening her slowly without guiding her comments.

"She doesn't play with anyone. She hardly talks, except to Grandpa Dan and animals. She knows things. People are afraid of her."

"Ah. So their fear causes your fear."

"It scares me when she knows things or does things like talking to the animals or picking up birds."

"Grandpa Dan says she has an old spirit," Donnie added.

Benais smiled. "And so you bring her to me?"

"Grandpa Dan says she is like his sister," Angie said, "and that you knew his sister. He said you will understand her knowledge. We hope you can help us, Grandfather."

He nodded and stared at the earth.

"This girl," he said, pointing toward Jumbo and Zi at the edge of the clearing. "Is that her over there with the large man?"

"Yes," said Angie. "Should I get her?"

Benais lifted his hand. "No. I will watch."

Zi was standing between Jumbo and Festus. The sky in front of them was moving in waves.

"Do you know of these lights in your country?" Benais said to Donnie.

"Yes, Grandfather," Donnie said. "In our country they are called *Wanagi Wacipi*. Ghosts dancing. But we don't have them like this."

"Do you hear them?" Benais asked. He pointed upward. Sharp cracking and popping sounds were coming from the sky. I had assumed they were branches breaking or sounds in the forest.

"They are not like the stars, who care nothing for us. Listen." The cracking continued. "They talk to us," he said.

Once Benais had drawn our attention to the sounds, it was obvious that they were coming from the sky and not from the surrounding forest.

Zi had lifted her hands toward the flowing lights and was moving back and forth, almost dancing, in time to their movement.

"Ah," said Benais. "She hears them. That is good."

Angie looked at him with surprise. She was unused to hearing anyone speak approvingly of her daughter's actions.

"Yes, she is a good girl," Benais repeated. He pointed at the sky. "The fires of the grandfathers. She is dancing to them. They are talking to her."

The strange popping was getting louder, accompanied by chirping, like undersea sonar or the sounds of whales. I had never heard such sounds before. The sky moved and twisted and flowed. Zi was dancing, as if at a powwow, circling and dipping and weaving.

From his seat by the fire, Dan followed her movements and smiled.

Donnie and I looked at each other. All around, shadows moved in the shifting light.

Grover had moved off to the edge of the forest. Only the rising and falling of his orange cigarette ash betrayed his presence.

"He is a protector," Benais said.

Dan nodded.

"We have them among our people, too."

The two men smiled at each other in their common knowledge.

Jumbo, seeing that Dan and Benais had arrived, hurried over, leaving Festus to stand watch over little Zi's dancing. His eyes were wide.

"I won't leave her for long," he said to Dan. "But I never seen nothing like this."

Benais shook his head and put his finger to his lips.

"Sorry," Jumbo whispered. He stood, awestruck, gazing up at the moving sky.

"They are talking. She is listening," Benais said. Festus stood beside her, alert and vigilant, as she swooped and danced beneath the shifting, whorling lights.

After a moment, Benais turned to Jumbo. "I see you are her friend," he said.

"Yes, Grandfather," Jumbo answered in an uncharacteristically soft voice, "I try to take care of her." I was sure it must have been the tone he had used when he had talked to his own grandfather.

"And what are you called?" Benais asked.

"Everyone calls me Jumbo, Grandfather."

"That does not sound like a Lakota name," Benais said. His eyes crinkled with a distant mirth.

Jumbo looked around at all of us, as if embarrassed to speak in our presence. "My Indian name is Tatanka Cicala. It means Young Buffalo. My grandfather gave it to me. People call me Jumbo because..." He blushed slightly and looked down at his stomach.

Benais held up his hand to stop him from saying more.

"Tatanka Cicala. Now, that is a good name. Do you try to live up to that name?"

"My friends said I was given it because I snore so loud."

"I do not think your grandfather would have given you a name to honor your snoring. There is more to the buffalo than the sounds that he makes," Benais said. "Tell me about this *tatanka*, as you call it. What do you know of it?"

It was fascinating how Benais was able to draw Jumbo out. I had never before heard Jumbo utter his Lakota name. He looked around sheepishly.

He began slowly, as if reciting something he had learned years ago.

"I watch *tatanka*, Grandfather," he said. "My grandpa told me I could learn from him."

"And what have you learned?"

"*Tatanka* is a noble animal. He cares for his children until they are old enough to live on their own. He never fights with other animals unless he is attacked."

Jumbo paused. Benais nodded for him to continue.

"He gives everything he has for the humans. He gives his coat for shelter and clothing, his bones for needles, his horn for drinking cups, his flesh for food."

"Is there more?"

Jumbo squeezed his hands together. "He can read our hearts," he said softly.

Benais nodded his approval. "I think Tatanka Cicala is a good name for you. Even if you wear the name Jumbo on the outside, you should hold close to the name of Tatanka Cicala on the inside. It is a great gift to be able to read people's hearts."

He turned his attention to the rest of us gathered around the fire. "I am pleased you are all here. We should smoke now. My friend, we will use your *Chanupa*," he said to Dan, honoring Dan's tradition by using the Lakota word for the sacred pipe.

Dan had carried his pipe out from Benais's trailer. He unfurled the buckskin roll and fastened the red pipestone bowl to the wooden handle, then handed it to Benais.

Benais took some tobacco or *kinnikinnick* from a pouch on his belt and carefully packed the bowl, tamping it down with his finger after each pinch.

Everyone moved closer. This was a ritual they all knew — the common ceremony of all Indian people — the coming together around the pipe to send the smoke of the earth to the four directions, down to the earth, and up to the heavens to honor the Creator.

Benais took a coal from the fire and lit the bowl, drawing hard to bring the *kinnikinnick* to a glow. The smoke rose into the night air. He then extended the pipe in front of him and rotated it slowly in a complete circle, before handing it to Dan, who did the same, then passed it on.

One by one we took the pipe, drew the *kinnikinnick* into our lungs, and performed the ceremony of sharing the Creator's smoke in the manner in which we each had learned it. They were private gestures, performed like prayers.

When the pipe came to me, Benais relit the *kinnikinnick* with an ember, and I prayed silently for peace for Donnie and Angie and Dan and Zi. Benais watched me as if he was reading my heart. He smiled slightly as I finished and passed it to Jumbo.

Above us the sky moved from unearthly greens to brilliant reds and lavenders. The lights shot upward, then wrapped around us like the smoke rising from the pipe.

When each of us had finished with the pipe, Benais turned to Jumbo. "Get your young friend, Tatanka Cicala," he said.

"I will, Grandfather," Jumbo said. He pushed himself upward and hulked across the crusted snow to where little Zi was still dancing on the edge of the clearing.

Angie and Donnie sat silently with their heads down. I moved closer to Angie and put my arm around her shoulder.

Jumbo came hurrying back with Zi, holding her hand in his. She could barely keep up with the huge man's stride. Festus was close behind.

"Here, Grandfather," Jumbo said. He led Zi to the circle and positioned her directly in front of Benais. Zi said nothing, just stood motionless in her dirty pink parka with her chin down and her little wool cap pulled down over her ears. Festus stood protectively by her side.

"*Animosh*," Benais said, and gestured toward the ground. Festus immediately lay down.

"Come," he said to Zi. She moved closer, staring directly at him from beneath her bangs.

He took her face in his aged hands and stared at her for what seemed like minutes.

"*Noozhishenh*," he said softly, using the Ojibwe word for "my grandchild." Zi's dark, liquid eyes were locked on his. Without averting his glance, he reached his left hand toward Donnie and Angie. "What is her name?" he asked them.

"Zintkala Zi," Angie answered. "Grandpa Dan gave it to her."

"And what does it mean?"

"It means Yellow Bird, Grandfather," Donnie said.

"It's the same name as Grandpa Dan's little sister that you knew," Angie added.

Benais nodded and began speaking in Ojibwe. His manner was formal and ceremonial. When he finished in Ojibwe, he repeated what he had said in English.

"Zintkala Zi. You are finally here safe. You came running to be born. We will take care of you good and support you. Zintkala Zi. You are finally here safe. You came running to be born. We will take care of you good and support you."

The doubling of the phrase made it seem like an incantation, formalized over many generations.

He spoke another phrase in Ojibwe that sounded like *Gizhawendaagoz*. Then, in English, he said, "Everybody loves you, including the spirits, too." He repeated the phrases a second time, keeping her face in his hands.

Zi did not move, but stood, passive and compliant, as the ancient man stared into her eyes and spoke.

She said something very softly, and Benais responded in kind. She looked at the sky and moved her hands in the direction of the dancing lights.

"Go," he said. "Go to them."

She walked back toward the edge of the forest clearing where she had been dancing. Festus stayed right at her side. She turned and waved to Benais. Benais waved back. I had never seen her wave at anyone before.

"I know her," Benais said.

From his place on the log I could see a small smile creep across Dan's face.

Angie moved closer to Donnie. She tugged slightly on his sleeve and pushed at him.

Donnie whispered something to her, then stood up and approached Benais. His eyes were down and his hands were shaking. "I would like to offer you a gift, Grandfather," he said.

He reached into his jacket pocket and pulled out the buffalo stone he had carved. He had polished it to a buff smoothness, but it still retained the perfect balance between the image of a buffalo and the natural form of a stone. It was truly a beautiful work.

"I carved this for you," Donnie continued. "Zintkala Zi

helped find the stone. It came from a place on our reservation where the stones sit up high and look at the sky all day. It had not been touched. It came up from the earth on its own. My teacher said it knew where it wanted to go when it called to us. He said I should offer it to you, Grandfather."

It was a formal statement, obviously prepared. Donnie's voice wavered as he spoke.

Benais's eyes crinkled, and he held out his hands. Donnie placed the stone in them. Benais said something low in Ojibwe.

"This is a good thing," he said in English. "I can feel the earth's heartbeat."

With his hands still shaking, Donnie reached into his pocket again and pulled out a packet of Prince Albert tobacco and held it out to Benais. Benais looked at it, then at Donnie, then back at the tobacco. Slowly he nodded, took the tobacco in his hands, and held it with the buffalo carving. "*Miigwech*," he said — the Ojibwe word for "thank you."

"Grandfather, may we ask you a question?" Donnie said.

I had seen this ritual many times before — even participated in it: the offering of tobacco as a gift for the right to ask for the gift of another person's knowledge.

"What is it you would like to know?" Benais said.

Angie stepped forward, as if this was her cue.

"Grandfather," she said, "should we listen to the white doctors? They tell us our little daughter is sick."

Benais smiled and took her hand in a fatherly, caring gesture. "White doctors do not understand this," he said, looking out over the snows at little Zi dancing in the glow of the flowing lights. "There is no sickness here. This has been passed to her."

Angie held tight to Benais's hand. "What do you mean, Grandfather?" she said.

"The old ones called to your daughter when her spirit ran by to be born. They said, 'We know you, little one, and you will remember us. You will remember us and we will remember you.' That is what she is doing. She is remembering."

"But what shall we do, Grandfather?" Angie persisted. "The white doctors want to give her white-man medicines."

Benais held up his hand to silence her.

"The white people always try to destroy what they do not understand. Their world is too small and they protect it with violence. These doctors, they are trying to destroy your girl with the violence of their medicine. Do not be angry with them. They are not cruel, they are afraid. But they have made their fear your fear. You should not fear for your daughter. Her world is rich. You should not fear her knowledge. You should protect it."

On the rise at the edge of the clearing we could see Zi dancing to the luminous, snaking bands of purple and green phosphorescence floating across the sky. Her tiny voice could be heard against the crackings and poppings of the celestial movements.

"You," Benais said, gesturing to Donnie. "You tell me this stone came from the place where the stones look at the sky. You say it had not been touched. You say it came up there from the earth and lay there waiting. Many people passed it and it did not speak. Then your daughter came by. The stone knew your daughter and spoke to her. She did not choose it; it chose her."

Donnie nodded.

"That is the way the spirits of the old ones work," Benais continued. "They are almost silent now. They speak only when someone passes who can hear their voice. They know the white world is a world of noise, and they do not shout. They wait. They have the patience of the earth, like this stone. When your daughter came running to be born, they spoke to her. She listened.

"She has been given the gift of the old knowledge, just like this stone was a gift to you. Now she must shape it. You must help her."

"But how can we do that?" Donnie said.

"You should keep her from the white people. Her knowledge

is not meant for them. Keep her close to the elders. They will teach her. Keep her close to the animals. She hears them and they hear her.

"Remember that she is not yours. She is a gift to the Indian people to remind us that the old ways are not gone, they are only keeping silent. She is like her name, the Yellow Bird, who rises up in springtime from the dark of winter. She is a voice of hope for the people in the time of darkness."

Dan was smiling slightly, with closed eyes. This is what he had hoped to hear.

I thought we were done. But Angie wanted more. She was a mother protecting her child with a warrior's heart.

"Thank you, Grandfather," she said. "Your words are good, but they are only words. How are we to know she has the old knowledge? How are we to know the old ones are speaking to her? How are we to know this is not a sickness, as the white men say?"

Benais smiled a tiny ferret-toothed smile. "When one has the old knowledge, it is shown," he said. "It will be shown."

He brushed his hand across the sky.

"It will be shown," he said again.

Then he turned abruptly toward the trailer, holding the buffalo stone Donnie had given him in both hands.

It was an unexpected departure, and surprising in its finality. We all stood, silently, watching the hunched little man with his shock of white hair make his way across the snows back to his trailer.

I looked at Donnie and Angie. I couldn't guess what they were feeling. They had come hundreds of miles with the promise of learning something that would set their minds at ease about their little daughter, and Benais's talk seemed more like a benediction than any sort of corroboration or proof.

I slid over closer to Dan. "Is that it?" I said. "I thought you said he was going to show us something."

Dan raised his hand, as if telling me to have patience.

Benais had almost reached the trailer steps. He turned and smiled his animal smile toward Angie and Donnie.

"It will be shown," he said.

He flapped his hand toward Dan and Grover. "You two. My brothers. Come. We will smoke more."

Then he opened the door and disappeared into his home.

Grover and Dan stood up and followed him. Grover held Dan's arm as Dan used the crooked stick to support himself on the hard-packed snow. They did not look at us as they climbed the steps. They opened the door and walked into the trailer, leaving us alone in the great winter darkness.

CHAPTER THIRTY-ONE

THE SINGING SKIES

*T*he men entered the trailer and pulled the door shut behind them. It was as if the forest had closed in around us. The air was suddenly colder, and the fire seemed but a small flicker of light in the great northern darkness. The aurora danced above us like retreating ghosts.

We all gathered in closely around the fire. The flames had settled to a low orange glow, and the dying embers spat sparks into the night. The chill from the winter darkness cut into our backsides as we leaned in to get the last vestiges of warmth before the night overtook us all.

"I guess we should go get her," I said, gesturing toward little Zi, who was still dancing at the edge of the clearing.

"Leave her," Jumbo said. "At least she's happy." There was an unspoken sadness in his comment, as if he, too, felt a hollow incompletion at the way the journey was ending.

Donnie and Angie huddled together and whispered. I could see the confusion in their eyes.

Donnie took off his thin leather jacket and draped it over his young wife's shoulders. She pulled her hands inside the sleeves of her grey hooded sweatshirt and clasped her hands around her belly.

Jumbo leaned in toward the dying fire and rubbed his huge hands together, trying to get the last warmth from the flames.

The lights in the sky were shifting again, turning from a phosphorescent green to an iridescent purple. They snaked across the heavens, shooting shafts of light upward through the firmament of stars.

"Sometimes I wonder if it's all gone, Nerburn," Jumbo said. "All of it. The old people chasing their memories. Us young people hoping for something we never knew. I wanted there to be something for little Zi. I don't know — just something." He wrung his hands and stared into the embers.

"I just don't know what's right," he said. "You can't give up hope, but it ain't no good to live in pretend. We try to live right, but we just can't seem to touch the old places." Donnie and Angie nodded.

We all stared across at little Zi as she danced to the swirling lights — a tiny priestess of a forgotten rite, moving in time to some celestial music from a world where animals spoke and stones sang out their songs.

Jumbo pointed up to Benais's trailer and the thin rim of light coming from around the blanket-covered window.

"What do you think it's like for them, Nerburn?" he said. "I mean, is it real for them?"

"Probably not for Grover," I said. "Dan? He wants it to be. Benais? I think he knows things we can't even imagine."

Jumbo let out a sigh of weariness. He stirred the fire with

a stick, sending sparks flying into the sky, then pushed himself upward and turned toward the clearing. "I'm going to go get her," he said. "It's getting too cold. I don't like her being out there by herself."

He took several steps toward Zi, then turned back to us.

"Where is she?" he said.

We turned as one in the direction of the field. The lights in the sky were rising like ghostly green campfires from the horizon, illuminating the snow with an unearthly glow. But Zi was nowhere to be seen.

Panic swept across us. It couldn't have been more than a minute since we had last seen her. We all had been keeping watch over her, figuring that so many pairs of eyes would keep her safe.

"Maybe she's just over the hill," I said. "I'll go see."

I ran to the top of the rise and looked across the field. Zi was nowhere to be seen.

"I don't see her," I shouted.

Angie let out a gasp and pulled away from Donnie. She rushed toward where her daughter had last been standing. "Where is she?" she said, the fear rising in her voice. "I just saw her."

"I'll check the woods," Jumbo said. He lurched off toward the bank of trees where the buffalo had been standing.

Angie was quickly becoming frantic. "Where's my baby?" she said, searching the wind-blown snow for footprints. "Someone find my baby!" The night air cracked at the sound of her voice.

Jumbo lumbered across the snow in his huge coat and heavy boots, shouting out Zi's name. His cries were like the bellows of a wounded animal.

Donnie ran back toward the truck to get a flashlight.

I thought of running to the trailer to alert Dan and Benais and Grover, but there was no time to waste. They were too old to help, and we needed to find Zi before she got lost in the tangle of woods. Her ragged thrift-shop jacket wasn't warm enough to stand a night outside in this cold.

The yard was a chaos of shadows and confusion. Jumbo shouted from the trees for us to follow him. Angie and Donnie ran to opposite corners of the field, calling out their daughter's name. The aurora above us flashed and moved, shifting from green to red to an otherworldly purple.

I headed across the clearing toward the woods where Jumbo was yelling. I could hear him thrashing among the branches and the tree trunks. I had no idea where his strength and stamina came from. I could hardly catch up to him as he crashed through the ankle-deep snow, snorting and wheezing and shouting out for Zi.

Finally, exhaustion overtook him. Unable to go farther, he bent over and rested his hands on his knees. "We got to find her, Nerburn," he gasped. "We got to. She's my best friend." He looked up at me with an innocence that was heartbreaking. "I let this happen. My grandpa told me I had to take care of people. I let this happen."

He pushed himself upright and surged forward again, his chest heaving.

Donnie was to the left of us, shining his flashlight across the snow, looking for footprints. From somewhere in the clearing Angie was crying out her daughter's name.

Jumbo tore through the trees, cracking branches and snapping limbs.

"I found a path," he shouted. "She must have gone through here."

The others rushed over. We stopped for a moment to catch our breath, then fell in behind him as he pushed along the path. The moon shone cold and distant through the breaks in the branches overhead.

Slowed by an old leg injury, I was about ready to fall back and let the rest of them go on ahead, when the path opened into a broad, snow-covered valley. It spread out before us, silver in the spectral moonlight, for at least a mile in either direction. At the far horizon, the haunting lights of the aurora rose like searchlights into the dark dome of the night.

We all stopped, brought up short by the awesome majesty of the scene before us.

"Jesus," said Jumbo, pointing to the luminous, snow-bright earth. "Look at that." All across the hillside and valley, alone and in groups, stood silent, stolid forms — dozens, maybe a hundred, buffalo, breathing steam from their nostrils into the frigid northern night. They looked like boulders in the strange nocturnal light.

In a moment of recognition, my dream came rushing back to me. These were the same forms I had seen as Yellow Bird walked away from me in my dream, beckoning me to follow. They were exactly as I remembered them, but now they were clear and recognizable.

The buffalo stood dark against the midnight snows, grunting and lowing and pawing at the earth.

I grabbed Jumbo by the sleeve. "She's out there," I said. "She's out there with those buffalo. I know it."

Jumbo nodded amid his gasps for breath. He did not ask for an explanation.

The others moved in around us. "I don't think she'd go out there," Donnie said. In the distance, the buffalo made deep, rumbling sounds and shifted slowly in the snows.

"Come on," Jumbo wheezed. "We've looked everywhere else."

Without waiting for more discussion, he pushed forward onto the open hillside.

We pulled in tighter to one another and fell in behind him. We were all happy to let him lead. The beasts snorted and chuffed and gave off steam from their backs and mouths and noses as we moved into their valley.

In spite of my dream, I was nervous about entering the valley. I had read too much about the unpredictability of buffalo, seen too many videos of them goring unsuspecting tourists who thought approaching them was a game.

We moved as carefully and quietly as we could. Some of the beasts jumped and snorted as we moved down into their valley. There was something dark and threatening about them. They exuded a potent and ominous indifference.

Donnie leaned in close to me. "My uncle raises them," he said quietly. "He would never go out in a field like this."

"Do you think we're making a mistake?" I said.

"We don't have any choice," he said. "We've got to look everywhere."

We pulled close together and moved as a group. Alerted by our presence, the huge animals began to rustle and shift. Slowly, they turned in our direction, as if acting from a common mind.

One by one, they moved from their places on the hillsides and the edge of the woods and began walking toward us. It was as if we had aroused their curiosity and they were slowly closing in to see what had entered their land.

Soon they were all headed in our direction. They moved without hurry, grunting and snorting, as if speaking to one another.

"Do they attack?" I whispered.

"They can," Donnie answered. "Just keep walking." He had his arm around Angie, who was holding her stomach protectively.

I put my head down and kept my eyes on my feet. The dark presence of the approaching animals filled me with fear.

Jumbo was five paces ahead of us, moving with a sense of purpose.

"When my grandpa gave me my name he said I would have strong power with *tatanka*," he said. "We're going to just keep walking. We're going to find little Zi." It was the most forceful statement I had ever heard him make.

The buffalo had moved in close. They formed a dark wall on either side of us, no more than ten feet away. They moved along with us, grunting and snorting and tossing their heads. Their shoulders stood level with our eyes.

I could not tell if they had come down to us out of curiosity or if they had some darker intent. Donnie spoke softly. "Just keep walking, Nerburn," he said again. "They can feel what you're thinking."

Angie moved in between us. She kept her hands clasped tightly around her belly in an unconscious gesture of protection of her unborn child. The grey hood of her sweatshirt was pulled up over her head.

The buffalo were so close we could touch them. They moved alongside of us — shaggy, matted, with eyes as lightless as lumps of coal.

The snow crunched beneath our feet. The sky popped and whorled as the carnival of lights flashed from horizon to horizon. On all sides of us, the great beasts grunted and snorted and filled the air with their overpowering musk.

I was almost immobilized from fear. I had entered into a frozen state of hyperawareness; I had no sense of time or movement or the presence of my own body. I had never been this close to such huge wild animals before, never felt so vulnerable. I had visions of us being gored or crushed and left to die on this lonely snow-blown field.

I looked at Donnie and Jumbo and Angie but could barely recognize them. They were like dream forms, moving beside me in slow motion.

The buffalo, too, seemed to be part of a different world. Their grunts and snorts sounded like talking and whispering and laughing.

My mind tumbled and raced. I remembered my first visit to Benais, when he had spoken with the birds and animals. Was this what he had been hearing? Was this how little Zi heard the world when rabbits climbed into her hands and stones cried out for her attention?

I moved with the others through the dark flowing night.

I don't know how long we went on this way. Jumbo had fallen silent, and Angie's sobs and whimpers had settled into a quiet shallow breathing. We moved across the valley as if lost inside a dream.

Then, without warning, a form flashed out of the darkness and hurtled into Jumbo's legs.

"Festus!" Jumbo said. It was the old dog, panting and coughing. He thrust his nose against Jumbo's hand and whined and wheezed.

The buffalo snorted and jumped back, as if surprised. As they parted, we could see, for the first time, the full extent of the valley that surrounded us. It spread out before us — a great bowl of land bathed in silver moonlight and rimmed with dark, impenetrable pine forests that seemed to stretch without limit toward the distant horizon. More buffalo — scores of them — stood alone and in small clumps as far as the eye could see.

Angie let out a tiny gasp. "We'll never find her out there," she said.

I looked out across the great, snow-covered hollow. The buffalo stood, dark as shadows, some milling, some motionless, some solitary under trees or on the distant hillside. On the far edge of the valley, against the dark barrier of the distant forest, one group stood silently in a circle. There must have been thirty of them, standing shoulder to shoulder, heads facing out. Clouds of steam rose from their shaggy coats. They swayed their heads slowly, but their bodies remained motionless.

"What are they doing?" I said.

"I don't know," Jumbo said. "I never seen nothing like that."

Elsewhere, small groups of the animals stood hidden in the

shadows — mothers with light-brown calves, bulls rubbing their flanks against trees or rolling on their backs in the snow.

The buffalo that had so recently surrounded us were slowly withdrawing to the hillsides and clusters of trees, where they faded into the margins of the darkness. It was as if they had guided us to this place and now were receding into the night.

"What's going on?" I asked.

"I don't know," Donnie said. "I don't understand any of this."

Angie began to cry again. "I wish we had never come to this place," she sniffed.

Jumbo placed his hand gently on her shoulder. "We'll find her, Angie," he said. "I promise." His tone was kind and comforting.

We stood, forlorn and confused, staring across the broad valley. The northern lights were quietly receding — ghostly trails disappearing into the purple night. In their wake, the stars burst forth in cold and icy brilliance.

We all scanned the valley looking for movement. A frightened little girl could be huddled down, almost invisible, anywhere in the snows.

"We just have to keep going," Donnie said. "Keep looking for tracks." But the hard crust and wisping snows made the search for tracks futile.

Festus continued to nose at Jumbo's sleeve with his wet, grey muzzle. Jumbo knelt down and took the old dog's head in his hands.

"Do you know where Zi is?" he said.

Festus wagged his tail earnestly.

"I think this dog knows something," Jumbo said. He pointed Festus in the direction of the valley. "Go," he said. "Show us."

Festus barked once and bolted off down the hill.

"We better follow him," Jumbo said.

Festus ran about twenty feet, stopped and turned to make sure we were still behind him, gave another yip, then took off again.

"Do you think that dog understands him?" I said to Donnie.

"You got a better idea?" he said.

We all pushed forward after the old dog, giving ourselves over to the faint hope that he might be able to lead us to little Zi.

With the aurora dimming and the sky darkening, the night suddenly seemed colder. Moments before it had been alive, magical, and dancing. Now it felt indifferent, icy, and distant. The wind was picking up and howling with an almost human sound as it funneled down the valley.

The buffalo seemed to have lost all interest in us. Those that had surrounded us had taken up positions on hillsides and in thickets and were watching placidly as we moved through the valley. The rest had returned to their private concerns and were chuffing and pawing in the night shadows. Only the group standing in a circle at the margin of the forest showed any interest in us, and they, too, seemed mostly unconcerned about our presence. We moved alone and unimpeded through the great indifferent night.

My fingers had begun to go numb, and the blowing snow had made its way into my boots and burned like fire against my ankles. Angie had her hands pulled up into her sleeves, and I could see Donnie shivering in his thin, hooded sweatshirt.

He pulled the sweatshirt hood up over his head. "If my little girl's going to freeze to death, I'm going to freeze to death with her," he said. He kept his voice low so Angie didn't hear.

He fell in behind Jumbo. We all did the same. In some unspoken way, Jumbo had become our leader.

We moved down the center of the ghostly silver valley. The world looked like a tintype from a different time.

At last, Angie could stand it no more. She began shouting, "Zi. Zi. It's your mommy. Answer me." Her voice violated the silence and echoed into the frozen dark.

"Angie, be quiet," Donnie said. "We don't want to spook *tatanka*."

Angie paid no attention but continued shouting. Her cries disappeared, unanswered, into the night.

Festus heard the distress in her voice and limped over to comfort her. He rubbed against her thigh and nudged at her sleeve with his muzzle.

She knelt down and hugged him tightly. "Can't you help me find my little girl?" she sobbed. Festus looked at her with earnest, sympathetic eyes. She had reached the point of hysteria.

Donnie tried to calm her, but she pulled away and took off, stumbling, through the snow. She lost her footing and fell, then got up and fell again. Festus ran alongside her, nosing at her legs, as if trying to assist her.

"I'm telling you, that dog knows something," Jumbo said.

We let Angie and Festus push on ahead of us. Donnie stayed right behind, keeping close to his sobbing wife.

Though we had moved deep into the part of the valley where the buffalo stood, they all gave Angie wide berth. It was as if they could sense her motherly desperation and were, in their own way, respecting her grief.

Eventually, even Donnie fell back. We all watched helplessly as the young mother pushed and sobbed and stumbled through the snow.

Jumbo had finally reached the point of exhaustion. He was bent over, wheezing, almost unable to move. Donnie's eyes had narrowed and his jaw was clenched. We almost dared not look at each other for the unspoken knowledge we all shared. Only Angie was moving forward with anything close to hope.

We had passed through the center of the valley and were now moving toward the distant wood. If little Zi had made it that far — a doubtful proposition — she would have been faced with a dense tangle of dark pine and deadfall that even the buffalo did not enter.

"We've lost her," I said, being the first to state the obvious.

Even Festus seemed to have lost the will to go farther. He pulled once at Angie's sleeve in an attempt to stop her, then returned to us, whimpering, with his head low and his tail between his legs. I reached down and patted his head. He looked up with apology in his eyes and nosed me several times on the hand.

"It's okay, buddy," I said. "You did the best you could."

He licked my hand and slunk off toward the trees.

Angie had sat down in the snow and was sobbing softly, her face buried in her hands. Donnie came up and knelt beside her and put his arm around her shoulder. "We'll probably have to wait till morning," he said.

"No," she choked. "It's too cold. She'll freeze. She's out here somewhere. She has to be. Please, let's look just a little longer."

Donnie stared up at us with sad, resigned eyes.

I looked out across the great expanse of valley. The wind was increasing and the gusts were lifting the snow into a blowing mist.

I shook my head slightly. Donnie nodded in acknowledgment.

I felt a twinge of shame. If it were my child who was lost, I, too, would insist on going forward. But the winds were getting brutal and the chill dark was overtaking the night. It would be challenge enough just to work our way back, much less to find a little girl who could be anywhere within miles of where we were standing.

"Come on, Ange," Donnie said. "Zi's a smart little girl. She'll figure out a place to stay warm until morning."

"She's four!" Angie shouted. "She'll die!" It was the first time anyone had voiced the unspoken fear that we all harbored in our hearts.

"Let's work our way backward," I said. "Maybe we've missed her." I gestured toward the dark tangle of forest ahead of us that was quickly disappearing in the mist of the swirling snow. "She couldn't have gotten any farther than this."

"Nerburn's right," Donnie said, trying to put a good face on things. "She's probably behind us, huddled under a tree some-where." He, too, was doing his best to lift Angie's spirits.

"Or maybe she's back at Benais's," Jumbo added. "She might have just wandered off where we didn't see her. We didn't look everywhere. She might be sitting there with Dan and Benais at the fire."

Our words echoed hollow, but we pretended to believe them. Except for Angie, none of us had the heart to go on.

Angie looked up at Donnie with tear-stained eyes. She, too, seemed to be realizing that further searching was fruitless. "We'll keep looking on the way back, won't we?" she said.

He put his hand on her shoulder. "We'll keep looking until we find her."

The moon had risen high in the sky and was moving, ghostly, behind the blowing snows. The winds howled like voices down the valley. Donnie helped Angie up and took her hand in his, and we began the long walk back to Benais's trailer.

CHAPTER THIRTY-TWO

TATANKA NEVER LIES

*W*e moved in silence, each lost in our own thoughts. Jumbo again was in the lead. He trudged forward with the same heavy stride he had displayed on the way into the valley. But now his head was down and his shoulders were slumped. The wind cut across us and pelted us with blowing snow.

We proceeded slowly, holding our jacket collars tight to our necks. I couldn't imagine how Donnie was surviving in just a thin sweatshirt, but he refused to take back the jacket he had placed over Angie's shoulders back at the fire.

Occasionally, Jumbo would turn to see if we were all together, then forge forward as soon as he was convinced we were all safe. We were like a string of refugees moving with resignation and defeat through the frigid winter night.

Jumbo's concern for us was touching. He would not force the pace if any of us seemed to be tiring. He would stop and pretend to be catching his breath or listening to the wind until we had all caught up.

We had all ceased talking. The only sounds were the winds, Jumbo's labored breathing, and an occasional sniffle or whimper from Angie.

Suddenly Jumbo stopped. "Where's Festus?" he said.

We all looked around. The old dog was nowhere to be seen.

Jumbo paused and looked off over the field. He leaned his head into the wind and gestured us all into silence.

"Do you hear something?" he asked.

"Is it Festus?" I said.

He held up his hand. "Maybe. I can't tell." His attention was focused on the distance.

I inclined my ear in the direction he was facing. I could hear nothing out of the ordinary. "It's just the wind." I said.

"No. I know wind. This is different."

The others had come up behind. We all stood motionless as Jumbo listened.

"It ain't normal," he said.

"You're not used to tree country," I said. "That's just how it sounds up here."

"Hold on," Jumbo said. "Listen."

There was an odd high-pitched keening weaving through the howlings of the wind. It sounded like a moan or an animal cry.

"I hear it, too," Donnie said.

We all remained silent, trying to identify the strange, distant sound.

"It's coming from over there," I said, pointing back toward the woods. We turned and squinted into the darkness. Through the blowing snows we could barely make out the group of buffalo we had seen from the top of the hill. They were still in a circle, standing shoulder to shoulder with their heads facing out.

The sound was coming from somewhere in their midst.

"Come on," Jumbo said, moving toward them. "We'd better go see."

It was a long way back across the field. The sound continued, carried faintly on the wind.

"That's a weird sound for a dog to make," I said.

Jumbo gestured me to be quiet. "It ain't a dog," he said.

As we got close to the ring of animals, Angie let out a gasp. "It sounds like Zi," she said. Through the whistling and moaning of the wind and the snorts and grunts of the buffalo, we could barely make out a tiny sound, like a child's voice singing.

"That's her," Angie said. "That's my baby. I'd know her voice anywhere."

She pulled forward in an attempt to get to her daughter.

Donnie held her back. "We can't just run up there," he said. "It's too dangerous." The buffalo were a living fortress, an impenetrable wall. Their blank eyes and guttural grunts were like barriers to any approach.

"Look," Donnie said.

A small, stationary form was stretched out in the snow, no more than ten feet in front of the circle of buffalo.

"Is that Festus?"

The old dog was lying flat on his stomach with his head on his front paws, facing directly toward the buffalo. His ears were pulled back and he was tense and motionless, like an animal sent forth to flush big game. He was growling and whining. The buffalo were facing back at him, grunting and pawing.

"She must be behind them," Jumbo said. "He's trying to get to her."

The buffalo were threatening and ominous. Festus was inching forward, crawling slowly on his belly.

"They're talking back and forth," Jumbo said. "Listen."

Festus's growling rose and fell. The buffaloes' grunts punctuated his snarling, as if in response.

"They'll kill him," Jumbo said. "I've got to stop him." He lurched away from us and lumbered across the snow toward the old dog.

"We've got to stay together," Donnie said. The snow was picking up. "Come on." He grabbed Angie's arm and took off after Jumbo. She was already pulling ahead, trying to get to her daughter.

I was terrified that the buffalo might charge. They could easily crush us if they spooked or decided we had gotten too close to their territory. But if that was indeed Zi we needed to get to her. I had to trust that the others knew more about buffalo than I did.

Jumbo had already reached Festus and was kneeling next to him with his hand on the old dog's head. The two of them were staring directly at the beasts. They seemed tiny and vulnerable next to the circle of snorting animals.

The rest of us moved up close and crouched down beside them. The buffaloes' heads were no more than a few arms' lengths away from us.

Snow had dusted their backs and heads, making them look ever more like a ring of boulders standing in the night. They began to paw the ground and snort more loudly as we drew closer.

I stayed to the rear. I remembered Benais's comment that the animals could feel my fear, and that fear was once again rising strong inside me. I did not want to give them more cause to turn on us than they already had.

The closest animal was grunting and pawing the ground with ominous intensity. I stole a quick glance in his direction. A shock of recognition ran through me. It was the rogue bull that had shadowed me on the hillside and moved behind us by the fire. He had that same dark, malevolent presence. He seemed to be staring at me. The fear that I was hoping to hide washed over me like a wave.

I crouched down and huddled close to the ground. I could hear the others whispering together while staring at the ring of snorting, agitated beasts.

"We've got to get to Zi," Angie was saying. "Listen to her." The tiny, pure sound of the little girl's voice was unmistakable. It cut through Festus's growlings and the dark, low grunts of the great animals.

"I'm going in there," Jumbo said. "My grandpa said I had strong power with *tatanka*. That's why I got that name."

"Be careful," Donnie said. "We don't want them to hurt her."

I watched as Jumbo stood up and stepped toward the rogue bull. Festus followed behind. The bull waved its head back and forth and made low, threatening sounds. Its horns moved like blades in the night. Far in the background, in tiny counterpoint, we could hear the soft voice of little Zi, only a few arms' lengths from us but as unreachable as if she were a thousand miles away.

Donnie grabbed Jumbo's sleeve as the huge animal slashed at him with its horns. "You can't get through," he said.

"Then what are we going to do?" Jumbo asked. The buffalo had moved closer together. Their flanks were touching. There was no space between them.

From behind us, Angie spoke. She stepped forward without looking at us.

"I'll get her," she said. "That's my daughter. We are Lakota. *Tatanka* is our friend." She pushed Jumbo aside and stepped to within a few feet of the great beast's horns. Its head was almost as big as she was. The animal snorted and looked at her with huge, empty eyes.

Angie stood straight and pulled back her hood. She stared directly at the bull and spoke a few words in Lakota. Then she began singing in Lakota, clearly and distinctly. All around, the animals stopped their pawing and grunting. They seemed perplexed and unnerved.

She stepped forward, as if to pass through their barrier.

Slowly, the rogue bull moved slightly to the side. The animal to his right pulled away, and a small passageway opened between them. Angie seemed to have them completely under her control.

We could see through the passageway to the center of the circle. There, cast in dark silhouette against the white midnight snow, two young buffalo calves were lying on the ground. They had not yet gotten their adult coats — they were reddish brown, almost auburn. They lay side by side, completely encircled by the adult animals except for the small pathway of entry that the two beasts closest to us had allowed. The sweet, tiny voice of little Zi was coming from near where the two calves lay.

Angie walked forward between the huge animals. She came up no higher than their flanks. She continued singing as she walked. Her voice and Zi's blended as one.

The buffalo shied back. It was as if something had changed. They no longer seemed ominous and threatening but acquiescent and submissive. The barrier they had formed to keep intruders out had now become a barrier protecting the center of the circle from the outside world. And in the center of that circle, barely visible between the two buffalo calves, we could see little Zi sitting in her dirty pink parka and her little white dress and snow boots. She was singing the same small, clear song she had been singing to the buffalo rock.

Angie walked between the animals and up to her daughter.

"My girl," she said.

Zi looked up at her with wide, liquid eyes. Wordlessly, she reached her hands up to her mother. Angie bent down, took her daughter in her arms, and lifted her to her chest. Zi clung tightly to her and buried her face in her mother's shoulder. "Momma," she said softly. It was the first word I'd ever heard her speak. Angie rocked her and began to sob.

The buffalo shifted. Slowly, they turned and faced in at the mother and child. The circle had become an enfolding, and the animals radiated an aura of calm and peace.

Donnie wanted to run to his little girl, but something about the moment belonged to the mother and child. The buffalo were facing them in what seemed almost like reverence. The animals swished their tails and kept their heads bowed.

"They were protecting little Zi, weren't they?" I whispered to Jumbo.

"That's how they are, Nerburn," Jumbo responded. "They ain't like other animals."

From within the circle, Angie looked out at Donnie and smiled. Her cheeks glistened and her round, girlish face was filled with joy and relief. Little Zi held tightly to her mother and kept her face buried in her shoulder.

"Come on," Donnie mouthed.

Angie smiled and took a step in our direction.

At the first indication of movement, Zi twisted and squirmed her way out of her mother's grasp. She got down on the ground and embraced each of the two buffalo calves, one at a time.

"Jesus," Jumbo said under his breath.

Zi walked slowly around the circle formed by the huge animals, touching them each on the head as she passed. She continued to sing in her tiny, childish voice. The animals seemed to be listening.

When she finished touching each of the buffalo, she took her mother's hand and led her through the small passage between the rogue bull and the large female. The two animals stood still, neither snorting nor pawing, as the mother and child passed.

Zi led Angie back to where Donnie, Jumbo, and I were standing. Donnie's strength and control dissolved as he took his wife and daughter into his arms. His chest heaved with silent sobs.

The buffalo watched them silently. Their stillness had become an act of witness.

"God, they've got a presence," I whispered to Jumbo. "I've never seen anything like it."

"They're our teachers," Jumbo said. "Creator gave them power."

Jumbo stood by while the family embraced. I could see he wanted to go to his young friend but did not want to intrude on the family's private moment. He had a humility and quiet patience that was every bit as strong as the buffaloes' aura of peace.

"You're a good man, Jumbo," I said.

"I'm happy for Angie and Donnie," he said.

We stood quietly as the young couple and their child held each other. The winds had calmed and the sky had cleared. The night was once again alive with numberless points of light. The moon was a distant, colorless orb, moving silently in the heavens.

"We should go," I said. I was concerned about the weather shifting again, but even more concerned about the buffalo. I did not know how long this momentary calm would last.

"Let them be," Jumbo said. "We'll go when they're ready."

Festus was wagging his tail desperately. He, too, wanted to get to his little friend. Jumbo had held him back when Angie walked into the circle, and now he was wild to get to little Zi.

"Go," Jumbo whispered, tapping Festus on his head. The old dog bounded over to Zi and pulled at her pant leg, wagging and making high, excited squeaks.

Zi wriggled down from her father's grasp and wrapped her arms around Festus's neck. Festus licked her face and she rubbed her cheek against his grizzled muzzle.

Jumbo stood smiling with his hands clasped behind his back. He made no movement or sound while the child and dog greeted each other.

"I can carry her," he said softly to Donnie and Angie. "It's a long way."

At the sound of Jumbo's voice, Zi looked up and ran over to him and threw her arms around his huge leg. He reached down and, in a single gesture, lifted her onto his shoulders, where she wrapped her arms tightly around his neck.

"You had a long journey, my girl," he said. "Let's go home."

It took us almost an hour to make our way back through the valley and the forest to Benais's trailer. The air had taken on the fresh smell of approaching dawn, and the buffalo that had been so intent and curious upon our arrival watched our return journey with disinterest. We walked without speaking, listening to the sharp crunch of our feet on the frozen snow.

Festus took the lead, running ahead, then stopping and turning to make sure we were following. Zi rode on Jumbo's shoulders, nodding off periodically and slumping over on Jumbo's head like a fallen marionette. Donnie and Angie walked side by side, holding hands. I brought up the rear, staring at the star-filled northern sky and the occasional solitary shooting star that cut across the heavens in a long, lonely arc.

I was filled with a peace that bordered on exhaustion. I cast about for a way to make sense of what I had seen, but none was forthcoming. I felt like the buffalo had understood me far more than I had understood them. They had touched a place in me that I could not comprehend.

I looked up at the North Star, solitary and brilliant in the winter sky, and thought of how Jumbo had once told me that his grandpa had instructed him to learn from that star. "*Wichapi Owanjila* — the star that always stands in one place," he'd said. "It is the one star that can always be trusted. It is a good lesson for our life."

I watched the hulking man who was trudging through the

snow with the sleeping child on his shoulders. "Your grandpa would be proud," I thought.

Soon we came to the trail through the forest. In the distance we could see the dim outline of Benais's trailer reflected in the low glow of the fading campfire. As we got closer, I could make out the forms of Dan and Grover and Benais standing on the steps. They showed neither curiosity nor relief at our arrival, though we had been gone for more than three hours.

"Should build up that fire, Nerburn," Grover shouted as we got within earshot. "You let it get pretty low."

Benais made his way down the steps and across the snow toward us. He had on his knee-high moccasins, some black trousers with ribbons down the side, and an ill-fitting flannel shirt. He walked past the rest of us and went directly up to Jumbo and Zi. His head barely came up to the huge man's chest.

"Tatanka Cicala," he said, using Jumbo's Lakota name. "You have done well."

He looked up at little Zi, slumped over on Jumbo's shoulders, and gently reached up to touch her hair. She awoke and blinked her eyes several times. He took the buffalo sculpture from his pocket and held it toward her.

She placed her hand on it. The two of them remained there, sharing the touch of the stone. Benais nodded slightly and smiled, as if he knew what had just taken place out in the field. Their dark, unfathomable eyes seemed to connect in some common understanding.

Donnie and Angie stood off to the side with me, watching their young daughter and the ancient Ojibwe man share a knowledge that the rest of us could not comprehend.

"He knows her," Donnie said.

Dan limped his way over to us. He was breathing heavily and leaning on his makeshift crutch. "Hell of a place, eh, Nerburn?"

he said. He looked up at the star-drenched sky. "To think we used to live in this country."

He limped over to the fire and sat down heavily on a log.

"I like it better out where we are now," he said. "At least there you can see everything coming, and everything coming can see you."

I looked at him quizzically. His lack of excitement and relief at our return was perplexing for a man who had once said that the little girl was the most important thing in the world to him.

"Didn't you guys worry about where we were?" I asked.

"Nope," he said. "You had that Festus with you. If you can't trust a dog, who can you trust?" He scratched at a spot of soot on his dirty khaki pants.

"Dan," I said, more than a little exasperated, "little Zi got lost. We were lucky to find her. She could have been killed by the buffalo."

"Was she?" he asked.

"No."

"Well, there you are."

It was as if he was indifferent to everything that had happened.

"Dan, what's going on?" I said.

He poked at the fire with the end of his walking stick. "Benais said he was going to show you something. Did you see something?"

I had expected joy, relief, maybe even anger — anything. But not this matter-of-fact indifference and coy game of cat and mouse.

"Yes, we saw something, and it could have ended in the death of a little girl."

"But it didn't," he said. "Did it?"

Angie and Donnie were paying close attention to the conversation. They seemed to understand better than I what was going on.

"Grandfather," Donnie said. "She had strong power with *tatanka*."

"And did she need white-man medicine to have that power?"

"No."

"Does *tatanka* lie?"

"No, Grandfather. *Tatanka* never lies."

"Then you saw something."

On the other side of the fire, still perched on Jumbo's shoulders, little Zi had taken the buffalo rock from Benais and was singing softly as she turned it in her hands. Festus was right at Jumbo's side, wagging and staring up at the little girl. His tail seemed to be moving almost in time to her song.

Benais had not moved. He stood, small and ancient, facing the huge man and the little girl as she sang. He was nodding and smiling.

Grover walked over and stood silently next to me. He cuffed me playfully on the shoulder.

"Welcome to Indian country," he said.

CHAPTER THIRTY-THREE

THE GIFT

*D*an sat drinking a cup of weak truck-stop coffee. Grover was at the checkout counter examining some moccasin key chains and finger-puppet headdresses. "Authentic," he said, and made a few war whoops as he danced the finger puppets back and forth on his index fingers.

We had left Benais's trailer just as the first light of dawn had creased the eastern horizon. He had not offered us a place to stay, and none of us had felt inclined to ask. Though we were tired to the point of exhaustion, we were all ready to be back in our own homes.

At Jumbo's suggestion we had stopped for breakfast before beginning our long day's drives. I needed coffee, and all of us — especially Jumbo — were more than ready for a plate of·greasy roadhouse food.

Donnie and Angie and Dan and I were seated at one table. Zi and Jumbo had taken a table by themselves near the window where they could see Festus staring in at them from inside the pickup truck with hungry, yearning eyes.

Jumbo had ordered what was described in the menu as a "kitchen sink omelet," along with a plate of pancakes and a side of bacon. He was feeding bites to little Zi, who was swinging her feet and sucking on a cherry Coke. Dan was busily engaged in opening pack after pack of sugar and stirring them into his coffee with the handle end of his fork, while I happily finished off a heaping plate of hash browns covered with scrambled eggs and cheese.

"You've gotten kind of fond of eggs, haven't you, Nerburn?" Grover said. "Must have been the rez mash I made you back at the old man's house."

He had already finished his single piece of toast and was examining the various tchotchkes and trinkets that hung on racks next to the candy bars and packets of hangover medicines.

Donnie and Angie were huddled close together, speaking intensely to each other.

"Should I ask him?" Angie said.

Donnie nodded.

She lifted herself heavily from our table — the night had obviously been hard on her — and went over to where Jumbo and Zi were sitting.

She took out a pack of Prince Albert and handed it to Jumbo. "Can I ask you something?" she said.

"Sure," Jumbo answered quizzically. He was unaccustomed to the formality of a tobacco offering from his friends. "I'd be honored."

"Well, Donnie and I have been talking. We were wondering if you would like to be Zi's *hunka* brother?"

Jumbo's face widened in a look of childlike wonder.

"You would do that? You want me to be *hunka* with her?"

Angie nodded.

"What's *hunka*?" I whispered to Dan.

"Shh," he said.

"I would be the best *hunka* brother ever," Jumbo said, breaking into a huge grin.

Dan leaned close to me. "*Hunka* is the greatest gift," he said. "It means you will do anything for the other person, even give up your own life. It's a sacred bond."

Jumbo was near tears. "I will take care of this girl," he said, adopting the formal voice he had used when speaking with Benais. "For my whole life I will help her." He was like a child trying not to cry after receiving a wondrous and unexpected gift.

"I think Odell can perform the ceremony," Angie said. "We'll ask him when we get back."

"I will do this," Jumbo said. "This will be the most important thing in my life."

He looked across at us. We were all staring at him.

"I'm going to be her *hunka* brother," he said, beaming. "Donnie and Angie said so."

Grover had returned to his seat next to Dan. The two of them lifted their coffee cups in Jumbo's direction. "Hau, hau," they said.

"Festus can be the best man," Grover said.

Dan hit him in the thigh. "Don't joke about this stuff," he said.

The old dog, unaware that he was being talked about, kept mooning at Jumbo's half-eaten omelet through the plate-glass window.

"That old dog protected her," Grover said. "I got to give him that."

"I told you," Dan responded. "That dog's a guardian. I tried to tell you. You should listen to me more."

"It would be easier if you didn't think every damn thing that happened was a direct pipeline from the Creator."

"I'm just paying attention. Not like you young guys who don't pay attention to nothing unless you see it on a screen."

Jumbo pushed up from his table. He took Zi's hand and helped her off her seat. "Me and Zi are going out to see Festus. I want to tell him."

He reached into the side pocket of his pants. "This is an important day. I want to leave a big tip. Where do I put it, Nerburn?"

"Anywhere the waitress will see it," I said.

He dug around and took out a handful of pennies and dimes and stacked them like poker chips by the side of his plate.

"I'll bet there's almost a dollar there," he said proudly. He nodded to all of us and lumbered out with little Zi at his side, her small mittened hand held tightly in his great syrupy paw.

Dan was holding his coffee mug up to his mouth and banging on it with a spoon, trying to get the last of the sugar to slide out.

"So, what do you think, Nerburn?" Grover said.

"I think that Benais is one of the strangest men I've ever met."

"He'd probably say the same about you. Drive all the way out to his house in the woods and steal his words with a little machine."

"Do you think he really knew we were coming?"

Dan set his coffee mug heavily on the table. "I told you, he's one of the old ones," he said. "He knows what he knows." Tiny streams of sugar-laden coffee dribbled down the sides of his mouth.

Through the window we could see Festus licking feverishly at Jumbo's fingers.

Dan pushed away from the table and stood up unsteadily. "Come on, let's pay up. We've got a long way to go."

He grabbed his crutch and headed for the door. It was clear he was not going to pay for his breakfast; that was his right as an elder.

I waited for Grover to offer something toward the cost of the meal, but he just sat, poker-faced, across the table from me, not

moving a muscle. Finally, I reached into my billfold and took out
several twenties.

"Can't find your wallet, eh?" I said, not very graciously.

Grover picked at his teeth with a toothpick.

"How do you think he got his Indian name?" Dan said from
the edge of the doorway.

"What's that?"

"*Last Hand in the Pocket*. He earned it fair and square."

Outside, Donnie and Angie were adjusting everyone's luggage in
the truck. We had come to the moment when they had to head
south and west, and I had to turn off toward the east.

Angie came over shyly and put her hands on mine. "Thank
you, Mr. Nerburn," she said, "for what you did."

Donnie nodded his assent.

"I didn't do anything," I said.

"Yes, you did. You're a white man who didn't tell me to follow
the white man's ways. You brought us to Mr. Benais."

"I just drove the car," I said.

"Been doing it since he was a baby," Dan said from across the
lot. He did the same pantomime of holding a steering wheel he
had used when talking to me about child rearing.

Little Zi was standing at her mother's side, staring at me.
Without any warning, she ran over and wrapped her arms around
my leg.

I bent down and took her hands in mine. "Thank you, Zi," I
said. "You're a very special girl."

For a moment, it looked like something close to a smile
crossed her face. She clasped her arms tightly around my neck,
then ran back and hid behind her mother.

Dan came over and stood next to me, rocking back and forth,

like a man hearing a distant tune. He seemed pleased and at peace. I thought I would try one last time to find out what he thought had transpired at Benais's.

"I know it sounds stupid, Dan," I said. "But did Benais have anything to do with those buffalo protecting little Zi?"

"Humans don't tell *tatanka* what to do," he said. "*Tatanka* tells humans what to do."

"But do you think he knew? He didn't seem worried or surprised when we got back."

"He ain't the kind of guy to get worried or surprised."

"But what about my dream? It had the same buffalo we saw in the field."

"Good thing that Mary was an Indian," he said. "She had some extra room in that dream, so she threw in those buffalo to give you a hint. We Indians don't waste nothing."

I shook my head in frustration. It was clear that I wasn't going to get any straight answers, so I gave up and went to say my good-byes to Jumbo and Festus. Jumbo was seated on a rock at the edge of the parking lot, combing the old dog's matted fur with a broken pocket comb.

"I mostly don't share this," Jumbo grinned. "But for this here Festus, I make an exception."

"I'm sure he's honored," I said.

Festus thumped his tail at the mention of his name.

"I wanted to thank you," I said. "You really saved us last night."

"I just trusted my grandpa. He didn't give me my Indian name for nothing."

"I guess nothing in Indian country's for nothing."

Jumbo ran the comb through Festus's fur. "That's pretty much the way it is."

Festus lifted his paw and brushed it against me, as if demanding my attention. "Yeah, yeah, I'm not forgetting about you," I said. "You really snookered me out there in that park."

"Glad he did," Jumbo said. "Now I got a guard dog like one of those high-class junkyards."

Donnie had finished packing up the truck. "Come on, everybody. Time to saddle up," he said.

We all made our way to the truck to say our final good-byes.

Donnie buckled Zi into her car seat, then assisted Angie as she climbed into the passenger seat. Jumbo grunted his way into the rear after helping Festus clamber in ahead of him.

I reached in and shook Jumbo's hand one more time. I touched the shirt pocket where I kept the bone he had given me. "You're a good man," I said. "I'm lucky to know you." He smiled sheepishly and looked away.

Dan and Grover had wandered over and taken a position directly behind me. They each had on their fake Ray-Bans.

"We have a gift for you, Nerburn," Grover said. He was holding a small object tied in a piece of buckskin.

"*Pilamaya*," I said. I was already feeling privileged and overwhelmed by the kindnesses that had been shown me.

Grover reached out and placed the object gently in my hand. I accepted it formally, gratefully.

"We know that you are not like most white men," he said. "That you try to serve the Indian people with honor. So we want to offer this to you." Dan nodded in agreement.

I carefully untied the small laces, trying to give their gift the ceremonial significance it deserved.

The two men stood quietly with their heads bowed as I slowly unrolled the scroll of buckskin.

Inside was a tiny red-and-yellow plastic tomahawk on a key chain.

I looked at Grover with amazement. His eyes were hidden behind the reflective lenses of the sunglasses.

"For you," he said. "Blessed by the eagle man."

Dan burst out laughing until I thought he was going to choke. Grover joined in, and the two of them stood there guffawing in the middle of the lot like a couple of kids who had just pulled off the greatest prank in the world.

"Come on," Donnie said. "Zi needs to get home."

Grover helped Dan into the front seat next to Angie, then climbed in the back next to Jumbo and Festus. Neither of them could stop laughing.

Donnie fired the engine into life. He shifted into gear and started slowly across the lot.

Grover stuck his head out the window and gestured me over. "Hey, Nerburn," he said. "Come here." He was already puffing on a cigarette.

I hurried over, thinking perhaps he or Dan had one more thing they wanted to say.

He pointed to Festus, who was sitting up, alert as a sentry. "You didn't really think this dog was a stray, did you?"

EPILOGUE

The following summer, on my way to a conference in Denver, I had just enough time to make a quick stop at the rez. No one was home at Wenonah's or Dan's, I couldn't remember how to get to Donnie and Angie's, and Jumbo's garage had a sign taped to the door that said "Gone to Speerfish." So I headed up the road to Grover's in hopes of learning how all my friends, especially little Zi, were getting on.

Grover's old Buick was sitting in the dirt on the side of his trailer, covered with dust. A pearlescent white SUV occupied the concrete slab where he normally parked. It saddened me a bit to think that he had put his pristine '71 Buick out to pasture in favor of an expensive but soulless hunk of contemporary American metal.

He met me at the door with a smile on his face and a cigarette in his hand. He was wearing no shirt and seemed unusually relaxed.

"Well, well, Nerburn, long time no see," he said.

"I've got a conference in Denver. I figured I'd swing by to see how things are going."

We sat on the front steps and reminisced about old times and our friends on the rez. The most gratifying information he offered was that the Indian Health Service had hired a new doctor who was trying to combine traditional Native healing practices with modern Western medicine. He had placed little Zi under a tribal medicine man's care, and she was now doing fine without the use of modern drugs.

As we talked, a strange, overpowering scent wafted out from the interior of his trailer. It was heavily perfumed but seemed to have a pungent herbal smell at its base.

"What are you burning in there?" I asked.

Grover picked at his teeth with the buck knife he always kept in a sheath on his belt. "Lavender and sage," he said.

"I've never known you to be much for designer scents," I said.

"There's a lot you don't know," he answered.

Just then a woman's voice came from somewhere deep within the trailer. "Grover," she said. "Is your friend staying for dinner?"

"Nah, he's just passing by," he answered.

"Well, you let me know if he changes his mind."

I caught just the tinge of a German accent in the woman's voice. I looked at Grover and then at the SUV.

"Oh, no," I said. "You didn't."

The powerful scent of the perfumed herb floated out from inside the trailer.

"Lavender and sage?" I said. "House blessing? Native American aphrodisiac?"

He grinned wickedly. "Didn't need none of that."

Behind us the woman from the shaman shop appeared in the doorway.

"Just gave her my Indian love bundle," he said. "Works every time."

POSTSCRIPT

*I*n 2011 the state of South Dakota erected a roadside historical marker commemorating the Hiawatha Asylum for Insane Indians (asylum pictured above). The marker stands in a pull-off on the side of South Dakota Highway 18 just east of the town of Canton, adjacent to the signs commemorating Augustana College's "rolling campus" and a long-dismantled wooden ski jump. Its installation came seventy-eight years after the closing of the asylum.

FOLLOW DAN DOWN
FORGOTTEN ROADS

If you appreciated *The Girl Who Sang to the Buffalo*, be sure to check out the first two books in the trilogy, *Neither Wolf nor Dog* and *The Wolf at Twilight*.

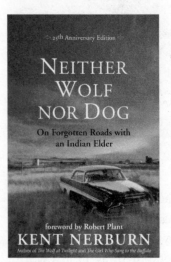

"This is one of those rare works that once you've read it, you can never look at the world, or at people, the same way again. It is quiet and forceful and powerful."
— American Indian College Fund

"Emotionally arresting...Nerburn shines when describing the humor and heartbreak he finds on South Dakota's Pine Ridge Indian Reservation....Heartfelt wisdom is found throughout Dan's quest for closure and the tale is beautifully told."
— *Publishers Weekly*

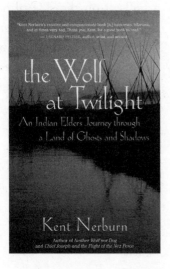

ABOUT THE AUTHOR

*K*ent Nerburn is widely recognized as one of the few American writers who can respectfully bridge the gap between Native and non-Native cultures. Novelist Louise Erdrich has called his work "storytelling with a greatness of heart." Nerburn is the author or editor of fifteen books on spirituality and Native themes, including *Chief Joseph and the Flight of the Nez Perce, Simple Truths, Small Graces,* and the two earlier volumes in this series, *Neither Wolf nor Dog: On Forgotten Roads with an Indian Elder* and *The Wolf at Twilight: An Indian Elder's Journey through a Land of Ghosts and Shadows,* both of which won the Minnesota Book Award. He lives on a pine-rimmed lake in northern Minnesota with his wife, Louise Mengelkoch, and an earnest yellow Lab named Lucie. His website can be found at www.kentnerburn.com.